PRAISE FOR *THE DARK LAKE*

'*The Dark Lake* is a thrilling psychological police procedural as well as a leap into the mind of a woman engulfed with guilt.' *New York Journal of Books*

'*The Dark Lake* hooked me from page one! Sarah Bailey combines the very best elements in this stunning debut thriller—a troubled detective still trying to find her way as a female investigator, a small town haunted by secrets both past and present, and a beautiful victim whose unsettling allure appears to be her biggest asset and largest downfall. With clever twists and all-too-human characters, this book will keep you racing toward the end.' Lisa Gardner, #1 *New York Times* bestselling author of *Right Behind You* and *Find Her*

'This polished debut is a winner from the first page.' *Daily Telegraph*

'I read *The Dark Lake* in one sitting, it's that good. A crime thriller that seizes you from the first page and slowly draws you into a web of deception and long buried secrets. Beautifully written, compulsively readable, and highly recommended.' Douglas Preston, #1 *New York Times* bestselling author of *The Lost City of the Monkey God* and co-author of the bestselling Pendergast series

'An addictive and thoroughly entertaining read.' *Weekly Review*

'*The Dark Lake* is a mesmerising thriller full of long buried secrets that sucked me right in and kept me up late turning pages. Gemma Woodstock is a richly flawed and completely authentic character—I loved going on this journey with her and the way the truth of her past was revealed in bits and pieces as we went along. Sarah Bailey has crafted an exquisite debut—I can't wait to see what she does next!' Jennifer McMahon, *New York Times* bestselling author of *The Winter People*

'So many people have compared Sarah Bailey to the likes of Gillian Flynn and Tana French, and they're so right. The prose is incredible.

Poetic and perfectly constructed . . . I recommend this book if you're into crime thrillers with a strong female lead and lots of twists and turns. I can't wait to see what Sarah [Bailey] does next.' A Girl and Grey

'Debut author Sarah Bailey depicts both the landscape and Gemma's state of mind vividly, bringing into focus the intensity of Gemma's physical and emotional pain and her increasing discontent. *The Dark Lake* adds to the trend of haunting, rural Australian crime fiction, and provides a welcome addition to the genre for those left bereft after finishing Jane Harper's *The Dry*.' *Books + Publishing*

'*The Dark Lake* is an absolutely stunning debut. This is such a beautifully written and utterly absorbing read, it's hard to believe that it's the author's first novel. I love to get my hands on a good character-driven murder mystery—especially one with a complex protagonist and a plot that keeps me guessing. *The Dark Lake* delivers all of this and more. The characters and relationships portrayed are so intricate and messy and real . . . it was a real struggle for me to put this book down.' Sarah McDuling, Booktopia

'. . . a page-turner that's both tense and thought provoking.' *Publishers Weekly*

'*The Dark Lake* by Sarah Bailey is a brooding, suspenseful and explosive debut that will grip you from the first page to the last.' *New Idea*

'A compelling debut.' *Booklist*

'I raced through this deliciously complicated, mesmerising debut at warp speed. Sarah Bailey's *The Dark Lake* is sure to keep readers awake far too late into the night.' Karen Dionne, author *The Marsh King's Daughter*

'Enthralling . . . Bailey uses solid character development and superior storytelling, rather than violence, to fuel *The Dark Lake*, and she is off to an excellent start in this launch of a series.' Oline Cogdill, Associated Press

Sarah Bailey is a Melbourne-based writer with a background in advertising and communications. She has two young children and currently works at creative projects company Mr Smith. Over the past five years she has written a number of short stories and opinion pieces. *The Dark Lake* was her first novel. *Into the Night* is her second book featuring Detective Sergeant Gemma Woodstock.

INTO THE NIGHT

SARAH BAILEY

ALLEN&UNWIN
SYDNEY·MELBOURNE·AUCKLAND·LONDON

First published in 2018

Allen & Unwin
83 Alexander Street
Crows Nest NSW 2065
Australia
Phone: (61 2) 8425 0100
Email: info@allenandunwin.com
Web: www.allenandunwin.com

 A catalogue record for this book is available from the National Library of Australia

ISBN 978 1 76029 748 0

Set in 12/17 pt Minion Pro by Midland Typesetters, Australia
Printed and bound in Australia by Griffin Press

10 9 8 7 6 5 4 3 2 1

Melbourne, this one is for you

'The eternal stars shine out again,
so soon as it is dark enough.'

Thomas Carlyle

Tuesday, 14 August
12.14 am

Freezing air slices my lungs every time I breathe. I walk to the other side of the tunnel in an attempt to shift blood into my numb feet. I peer into its black depths. I assume it's just a long stretch of concrete and rubbish, shelter for rats and mice, that eventually merges with other concrete passages running underneath unsuspecting roads and buildings. Faded graffiti hugs the curved wall, the colourful scrawls harshly exposed by a mobile spotlight and fresh police tape across the entrance is taut, barely shaking in the breeze. The nearby asphalt path is slick with recent rain. High above, a plump moon peers down at the blunt edges of the city. As the white puffs exit my mouth, I think about how much grittier the crime scenes always seem here than they did in Smithson. So much more sinister somehow.

I was drifting into my second hour of sleep when the call came through. A fatal attack in Carlton. Putting the phone down, I threw a glance at the lightly snoring man in the giant bed beside me. I slipped out of the warm cocoon, stumbled into the small lounge, then quietly pulled on the clothes I'd stripped off only an hour earlier. After easing the door shut, I made my way to the lift and rushed through the gleaming lobby, eyes on the floor, before jumping into a cab. The city is smaller at night, and less than fifteen minutes later I'm staring into the face of a dead man, the wind biting at my nose and ears.

My body aches for rest. I taste wine on my breath. Sex is still fresh on my skin. I pull my wool coat tighter around me and shake my head, forcing my brain to accept that for the next few hours at least, sleep is out of the question.

The forensics officers are silent as they go about their business, glowing in their puffy white uniforms. Their jaws are set as they pluck items from the ground with gloved hands and tweezers, dropping them carefully into evidence bags, their experienced eyes taking in the story of the scene.

All I can hear is the endless buzz of the sprawling night.

I jump slightly as a camera flash lights up the dingy surrounds— once, twice, again—and it reminds me of a music video. But in place of curvy dancing silhouettes, there is only the profile of the victim, his head hanging forward into his lap, his back hard against the wall. In death, the old man's gnarled fingers curl gently into each palm. His bald head is partly shielded from the cold; a woollen beanie dotted with holes grips his head. His tracksuit pants are down around his knees but his oversized shirt grants him some dignity. His hands are slick with drying blood, indicating that he tried to keep the life inside his body. He didn't want to die despite living like this. The dark red mingles with the rubbish on the ground, creating a murky, smelly puddle. I wonder if anyone is left alive who remembers him as a child. I wonder about his mother.

The glowing tip of a cigarette bobs into my vision.

'What a place to go,' says Detective Sergeant Nick Fleet, extinguishing the smoke and placing it in a plastic bag before shoving it into his pocket.

The familiar smell finds my nostrils and instantly triggers a craving.

'It's pretty isolated,' I observe. 'And badly lit. You'd be fairly safe to assume that you could get away with pretty much anything out here.'

Fleet snorts. 'Well, if it wasn't for the witness I'd guess it was a gay hook-up gone wrong, seeing as our guy's half naked.' Fleet squints into the tunnel at the body, wrinkling his nose. 'But it was probably drug payback. Usually is.'

'Maybe,' I reply, 'but I don't think so. Everything here suggests that he was taken by surprise. I think he was urinating against the wall when someone attacked him.' I point to the rancid wet circle not far from the body.

Fleet clears his throat loudly and the rattle of loose phlegm nauseates me. 'My money is still on drugs.'

'It's possible,' I say, 'but there's no suggestion that he was using or selling. No track marks, no drug paraphernalia.'

'Maybe he pissed someone off.'

'Maybe,' I say curtly.

Fleet clicks his tongue. 'We must keep an open mind, Gemma,' he says in a faux-wise voice. 'It's early days after all.'

A familiar surge of frustration flares just as headlights swing across the darkness nearby. The bark of a dog explodes behind us. Moments later, our boss, Chief Inspector Toby Isaacs, ducks under the tape and into the mouth of the tunnel. He nods at me, then Fleet, before surveying the scene with wide grey eyes. His features don't move but his gaze lingers on the dead man's worn boots; the sole of the left one gapes open at the toes like a howling mouth.

'What do we know?' asks Isaacs.

'He was stabbed,' I say, straightening my shoulders and forcing strength into my voice. 'Looks like a single wound, though we haven't moved him yet. No sign of a weapon. I'll arrange for a field team to do a search at first light and see what CCTV we can pull from the area, but I think we'll hit a dead end on that front. I can't see any cameras.'

Isaacs nods briskly. 'And we're sure he was homeless?'

'It certainly looks that way,' I confirm.

'And smells that way,' says Fleet. He points past the forensics team to a blanket and a tatty backpack. 'That looks like his bedroom over there.'

'We can't find any ID,' I add.

'Where's the witness now?' asks Isaacs, looking around.

'She's at the station,' I tell him. 'We'll head back there and take her statement once we're done here. Apparently she's elderly and homeless herself. On my way here I spoke to the constable who's with her, and he says she's in a bad way.'

'She definitely doesn't have anything to do with it?'

'It doesn't sound like it. He said she's terrified.'

Isaacs purses his lips. 'Do we have a description to work with?'

'A man in a hoodie,' I reply. 'We'll push for more details but it's so dark out here I doubt she saw much.'

'Men in hoodies really are the root of all evil, aren't they?' quips Fleet.

I watch as he scratches his elbow and pushes a hand roughly through his wiry hair. Isaacs seems to tolerate rather than favour him, which he never seems too fussed about—but, then, Nick Fleet never seems particularly ruffled by anything.

In the three months I've been in Melbourne, I've worked more closely with him than anyone else on the squad. He's a detective sergeant like me but at least a couple of years older—I'd be surprised if he's forty. I get the feeling he had another life altogether before entering the force. I also quickly learned he has a massive reputation with the ladies, though I'm yet to see the charm.

He's unappealingly hairy and frequently rude, and he has a rough, primal quality: a harshness.

The forensics officers begin to trawl through the pile of bedding. The camera strobes again before a jumper and a faded picnic blanket are swiftly bagged.

Isaacs rubs his hands together and breathes into them. 'Hopefully it was someone he knew. A random attack on the homeless is the last thing we need.'

'I'm going to have another smoke,' announces Fleet. 'I'll have a bit of a look around while I'm at it.'

Isaacs just clasps his arms and rocks back slightly on his heels. He turns his head to look out across the parkland, his angular profile sharp. The moonlight paints his hair silver. As always, I can't tell what he's thinking.

I shift my gaze past Isaacs to take in the maze of lights and uneven rooftops. I feel uneasy, not knowing who might be watching from the darkness.

'Detective Woodstock?' says Brenton Cardona, one of the senior techs. 'We're going to move him in a minute. That okay with you?'

Aware that Isaacs' eyes are on me, I give Cardona a firm yes before squatting next to the nameless victim one last time. Careful to avoid the blood and debris, I look into his face. His bottom lip hangs open slightly and shines with saliva. His unseeing eyes are fixed on his broken shoes. I would place him around sixty-five but the layers of grime on his leathery, pockmarked skin make it hard to tell. He might be much younger. My back teeth grind together as I play out his macabre demise in my mind: the split-second register of a presence, his surprise at being grabbed from behind and spun around. The blinding pain as a knife is pushed into his chest, eyes widening as his blood flowed straight from his heart and onto the ground. His panic as he realised he was dying. His terror.

It's impossible for me to know if he was good, bad or any of the shades in between. But no matter what happened at the end, right now—punctured, slumped forward and drained of life—this dead old man looks like an abandoned little boy.

Tuesday, 14 August
7.43 pm

The heavy door thuds shut behind me and I stand in the dark boxy entrance for a moment. I just want to be perfectly still as the day fades away. The brutality of the homeless man's death has pulled me down, his crumpled corpse heavy in my thoughts. I walk over to the lounge-room window and take in the sprawl of activity below. Cars creep along the ruler-straight roads, the angry glow of red tail-lights evidencing the collective frustration of their drivers. Everyone here is so impatient to *be* somewhere.

My apartment is at the top end of Melbourne, near the corner of Little Collins and Exhibition streets. It's eight floors up and the view gives the city such a sense of grandeur. Smithson, my home town in regional New South Wales, is definitely growing, but its 25,000-odd people has nothing on the crazy melting pot of lives that Melbourne homes.

Dropping my keys onto the kitchen bench, I shake off my jacket and flick on the ancient wall heater. It chokes into life, half-heartedly filling the room with warm stale air.

I ended up leaving the station just before 3 am, wired on caffeine, my eyes like two hot discs in my face after interviewing

Lara Maxwell, the terrified witness. Lara couldn't tell us much and knew the victim only as Walt. Both homeless, they'd spoken occasionally but she said he'd mainly kept to himself. She described him as simple but harmless; she often saw him talking to the pigeons and whistling show tunes. The perfect sitting duck.

Fleet and I calmed Lara down and arranged some temporary accommodation for her before heading home.

By the time I returned to the station at midday, Isaacs had appointed Ralph Myers as case lead and we'd confirmed an ID. Swallowing my disappointment at being overlooked again, I sat through the formal briefing.

Our victim, Walter Miller, a 62-year-old perennially homeless man with a staccato history of mental illness, had been living rough for over two decades. He last had a fixed address in the early nineties. Tammy Miller, his 33-year-old daughter, hadn't seen her father for almost twenty years, after her mother, Walter's ex-wife, decided she wanted nothing to do with him. Tammy, now an event planner with two young children, is clearly bewildered about what to do with the news of her estranged father's murder. She's suddenly grieving for a man who in many ways was dead to her years ago. Her mother died in 2013, and the shock of her orphan status and the horrific circumstances of Walter's death were written on her pretty face as Ralph led her to an interview room.

At around 3 pm I was sent back to the crime scene to interview workers in nearby factories. Had they seen anything the previous evening? They hadn't. They were all long gone and tucked up safely in bed by the time Walter met his grim fate.

So far, our investigation has revealed a life as lonely as his death. There's no sign of chronic drug use and no criminal record. There is no apparent motive for the attack at all, unless the objective was a cold-blooded kill. We'll continue to pull his world apart, analyse his recent interactions and track his movements, because someone is better than no one to blame, even if it's the victim himself. I'm already getting the feeling that Walter's death will remain an inexplicable cruelty. A nasty statistic. Sometimes you can just tell.

Walking past my tiny bedroom, I consider collapsing straight into my unmade bed. But not yet. It's a Ben night and it's almost time for our call. I should eat now so that I can put all my focus into his face and voice. The slow turn of my stomach is familiar, my pre-Ben conversation physiology always the same. I've come to recognise it before I'm consciously aware of it. It's similar to the feeling of having a crush but with a ribbon of melancholy tied tightly around it. I love talking to him but it is somehow also very unsatisfying, the pain so acute when he hangs up that I'm still not convinced the high is worth the crashing comedown. But, of course, none of it is supposed to be about me.

In the end, my relationship with Ben's dad Scott simply faded away. After working a major murder case a few years ago, where the victim was an old classmate of mine, I was empty. Rosalind Ryan's murder had completely broken me. It forced so much of my past into the present that eventually I collapsed under the weight.

In the immediate aftermath of Rosalind's case Scott and I came together, but ultimately we ended up even further apart. Scott tried, I know he did. He is a solid person, inside and out: broad-shouldered and stocky with a thick crop of dark hair and a sense of reliability that always sees him called upon for favours. His kind eyes, full of hope and effort, followed me around the house. He wanted to be close to me, to connect with me, but I'm ashamed to say, that after a few months of hypervigilance in regard to taking it easy, and giving our relationship the attention it deserved, I regressed to my old ways and funnelled my scant energy into work. I was an exceptional detective but a shitty partner and a barely passable mother. Rosalind haunted my dreams and I was grieving badly for Felix, my colleague who had transferred to a Sydney squad. Our affair, and the resulting miscarriage I'd endured, paired with the emotions Rosalind's murder unearthed, left me badly bruised. Over time the pain faded to apathy, and I found myself directing that toward Scott. It was as if I'd decided that if I couldn't be with Felix, there was no point in trying to make it work with anyone else. I was high-functioning but deeply broken and eventually something had to give. When the opportunity to transfer to Melbourne arose, I needed to take it. Living in Smithson was slowly killing me.

I lean against the bench, looking at my poky kitchen. I can't be bothered to cook but I know I should eat, especially after my coffee lunch and afternoon snack of crackers and chewing gum. I've lost over five kilos since arriving here. I fire up the gas. Grate some bright yellow cheese and pour the dregs of some fading chardonnay into a wineglass. As the water begins to boil I dump half a cup of pasta into the saucepan.

I close my eyes as I tip the wine down my throat. Next door a man's voice yells through the thin common wall and a woman's sharp voice retorts loudly, sparking a ping-pong argument; it penetrates the soothing shield that alcohol is gallantly trying to form around my brain. I picture the cold grey tunnel that Walter Miller called home and shiver, turning the heater up higher. I open a new bottle of wine and pour another glass. It seems that the TV options on Tuesday night are no better than those on Monday.

I flick from an episode of *The Street* to the news, and my boss's face fills the screen. I sit up a little straighter and note how Isaacs' grey stare holds the reporter's as he calmly answers her questions about Walter Miller's death.

As I shovel my unappetising dinner into my mouth, I have to admit my boss is compelling on TV. His thick grey hair obediently falls into place every time he shifts his head. His nose hooks slightly, set above full lips. His movements are slow and deliberate, like those of a lizard whose blood needs warming in the sun. His low voice is steady, an authoritative baritone.

Isaacs is polite to me, polite to everyone, but everything about him feels distant. I sense it's intentional: he seems determined to keep everyone at arm's-length. Our relationship is formal, forced, and so far I feel like I've struggled to transcend the job interview phase, which is unsettling as I'm still technically on probation. Nan, Ralph and Calvin are his clear favourites but even with them he is frosty. He's so unlike Ken Jones, my old station chief who wore his heart—and every thought that ran through his head—prominently on his sleeve.

Rumour has it that everyone thought Isaacs was a shoo-in for the commissioner role a few months back, but instead Joe Charleston, a well-regarded inspector from Tasmania, got the gig. Allegedly Isaacs has been even more aloof since then.

The news shifts a gear and a reporter is now talking excitedly about the Hollywood movie *Death Is Alive*, which will begin filming in Melbourne tomorrow. I'm vaguely aware of the production— a bunch of our guys have been working with the film's security team and the council for the past few months, and Candy keeps mentioning it because she has a crush on the lead actor.

Candy Fyfe is a reporter back in Smithson and probably my closest friend. She is a force of nature, the first indigenous journalist Smithson has seen and probably the most dedicated. We weren't friends initially, in fact we were openly hostile, but I've grown to love her relentless energy. She is single-handedly trying to keep our friendship alive via various forms of electronic correspondence. With a stab of guilt, I realise I never got back to her most recent message, which she sent over a week ago. I pull it up on my phone, laughing as I reread her updates about our home town. She's heard a rumour that the local Presbyterian minister is having an affair with the funeral director, so she's been fronting up to church every Sunday to investigate. I can just imagine Candy, her athletic brown body poured into one of her trademark tight-fitting outfits, lurking around the church trying to catch the unlikely couple out.

Famous faces flash onto the screen as the reporter chatters on. Having zero interest in celebrities, I barely recognise any of them. I yawn and get up to pour another wine. My hips creak as I rise and stagger the few steps to the kitchen. I might be losing weight but my fitness is at an all-time low. I've stopped running. I do enough at the squad gym to pass for trying, but I'm only going through the motions. I need to get into a better routine.

I need to do a lot of things.

Checking the time, I head onto the tiny balcony for my daily cigarette, eyes on the twinkling dots in the sky as smoke fills my lungs. I begin to picture Ben's face. His pale green eyes, identical to mine. His smattering of freckles. The sweet curve of his mouth. 8.28 pm. He will ring any second now. He is punctual, a trait inherited from his father.

Scott sometimes says a quick hello to me but we spoke on Sunday so it's unlikely that we will this time. The finances are agreed for now, Ben is fine, so there's nothing for us to talk about.

Shoving the cigarette into the growing graveyard of yellow butts in an empty flowerpot, I go back inside and pull the door closed. I drink more wine, wrestling with the memory of the hotel room from last night. The abstract art on the walls, the strong eager hands on my body. I cringe slightly, my head pounding. I realise the bottle of wine is already half empty.

My phone buzzes and I scramble to mute the TV. Wipe my mouth. Pull my legs underneath me and curl into a ball to Skype with my son.

'Hi, Mum.' His face fills the screen and he waves at me.

'Hey, Ben!' I summon my best smile and push my guilt firmly aside. 'How are you, darling?'

'Good.'

My chest tightens at his little boy nonchalance. He's not obtuse; he just doesn't go into detail. Our conversations are a blissful jumble of simple words and sweet silences. They are everything. They are not nearly enough.

'Did you have sport today?'

'Yep.'

I smile, just taking him in. He always sits up straight when he talks on Skype. It's still a task that requires his full concentration, like he's worried he'll get the next answer wrong if he relaxes. Ben has just turned five and I often struggle with the thought that he's not that many years from being the same age as so many of the kids I deal with at work. The kids who are tangled up in the bad situations I'm trying to figure out. Kids who've been around evil for so long that it has seeped into their souls and erupts in all the worst ways. I swallow past an image of a future Ben, broken by his mother's rejection.

'Soccer, right?' I say.

'Yep. And my team won again!' He beams at me.

'That's great, sweetheart! And do you have footy on the weekend?'

'Yeah, this Saturday, and then we have a week off. That's what Dad said.'

We chat about his friend's mini-golf party, and he asks about my goldfish.

'Frodo is fine,' I tell him, shifting the phone so he can see the fishbowl. 'He told me to tell you he says hi.'

Ben giggles and I smile again before sadness bubbles inside me. Oblivious, he chatters on about school, his teacher and what he ate for lunch.

'Do you want to look at the stars now?' he asks, already knowing the answer.

'Of course,' I say, careful to hide the crack in my voice. 'I bet I know which one you're going to talk about first.'

'Well . . .' He moves toward the window in the lounge. 'There's that big one right in the middle of the sky. And like, three little ones in a little line next to it. Can you see the one I mean?' He turns the phone around and I get a sweeping glimpse of the familiar room before hazy sky fills the screen.

'Sure can,' I tell him. 'That's a good one. Can you see the sneaky sparkly one on the right? I think it's right near my apartment.'

'Oh yeah,' he says, eyebrows shooting up, 'it's kind of yellow. Cool.'

He stifles a yawn and his eyes drop away from the heavens. 'Time for bed,' I say firmly—still able, occasionally, to be his mother.

'Okay,' he agrees, yawning again. 'Speak to you on Thursday, Mum?'

'You bet. Have a great day tomorrow. I'll give Frodo an underwater kiss for you.'

We blow a kiss to each other and, as I hang up, I realise that my hand is flat across my heart.

I brush my teeth, use the toilet and undress, sliding into my freezing bedding. My head spins and my stomach cramps uncomfortably. In the lounge, the heater makes an unhealthy ticking sound. The TV next door mumbles. Rock music thuds through the ceiling. Glass smashes on the street. A cat meows. I toss and turn, picturing first Ben sleeping peacefully in his bed and then Walter Miller slumped forward in his cold bloody puddle. Until finally, I am asleep.

Wednesday, 15 August
5.55 am

I wake before the alarm goes off, my eyes sore and grainy, traces of wine fixed offensively to the walls of my mouth. Rolling over, I stare at the ceiling for a few seconds, considering the day ahead. I expect it will mostly consist of attempting to confirm Walter Miller's final movements, trying to work out why the hell someone wanted him to exit the world so dramatically.

I pull myself up and throw the blanket roughly back over the bed. Turning on the shower, I let the steam warm the air before stepping in. Wash, dress. Blast my hair with the dryer and I'm ready for whatever the day hurls my way. I tap some flakes into Frodo's bowl and give him a half-hearted kiss for Ben. As I thump down the stairs, I swallow the tail of an overripe banana.

At the base of my apartment block is a tiny cafe called The Boil, which does a strange mix of breakfast food and noodles. I order two takeaway coffees and pick up the newspaper. A grainy, decades-old photo of Walter Miller and his daughter is on the front page, the bold headline above his face screaming 'Homeless and Hunted'.

When I step back outside, the cold air fingers my scalp and flicks up my hair. I pull my scarf around my head in an attempt to pin it down. I walk up to the corner where, behind a bench seat, a little concrete alcove is cut into the base of an old office building.

'Morning, Macy,' I say, relieved to see the familiar mass of blankets. I hold one of the cups out to the large woman curled underneath the hard grey overhang. A giant beanie rests just above her eyes and her round chin juts out above her tatty coat collar as she appraises the new day. She heaves herself up, her face cracking into a smile as she takes the cup from me. This alcove, about two hundred metres from my front door, is the closest thing Macy has to a home. Everything she owns is in an ancient North Face backpack that she uses as a pillow.

A few weeks after I arrived in Melbourne, I locked myself out of my apartment block after a night shift. Tired and alone, I collapsed on a park bench crying my eyes out. Macy emerged from her alcove and sat with me for over an hour listening to my story, while I waited for the property manager. And then she shared hers. It turned out we both have sons we don't get to see anymore. These days I find it easier to talk to Macy than anyone else I know. Surveying Walter Miller's crime scene had reminded me of her modest jumble of earthly things more than I'd wanted to admit to myself.

'What's news today, big cop lady? More of my fellas turning up dead?' She's smiling but I think she must be so scared about what happened to Walter. She must feel so vulnerable out here. Not for the first time I think about helping her in some way. Finding her somewhere to stay or inviting her into my apartment, but when I alluded to this a few weeks ago it was clear it made her uncomfortable. She is such a proud woman and wears her resilience like an invisible badge. So I settle on buying her coffee and the occasional snack but anything beyond a token gesture feels like it's off limits.

'No news yet today, Macy,' I tell her, sitting on the bench, 'but it's still early.' I pause, then say, 'You didn't know the man who died, did you?'

She wipes her nose on her sleeve. 'Not really. Met him once or twice. But my friend Lara, she knew him. She said you spoke to her the other night at the cop shop. She's not doing so well. Keeps remembering what she saw.'

I instantly summon Lara's terrified face, her jerky movements and nervous glances as Fleet and I interviewed her about what she witnessed at the tunnel. I wonder if she's back on the streets already; I don't know how far the empathy of the tax-paying dollar stretches to a homeless witness.

'I'm sorry to hear that, Macy,' I say. 'We're doing everything we can to find the person who attacked Walter.'

She shrugs and sips more coffee, suggesting little faith in the like-lihood of this outcome. As she pulls her mouth into a smile again, her stained teeth gleam in her dark face. 'Well. Anyway, enough sad talk. There's big excitement around here later today. They're shooting a movie along the top of Spring Street.'

'That's right,' I say, putting my coffee down so I can make jazz hands, 'the big Hollywood film.'

'They're blocking off all the cars, you know. Your lot are gunna be everywhere, keeping people out of the way. I read the information flyer they were handing out. There's gunna be some big action scene. With real movie stars.' Her gravelly voice rolls across the path, and we get a few odd looks from eager corporates in tailored suits and sleepy shift workers heading home. 'I'm going to get myself a front-row seat. Try to get Lara to come.' She knocks back more coffee and closes her eyes. 'Man, this is good stuff. Just a beautiful, beautiful thing.'

I tuck my feet in their new boots under the bench as I notice her woollen socks sticking through holes in her worn broken ones.

'How is your little boy?' she asks.

I sigh and have some of my own coffee. 'He's fine. He seems happy. You know, with school. With his sport.'

'Well, that's the main thing. And don't you go worrying about things that aren't really there. If he's fine, then everything is. Remember?'

I nod and try to smile. 'I know you're right. But look, I gotta get going, Mace,' I say, already on my feet.

She gives me a reproachful look. 'You take care out there, Detective Gemma.'

'You too,' I say, giving her a pointed look. 'I mean it, be careful.'

'Yeah, yeah,' she says, but I see a flicker of fear in her eyes again.

I smile at her. 'I'm looking forward to hearing about your day at the movies.'

—◀○▶—

I don't know why I went to the hotel that first night. It was a Thursday. I'd been in Melbourne for exactly one week and had barely spoken to a soul. I was still staying in a serviced apartment, applying for rentals and due to start work the following Monday.

I'd spent the day wandering aimlessly around the city, up and down the corridors of the Queen Victoria Market, sitting in cafes, nursing coffees until they became cold. Just before five I went back to the apartment and had a shower. I craved a drink and figured I may as well make myself look half decent and go out somewhere. Maybe I could pretend I was here on business, I reasoned. I put on the only dress I owned and dried my long hair. Stepping outside and walking along Exhibition Street toward the heart of the city, I saw a stream of taxis rounding into a hotel entrance. There would be a bar there, I thought, and it would be nice to look out over the main street. It started to rain, fat droplets splattering onto the pavement, and I hurried across the road and through the glass doors, past the smiling concierge.

I ordered a wine and sat on a velvet-covered chair, watching night-time take hold of the city. Every surface shone and I was mesmerised by the glittering chandelier. I felt gloriously at peace, more relaxed than I'd been in weeks. I took off my jacket and crossed my legs, leaning back against the plush cushions. The waiter returned, a full glass of wine already perched on his tray, and told me that the gentleman at the bar had bought me a drink.

I looked over to see an olive-skinned man in a navy suit smiling at me.

I smiled back and picked up the drink, my eyes still on the man as I took the first sip.

Just as I was finishing the wine, he came over carrying two fresh drinks. 'What a day, huh?' he said, handing me a glass. Underneath his smile his gaze was intense as it raked over my body.

'Yes. It's nice to relax now though.'

'How long are you staying here?' he asked me.

I blinked. 'Home tomorrow. Back to Sydney.'

'Me too—I'm based in Auckland,' he said, and I detected the hint of an accent.

We exchanged looks before I pulled my eyes away. My breathing was all through my mouth.

I was drunk when we got to his room. My arms were above my head, pinned against the wall before the door shut. I let him strip off my clothes; I let him take control. I felt like a piece of driftwood, tossed around by the raging water. It felt good to be held by this stranger. For him to know nothing about me. He held my wrists and threw me onto the bed. His long lean body was heavy on top of me and he pushed so far inside me I winced.

Hours later, in the dead of the night, I crawled into my own bed, breathing as if I'd been chased. The room danced around me, my pulse pounding through my whole body, while I thought about how I wanted to do it again.

Wednesday, 15 August

7.29 am

'Morning,' says Calvin Atkins perkily as I drop my bag on my desk. Coffee churns in my guts, lonely with only the banana for company.

'Hi,' I say, my eyes already trained on my computer screen, blocking off more chat.

Calvin agreeably busies himself with a pile of paperwork, the angles of his thin face emphasised by the glow of his computer screen.

Nan Sheridan walks in, grunts, and deposits her sizeable bulk into her worn office chair, which groans in response. She plucks out her earphones and rustles in her bag, dumping a worn-looking Val McDermid novel on her desk next to a haphazard stack of crime novels. Emptying her handbag of fast-food wrappers, she snaps on her computer and stares at the blank screen as it whirs into life.

'Want a coffee, Nan?'

She looks at Calvin right between his eyes, which he seems to understand means yes because he nods and scoots off to the tearoom muttering, 'Long black, no sugar.'

I don't say anything to Nan and she doesn't say anything to me. I think we like this about each other.

There are just over a hundred detectives in the Melbourne homicide squad. Nan, Calvin, Fleet and I are in one of the sixteen groups along with Billy Benton, Ralph Myers and Chloe Senna. Each group has a mix of experienced senior detectives like Nan and Ralph, and then junior detectives like Chloe, with people like me falling somewhere in between. Nan has been a senior DS for almost a decade and surely must have her eye on Isaacs' job. She's good, I'll give her that, ferocious—though I'm not sure how well she'd go at managing people. She has slightly more patience with the dead than with the living but not much. I watch as she jabs a single finger at her keyboard. Technology is another thing that Nan merely tolerates—if she could do the entire job with her bare hands, she would.

A small commotion flares up a few pods along. One of the juniors is back from a holiday and there's a lot of excitement about her tan. I stay at my desk, working steadily through my emails. Ralph is usually in early but I assume he's at Walter Miller's autopsy, which was scheduled first thing this morning. Billy is probably there with him too. Isaacs has set a ten-thirty meeting to review the Miller case and any updates on the Jacoby case, and until then I have plenty to keep me busy.

I briefly wonder where Fleet is before I firmly shove the thought away. I'm not Nick Fleet's keeper. He'd have to be missing for days before I would call his mobile. Fleet isn't the kind of guy who likes to be managed, and I wouldn't want him to know that I've noticed he's missing.

The three of us work in silence for a while and just as I'm considering another coffee, my personal phone buzzes. It's a message from Josh Evans, wondering if I have time to meet him this morning. I feel a pulse of guilt at not texting him back all day yesterday.

I look at my desk, piled high with papers. Seeing as I'm not lead on the Miller case, I should be able to get through it all later. I can always stay back anyway—it's not like I have a family to go home to. Placing the papers in my bottom drawer and locking it, I grab my coat. 'I'm heading out for a bit,' I tell Calvin. 'I'll be back for the case briefings.'

He nods, looking slightly bewildered.

Nan grimaces as I push in my chair. 'Don't be late,' she says bluntly.

◄○►

'Hey,' says Josh, flashing me a big white smile as I approach the table. 'I've ordered for you already. A latte.'

'Oh, okay, thanks,' I reply, smiling back as I sit down across from him and toy with my watch. 'Sorry I've been a bit AWOL this week. Things have been intense at work.'

He grabs my hands, pulling them over to his side of the table. 'Don't be silly, Gemma. I know you're busy.' He leans forward and gives me a quick kiss. My eyes close and I breathe in the musky scent of his cologne. Not for the first time, I wish I liked Josh as much as he seems to like me. He is so good-looking, so uncomplicated. As I pull away, a businessman at an adjoining table raises a bemused eyebrow at me, and I wonder if my thoughts are that obvious.

'It feels like ages since I saw you,' Josh says.

'I saw you on Thursday night,' I reply lightly, gently tugging my hands free.

He laughs. 'I know it hasn't really been that long—it just feels like it. You should have come out on Saturday, it was such a fun night.' He goes on to describe the evening in detail.

With Josh has come an instant social life: noisy busy people with interesting jobs who hang out in achingly small bars that turn fifteen dollars into a swish of wine. His cool breezy world has been intoxicating from the moment we met, just over a month ago, and part of me wants to tumble in. To relax into his strong arms. The other part of me stubbornly rejects it. The closer he inches toward me, the further I lean the opposite way. So that I don't feel so bad, I tell myself he's probably seeing other people too.

He ends his story with a sip of coffee and says more seriously, 'So the homeless man's murder sounds pretty brutal. Are you working on it?' His dark eyes are bright with interest as he runs a hand through his short gold hair.

'Yeah. I got called out there on Monday night.' I picture Walter's broken body again. 'It wasn't very nice.'

Josh gives a low whistle. 'Poor bugger.'

He finishes his coffee just as mine arrives. He orders another and I curl my hands around the warm glass, watching as a little boy seated near the door drives a toy car across the table in front of his plate. He dips the car into his steaming hot chocolate. He is small, his narrow shoulders only a ruler-width apart. Thick white-blond hair falls in cartoon-like chunks toward his eyes. His furious mother swats at his hand as she admonishes him and I look away, focusing back on Josh.

'Anything else exciting happening at work?' he asks.

'Just your standard bashings, shootings and suicides,' I say flippantly. His tan face remains serious and I drop the humour, adding, 'This murder case is a big one, especially if it really was a random attack.'

'Are you still working on all your other cases too?'

'Yep,' I say. 'Though, I think this one will become a focus now.'

'Sounds like you'll be pretty busy then.'

I shrug. 'Always.'

'I don't know how you do it, Gemma,' he says. 'You're amazing.'

I duck my head, brushing off his praise. Josh seems fascinated by my job and appears to understand the unpredictable nature of my world, which is a welcome change—and in stark comparison to Scott's steady stream of exasperation and judgement. Josh rubs his foot against mine under the table and winks at me, causing a deep wave of shame about Monday night to swirl through me. And Saturday night. All of it. I know I need to stop. Or I need to stop seeing Josh. It's not fair to string him along. But at the same time, it's so nice having someone here to rely on, having someone be so into me. And so far, Josh seems fine with taking things slowly, though surely at some point that will change. I imagine being in bed with him but my bones get twitchy and my insides squirm. For the hundredth time, I wonder why I'm so much more comfortable being intimate with complete strangers. Somehow it seems less dangerous than being with Josh.

'What about you?' I ask.

'I'm good,' he says. 'Work is really busy. I think I'll need to stay back late tonight and maybe tomorrow too, which is why I wanted to see you this morning.'

Josh is a junior lawyer at a huge firm with a string of letters for a name. His weekdays are a blur of court, research, teleconferences and coffee.

'So, did you have fun with your friend on the weekend?' he asks me.

'Yeah, it was great to catch up with her,' I lie. 'It was low-key though, just dinners and sightseeing.' I wave my hand to emphasise the fun of my imaginary weekend.

'Sounds great,' says Josh, clearing his throat. 'So, hey, I thought it might be nice if you come over to my place on Saturday. I'll cook us dinner.'

I smile and nod, alarm bells sounding at the potential awkwardness of this scenario.

The woman at the table near the door leans close to the little boy, angry-whispering in his ear. He keeps his eyes steadily trained on the tabletop where his toy car sits, sticky with chocolate. She straightens, still scowling, and her eyes meet mine. I try a tight smile but it is not returned: she doesn't recognise any maternal solidarity in me.

'That sounds great,' I say when I realise Josh is waiting for an answer. 'As long as things don't get too crazy at work.'

He takes my hand and laces his fingers through mine. 'Cool. We can meet some of my mates afterwards if you like, or we can just have an early one if you're tired. I want to spend some proper time with you.' His voice lowers. 'You can tell me all about your week and maybe I can even give you a massage or something.'

Outside, the wind has picked up and it's raining again. Sheets of water are falling at an angle, sneaking under the edges of umbrellas and threatening expensive handbags. Parents clutch their children, yanking hoods onto small heads in futile attempts to keep them dry. I think about Macy and hope that she's found shelter. Suddenly anxious, I rub at my face: my skin feels sallow and dry, like a rubber mask. Josh is stroking his fingers in circles on the top of my other hand, making my eyes droop.

'I've got to get going,' he says, frowning slightly and looking at his watch. 'I'm due in court soon. But hey, I'm really glad you could meet me. I'll call you about Saturday. Don't work too hard.' He stands up. 'God, I can't wait for summer,' he mutters, seeing the rain.

He aims another kiss on my lips but I turn my head and he catches the side of my face instead. I watch him pause to collect his golf-sized umbrella from the bin near the door and carefully open it into the rain, his tall figure crossing the road and disappearing into the gloom. Once again, I'm struck by how attractive he is.

How attentive and fun. I have to admit I feel like I've known him a lot longer than a few weeks.

I look back at the little boy and his mother. His face and hands have been cleaned, and he is picking at a scab on his hand, his mouth in a pout. The mother is frowning too, her thumb scrolling on her phone.

I sigh heavily as my conflicting thoughts battle each other. I down a glass of water to drown them out. There's so much that Josh doesn't know about me; I imagine how quickly he would back away if he knew even half of it.

Noting that the rain is fading to drizzle, I stand up and rally myself for what is sure to be a long day. I can worry about Josh later. Right now, I need to get my head firmly in the Miller case.

Wednesday, 15 August
10.29 am

Fleet slides into the case room just as Isaacs is closing the door. He tosses a nod in my direction, and I dip my head and push stray hairs behind my ear in response. The smell of fresh smoke wafts off him and gropes at my edges.

Ralph stands at the front of the room, legs spread wide, and launches into an overview of the Miller case. We have accessed some grainy CCTV footage from a nearby car park, which shows a shadowy figure walking quickly across the corner of the screen around the time Walter was attacked. The figure appears to be male and young, matching the description that Lara gave us, and is perhaps slightly taller than average, which hardly narrows the field. Walter himself appears to have had no apparent enemies. Although his flimsy medical records show a mild learning disability, it seems he kept to himself and, until now, avoided trouble. Preliminary autopsy findings reveal a single deep stab wound to the chest and some bruising along his collarbone where the killer probably pinned him against the tunnel wall with his forearm.

Looking at the grim photos, I try to see all the things around the violence: pale wrinkled skin, spidery veins, a rangy beard and dirty broken fingernails.

After Ralph has run through his updates, Isaacs joins him at the front of the room. Looking at the small group, he doesn't speak for a few moments and I sense that we collectively become self-conscious. I cross and uncross my legs, trying to mute my growling stomach.

'While we know our victim was homeless and had been for a long time, what we *don't* know,' Isaacs says, eyeing each of us in turn, 'is if he was killed *because* he was homeless.'

I know what Isaacs is referring to, thanks to Calvin, who got me up to speed just before the meeting started. About two years ago there was a spate of homeless bashings across Melbourne. Back then the media embraced the story, with one journalist even sleeping on the streets for a week and reporting from the 'front line of poverty'. One of the four men who were attacked died from his injuries, and the entire city was on edge for months. A couple of the incidents were captured on film, though tragically the perpetrators were never caught. At the time, it seemed most likely that the trio of young thugs had desired to inflict pain and found the perfect victims on the streets: alone, weak and vulnerable, with no family waiting for them to come home. No one looking out for them.

'Well, he certainly wasn't killed for money,' says Fleet, smiling at his own joke.

Isaacs looks at him blankly for a long beat before saying, 'I'll be confirming the number of extra uniforms we're putting on at nights to the press this afternoon.' He scans the room with his grey gaze and continues, 'Fleet, Woodstock and Senna, you will work with Myers on the homeless-shelter interviews and the secondary-witness reports.'

In the row in front of me Chloe Senna nods, the straight line of her thick blonde hair shifting up and down on her shoulders. She absently rubs her pregnant belly. Fleet shifts next to me, kicking the side of my shoe.

Ralph clears his throat. 'We've identified three other homeless men who frequently spent time with Miller and we believe two of them saw him the day before he died. We obviously want their statements as soon as possible. And we need a clear view of Miller's regular habits and movements. We want to know if anyone was hassling him or if he'd been involved in any conflicts recently, or if he mentioned anything that might be linked to his murder. I want reports by Friday if we can manage it.' Ralph puffs out his chest, revelling in handing out orders.

Isaacs is nodding his approval at this action list. 'It's a shame we're still thin on the ground because of the Jacoby case but we'll just have to make do,' he says. He turns to Nan pointedly before his eyes stray to me. 'I don't want to lose focus on Jacoby.'

Next to me Fleet muffles a burp.

I'm unsure which group I've been lumped into. Clearly I need to help Fleet with the statements from Miller's contacts but it seems like Isaacs also expects me to help Nan on the Jacoby case.

Before I have time to confirm, Isaacs reels off a list of things he wants me and Fleet to follow up on top of Myers' tasks, including retrieving the footage from the 2016 bashings. Isaacs' gaze seems to rest mainly on me; I can't shake the feeling I've done something wrong. The energy I summoned earlier has fizzled, and I look around at the others, convinced I'm the odd one out. Glancing at Miller's autopsy photos again, I feel so frustrated. I want to be leading the case but Isaacs obviously doesn't trust me enough, even though I was first to the scene. I clench my jaw and, for a horrifying second, I think I might cry.

It's hard here, I admit to myself. Harder than I thought it would be. There's no special treatment, no reassuring winks from Jonesy. No end-of-day cuddles from Ben. Not for the first time, I wonder if I've made a terrible mistake. I do wonder what the point is sometimes. I am a mother to a son I can't seem to look after, and his father wants as little to do with me as possible. My old life, the only one I've ever had, is over a thousand kilometres away. There's nothing I'm looking forward to, I realise, the thought like a laser beam into my brain. And in the meantime, I'm wrapping my body around strangers, pretending to be someone else, when a perfectly good man is interested in me. Outside the window, a crow tips its head from side to side and looks down its beak at me. In the end, I have to look away.

I love being a detective, I'm instinctively driven to right wrongs, but truly ridding the streets of crime wouldn't suit me at all—the death and horror keep me going. I have nothing else: no hobbies, nothing to fill the minutes, let alone the hours. In a utopian world of pure white goodness, I would be lost. If the killing and the pain and the hurt all stopped, I'm not sure what would become of me. Deep down I suspect that I would probably stop too. Luckily, we humans seem hell-bent on ensuring I won't need to contemplate that scenario any time soon. We enjoy hurting one another too much.

Isaacs asks Nan to give the room a brief update on the Jacoby case. Now that it's almost six weeks old, everyone is starting to acknowledge the possibility that a solve may not happen. You can literally sense the shift: hope and optimism have a certain smell to them, while defeat emits a very different scent. Full credit to Nan though: she's convinced she will get her man and is studiously ignoring the increasingly pungent stench of hopelessness wafting from her colleagues.

The Jacoby case is one of those complicated puzzles you dream of taking on when you're a young idealistic detective with a genuine belief in the justice system. For a bunch of sceptical detectives who've been around the block a hundred times, it's mainly just a pain in the arse. A woman turns up dead at the base of a luxury apartment complex one Sunday morning. It's quickly established that she fell from the penthouse suite, where she'd attended a Christmas-in-July party the night before. Ginny Frost was a 37-year-old escort. The post-mortem was inconclusive but several of her injuries indicate that she was pushed.

To complicate matters, the suite is owned by Frank Jacoby, a retired chief justice in his late sixties. Charming and connected, he has the rich and powerful firmly in his silk-lined pockets. He's married, to high-profile academic and artist Ivy Strachan, but that hasn't stopped him having a 'healthy interest in all kinds of women', which was how he referred to his philandering in one of the many interviews Nan has subjected him to.

'If those walls could talk, they'd talk dirty,' Nan has taken to saying as she sifts through the seemingly endless pile of photographs that detail every square inch of the apartment.

But the walls can't talk and neither, it seems, will any of the people who attended the elaborate party hosted by Jacoby that fateful night. The only lead we have is the statement from Ginny's friend Sasha Cryer: she claims that she witnessed—through a guest bedroom window that night—Jacoby and Ginny arguing on the balcony. Unfortunately, Sasha is also an escort with a history of drug use, and the attractive blond man who she claims also witnessed the argument has either disappeared off the face of the earth or is a figment of her imagination.

Nan is as determined as ever but I can tell that even she is tiring of Jacoby's endless denials, fiercely loyal mates and passive-aggressive threats toward our department. The media isn't helping: their insane theories and rogue investigations have choked the front pages and dominated social sites for weeks, the general incompetence of the homicide squad a key part of their narrative.

Now Nan runs through the latest leads on the case, which almost all involve hunting down the missing male witness. I pick at some skin under my nail. Pulling at it with my teeth, I'm surprised to taste blood as it breaks away. I suck on my finger discreetly, enjoying the coppery taste, before realising that Isaacs is looking at me, his brow creased. I yank my finger out of my mouth and focus studiously on my notebook.

I glance at Fleet and wonder if he is also pissed off about not leading the Miller case. I can't help feeling that we're on the outer— that Isaacs is toying with us, considering us for a bigger role but only when he thinks we're up to it.

I sigh, forcing my attention back to Nan. Even though I find her prickly, I'd prefer to work more closely with her: perhaps some of the glow Isaacs obviously sees in her might rub off on me.

'Alright, let's get moving,' says Isaacs. 'I want a big push to pin something on Jacoby. Let's find that missing witness or put it to bed. I don't know if we'll be able to avoid an inquest but let's give it our best shot. And let's get this homeless man some justice. If this thing is linked to those old bashings, I want to know about it. Is everyone clear?'

'Yes, sir,' we chorus as he exits the room.

I rise, trailing after Nan and Calvin like a puppy.

Fleet brushes past me roughly, still reeking of cigarette smoke as he heads toward the car park. I stand watching his retreating figure, annoyed, my finger throbbing, before I head back to my desk to watch grainy footage of faceless young men beating fellow humans into oblivion.

Wednesday, 15 August
4.04 pm

The wind tangles the rain. Leaves and rubbish swirl in a wild dance outside the office windows. After watching several unpleasant hours of violent footage from the 2016 bashings, I'm down a red-herring rabbit hole, following up a lead at a shelter where Walter Miller possibly stayed for a few days in late July. One of his friends told Chloe he'd run into some trouble there, that he'd argued with a fellow guest, but I'm struggling to find someone on staff who can corroborate this. I narrowly avoid sighing into the phone, mid-conversation. I leave my details and thank the person on the other end of the line before I hang up.

I stretch my arms above my head, gearing up to go find Ralph and give him my updates, when a jolt of electricity seems to pass through the room. A chill runs down my bare arms, rousing the downy hairs. I pull my shirt sleeves to my wrists and look outside. Everything is still; the wind has dropped. Wet leaves form sloppy piles on the walkways. People are still carrying umbrellas but angle them away from their heads, checking whether it's still raining or if the drips are just falling from trees and awnings. The light is caught between day and night, an eerie alien colour that seems to carry wafts of smoke, just like the way rainbows form in dregs of sunlight.

Without warning, the switchboard explodes behind me. The terror alert goes off and the office breaks into well-practised action. Eyes widen. Everything speeds up. The air is flush with the taste of danger.

Fleet is coming back from the tearoom, a mug in his hand, and comically stops to survey the madness. Isaacs charges toward his office, his phone against his ear. I jump as he slams his door shut behind him. A thrill runs through my middle, forcing me to my feet.

I join Fleet, who is casually sipping his tea with raised eyebrows. 'Shit's going down,' he says unnecessarily.

A young, pretty cop stops next to us, slightly breathless. 'Something's happened at the top of the city,' she says. 'My friend's a journo and she just texted me.'

'Great,' says Fleet. 'I'm glad the experts are leading the way when it comes to crime in the city.'

'Look,' I mutter.

Isaacs yanks his office door open and thrusts a hand out, gesturing at Nan, Calvin, Fleet, Chloe and me. We all head his way.

His mobile starts up a wail again and he swears, holding out a hand to pause us mid-step. He disappears into a small meeting room a few metres from his office. We stand in an awkward circle around the doorway, waiting like naughty children. We can hear bits of his conversation, harsh short words muffled by the trills of office phones and the calming voices that answer them.

Isaacs reappears and we fall into an obedient trot behind him.

Last inside his office, I pull the door shut. Isaacs laces his fingers, agitated, and looks at each of us in turn.

'What's up?' says Fleet nonchalantly.

'A terror attack?' asks Nan, back straight, ready to pounce, eager to clean up whatever mess her fellow humans have made this time.

'No,' says Isaacs. 'There's been an incident on the corner of Spring and Collins. On the film set. An adult male was stabbed, just over twenty minutes ago. He's critical and has been rushed to hospital.'

'The big action scene,' I say, remembering the news report and my conversation with Macy.

'Yes,' Isaacs says, turning to me. 'The incident happened live on one of their takes or whatever you call it. It's a cast member who was injured.'

'So, it's on camera?' Fleet snorts out a laugh. 'That's kind of funny.'

Isaacs continues as if he didn't speak. 'The injured man is Sterling Wade. I probably don't need to tell you that this is going to be huge.'

No one speaks for a moment but the room crackles with energy. I recognise Sterling Wade's name—he's the movie star my friend Candy calls her 'Aryan God'. It takes me a moment to summon an image of a flawless young blond man. I recall Candy mentioning that his family lives in a town near Smithson as she joked about inviting herself over for Christmas lunch.

Chloe swallows loudly, her eyes enormous.

'The guy from *The Street*?' says Calvin slowly. 'My daughters are obsessed with him.'

'Yes. I'm told there are already about a hundred distraught teenage girls at the scene refusing to leave. They've started turning up at the hospital too.'

Nan narrows her eyes. Teenage girls are her least-favourite type of human. 'Good lord,' she mutters.

'Was anyone else injured?' I ask.

'It doesn't appear so. But it's absolute chaos down there. Over three hundred people were running around with masks on, in zombie costumes, plus the crew and general public who were watching, so it's near impossible to do a stocktake on everyone.'

'Do we know what happened?' I press.

'The reports coming through from the security firm aren't clear, but I'm marking it as suspicious for now though I assume it was probably some kind of accident. An issue with one of the props, or maybe a mental-health issue with a cast member, but we'll need to do due diligence and a full review. Especially if there was a security breach.' Isaacs rolls his shoulders back in their sockets. 'We'll need to conduct formal interviews with everyone who was in the proximity of Wade and work the scene as soon as possible.'

I've heard about terrible accidents happening on film sets: faulty props or stunts that backfire, silly pranks with serious consequences. It's not hard to imagine how things can go wrong with so many people working under pressure and acting out such dramatic scenes.

Fleet rubs his hands together. 'Okay, so, who'll do what?'

Nan's pale eyes are shining sharply in the yellow office light. With her grey cropped hair, she looks like a wild wolf.

Isaacs glances out his window. 'Woodstock and Fleet will lead,' he says after a moment. 'Senna to support. I want your full attention on this now. If it turns out to be a simple accident, you can get back to business as usual tomorrow. But if it's more complicated, you will handball your existing case load, and that includes the Miller case.' Isaacs looks like he's about to say something else but shuts his mouth instead. His phone rings again and he talks quietly with the caller for a minute.

Endorphins zap around my body. Even though I know this whole thing is probably some kind of accident, I'm slightly disoriented by Isaacs' decision. And I can sense the surprise in the room. I glance at Fleet, who sees me looking at him and winks.

Isaacs ends the call and I notice little pulses of adrenaline rippling across his face. It's flowing through all of us. I want to say something, to assure him that I've got this and have already worked out the next logical step, but he speaks first.

'Get to the hospital,' he says to me and Fleet. 'Talk to anyone you can who saw what happened and speak with the ambos who brought him in. Apparently it's not looking good for the Wade kid.'

—◀o▶—

'I can't live with your sadness anymore, Gemma,' Scott said to me abruptly one night in early December, after he put Ben to bed.

I blinked, looking up from a magazine article I'd been half-reading. I marvelled that Scott couldn't see that I could barely live with it either.

'We need to get on with our lives,' he said. 'I want you to leave. Or I will.'

I left the next day. I called in sick, packed a small bag, dropped Ben at school and drove to Dad's.

Dad opened his door to find me clutching my overnight bag. He held me in his arms as I cried. Years of tears poured out of me, breaking down my bones, making them soft and floppy. All I could think was 'we didn't make it', until I couldn't tell whether I was thinking it or saying it. Even after I stopped crying, I barely spoke for days.

Our split brought back all the old grief. I cried for Mum, who was taken from me so suddenly when I was only fourteen. I cried for my dead high-school boyfriend, Jacob. I cried for the way I'd treated Scott, for how things ended with Felix, my miscarriage and my broken heart. Most of all I cried for Ben and the mess I was about to make of his life.

Three weeks later I left Dad's, moving into a tiny rental cottage not far from my work. Scott and I grimly worked out how to share Ben. Scott's resolve terrified me but I was grateful for it too—I didn't have his strength and I needed him to show me how this could work. Show me that it was going to be okay.

There were no rings to take off. No papers to sign or names to change. We were able to detach instantly, as if we'd never happened at all.

I threw myself into caring for Ben, willing the time I spent with him to mean more than it ever had. We fumbled through Christmas, and I sleepwalked through work, navigating the terrible crimes, the stupid ones and everything in between. But Smithson was closing in on me, and the anxiety I've always battled became overwhelming. Every night as I lay in the tiny cottage, trying to sleep, I could feel the town talking. The endlessness of the bush pawed at me through paper-thin walls. During the day, the open spaces and lonely roads taunted me. The need I had for Ben felt dangerous. My mind pushed me into darker and darker places, and I was scared to be alone with him. Scared to be apart from him. Scott became wary, worried. For a while there, I'm not sure he trusted me with our son—and, if I'm honest, I didn't trust myself.

Three months after our split, Jonesy sat me down for a serious chat. 'I have news,' he said, before detailing a senior position that had come up on the Melbourne homicide squad.

'Your work is still exceptional, Woodstock,' Jonesy said. 'I rely on you more than I should. But I don't want to watch you fade away.' He lifted heavy, water-filled eyes to mine. 'I can't have that.'

I went ahead with the application and summoned the energy to do the interviews.

When the offer came through, Jonesy firmly suggested that I accept it. My body exploded with fear: it knew before I did that

I would go, that I had to, and that this would rip me apart but save me at the same time.

'But I can't go,' I said, Ben's little face sharp in my mind.

Jonesy just looked at me sadly, already knowing I could.

I arrived in Melbourne halfway through May and was greeted by vivid green lawns, naked trees and raincoats covered with metallic polka-dots that had obviously become a fashion statement when I wasn't looking. Standing outside my serviced apartment, battered by chilled wind and doused by fine misty rain, I was buffeted on both sides by people who were busy in a way I'd never known before. I was completely disoriented but wildly, heart-thumpingly alive.

Saying goodbye to Ben was like a stake to the heart. In my memory, the locked-off shot that I play over and over has the smell of death around it. My beautiful son, always a solemn child, stood next to Dad's car, his hand in mine, and looked at me, looked inside me. In that moment the natural order switched. I yearned for his permission and he gave me his blessing. I think he understood that I had to go.

Wednesday, 15 August
5.21 pm

I scroll through an endless stream of Google images and news articles about Sterling Wade as Fleet steers us toward the Royal Melbourne Hospital. He's weaving in and out of the traffic like a race-car driver. The day has broken into a moody tantrum. Sections of the mostly grey sky are bruised a soft blue. Fleet seems to be in a mood too, making strange little noises every minute or so and fiddling with the heater dials.

'Wade's twenty-three,' I tell him. 'He won a Logie a few months ago. And he was rumoured to be leaving *The Street* at the end of the year to move to LA.'

'No Hollywood break for him anytime soon now,' comments Fleet darkly.

'Obviously,' I say, rolling my eyes, 'though you never know. If he survives this, it's a great story. It could be his golden ticket in LA.'

Fleet snorts.

'His girlfriend is in the film as well,' I continue. 'There are heaps of local actors in it. Even I recognise some of their names.'

'Maybe you can get some autographs, Woodstock.'

'Good idea,' I reply calmly. 'Here's another fun fact for you. Wade grew up right near my home town. His family live on a farm just outside of Karadine in New South Wales.'

Fleet snorts again, slowing to turn into the hospital entrance. 'If only your paths had crossed years ago, imagine how different your life might have been.'

'Don't be an idiot. He's almost a decade younger than me.'

Fleet starts to say something but his personal mobile lights up. I catch a row of emojis before he snatches it out of the centre console. 'You talk, I'll watch,' he says, sliding into an emergency-vehicle parking spot and flicking off the ignition.

'Sure.' I shrug agreeably. 'That works.'

After dealing with security—who are trying to contain at least fifty teenage girls at the main entrance—we present our IDs at the reception desk and ask to speak to the manager. Doctors and nurses are buzzing everywhere like bees in a hive. I hear Sterling's name whispered, faces flushed with the drama of such a high-profile victim. A frazzled woman appears, telling us she is Lauren Klein, the hospital operations manager. She ushers us toward a small room at the far end of the main corridor. Fleet's eyes dart around like he's casing the joint, which I find strangely reassuring; I know those eyes won't miss a thing.

We rush to keep up with Lauren, who walks surprisingly quickly. I suddenly feel as if I'm under observation, so intense are the stares from everyone we pass. Lauren pauses, her hand on a creamy door, and gives us a look full of something that I can't quite decipher before she pushes it open and steps inside.

Two constables flank a young woman on a rose-coloured couch. She is well past shock: she's expressing the kind of despair that most people find jarring because they're so unused to seeing it in real life. The space is softly lit, and not unlike a dated lounge room. Three tissue boxes sit on the coffee table, and the couches and armchairs are crowded with limp cushions. I can feel the ghosts of bad news past hovering above us in the lavender-scented air.

As my eyes adjust to the dim light, I realise a man is sitting in an armchair on the other side of the room. His long legs make him look too big for the furniture and his knees jut out, pointing awkwardly to the ceiling. He's staring at the wall, unblinking. Despite his long stylish haircut, I guess he's about forty.

One of the constables gets to his feet, clearly relieved that we have arrived.

'Detective Sergeant Woodstock,' I say, 'and this is Detective Sergeant Fleet.' My strong voice seems harsh in the soft cloud of the room.

The girl looks up and tears drip down her face. She's still wailing, her mouth open and clenched around her fist as she heaves through another sob.

I raise my eyebrows at the constable, noting that his badge reads 'Roper'. 'Let's talk outside for a minute,' I say to him.

He exchanges a look with the other constable, who nods. Then he glances at the man in the corner of the room, who still appears to be in a daze.

When Constable Roper has joined me and Fleet, I pull the door shut behind him and we duck into a small alcove.

Lauren glances down at her squawking pager. 'I'll be back in a minute,' she says.

'So, what's the deal?' asks Fleet, leaning against the wall.

Roper's eyes flick anxiously between the two of us. 'I was doing crowd control when they were shooting the scene. I was probably the officer closest to Wade when he was injured.'

'Did you see what happened?' I ask him.

'No, I was facing the other way but the security was solid. We had large barriers on both sides of the street and guards everywhere ID'ing the cast and crew. Plus, we had at least twenty of our guys around the perimeter by the time filming started. I don't think anyone got in. I don't see how they could have.'

I try to picture it. 'When did you realise that something was wrong?'

'Well, it was weird. There was already so much screaming. They were all supposed to be doing that as part of the movie, you know, hundreds of zombies running along the road toward Wade. It was raining a bit—made it a little hard to see. And like I said, I was looking the other way. But after a while I could hear this one girl screaming, and it sounded different from the others. Some of the crowd started to point, and when I looked back I saw Wade on the ground with his girlfriend. She was trying to hold him up. That's her in there,' he says, cocking his head at the room. 'Elizabeth Short.'

'Who's the other guy?' asks Fleet.

'The film director. Cartwright. Riley Cartwright. They both went in the ambulance with Wade—they wouldn't take no for an answer.'

'What do you think happened?' I ask him.

'It's hard to say,' he replies. 'My guess is that it was an accident. Someone got carried away with a prop and stabbed him. Probably panicked when they realised what they'd done.'

'Did you see anyone leaving the scene?' I ask.

'People were running all over the place. It was a mess.'

'I thought you said security was everywhere?'

'Yeah, but everyone just went mad. I've never seen anything like it. People were running around in costumes. The security guards were yelling for everyone to stay where they were, and our guys were just trying to control the general public, but it was pretty

crazy.' Roper's voice takes on a mild whine; he wants us to understand. 'I mean, people were screaming out that there was a terrorist
attack . . . For a minute I was worried too. I jumped the barrier and
got to Wade as soon as I could, but by then he was already in a bad
way. Blood everywhere.'

'Was there a doctor onsite?' Fleet asks.

'There was a first-aid team, and they got to him pretty quick
once it became clear something was wrong. They didn't work on
him for long—I think they knew straight away that he needed
to get to a hospital.' He bites his lip. 'I heard the ambos say he'd
need surgery. I just tried to contain the people who were near him
when it happened and comfort his girlfriend. She was completely
hysterical.'

'Did anyone you spoke to say what happened?' I ask.

'Everyone just said they saw Wade suddenly collapse. The other
officers at the scene were getting statements when we left—but
we're talking about a lot of people.'

I nod, starting to appreciate the scale of this thing. Often all we
want when we work a case is more witnesses. It sounds like that
won't be a problem in this instance.

'Alright, well, we'll take it from here,' I tell Roper. 'It would be
great to get your reports as soon as you can manage it.'

He nods. 'Of course.'

When we return to the room, Elizabeth has stopped crying but
her blotchy face is tear-stained. Riley Cartwright is still hunched
over in the corner, staring into space.

'We'll leave you with the detectives now,' Roper says to the two of
them. He nods to the other constable, who puts a reassuring hand
on Elizabeth's shoulder before he stands. He takes a deep breath
and puffs his cheeks, releasing the air slowly. Angry blemishes form
a red crescent across his jawline. He looks exhausted.

'We'll send through our statements as soon as we can,' confirms Roper as they escape into the hallway.

The door shuts behind them and it immediately feels like we're in a tomb. The heater has switched off and the air hovers, unmoving. Fleet walks across the room and sits on one of the armchairs, eyeing Riley. I can tell he is leaving Elizabeth to me.

Swallowing, I walk over to sit on the couch next to the grief-stricken girl. I gently tuck my hand into the curve of her elbow and duck my head, encouraging her to meet my gaze. 'Elizabeth?'

She's obviously in costume—even though she must be at least twenty, she is dressed like a schoolkid. Her wavy brown hair is pulled back from her face, seventies style, and she's wearing a white shirt and a tartan skirt. She is slight but long-limbed. Flat-chested with elfin features, she reminds me of Mia Farrow. Despite knowing she's an actor, I'm not sure I recognise her.

She squeezes her eyes shut and rocks forward in another bout of sobbing. It echoes around the room.

'Elizabeth, I understand this is a terrible shock but I need to ask you some questions.' I spy a glass of water on a coffee table and offer it to her. 'Come on, here, have this.' She takes it and gulps down a few mouthfuls, then gives it back to me. Blood stains the skin of her hands and wrists: a light rust-brown has set into the creases of her knuckles, and dark red lines curve under her fingernails.

'I heard the ambulance officer say that he lost a lot of blood,' she whispers.

'How about we take a walk?' says Fleet to Riley. The director reluctantly unfolds his body from the chair and stands up. His whole body seems to shake.

Elizabeth lets out a jerky sob as the door clicks shut behind them. 'When can I see him?' she asks me.

I rub her back and breathe deeply, encouraging her to mirror me. 'I'm not sure,' I admit, 'but I know everyone here is doing everything they can to help him.'

She tips her head forward as if she is praying, her hands clasped together.

'Elizabeth,' I say gently.

'Lizzie,' she says. 'Everyone calls me Lizzie.'

'Okay. Lizzie. You were there with Sterling today?'

'Our scenes together were finished.' She paws at her hair. 'But Sterling had the big zombie scene today. He was so excited about it.' Her face crumples again.

'So, you were just there watching?'

She nods and shudders, forcing herself to breathe and answer my question. 'Yes. Just hanging with the crew.'

'I know this is hard, but it would be really helpful if you could tell me what you saw happen.'

Her tears spill over again. 'I was watching Sterling. Everything was going well, the scene looked great, but then after a while I could just tell something was wrong. He just stopped all of a sudden. He was trying to say something but because there were so many people it was hard to see, but I *knew*, I just knew . . .' Her hands squirm on her lap and she talks around fresh sobs. 'I could tell he was hurt but I didn't understand what had happened. And then he just dropped to the ground. I thought he'd fainted. But then I saw he was bleeding for real and I just started screaming. I think everyone thought I'd lost my mind. Everyone was just staring at me. No one was doing anything to help . . . Oh god—' Lizzie's voice gives way to her sobs for a moment. 'I just want to know he's going to be okay.'

'It must have been horrible,' I say.

'I can't believe this,' she says, crying into her hands. 'What happened?'

'That's what we need to work out.'

'I should call his parents.' She moans. 'And Brodie.'

'Who's Brodie?' I ask.

Lizzie brushes more tears away. 'Sterling's best friend.'

There's a knock on the door, and the frazzled-looking hospital manager sticks her head inside. 'Elizabeth,' she says, 'your brother is here.'

A young man enters the room in a flurry and makes a beeline for Lizzie. I can't tell if he's older or younger but they look alike: he's tall and there's a similar shape to his face, the same chestnut hair, but his complexion is darker. Right now, they have an identical pull of shock in their expressions.

'Thank god you're here,' wails Lizzie, sobbing noisily into his chest. 'They don't know if he's going to make it. They keep talking about surgery.'

'This is awful,' he murmurs, hugging her and stroking her hair. 'I can't believe it.'

'I know.' She falls back against him again, cupping her mouth with her hands.

'I'm so glad I didn't get on the plane before I got your text,' he says.

Lizzie nods as she begins a fresh wave of tears.

I introduce myself to him.

'I'm Kit,' he says distractedly. 'Lizzie's little brother.'

The door swings open again and we all jump. This time a beautiful young woman stands in the doorway. Her otherwise perfect face appears to slide downward thanks to dark trails of running make-up. The hospital manager, Lauren, stands behind her looking agitated.

'They wouldn't let me in,' the woman announces in a strong American accent, tossing her long fiery hair behind her shoulders and apparently making an effort to control her emotions. 'I've been waiting outside for ages. Where is Sterling? Can we see him?' Her shiny blue eyes are wild and leap around the room.

'He's in surgery,' whispers Lizzie, who has noticeably stiffened beside me.

'What the fuck happened out there?' the redhead implores.

Before anyone can respond, Fleet joins her in the doorway with Riley Cartwright trailing behind him.

The woman shoots Cartwright a furious look and moves away from him into the room. I slowly recognise her from glossy magazine covers and a hair-dye commercial claiming the 'perfect colour every time'. She doesn't usually have red hair but her surname is James, I think.

I stand up and walk over to her, introducing myself and Fleet.

'Ava James,' she says to me. Despite her tears she tilts her chin in reflex with her handshake, with the confidence of a Bond girl. Or perhaps James Bond himself. 'I'm in the movie with Sterling. I'm his co-star.' Her tone is clipped, professional.

Fleet lifts his hand in a lazy wave, brazenly looking her up and down.

Ava spins back to Lizzie. 'What kind of surgery?' she demands.

Lizzie raises her shoulders in response. 'I don't know. I guess they need to try to—'

'How could you let this happen?' Ava snaps at Cartwright.

The room has grown crowded and hot. Waves of perfume compete with body odour and swirl around the space, buoyed by the heat now blasting from the wall vents. Lauren's beeper starts to bleat again, and she glances at us apologetically as she backs away and closes the door. Lizzie continues to cry into her brother's chest. Cartwright comes to life in the form of a coughing fit. This earns him another glare from Ava, who with hands on her hips seems more furious than upset. Fleet gets up and slaps Cartwright on the back until the coughs turn to heaving tears, and he clutches his knees as he splutters.

I can't shake the feeling that I have wandered onto a TV set. Fleet manages to seem mildly amused by the entire scene.

The door opens again and everyone looks up expectantly.

'I'm very sorry,' starts Lauren, clearly wishing she was anywhere else but here. 'I'm afraid Sterling Wade has just died.'

Ava screams. Cartwright drops to the ground, his face in his hands.

'Oh shit,' whispers Kit.

Next to him, there's a whooshing sound as all the air leaves Lizzie's body. She slumps back against the couch, her eyes huge and her knuckles white as she grips her brother's hands with her bloodstained ones.

Wednesday, 15 August
9.16 pm

The top stretch of Spring Street is empty, barricaded off at the start of Collins all the way to the beginning of Flinders and lined with security. The glow of the streetlights warms the shadowy gutters and the navy sky wraps around everything like an icy blanket. The curious eyes of the stars peer down from their endless dome. A possum jumps from a powerline into a tree above us and I spin around at the sound, hairs prickling on my neck.

'Jeez,' says Fleet, whistling.

'What?' I say self-consciously, my heart thumping loudly.

'It's like a zombie apocalypse out here.' He says it seriously but tosses me a wink. He taps out a cigarette from his signature soft packet and shoves it in his mouth like a badly groomed James Dean.

While we were at the hospital, Isaacs, Nan and Calvin went to the crime scene and assisted the first responders: sixteen over-whelmed street cops who had worked with the film's security crew in an attempt to control the panicked crowd. Between them, they locked down the scene, taking as many initial statements as they could, and bagging blood-spattered costumes and props. A fresh wave of uniforms turned up at about 6 pm and are still dotted along the edges of the streets, keeping the crowds of onlookers at bay.

Amid the initial madness, a female zombie, her forehead split open above her right eye, nervously handed in a bloodied knife she'd found about twenty metres from where Wade was attacked. She'd recognised that it was heavier and sharper than the other prop weapons littering the ground. Covered in shoeprints, fingerprints and the grime of the city, the knife suggests something far more sinister than a stunt gone wrong.

I step onto the path and look down into the Treasury Gardens. White-and-blue-checked police tape flaps in the breeze. I turn to take in the empty road. Fleet's right: the scene instantly conjures up memories of doomsday films. Odd how eerie an abandoned city street can be. So unnatural.

A clumsy wall of flowers already rests against one of the plastic bollards. Random props are scattered haphazardly on the ground: masks, strips of black cloth, chewing-gum wrappers and folded sheets of paper. I bend to pick up one with my gloved hand. It's a list detailing the day's filming. Along the top of both pages is the movie title, *Death Is Alive*. The 'mass zombie street scene' was scheduled for 4.45 pm. The names 'Wade' and 'James' are listed next to it. Wade's final act, I think grimly.

'Find something?' calls Fleet from behind the barricade, breathing out the last of his cigarette.

'It's a list of all the scenes they were shooting today.'

'Give us a look,' he says, walking over and taking it. 'Yeah, this is the call sheet. So, this zombie thing was the first scene today that had extras. All the other ones were with the main cast in other locations.'

I look at him, little lines forming on his forehead as he skims the list again.

'Since when are you so down with the movie lingo?' I ask.

He wiggles his brows at me. 'Did a bit of acting in my time. Even had a few guest appearances on *Neighbours* back in the day.'

'Really?' I can never quite tell when he's being serious.

'Uh-huh,' he says, reaching for another cigarette. 'I have legit qualifications. Don't tell me you haven't noticed my drama skills.'

'You shouldn't smoke so much,' I say, as a nicotine craving hits me square in the gut.

'Correct,' he says.

I roll my eyes. 'What do you think happened out here today?'

He sucks on the cigarette, pulling in his cheekbones. 'No idea. But that knife changes everything. Someone either planted it as a joke and it ended up going way too far, or we have a genuine homicide on our hands.' He taps the ash from the end of the smoke. 'Or a manslaughter, at least.'

'Yeah.' I put my hands on my hips as our eyes meet. 'Something's definitely not right. Even if it was a hoax that went too far, no one's come forward.'

I look at the small huddle of our forensics team, diligently toiling in the area at the top of Collins where Sterling Wade was stabbed. 'Come on,' I say, leading Fleet over to them.

Wade left behind a neat circle of blood bordered by a few uneven spatters. It's the only indication that something bad happened here. Everything else suggests a roaring party.

'How are you guys doing?' I ask as we approach the team.

Brenton Cardona is meticulously studying sections of the bitumen with a small torch but he tosses me a toothy smile. 'Fancy bumping into you like this again.' He arches his back into a stretch. 'We'll be here a while yet.'

I crouch down next to him. 'Have you found anything?'

Cardona rocks back onto the balls of his feet and looks at me, his dark skin velvety in the moonlight. 'We found lots of things,' he replies, 'but in terms of useful stuff, we found shit so far. This whole scene is a mess.'

'Yeah,' says Priscilla Godfrey, one of the junior techs. 'No body, and the leftovers of hundreds of random people dressed in costume and dripping fake blood. Plus, there's general day-to-day shit, ambo footprints all through Wade's blood and crap like this.' She holds up a fake knife in one gloved hand and a fake gun in the other.

'Definitely one for the memoir,' quips Fleet, sidling up beside me. 'Hey, Pris,' he says, leering at her.

'Hey, fuckhead,' she replies, all but confirming the rumour I heard about them hooking up.

'So basically, we're starting at zero,' I say, forcing the conversation back to the case. I look out across the park again, my breath making white trails in the air. My work phone rings and I mask a slight jolt as the electronic tones beat out into the darkness. It's Isaacs. I step away from the group and tell our boss that we're on our way. I give Fleet a quick nod. 'We need to get back.'

'Not much to see here anyway,' says Fleet, looking directly at Priscilla again. She tosses him a nasty glare and then busies herself with tweezering a piece of fabric and a cigarette butt into a plastic bag.

Cardona rolls his eyes at them. 'Hopefully that knife is smeared with a generous dollop of our guy's prints and DNA,' he says, 'because apart from that, we're pretty much nowhere.'

'Don't worry too much, mate,' says Fleet, over his shoulder as he walks off. 'Apparently the whole bloody thing is on tape.'

Wednesday, 15 August

10.38 pm

At least thirty reporters ambush us at the main entrance of the police station. They're like a mob of crazed zombies from Wade's movie, armed with phones, recording equipment, cans of Coke and takeaway coffees.

'Are you on the Wade case?'

'How was it at the hospital?'

'Did someone plant a weapon in the props?'

'Was it a crazy fan?'

'Was it a random attack?'

'What is the security company saying?'

'Did Sterling Wade have a stalker?'

'How is his girlfriend coping?'

'Was Sterling having an affair with Ava James?'

'Are there any developments on the homeless man's murder?'

I keep my eyes on the ground. An enthusiastic young reporter with a halo of blonde frizz yells, 'Gemma! Gemma!' as she shoves an iPhone in front of my mouth. Shaking my head and pushing the phone away, I step around her and into the safety of the station. The door seals shut behind me and Fleet, neutralising the desperate symphony.

We exchange looks before he breaks the stare with a quick trademark wink, but I can tell he's frazzled. I've dealt with the media before, had my fair share of hassles, but I've never witnessed anything quite like this frenzied desire for information. Leaving the hospital had been bad enough: a mob of reporters circled the building, joined by at least two hundred devastated teenage girls who wanted answers as badly as the journos did. Death is interesting, I get that. Especially when a victim is young and their death is violent. But Sterling Wade is clearly in a different league altogether. The journalists have their fangs out and they want blood.

'In here, you two,' says a gruff voice from behind us. Isaacs is standing next to a water cooler in the half light of an office doorway, drinking out of a mug that reads 'Cop This' and staring at the mob of reporters outside.

The artificially lit main room is a thrum of activity. Phones bleat, printers whir. I can hear the drone of a news report and a heavy thud as someone moves one of the case boards without releasing the wheels properly.

All attention is on us as we follow Isaacs to his office. I notice a gleam in the eyes of the juniors—they are primed for hunting. We are more like the journos than we like to admit: we all want the answers, we just tend to have different ways of getting them. And whether we like it or not, we're all addicted to the story.

Nan and Calvin are already here, as is Chloe. They all look wired, riding high on the fresh pulse of death. I can feel it in me too.

'How was it at the hospital?' Isaacs asks, echoing the reporters.

'Pretty intense, sir,' I reply, taking the group through what transpired in the lavender-scented room. Eyebrows shoot up when I mention Ava's name. 'There wasn't much hope when they brought him in, but once the hospital staff confirmed Wade had died, none of them were in very good shape. The girlfriend was bawling,

demanding to see the body, and Ava went full diva, requesting seda-
tives and a private room. She had her own security there too—it
was pretty surreal.'

'What about the director?' asks Isaacs. 'Riley Cartwright?'

'Weird guy,' says Fleet. 'He barely spoke. Then again, he's lost a
mate and probably a movie. That's a pretty shitty day by anyone's
standards.'

'We spoke to the ambos who brought Wade in,' I say, 'but they
couldn't tell us much that we didn't already know. They said they
thought it was touch and go from the start because of how much
blood he'd lost at the scene.'

'The surgeon said the wound was straight to the heart,' Fleet
says. 'The guy had no chance.'

'Did any of the cast or crew shed more light on what happened
out there?' I ask the group.

'Nope,' says Nan loudly. 'No one has a clue. One second Wade
was fine, you know, acting, the next he's on the ground screaming
in pain. They were all very emotional,' she adds with disdain.

'So did one of the zombies stab him or not?' asks Fleet. 'Or was
there a surprise guest appearance on set that we're not aware of?'

Nan shrugs. 'My money is on a lunatic fan turned cast mate.
That knife and the force that must have been used makes it seem
pretty deliberate to me.'

'Calvin spoke to the film's producer at the scene,' says Isaacs,
'a Katya March. She's getting us the footage from the shoot this
afternoon as soon as possible, so hopefully that will provide some
clarity. But based on the circumstances, we're definitely treating
this as suspicious. It seems likely that Wade was targeted.'

My pulse quickens. If Isaacs is right, this is huge. Until now
I hadn't really let myself believe that Fleet and I had a full-blown
case on our hands.

57

'We informed Wade's parents earlier,' Isaacs announces, inter-rupting my thoughts. 'They live in regional New South Wales, a tiny place called Karadine. I had some local uniforms get to their house before the press did—which was something, at least. I spoke to them briefly. They're in complete shock. I'm actually not sure that they really took in what I was saying or have got a grip on what's happened, but they're on their way here now.' He glances at his watch. 'They will be flying out of Sydney shortly.' Straighten-ing his head, he looks first at me and then at Fleet. 'I want you two to meet them at the hospital morgue first thing in the morning. I'll get someone to pick them up from their hotel. Get them to do the ID and then find out when they last spoke to him. Maybe he mentioned something that in hindsight seems important.'

'We'll need to speak with Wade's management too,' I say. 'Don't they normally manage the social media accounts and publicity? They might know if he's received any threats.'

'Yes, good idea. Try to speak with them tomorrow as well.' Isaacs leans forward. 'I want us to make contact with everyone we can who was connected to that movie. The security plan needs to be gone over with a fine toothcomb. I want to know how people were allowed access on set and if anyone unauthorised could have gotten through.'

I start to make a list in my head. Isaacs is right: we need to know absolutely everything we can about the film set, and Sterling Wade. By unpacking his world, we'll have a better chance of working out what happened today. Of course, the attack could have been completely random, a bizarre impulse that overtook one of the cast members, in which case our historical legwork will be a waste of time. But all the precedent on the planet suggests that there will be some kind of sign. People tend not to kill on a whim unless it's in the heat of an argument. And Fleet's right, that knife changes everything—it screams deadly intent. My skin is literally sparking with static electricity and a small shock jumps from my fingers as I lay my hand on the metal frame along the back of a chair.

'Wade's sister lives near the parents but I don't know if she's coming to Melbourne,' Isaacs continues. 'They have another son as well, living in country Victoria. Speak to both siblings if you can. Wade might have confided in them. His father, Matthew, also mentioned that Wade spent quite a few years staying with another family when he first moved to Melbourne, so we need to speak with them too. And find out who else he was close to. Talk to the tech guys tomorrow. I want all of Wade's private and public correspondence reviewed. As far back as eighteen months. Maybe there are signs of stalking. Speak to his girlfriend and any close friends about that—they might have noticed something.'

'Yes, sir,' we say in unison.

'If the parents do the ID first thing, we can move forward with the autopsy tomorrow afternoon. I spoke to Mary-Anne about it earlier. She's back from leave tomorrow and will do it herself.'

'Yes, sir,' I reply.

'What else?' says Isaacs, looking at us.

'We'll start pulling CCTV from the city precinct tomorrow,' I say. 'So if someone fled the scene, there's a chance we'll be able to identify them.'

'And I guess we'll need to start going through the five hundred zombie witness statements at some point,' says Fleet wryly.

'How many uniforms can we have on this?' I ask Isaacs. 'We can manage the Wades tomorrow, maybe his agent and loved ones, but Fleet's right, we need to start locking down the witness statements and there are a lot more than usual. We might need to set up a mass-processing area.'

Isaacs sighs. 'We're pretty stretched, as you all know, and another suspected homicide has been called in tonight already. But this is the priority for obvious reasons. I've pulled in a few extra boys and girls—they'll be here first thing. Hopefully we'll have thirty bodies confirmed by tomorrow morning. To be honest, you'll be turning uniforms away. Everyone's desperate to be close to this.'

I nod slowly, Walter Miller's face springing into my vision. I realise I haven't thought about him all afternoon.

'What about the Miller case?' I ask.

Isaacs looks at me. 'Would you prefer to stay on the Miller case, Woodstock?'

There's an uneasy silence. Nan looks back and forth between the two of us with a barely perceptible smirk.

'No, sir,' I say. 'I just hope it will remain a focus.'

'Ralph has the Miller case in hand and we'll assign some of the juniors to assist him.' Isaacs' voice deepens. 'With so much media attention on what happened this afternoon and the force's link to the security plan, we need to be meticulous. Is that clear?'

'Yes,' I say, my face growing hot.

Isaacs turns to Nan. 'I want you to help out on this when you have free time around the Jacoby case,' he tells her, then looks at Chloe and says, 'Stay back after this so I can brief you on the other homicide. We might need to shuffle some of the uniforms around.'

In my mind, I arrange Walter Miller's worn face next to Sterling Wade's glossy head shot. Even in death, Walter Miller's life will be overshadowed by the more privileged, the more popular. The state's stretched resources will continue to let him down.

Isaacs taps his foot on the ground, gearing up to dismiss us. 'Clearly this isn't what we need right now with our current open cases,' he says. 'And the media attention is going to make things extra challenging. The networks will have just as many people on this as we will, so we need to run a tight ship. Encourage everyone you interact with to avoid talking to journalists. That includes Wade's loved ones. Let's keep as much control over this as we can. I don't want anything biting us on the arse.'

We march out of Isaacs' office full of purpose. I square my shoulders and feel a pop in my chest as the stretch spreads down my spine. I consider setting up the case room before I leave, but it's pretty clear that sleep won't get much of a chance for the next few days and I have nothing in the bank, so I need to get as many hours as I can tonight. I'm old and ugly enough to know that pushing through on the first night of a case is a bad idea. Tempting as it is to let the rush take over, all you end up with are shitty decisions and a cowboy reputation. Fleet and I need sleep. The blue crescents under his eyes are no doubt mirrored beneath my own. I shake out my long hair and retie it in an elastic, forcing myself to focus for a little longer.

We quickly plot out a basic plan of attack for the next forty-eight hours. As always, the task ahead feels insurmountable, epic, but the thirst for figuring it all out has well and truly set in. I'm already completely consumed by what the hell happened on that movie set today.

Little red veins snake around Fleet's eyeballs and he rubs at them roughly, digging his fingers into the corners and making me wince. 'What a day, huh?' he says.

'Tomorrow will probably be worse,' I reply.

'No doubt you are right, Gemma Woodstock. You usually are.' He says this like he's imitating a BBC news anchor, but with a generous layer of sarcasm.

I swat at him half-heartedly. 'Whatever. Right, well, I'm heading home.'

Fleet slides off the table. 'Want a lift?' He leans toward me, too close, and for a second I think that he is going to touch me. 'I've got a spare helmet.'

I step backwards. 'Nah, I'm good,' I say lightly. I picture myself on the back of his bike, holding on to him as we tilt into the corners, the ice wind numbing my face. 'I hate motorbikes.'

'I love them,' he says, smiling.

'See you here early tomorrow.' It's not a question but I pause, expecting a response.

Fleet nods slowly, looking at me as he scrapes his front tooth with a fingernail. His pores are fast filling with dots of dark hair. 'Yep, I'll be here with the birds and the early worms. Fresh as a fucking daisy.' He pulls his cigarette packet out of his jacket pocket and walks toward the car-park entrance. 'See ya.'

I grab my bag and pull on my coat, wrapping a scarf high around my head. After I've given him a few minutes to clear out, I leave the station via the car park too, noting a couple of straggling reporters huddled near the concrete wall by the fire escape, smoking and talking.

I walk a block before pausing under the dim circle of light cast by a street lamp. I locate the packet of cigarettes at the bottom of my bag. Sliding one into my mouth, I close my eyes and suck in the smoke, holding it in before releasing it into the freezing air. I resume walking and check my personal phone. A missed call from Scott a few hours earlier. A missed call from Josh, who obviously wants to get all the gossip on the Wade attack, and three calls and a text message from Candy, who must be losing her mind over this. I read her text: 'OMG Gemma! I totally can't believe this. My number one toy boy is DEAD? Please, please tell me you are working on this. And call me back for fuck's sake. I need to know everything.' I text back that I will call tomorrow.

I see there's also a text from Ben on Scott's phone: a photo of his new soccer uniform laid out on his bedroom floor, sent around the time I was helping a hysterical Lizzie Short get into the back of her brother's 4WD in the hospital car park.

I start flicking through a couple of emails but the words blur on the screen. Rounding the corner, I extinguish my cigarette stub on the side of a bin and toss it in. I narrowly avoid stepping into a pack of drunk men who leer predictably at me. Water drips noisily from the end of a rusty drainpipe.

I buzz into my apartment and brace myself to push open the heavy main door. The air trapped in the stairwell is full of dinner and laundry. My thighs burn as I climb the stairs, imagining the moment Sterling Wade realised he'd been stabbed, that knife hitting his heart, the shock he felt as his fake world merged with his real one, and I wonder whether in those moments he knew who had attacked him, whether he knew who was behind the mask. Or did he die like Walter Miller probably did, his brain racing as the blood flowed out of him, trying to work out what was happening?

I pull on an old tracksuit and crawl into bed. As I drift off, I picture a crush of zombies, their gruesome faces morphing into one another until my mind is blank and the only thing left is the dark circle of Sterling's blood on the cold empty street.

◄○►

After two weeks in the soulless serviced apartment I took a twelve-month lease on my overpriced, run-down shoebox high up in the air on Little Collins Street. It was empty and therefore available straight away. Impressive rings of mould circled the bathroom ceiling and dead flies littered the windowsills, but the real estate agent assured me that the location was 'to die for'. The cottage back in Smithson had been the first place I'd ever lived in by myself and the aching silence had slowly boiled my blood. This was different. I was alone but it was noisy. Elevated. People surrounded me. I felt safer in the pounding heart of Melbourne than I ever had in Smithson.

It's not like I'd never spent time in large cities. I had visited Sydney and Newcastle, but I was woefully unprepared for the permanent change of pace in Melbourne. The constant sounds, the steady flow of people. The height of the buildings. The colours. Everything was amplified. Teenagers here were moodier; professionals were more polished. The art was artier and the music was louder. I arrived sad and flat, but in spite of myself I was quickly charged by the beat of the city.

My apartment has one bedroom plus an open nook, pitched to me as a study but which I immediately turned into a quasi-bedroom for Ben. I bought his bed before mine, and slept in the narrow space for over a week. I put up posters of his favourite soccer players and carefully arranged glow-in-the-dark stars along the cracks in the wall.

He's only been to stay with me once, in the mid-year school holidays. Dad came too, along with Rebecca, his new girlfriend. They'd started seeing each other around the time that I split with Scott. I was dreading spending so much time with Rebecca—seeing as our relationship in Smithson had been quite frosty—but thankfully Dad seemed to pre-empt this and booked them both into a modest hotel nearby. Ben stayed with me and I spent the entire four days of their visit fantasising that it was real, that I was a single mother who lived with her young son in the middle of the city.

Ben loved his tiny room. Loved Frodo the goldfish. Loved the swarms of pigeons and seagulls. But he didn't like the noise: the constant grind of the traffic, the dinging of the trams, the thump and pull of the garbage trucks. He had two nightmares in as many days and I couldn't get it out of my head that he was allergic to my new life.

I took them all out for dinner on their last night in the city. The restaurant was loud and full of tourists. The ceilings were low and the menu was written on a wooden board that sat at an angle along the back wall; Rebecca couldn't read it from where we sat. Ben's meal had too much chilli and Dad could barely hear me over the relentless chatter.

The next morning we had a coffee at Federation Square. Rebecca wanted to sit inside out of the cold. Dad had a headache. I pointed out my regular haunts and told them about Fleet and Nan and Isaacs, people they would never meet.

I bought Ben a helium balloon from a roadside florist. It was printed with a happy birthday message, even though his birthday had been two weeks earlier. He looked up at me, shivering but with a smile—purely for my benefit, I am certain. I caught Dad looking at me too, his eyes creased with confusion as he tried to figure it all out. Figure me out. He didn't understand this place or my life here.

I caught the taxi out to the airport with them that night, wanting to soak up every last moment with Ben. I held his hand as Rebecca prattled on from the front seat about her fear of flying. I studied my little boy's gentle profile, memorising his face all over again. I bought him a book and a model plane, and then they had to go and I hugged Ben, squeezing my soul into him, praying that he understood what I couldn't find the words to explain.

Afterwards, I watched the planes come and go into the night before heading to the airport sports bar. I drank two large glasses of wine as I went over some case notes, half-watching tribes of businessmen slap each other on the back as they downed beers and mopped up sauce with chips. Emboldened by booze, one of them tried to talk to me, offering to buy me a drink, but I shook my head and kept my eyes on the table.

I escaped to the bathroom and sat on the closed toilet with my head between my legs, panic churning until I abruptly spun around and yanked the toilet lid up before being neatly sick into the bowl, completely purging myself of the day with my son. Crying, I stayed in the stall for almost thirty minutes listening to the sounds around me: kids fighting, mothers pleading, cleaners bitching, all between the blasts of water from the tap and the whir of the hand dryers. I was too tired to get up, too tired to get back to my apartment, too tired to keep doing this anymore. All of it.

Eventually I stood, legs shaky. I rinsed my mouth and washed my face in the sink, then patted it dry with a paper towel before making my way to the taxi rank, the taste of vomit making me retch. I stood shivering in the line between the weary but excited travellers and their giant suitcases. In the taxi, its driver complained about the tax system, the politicians, the weather, his bad back. I let his voice fade away while I watched a plane move through the sky, its tail-light flashing in time to my heartbeat as we rounded into Melbourne. Streetlights blurred as I stared into them and the stars did the same above us until the sky was a reflection of the world below. Amid the stream of the driver's gripes, I let the city pull me back in. I felt calmer, but already it was hard to remember the pitch of Dad's voice. The way Ben's small hand felt in mine.

After directing the driver to drop me off near Bourke Street, I walked through Chinatown, breathing in the smells, soothed by the bustle. I was alone: barely a mother, barely a daughter. But somehow, despite my guilt and melancholy, I had slotted into my new home more easily than I had intended.

Thursday, 16 August
7.36 am

Sterling's parents arrive at the Melbourne morgue, bent over and blinking into the fluorescent glow. I notice that Matthew Wade has a tiny piece of hay clinging to the pocket of his flannel shirt. They identify their son's body, as naked as he was the day they met, his shock of thick blond hair angelic in the white light. Afterwards, at our office, they hold hands like lost children in one of our interview rooms, huddling across from us on a worn couch, behind the haze of steam that rises from overfilled mugs of tea, and answer our gentle questions softly. While this scenario is cruel and challenging for any parent, they seem particularly timid. It's hard to imagine them navigating life with such a famous child.

Matthew is slim but tall, with kind blue eyes and a face folded by the sun. His wife, April, is a fawn of a woman: petite, with deep-set brown eyes bordered by comically long lashes. She twists her plain gold wedding band while she speaks, her eyes leaking as the shock cuts more deeply through her by the minute. They haven't slept and it shows.

'Sterling was a good boy. He always was.' She looks first at me and then at Fleet, her head bouncing on her tiny neck.

'When did you last speak to him?' I ask, nudging the hot tea toward her. As much as my heart breaks for these poor people, I'm keen to keep our conversation moving. I'm impatient to see the film footage of the attack that Cartwright's producer, Katya March, sent to Isaacs overnight.

'Oh, well.' April grips her throat as if she's trying to help let the air in. Her eyes already seem to have sunk back into her skull, scared away by death. 'Maybe Monday? He usually calls once a week, doesn't he, Matt? He always calls.'

Matthew looks at his wife as if she's just woken him from a deep slumber. He rubs at his eyes. 'Yes, he does. He always calls.'

'Do you have other children?' I ask, even though I already know the answer.

'Yes. We have three children.' April reaches out for her husband again, who obediently takes her hand.

'Are they close to each other?' asks Fleet.

The Wades pause in their grief to exchange a look.

'They were as children, but Sterling's, ah, situation has made things hard,' says Matthew quietly, as if he's worried that Sterling will hear him. 'He moved to Melbourne when he was thirteen to work on *Team Go* and lived with another family, the Beaufords. They're lovely people but it was an unusual situation.' He pauses then says, almost as an afterthought, 'We probably should call them.'

'It was wonderful for Sterling, of course,' April rushes to add, brushing tears away. 'It's just such a different world, and Melissa and Paul found it a bit challenging. Sterling didn't really understand life on the farm.'

'Where do your other children live?' I ask, sensing an undercurrent worth riding.

'Melissa lives with her husband in Karadine, just down the road from our farm. And Paul moves around a lot, doing all kinds of jobs.'

'Melissa and Paul are pretty traditional names,' I venture, 'especially compared to Sterling.'

April's mouth tugs into a reflexive smile before she remembers what has happened. I can see a hint of Sterling's famous face across her cheekbones. 'Yes. He used to tell us that everyone thought he'd changed his name, you know, to be more memorable for TV or something. But Sterling is actually an old family name.'

'Does Sterling still see the Beaufords?' I press, noting the slump to their postures. They don't want to be talking about this, they don't want to be doing anything, but I know that this is the best time to get them talking. Information will flow freely from their mouths as their minds are distracted by shock. Little things that seem insignificant might emerge, things that in a few days' time they won't have the energy to conjure. We need to keep the words coming because soon April and Matthew will leave this room and head toward their first day in a world without their son.

For a small window of time there's a sense that it might all be a terrible mistake. A few victims' families have confided this to me, and I have experienced it myself, that the first day after real sleep is the worst one, because it's the point at which reality hits. A woman whose brother was murdered in a drug deal gone bad told me that on the night he died she held on to a tiny glimmer of hope that there was a crack in the universe, a programming error that could be corrected with the rise of the sun. She said she'd never felt so cheated as she did the next day when she woke up and her brother was still dead, the sun blazing down from the heavens.

Matthew takes a sip of tea before answering my question about the Beaufords, but he seems to struggle to keep the liquid in his mouth. Fleet and I avert our gaze as he dabs his chin with a tissue.

'I think so,' he says. 'Sterling used to talk about them quite a bit and they live in Melbourne so it's easier for them to see him.'

There's a mild bitterness to Matthew's tone and it prompts me to imagine what it would feel like if Ben replaced me with another parent, for him to slot so neatly into a new family.

'Were Paul and Melissa still in touch with Sterling?' I ask.

Matthew sighs deeply. 'Well, I guess it's no secret that they had a bit of a falling out. It started when he got the role on the show, you know, *The Street*, and got worse over the years. Broke April's heart.'

'I just wanted them to get along. They are all good kids.' April crumples a little and starts to cry again. I can tell her brain is still dipping in and out of accepting this new reality. She is now the parent of a dead child, surely the most unenviable role in the world.

'It's the money, I think,' says Matthew gruffly. 'Too much money is never a good thing. Our other kids, and our son-in-law, they work so hard, I think it made them uncomfortable, all that money Sterling had access to. We're not from that world.'

'Do they come to the city much?' Fleet asks.

The Wades shake their heads, little birdlike movements. 'Melissa hasn't been to Melbourne for years,' Matthew tells us. 'She and her husband, Rowan, their whole lives are in Karadine. Paul comes down here occasionally, I think. He has a few schoolmates who live in Melbourne. He's a quiet boy and his work takes him all over. He comes and goes. I don't think he sees Sterling when he comes to Melbourne. Sterling was always so busy.'

'What kind of work did you say Paul does?' I prod gently.

'Sometimes he gets a few weeks' house painting. He builds decks, drives trucks.' Matthew sighs again and it turns into a rasping cough. 'Paul will take over the farm when the time comes. It's always been the plan but I wanted him to have a few years away from the place. He had a bit of a hard time settling in Karadine after he finished school.'

'What kind of hard time?' I ask.

'Oh well, it was nothing really. He just got into a few fights. Silly, really. Typical for boys that age.'

Fleet and I don't say anything and Matthew Wade looks apprehensive.

'I wanted him to get some experience away from the farm,' he repeats. 'And any good honest work has always suited him just fine.'

The implication that perhaps Paul's younger brother was a different story hangs in the air, and we let it breathe for a few moments.

'Where are Paul and Melissa now?' I ask.

April muffles a sob with her hand and then tries to calm herself with some deep breaths. 'We called Melissa last night, straight after we heard. Rowan had already seen something online about it but he thought it was just a silly rumour. She called Paul for us . . . I couldn't bear telling him too. He's been housesitting a friend's farm in Castlemaine these past few weeks while he paints their new extension.'

'They're both coming to stay with us at the hotel tonight.' Matthew glances at his watch and then at his wife. 'Look,' he says with a slight firmness, 'Melissa and Paul weren't close to Sterling, especially not over the past few years, but they loved each other. We're a family,' he says, as if this proves a point, and I nod reassuringly.

April's sunken eyes seek out mine. 'We'll need to stay here for a while, won't we?'

'Yes,' I tell her. 'It will be easier if you're in Melbourne for at least the next few days. There are things that you will both need to do.' I pause. 'The initial autopsy will be conducted later today. And then funeral plans will need to be made. You should probably speak to Lizzie about that.'

April looks at me blankly, her mind clearly sorting through all the unthinkable things that are yet to come, as if seeing her son's cold, dead body wasn't horrific enough.

I hold her stare, silently urging her to dig for the reserves of strength that I hope are buried deep inside. 'The media coverage will remain very intense,' I say.

She nods absently but I can tell she doesn't comprehend just how bad it will be.

'There were reporters at the hotel this morning,' says Matthew.

'If they really hassle you, let us know,' I tell him. 'We can issue them with a warning.'

'We'd like to talk to Paul and Melissa too,' Fleet says.

'You need to talk to them about this?' says April, sounding surprised.

'We want to talk to anyone who knew Sterling,' confirms Fleet. 'Every piece of information helps. He might have mentioned something important.'

April closes her mouth and clutches the mug of cooling tea. Matthew attempts another sip of his before pushing it away.

We speak for a few more minutes but their shock has turned their helpfulness to helplessness. We bundle them into a car with one of the uniforms and send them back to the small boutique hotel in St Kilda that Sterling's management has arranged for them.

Fleet and I stand inside the hospital's front entrance, watching them go.

'Well, that was a fun start to the day,' says Fleet, leaning exaggeratedly against the wall and blowing a breath out forcefully.

'It must be strange to have a child who's so famous,' I say. 'Especially coming from a country town like that. Karadine is tiny.'

'But it's probably no different to how your folks feel about you, Gemma,' says Fleet. 'Their daughter suddenly a big important detective in the city.'

'Whatever. We should check out this foster family. The Beaufords. That's all a bit strange too, don't you think? Leaving home at thirteen and staying with another family.'

'So far it's all extremely odd, if you ask me.' Fleet stifles a yawn. 'Right, what's next?'

'Well,' I begin, just as a loud wave of taunting starts up from the pack of journos lurking near the hospital entrance—one of them has tripped over. I raise my voice above the clamour. 'I guess we should go check out this zombie movie.'

Thursday, 16 August
8.42 am

In Smithson we had an old TV in a small meeting room that we used to view case footage. Most files were sent out for analysis. Here we have a whole team of experts who sit in dark caves all day, dedicated to seeing more than the human eye could ever be expected to, extracting crucial information from hours and hours of captured time.

Fleet pulls open the heavy door of Video Room C and we step inside. Edo Ng, one of the video techs, lifts a hand in greeting, and my pupils shrink as I make my way to the back of the room. Fleet and I sit side by side on matching plastic chairs, facing the large TV in the corner as we wait to watch the moment that Sterling Wade was stabbed. Nan's solid frame is perched on the edge of the table that holds all of Edo's equipment, and she is typing quickly on her phone, her round face lit up by its glow. Isaacs leans against the back wall, his expression unreadable.

'Hang on just a tic,' says Edo, drawing out 'tic' in a way that I find inexplicably irritating. 'Okay, folks, here she goes.' He presses a button on his keyboard with a flourish. The vision cuts to a long shot along the asphalt at the top end of Spring Street.

A lanky guy wearing a headset appears in frame and smiles crookedly at the camera, holding a movie clapper. 'Scene twenty-four, take one, action,' he says half-heartedly as he snaps it together.

Sterling Wade appears, the camera trained on the back of his head. Even though I can tell it's Spring Street—I recognise certain landmarks, even a specific rubbish bin—it looks completely different through the frame of the camera. The edge of the city seems like another world, dark and sinister. Wade's blond head bobs along. He is impossibly handsome even though he's been dressed down to look like an average guy. He's nervous, sporadically turning around this way and that, eyes wide, anticipating danger. His heavy breathing is audible. Other people are walking past in the background but they are not in focus and seem separate from the scene. As the camera pans around to take in his face, his desperation is palpable, the suspense carefully manufactured: something bad is about to happen. His jaw is tight, and he's thrusting his hands through his hair. He's clearly running out of time to do something. My heart rate is picking up even though I know what awful thing happens next.

Suddenly something shifts and his eyes go wild. He starts to run. The scene abruptly ends, the camera cuts to black.

The vision returns and the lanky guy is back with a lopsided smile. He lifts the top of the clapper and drops it down again, saying, 'Scene twenty-five, take one, action,' before jumping out of the way.

The camera reels upward to show hundreds of creatures running straight toward it. This is bizarre to watch, like an unfinished painting. Uneven features, bulging eyes, gaping wounds that ooze blood and guts. Many are masked, others sport gruesomely realistic make-up, but there is still a fakeness about it. A lot of post-production trickery is yet to be done. Like a tidal wave, the homogenous mass flows closer.

Wade's character, who has tried to make his escape by veering left, is forced back into the centre of the street as the zombies close in from every angle. There's a feeling of inevitability as his circle of freedom grows smaller and smaller. The scene becomes more chaotic as the camera goes lower, and for a few seconds we are looking skywards, capturing the underside of the madness, limbs every-where, deformed faces overcome by agonising groans.

'No, no, please!' cries Wade, arms out, begging.

The camera is suddenly on the outer, and it reminds me of a football match when you lose track of the ball. Wade's head bobs among the darkness, but flashes of other faces fill the screen, twisted and blank, an unsettling vacancy to them. I spot a gloved hand on his shoulder and there's a moment when his head jerks up, but was that when the stabbing occurred? It's impossible to see exactly what is happening. Hands grab him, lifting him up, the faceless army pawing and pulling at him, his face in various stages of pain.

Until it shifts into something different, and I can tell he's forgot-ten about being on camera. Survival has taken over.

Stop, he mouths, though he has no volume. Only the symphony of moaning can be heard. He's grabbing at his chest, an arm up toward the sky, his eyes rolling back desperately. He is partly lifted off the ground as he slumps in midair. A few of the zombies shift away, but no one is making an obvious dash for it. The dark attire makes it hard to work out where one person starts and another ends.

The camera remains steady on Wade for around thirty seconds. And then the back of Lizzie's head appears, blocking him from view as she fights against the flow of bodies and makes her way to him. She gestures for everyone to move; she's screaming, veins in her neck raised, her teeth exposed as her jaw pulls against her mouth in panic. For a split-second I almost get swept away in the charged scene. Lizzie's arm whips out, pushing people away as she cradles

Wade, clutching at him when he folds to the ground. Blood appears on her hands and people fall out of character, moving off camera and exchanging worried glances.

The magic is gone. Abruptly it's a nightclub in the early hours after the lights have been turned on. Features twist into panic underneath the thick make-up and a strange uneven chorus is created by the words 'stop' and 'no' being repeated over and over. The scene deflates, the frenetic energy sucked away, leaving Sterling and Lizzie alone on the ground. She continues to hold him, pressing on his chest as she cries, her eyes to the sky in desperate prayer. A few zombies drop down to help, their caring gestures jarring with their monstrous faces.

Riley Cartwright appears, yelling over his shoulder for help. Lizzie gestures at him, her hands now dark with blood. Sterling looks steadily at the camera, his clear blue eyes turning cloudy as Lizzie strokes his face with her bloody hand. I've watched this moment a hundred times before: a beautiful young heroine caressing her doomed lover.

We all sit there as the tape plays on, Lizzie's screams becoming more primal and the hopeless panic on the sad zombie faces more intense. My brain is struggling to separate the familiar fiction from what I know has happened. I half expect Wade to open his eyes and sit up, ready to do another take.

Isaacs clears his throat as the ambulance officers reach Wade and the footage cuts to black. 'As you can see, it's not exactly conclusive.' He clenches his jaw, his face particularly stern in the dim light. 'Still, the guys haven't started going over it properly yet, so hopefully we'll be able to pick something up.'

'It's a bizarre way to attack someone,' says Fleet. 'It's quite complicated. Surely there would have been an easier way to kill him that was less obvious?'

'I don't know,' I reply. 'I think it's the perfect cover. Except for leaving the knife on the scene. I don't understand that at all.'

'Maybe it was some kind of stunt,' muses Fleet. 'Like a postmodern art piece.'

Isaacs grits his teeth. 'Yes, well, whatever it ends up being, let's just hope it doesn't spark off a spate of copycat attacks. At this rate, we'll need to provide security for the city's A-listers *and* the homeless.' He stands up and brushes at the lapels of his expensive suit jacket.

A sharp knocking on the door is followed by cracks of light materialising in the dark wall. Chloe's pale face appears. Her eyes dart around the room before settling on Fleet and me. 'Oh good, you're here. Um,' she bites her lip, reminding me for a second of Ben, 'there's a young man here to see you. About the Wade case. He's in quite a state.'

'Thanks, Chloe,' I say, standing. 'Who is he?'

She winces slightly as she guides her hands across the front of her swollen belly, and I wonder if her baby is kicking. 'His name is Brodie Kent. Says he's Wade's housemate. He's crying and was pretty worked up when he came in but he demanded to speak with the detectives in charge. Ravi's put him in one of the front rooms to try to calm him down.'

'Go,' says Isaacs to me and Fleet, his voice gravelly. 'We'll keep going over the footage until the case briefing.'

'Do we have a list of the cast and crew yet?' I ask him as we head to the door.

'Not yet. We only have the ones who stuck around yesterday, which is about a hundred and twenty out of four hundred. Apparently, a big group of them went to the pub. The rest we assume went home.' He frowns. 'It was a mess.'

'They went to the pub looking like that?' says Fleet, raising his eyebrows.

Edo snorts as he clicks the video back to the start. 'No one would have noticed, man. Have you seen what people wear out there these days? These dudes would fit right in.'

I bite my tongue, noting Edo's aggressive slogan T-shirt, army pants and brick-like boots.

Following Fleet out of the room, I feel a wave of frustration toward all those extras. Accounting for the zombie cast, let alone the crew, is going to be a nightmare.

◄○►

As Fleet and I enter the interview room, I take in the young man gripping the edges of the small table. His knuckles are white and his body is slumped forward as he cries. He looks up at us, radiating the wariness of an abused dog. He has what my dad would describe as a good head of hair, dense and dark brown. I suspect his skin is an attractive ivory when it's not flushed and blotchy with grief. His thick brows arch gently, framing large eyes, and he moves his mouth as if he's trying to talk to us but can't make a sound.

'Brodie, is it?' I say, before introducing us.

He makes an anguished sound as he thumps the table with his fists. 'I just can't believe he's dead. Just can't believe it.'

Fleet clears his throat loudly and the slightly off-putting sound is somehow comforting in the sterile room.

'They wouldn't even let me see him,' Brodie whispers. 'I wanted to say goodbye.'

'Do you mean at the hospital?' I ask.

He nods.

'Well,' I say slowly, 'I guess it was hard for the staff to work out who actually knew Sterling. After what had happened, they needed to be careful.'

Brodie lifts his head, his jaw shaking wildly. 'They let Ava in.' He scowls, his top lip curling before it lands in a pout. 'And Lizzie.'

'Okay, well, I can see that must have been very upsetting.' I ease into a chair and give Fleet a look to sit down as well.

'So why are you here, mate?' asks Fleet.

Brodie looks up through tear-filled eyes. 'Um, Lizzie gave me your card.' He nods at me. 'She said that you're the detectives looking after . . . Sterling.'

'Is there something you want to tell us about yesterday?' Fleet asks, leaning forward.

Brodie pulls back, his eyes wide. 'No! I don't know what happened if that's what you mean. I just wanted to find out what you know. I need to know what's going on.' He shakes his head like he's in a trance. 'I haven't slept at all. It just doesn't make sense that he's dead.' His voice cracks around the last word. 'I can't believe it,' he says again.

I study him. Sometimes people who proactively speak with us feel guilty—it might be that they had a fight with the victim the day they died and somehow feel responsible for what happened. Occasionally a perpetrator is looking to flaunt their proximity to the crime under our noses. And some loved ones simply get off on the drama and feel compelled to link themselves directly to the case; oddly, there is weighty social currency in having information about a murder, in being a part of the story.

In some instances, parents or partners become obsessed with having contact with the case detectives. Talking to us can be one of the few things that make them feel like they're doing something. Showing they care. Not forgetting.

And there's also a small chance that a loved one has something useful to tell us. This is what we're always hoping for. It's why we spend so much time with them, going over and over the same things, looking for an anomaly, a tiny clue in the blandness of a life.

As I take in the bewildered young man in front of us, I struggle to work out which category he belongs to. He doesn't seem to be a natural fit in any of them.

Starting work on a case is always like beginning a jigsaw puzzle without having looked at the picture on the box. We begin with finding the corners, then get the border locked down. The fuzz in the middle can remain unclear forever if you can't confirm some key pieces pretty quick. Ending up with a piece missing is every detective's worst nightmare. Those are the cases that wreck your brain. We've all got one: it's like a rite of passage, makes you legit, hardens your heart and sets your jaw. But you don't want to be in the habit of collecting them. I know that's what Nan worries about with the Jacoby case; I can see it in her eyes.

Fleet leans back and cracks his knuckles. Brodie flinches.

'Well, Brodie, it sounds like you were very close to Sterling,' Fleet says. 'We're really sorry, we know it's a huge shock. We're doing everything we can to find out what happened yesterday but we're not able to share too much at this point. Everything's still pretty sensitive and there's a lot that isn't clear. But even if you don't think you know anything, you might be able to help us. Can we ask you a few questions?'

Brodie nods slowly, as if his latest outburst of grief has left him completely deflated.

I flick on the tape and settle back in my chair, studying him. The room fills with the sound of his sniffing.

I reel off the formalities and then say, 'Let's start with your full name and date of birth, please.'

'Brodie John Kosmopolous. But I go by Brodie Kent. Fifth of February 1997.' I can hear the slightest twist of an accent as he says his name.

'And what do you do for a living?' asks Fleet.

'I'm an actor,' he says quietly. 'And a dancer.'

'You're not part of the cast from Sterling's film though, are you?' I ask him.

'No, no. I act in stage plays, mainly. Mostly in TV ads, really. Not film. I'm also in a dance troupe.' His speech wavers and I sense another wave of sorrow building.

I talk quickly, trying to keep him focused on our questions. 'And how long have you known Sterling?'

He shudders through a deep breath. 'About two years.'

'Where were you yesterday afternoon?' I ask.

'I spent the day in the city,' says Brodie. 'I was working on a new creative project so I was having some thinking time.'

'By yourself?' I say and he nods.

I tuck that information away for later—we'll need to look into his whereabouts more, but now clearly isn't the right time.

'When did you last see Sterling?' asks Fleet.

'Yesterday morning. He came into my room to say goodbye when Lizzie was in the shower. Early, like maybe 6 am. They both needed to be on set at seven.'

'Right,' says Fleet, sounding slightly puzzled. 'So how long have you been housemates for?' He flips open his notebook to where he's written down Wade's address.

'I moved in with him and Lizzie about two months ago,' says Brodie. 'I've been struggling to get work lately and Sterling said it would be fine if I stayed with them for a while. We'd talked about living together before.'

'He sounds like a good mate,' says Fleet.

Brodie looks up at each of us in turn, his black eyes huge. 'Yes. He was my best friend. But he was also my lover.'

Thursday, 16 August
9.41 am

I feel such pity for those in the orbit of the recently murdered. Out of nowhere, *bam*, not only is their loved one gone but their own carefully kept secrets are suddenly everyone's business. Their face is all over the internet for every old classmate and ex-lover to see, and every emotion they have is scrutinised, every action analysed. Although it's statistically likely that a loved one pulled the trigger or twisted the knife, that the husband strangled the wife or the son beat his mother, I feel sorry for the ones who are unwillingly along for the ride. It's a brutal journey.

Of course, I also feel sorry for the dead. Regardless of the manner in which they died—gentle, painful, public, private, quick or prolonged—very few escape intense judgement in the aftermath of their passing. They are fair game, and if their loved ones, enemies and my guys don't pick over their remains thoroughly enough, the media will always be happy to finish the job.

For all these reasons, I worry for the softly-spoken, pale-faced Brodie Kent.

'Well, that was an unexpected bit of gossip,' says Fleet.

A complicated-looking conference phone with a cracked screen sits on the table between us. Fleet's pupils are huge and his face is flushed. I know I look exactly the same. We've just summoned Isaacs to join us in here so we can update him privately on Brodie's revelation before the case briefing.

After his bombshell, Brodie sobbed his way through the tale of an eighteen-month secret romance with Sterling Wade. It was clear he was looking for validation—he wanted someone to give him permission to grieve as a lover—but all he got from us was a stack of questions. It's not that I necessarily think he was lying, but it always pays to be measured when secrets are revealed and it seems the only person who can verify or deny them is ice cold and horizontal in a morgue.

'So why keep it quiet?' Fleet asked Brodie bluntly.

The young man lifted his head, eyes brimming, and shrugged hopelessly. 'Because the truth would have cost him everything.'

'Being gay, you mean?' said Fleet.

'Do you really think that would have mattered these days?' I added more gently, trying to buffer Fleet's tone.

'Yeah,' Fleet chimed in, 'isn't everyone gay these days? Or at least bisexual.'

Brodie sat up straight and shook his head. 'No way. I mean, sure, some people have managed to make a career out of it, make it their thing, but for Sterling, the teenage girl's dream ... well, it might have been a disaster. Wendy even said so. She's Sterling's agent.'

'Did she know he was gay?' I asked.

'I don't think so. He was close to her but I doubt he would have spoken to her about it. She just always talks about stuff like that, how important his image is. She's pretty conservative and always has lots of opinions on what Sterling should and shouldn't do. He listened to her a lot.'

'Okay,' I said, 'so you were together but you both agreed to keep it a secret. I can see how that might have seemed important. But what about his relationship with Lizzie? Are you saying that the two of them weren't really together?'

Brodie's body language shifted and he set his gaze on the corner of the table. 'They were together, sure. Maybe even in love at some point. But then I think maybe Sterling just didn't know how to end it. He cares about Lizzie,' his lip wobbled, '*cared*. So do I. He didn't want to hurt her. He was pretty confused.'

'Did anyone else know about your relationship? Surely Lizzie suspected?'

Brodie shrugged. 'She didn't want to see it. She's not a confrontational person and Sterling had all the power in their relationship. I'm sure she worried he was slipping away but I think she just figured they were both busy.' He rubbed at his red eyes. 'And they *were* busy. Especially Sterling. I barely got to see him these past few weeks, between his work, his PR stuff and time he had to spend with Lizzie.'

'Why move in with them like that?' I asked gently. 'It must have been torture seeing them together.'

'I loved him,' declared Brodie, in the earnest way I'd expected he would. 'I just wanted to be close to him. I know it sounds kind of pathetic, but I did. And I didn't have anywhere else to go. Sterling wanted to help.' His whole body started to shake again as he smacked his fist on the table. 'Oh god, I just can't believe this. It's like my brain won't accept it.'

'Can you think of anyone who would want to hurt Sterling, Brodie?' I probed.

'A lot of people were jealous of him,' he said, his voice still thick with grief, 'but I can't imagine anyone who would do something like this.'

'So he seemed completely normal lately?' asked Fleet. 'Nothing struck you as odd?'

Brodie looked bewildered. 'He was busy. Stressed about the film. I thought he seemed distracted earlier this week so I asked him if everything was okay, but he said he was fine. Just tired.'

'Did you believe him?' I asked.

Brodie twisted his fingers together. 'I thought he had something on his mind. Figured it was just the stress of having to work with Riley Cartwright. Sterling thought he was completely crazy.'

'Crazy how?' I asked.

'Erratic. Moody. And his obsession with Ava was bizarre. Sterling said he took things too far with her and called him on it. I think things got pretty weird between them.'

'They argued?' said Fleet.

Brodie nodded. 'Yeah. Sterling was pretty upset about it.'

'When?' I asked.

'Last weekend. He didn't say much about it but like I said, he was definitely upset.'

'Upset or angry?' Fleet pushed.

'A bit of both, I guess.'

We spoke to Brodie for a few more minutes, trying to eke out anything else about Sterling that might be relevant, but Brodie just wanted to talk about their relationship.

As our case meeting loomed, Fleet's restlessness began to make me anxious. I ushered Brodie out with the phone number of a grief counsellor and promises to keep him updated about the case.

Now I glance up as Isaacs slips into the room, looking at his watch while he pulls the door shut behind him. 'Is this about the housemate who wanted to speak with you?'

'Yes,' I reply, before detailing what Brodie told us.

'It's almost like our own little twisted movie script,' adds Fleet sarcastically when I'm done.

Isaacs taps his fingers on the table. 'Jesus,' he mutters, after a moment. 'Nothing's ever bloody straightforward, is it?'

'Afraid not,' says Fleet, winking discreetly at me.

'We obviously need to touch base with these Beauford people and Wendy Ferla as soon as possible,' I say.

There's a sharp knock on the door, and I get a flash of deja vu as Chloe's head appears like it did earlier this morning in the video room. 'Hi,' she says nervously, 'something else has come up that I thought you should know about straight away.'

'What now?' exclaims Fleet melodramatically.

'Ava James has just accused Riley Cartwright of sexual assault.'

Thursday, 16 August
9.55 am

As always when I work a case, I feel time shifting around me. It seems unfathomable that Wade was alive twenty-four hours ago. And even more bizarre to think that we watched his parents identify his pale, cold body this morning. The dead tend to exist in a world that ignores traditional time zones, and a part of them stays alive until we find their killer. There remains for each of them a soft pulse of hope that justice might still be possible one day, lurking in the smallest of clues.

In the station bathrooms, I study my reflection. I wish I was tall like Nan. I remember the first briefing I attended with her and the way her stature immediately put her in control, her straight posture and no-nonsense manner giving the impression that everything she says is correct. I wonder how much of that is the success of a detective, simply looking the part. My face is serious too, but there's a blandness about my appearance—I'm easily forgettable. My pale green eyes are wide but dull as if the lights have been turned off inside. My dark hair is like a wild forest, swirling around my face and tumbling halfway down my back. Stuck between girl and woman, I appear slightly haunted, which I'm not sure is an ideal look for a senior detective.

I wonder what Ben is doing right now. He's probably at school, sitting on the floor surrounded by all his friends, his tongue peeking out of his mouth as he takes in what the teacher is saying. Sometimes the longing to hold him, to look into his eyes, is so intense I feel trapped in my own body. A big case always makes me feel guilty, as if I'm somehow being disloyal to him. It always has and I suspect it always will. *The price you pay*, I can almost hear Scott saying, followed closely by a helpful reminder that I actually have a say in the way I run my life. So many of our arguments ended with Scott telling me that I was acting like the victims I so desperately try to save. 'You don't *have* to do this, Gem,' he'd say earnestly. 'You don't have to be so torn all the time. Don't you realise you can walk away whenever you want?' I almost laughed at the insanity of his suggestion until I realised that he was completely serious.

I wash my hands and smooth some strands of hair behind my ears before heading toward the case room, taking slow, deliberate breaths. I always feel apprehensive before a briefing. I guess it's normal to question your own ability but there's nothing like the stares of keen-as-mustard eyeballs watching you, desperate to put their own mark on a case and one-up the boss, to make you self-conscious. The golden era of TV has made every young, ambitious uniform think that he can take on Jack the Ripper. Problem is, it's made every young ambitious criminal think that he could *be* Jack the Ripper. At least it's balanced, I suppose.

We're using the case room to the left of the main tearoom. It's not perfect—every time someone makes a coffee the wall shakes—but it's a decent size and it has one of the new, slick built-in case boards that you can magically attach photos and documents to, unlike the dinky cork pin boards we used in Smithson. It took me a while to get used to all the extra resources the city squad has. Not only is there an endless supply of decent biscuits on hand for staff, but there is also an abundance of stationery, and my computer can handle more than two files being open at once. Plus, there are more bums on seats. Something seriously bad had to happen in Smithson to warrant extra bodies being called in, so we were constantly justifying numbers and appealing for extra help.

Upon returning to the case room I find it empty. Checking my watch, I see it's still about ten minutes until we're scheduled to kick off. A shiver runs through me as my cold core adjusts to the heat of the room. I walk over to the case board, which is dotted with the basic info we have so far. Scanning it, I try to block out the noise of Wade's sexuality and Cartwright's alleged assault and take in the key facts of the attack, making sure I haven't missed something glaringly obvious.

Shifting my weight back and forth, I'm satisfied that nothing stands out so far. An up-and-coming movie star, stabbed in the middle of a big film set. If the intention wasn't to kill Wade, perhaps it was a scare that went too far? A dare? Could one of the props staff have planted a real weapon on set as a joke? Or maybe Fleet's onto something and it was some kind of fame kill. I've read about online forums where kids taunt each other to do outrageous things and then document the outcomes. Something like this would certainly fit the bill: just the right mix of profile and risk. But if this was true, that the knife was somehow added to the prop inventory, then what were the chances of Wade being the one hurt? Surely he had to be the intended victim. Or perhaps a cast member became obsessed with him, their fixation fuelled by the intimacy of the shoot, and the chance to have the ultimate power over him was just too tempting.

I've worked enough cases to know that what can seem like a harmless crush can easily teeter dangerously into a loss of reality and physical violence. We humans never have been very good about removing the concept of ownership from our romantic relationships. Maybe someone wanted Wade all for herself. Or *himself*, I think, recalling Brodie's tearful revelation. While I know to always expect surprises, his confession has thrown me a little— with the parade of glamorous women in Wade's life, I guess I expected some old-fashioned adultery of the heterosexual kind. If Wade really was gay, I wonder how widespread this knowledge is. There might be a small group of individuals in the know. Does that have anything to do with this?

And now there's the accusation that Ava James has made about Cartwright. I recall the lanky man in the hospital waiting room yesterday. Vacant and distant definitely, but there had been something else too: an underlying aggression that my body had immediately detected.

'She could be lying,' Fleet whispers in my ear as he suddenly appears behind me.

I steady myself just in time to prevent an obvious startle. 'I was thinking about the film footage, actually.'

'Sure you were.' Fleet takes an obnoxious slurp of his coffee. 'Seriously though, Ms James *could* be lying. And so could young Brodie. I mean come on, a secret gay relationship that he reveals now that Wade's dead? It's very convenient. Maybe he just wants in on the police action. Maybe they both do. They love the drama, right?'

'Brodie seemed pretty genuine to me,' I reply. 'And if he wanted attention he would go to the media, not us.'

'Well, he probably did have feelings for Wade. Loved him or whatever. Doesn't mean it was reciprocal.'

'I guess.'

Fleet takes another slurp of coffee. 'I saw that art-house movie Wade did last year,' he says, looking off into the distance. 'You know, with that hot-arse actress Jade Shaw, or whatever her name is.

There were some pretty raunchy scenes. I just can't see him giving it to a guy.'

'Oh, come on,' I say, exasperated. 'That's hardly relevant. The kid was an actor. His job was to make people believe. You know, some people can't see you being a half-decent detective but you sort of pull it off.'

'Likewise, little lady,' he says, as I turn back to the board, determined not to let him ruffle me. I attach a few more photos of the crime scene.

'Ready for us in here?' says a voice behind me a minute later.

I turn to see three young male uniforms filling the doorway. Fleet has disappeared.

'Of course, come take a seat. We're going to be here a while.'

'Fleet is taking a piss,' the prematurely grey one says. 'Said he'd only be a moment.'

'Great,' I mutter, walking out of the room to fetch a glass of water. As the cool liquid forges an icy path to my stomach, I watch another dozen officers file into the case room. Again, I feel insecure about my height—I'm pretty sure I'll be the shortest person in the room.

I suspect the young policewomen are desperate for some advice from me but struggle to work me out. I'm a mystery: a senior detective despite my young age, presumed single, with terrible outfits, a frosty disposition and no personal life to speak of. I have no wisdom to share about work–life balance. Nothing useful to offer about navigating a marriage around the demands of the job. No revelations about managing the challenges of motherhood in this harsh environment. The only person here who knows about Ben is Isaacs, and we haven't discussed him since my first interview, when I made it clear I didn't want to talk about my personal life.

I put on some lip balm and head back to the case room. At least I'm more approachable than Nan, I think, as I watch her ball up a piece of paper and throw it aggressively into a rubbish bin.

Fleet rounds the corner, texting on his phone, and almost trips over me. 'Sorry Woodstock, didn't see you there,' he sneers as he walks ahead of me toward the eager faces. 'Come on,' he calls over his shoulder.

Scowling, I start to pull the door shut just as Isaacs slips in. He nods at me and makes his way to the back of the room where he takes a seat away from the others. Clearly, we are being observed.

'Right,' Fleet barks, his voice like the crack of a whip to settle the room. 'This is a big one, so empty your calendars.' He walks over to the far wall and leans against it, looking at me expectantly. Everyone in the room follows his lead.

I clear my throat. I hate it when he does this.

'That's right,' I begin, trying to block out Isaacs completely. 'We have the stabbing and subsequent death of a young man in broad daylight, which would be bad enough but it's further complicated by the high profile of the victim.' I pause and look around the room evenly, a tactic I know projects confidence. 'Our actions will be monitored and reported even more than normal, so it's critical that we have our ducks in a row.'

A guy with sandy hair and a clammy complexion smirks, I assume at my cutesy phrase, and I give him a hard look.

Fleet snaps his gum loudly from the corner and I give him a look as well. I step around to the front of the case board. 'No doubt this face is pretty familiar to most of you. Sterling Wade. A big-deal celebrity if you're into that kind of thing. Twenty-three years old. Originally from Karadine, a small farming town in northern New South Wales. He's the youngest child of Matthew and April Wade. Two older siblings. Wade moved to Melbourne when he was thirteen and lived with another family, the Beaufords, until he was nineteen, almost like a foster situation.'

Most of the uniforms have their eyes fixed on Wade's picture. I can see them trying to reconcile his death with the face they've seen on TV and in magazines. It's always strange when you are familiar with a victim. Working in Smithson it happened to me frequently, and occasionally I knew a victim personally. And, of course, sometimes I knew a perpetrator. I know firsthand how much that can mess with your head. As a detective you want to be able to keep things separate, put up walls. Strong personal connections can seep through the most solid of barriers, and that's when you find yourself waking in a cold sweat and imagining your own loved ones twisted in pain or worse.

Sterling Wade is both familiar and remote. He feels like more than an acquaintance, perhaps almost a friend, yet we know virtually nothing meaningful about him. This creates an unusual vibe, a slight detachment from the pain and fear he must have experienced. Almost as if we are watching it on a screen. Like a storyline on *The Street*, his death could just as easily not be real. We're so used to owning our celebrities, demanding pieces of them, expecting them to just be there, that we all feel a sharp pang when they behave unexpectedly, are taken from us, are gone. In a way, Wade's death is simply something else for us to be a part of.

'There's video of the incident, one of the recordings from the film set,' I continue. 'You will all watch it straight after this. Unfortunately, because everyone is in costume it's not obvious who attacked Wade, but the tech guys are reviewing the files to see if anything can be picked up. At minimum, we want to narrow down the physicality of our attacker.'

A young constable at the front raises his hand. 'Are we sure it wasn't an accident?'

'It's possible,' I admit, 'but a knife was found at the scene. It's much heavier than the prop weapons, so a cast member should have realised it wasn't a prop pretty quickly. And no one has admitted to stabbing Wade. But even if the person responsible wasn't aware they held a real weapon, someone planted it on the set.'

I explain that we are pulling in CCTV from the entire top end of the city, along with all the other security information from the production company.

'Now, as you might have guessed, Sterling Wade was incredibly popular,' Fleet says, pushing his body smoothly off the wall and walking over to where I'm standing. He looks at our audience and juts out a hip. I catch one of the cops rolling her eyes and I have to stop myself smiling.

'We need to cast the net a lot wider than normal,' Fleet continues. 'Wade has three hundred thousand Twitter followers, the same number of Facebook fans and almost double that on Instagram. That's a lot of people knowing how pretty his breakfast looked last Sunday. We've got the tech guys started on his accounts but there's a fair bit to trawl through.' Fleet pauses and scans the room. 'I'd like you two'—he points at a young dark-haired girl and an Asian guy—'to work through everything they spit out and follow up anything that you think seems suss. We're going to get in touch with his agent about any communication she received from Sterling's fans directly. We'll throw everything to you for log and review.' Fleet stops pacing to sit on the corner of the front table, swinging his legs like a child. 'I want to know every single thing Wade did in the weeks before this happened.' He shoots a look at two young men with matching thick eyebrows. 'Can you guys map out his movements?' They nod, faces serious.

'And then we need to start working through the witness statements,' I say, walking in front of Fleet, and eyeballing two stocky guys with shaved heads. 'We're going to need to work with the film company and get the names of every cast member who was present yesterday. We've put in the request already but you'll need to follow it up. The uniforms on the scene last night could only account for about a hundred and twenty people of over four hundred cast and crew. I want the full list compiled today, then crosschecked against anyone who made a statement yesterday. Make sense?'

They nod. 'Good.' I point to two other young men. One of them, Amir Pavlich, worked on the Jacoby case with me a few weeks back and I'm impressed with his measured thinking. 'Can you two work together with these guys to arrange processing the list? Background checks and a crime-scene map as well as statements. I want this to happen as soon as we can manage it.'

'Yes,' they reply.

'But how are we going to manage processing that number of people?' wonders Chloe.

I nod slowly, thinking her brave to ask that question in front of everyone. 'It's not going to be easy,' I say. 'Let's speak to the film company and see if we can use one of their spaces. If it's big enough we can set up a rotation system and simply move through as many people as possible. It won't be as daunting then.'

'Thank you,' she replies, as she writes in her notebook and bites her lip.

I continue. 'We want everything we can get from these guys—how they got involved in the movie, if they've noticed anything unusual about Wade's behaviour, or anything odd at all. We need to know if they saw the attack and where they were when it happened. We also want to know what they did afterwards and whether they've spoken to anyone else from the cast since. Document everything you get.'

'Jesus,' says another guy. 'There's going to be a shitload of information.'

'Yes. There will.' I stretch my hands out behind my back and tip my head to each side. 'There've already been over two hundred calls to the hotline since nine last night. Clearly this isn't a normal case.'

A few eyes widen at the number and pens are pressed to notepads.

Fleet clears his throat noisily. 'Even though we're pretty sure there was only one attacker, it's possible they had a partner in crime. Maybe they passed the knife on to someone else and it was dropped accidentally. Maybe the attacker stuck around at the scene for an alibi.' Fleet scratches his groin unapologetically. 'We need to work our way through all the CCTV footage we can get our hands on.'

Ravi Franks speaks up, his gentle accent turning his words to melody. 'Was there any hint of Wade being stalked or threatened? You hear that a lot with celebrities.'

'Nothing has come up so far but that's definitely a possible scenario,' says Fleet. 'That's why we're asking his agent about any odd communication. So be on the lookout for anything that suggests he was followed or watched, even if it seems small.'

'Did he have a girlfriend?' asks a tall, wiry cop with a thick close-cut beard.

An older-looking blond uniform leans forward across his row of chairs to address the bearded guy. 'Yeah, he was seeing that actress. From that kids' show.'

'Elizabeth Short,' I say, cutting off the pop-culture quiz. 'She's an Australian actress and was in the movie with Wade. She witnessed the attack and went to the hospital with him. She wasn't in great shape last night, but we're hoping to talk to her again later today or tomorrow.'

A few of them nod in recognition. I exchange a quick look with Fleet. 'But we have reason to believe that Wade might have been in another relationship.' I look around the room seriously. 'This goes no further than these four walls. There's a possibility that he was also involved with a man, his flatmate Brodie Kent.'

Eyeballs bulge and one of the guys whistles.

'I mean it.' My voice is firm. 'That stays with us.'

Up the back of the room, a hand is raised.

'Yes?' I say.

'I heard Wade was involved with that American actress. Ava someone. My girlfriend was talking about it a few days ago.'

'Mate, this is a homicide investigation, not *Entertainment Tonight*,' says Fleet rudely and the guy turns a vibrant shade of red.

Isaacs' face remains impassive at the rear of the room.

'You two,' says Fleet, spinning around and cocking his thumb at a pair of young women sitting in the front row, 'check Kent out. I want everything you can find over the past two years. Woodstock and I will talk to him again, try to lock down a proper alibi and visit the alleged love pad, but I want as much background as you can get.'

'Maybe it was a lover's tiff?' ventures a tall young man with pretty blue eyes.

'I definitely got an odd vibe,' replies Fleet. 'He's one of those arty, spiritual types. And his whereabouts yesterday afternoon are vague at best.'

'Kent claims to have been in the city but can't recall exactly where he was when the attack happened,' I say, annoyed at Fleet's snap judgement of Brodie.

'Hence why we're looking into him,' Fleet cuts in.

'Maybe someone found out about their relationship and flipped?' says a woman with a thick plait hanging down her front. 'If Wade was gay, could this be a hate crime?'

'It's possible,' I say. 'We certainly need to look at any correspondence he received with that kind of flavour.'

'The false sense of familiarity people feel toward a guy like this is huge,' Fleet says with barely concealed contempt. 'At this stage, we're keeping an open mind about everything.'

I continue: 'We need you to dig up as much as you can. Just remember, the film set was under pretty tight security so it's likely the attacker had credentials or evaded the guards somehow. We need to find out as much as we can about how the production company managed access to the set yesterday.

'And just to add to the fun and games, Ava James contacted our station this morning to lodge a sexual assault claim against the film's director, Riley Cartwright,' Fleet tells the group. 'We're going to have the sex assault unit inform him of it today and start the ball rolling on that front, and Woodstock and I will speak with James today about Wade's death. We'll try to get to Cartwright about Wade tomorrow. For now we'll keep the two lines of inquiry separate. We have no idea if there's any link but it's something to be aware of.'

Heads dip forward as notes are scrawled.

I look around and shining eyes blaze back at me. They are ready.

'In a few minutes Edo will set the footage from the film up in here for you all to watch. And remember, keep things tight. The media attention is going to be intense and we can't afford to let anything slip.'

I swiftly walk them through our case meeting times, the shifts and the rules around overtime. They seem freshly charged, already looking forward to dinner parties a few months from now when this is all in the past and they can allude to the odd detail about the case and drop juicy information about the slain movie star. I get it: at the end of the day, not many people are immune to the lure of fame and, on the surface at least, the players we're dealing with here are a lot more intriguing than those in the normal hopeless cases we navigate.

Walter Miller's body bubbles up in my mind and I feel a wave of guilt at the speed with which this shiny new case has captured my attention. It's captured everyone's attention and I can't help but wonder how Miller's daughter feels about his death being so quickly pushed off the front pages.

I gather up my papers and turn to face Fleet, who's trying to dislodge something from his nostril with the tip of his thumb. 'Ready to speak with Ms James?' he asks.

'Yep.'

Checking my personal phone on the way to the car park, I listen to a breathless voicemail from Candy, berating me for not calling her back. She's planning a huge feature on Sterling Wade for her news website, and through her initial research has discovered that Matthew and April Wade appear to be in serious financial trouble. The word around town is that they're on the brink of declaring bankruptcy.

Thursday, 16 August
11.51 am

Ava James's hotel suite is less than two hundred metres from where Wade was attacked, a little further down Spring Street toward Carlton. With a start, I realise it's a hotel I've been to before. An image of the greying hair and lean body of a distinguished-looking businessman dances through my mind as Fleet and I elbow our way through grieving teenagers, pushy journalists, snap-happy tourists and grim-faced security guards. Entering the opulent lobby, we show our IDs and are directed into a gold-plated lift.

Emerging several floors up, we wait as a security guard with a deep pout solemnly reviews our credentials before rapping sharply on the hotel-room door.

Ava appears, clad in a huge white bathrobe, her long red hair combed and wet. She leads us into the main room where she collapses onto a garish floral sofa and proceeds to trace its pattern with her finger. A blonde assistant with a neat bob places glass bottles of sparkling water in front of us before disappearing into a bedroom and pulling the door shut behind her.

'Okay,' says Ava, taking a deep breath. 'Do you want me to tell you what happened with Riley Cartwright?'

'Yes,' I say, 'but let's talk about yesterday first.'

If she's surprised at this U-turn, she doesn't show it. She launches obediently into a detailed description of yesterday's events. She didn't see the attack; she was in a temporary trailer in the Treasury Gardens, but she was half-watching the scene on a split-screen. After a while, she could tell something was wrong.

'Was anyone in the trailer with you?' I ask.

'No,' she says flatly. 'I was meditating.'

Fleet snorts quietly and I cover it with an awkward cough, before asking, 'And how long had you known Sterling?'

'Only eight weeks,' she replies. 'Since I arrived here for rehearsals. But we hit it off straight away.' She squeezes her eyes shut. 'He was the most incredible person. So generous and so talented.'

'Did he ever mention anything to you about any unwelcome attention?' I ask.

'Only from the media,' she says. 'It was getting pretty intense. We were followed a lot of the time but he was always pretty cool about it.' She shakes her head in disbelief as tears drip down her porcelain-smooth cheeks. 'I really can't believe any of this. It's just crazy.'

'Okay,' says Fleet, shifting gears. 'So let's talk about Riley Cartwright. You called the station this morning to report him for sexual assault.'

She wipes under her eyes and nods. 'Look, I want to be clear that I respect him as a director. Working with him was the original reason I signed on to do the film—there's no question he's gifted. But I've decided he can't get away with this.' There's a defiant tilt to her head as she delivers her little speech and I remember the same movement when we met her at the hospital. She exudes an unusual confidence typically more evident in men. 'I know it might ruin his career and that's a shame but it's the right thing to do,' she continues. 'And I know Sterling would want me to come forward.'

'Tell us what happened, Ava,' I say, looking her in the eye and trying to convey that it's completely safe for her to talk to us.

She sighs, combing her long hair with her fingers. 'I so wish I hadn't been put in this position.' She breathes slowly in and out. 'Okay so, as soon as I arrived in Melbourne it was clear that Cartwright had a thing for me. At first it was just flirting, maybe he was a little too touchy sometimes, but nothing I couldn't handle.' She sits up straighter. 'But then it just became weird. During our run-throughs he would always ask me to stay back afterwards. He suggested we go out for drinks to talk about my character. He kept mentioning that we were both single. It was uncomfortable but not, you know, dangerous or anything.' She shrugs, her eyes set on the floor. 'But then last Friday it went too far.'

'What happened?' I ask.

'Well, it was the last day of rehearsals. Everything was going well. Sterling and I had nailed the big rescue scene, which is really full on.' She dabs at her eyes. 'We wrapped and I went to my dressing room and started to get changed.' Her gaze flits all over the place and she speaks more quickly. 'I had music on, I was kind of dancing around a bit, just unwinding, and then suddenly he was there putting his arms around me.'

'Cartwright?' confirms Fleet.

'Yes,' she says softly. 'He snuck in—I swear I didn't know he was there. He grabbed my breasts and was saying how he'd wanted me the whole time. How watching me with Sterling was driving him crazy.' She blinks. Her skin tightens around her jaw. 'He was really rough—he pushed me up against the wall and said he could tell I wanted it. He was pressing into me. I could feel he was hard, and he was grabbing me all over.' She shakes her head firmly, flicking her hair. 'I told him to get off me or I'd scream.'

'What did he do?' I ask.

'He asked me if I was sure.' She laughs bitterly. 'I told him to fuck off.'

'Then what happened?'

'I left. I didn't say anything to anyone, I just ghosted.' Fresh tears sprout from her eyes. 'Sterling was texting me, wanting to know why I didn't come out for drinks, but I just didn't want to be anywhere near Cartwright.' She chews on her pillowy lip. 'I didn't want to wreck the night for everyone. A good vibe was going with the whole crew.'

'But you ended up telling Sterling what happened?' I say.

'Yes,' she replies quietly. 'He'd noticed a few things and asked me about it before. He knew something was wrong. I met him for coffee on Saturday morning and ended up telling him everything. He went nuts. He said it was an abuse of power and trust, which I already knew, but he said Cartwright had to be told it was wrong and that he'd speak with him about it.'

'And did he?' asks Fleet.

Ava dips her head forward, huge eyes looking up at us. 'Yeah, he went into the studio on Sunday morning to confront him. Cartwright denied it happened the way I said and they had a big argument.'

'And where is this studio?' I ask.

She tucks her legs underneath her, hugs a cushion to her chest. 'At a warehouse in the Docklands. It's one of the main shooting locations.'

'You were there?' I press.

'I was waiting in the car,' she tells us. 'Sterling was pretty upset about the whole thing.'

'Was anyone else there?' I ask.

'I don't think so. Possibly the producer, Katya March. She's normally wherever Cartwright is—but I'm not sure.'

'Did the men fight physically?' Fleet asks.

She shakes her head. 'No, just argued. Cartwright said he'd only been "mucking around" and told Sterling to mind his own business.'

'And that was it?' I say.

'Yeah. Sterling drove me back here and said that if Cartwright ever touched me again, he would kill him. He really wanted me to report it but I didn't want to ruin the movie. I just figured we'd finish filming and I'd leave and, you know, whatever.'

'What was it like the next day?' Fleet asks. 'How was Cartwright?'

Ava shrugs. 'Everything was kind of normal. Cartwright was pretty frosty with me and Sterling, but I was fine with that. I just wanted to do a good job and I'm used to dealing with moody directors.'

'But you obviously want to take it further now?' I say.

'Yes.' Her jaw hardens again, her eyes flashing sapphire. 'I do. The movie is ruined now anyway. And like I said, I want to do it for Sterling.'

—◀○▶—

Fleet and I navigate through a mob of reporters to our car and make it to the Forensic Medicine Institute just in time for Wade's autopsy. We walk down the long hallway past the Coroners Court and ring the bell at the end of the corridor. Mary-Anne's assistant scans us in and we are immediately greeted by the distinct smell of dead flesh and chemicals. I know from experience that this means there is a decomposing body in the house today. I try to let the cool airless room calm my thoughts, but when I hear the snap of surgical gloves being pulled on, butterflies swirl in my chest. I take a deep breath and exhale slowly. Even after all this time and all those bodies, I still have to steady myself for this.

I focus my gaze on Wade. Odd to think that yesterday this lifeless man was the epitome of youth and health, headlining a major Hollywood production. Life is so binary, the moment of transition to death ultimately a beat in time, no matter who you are.

Dr Mary-Anne Tallis enters the room from her office, her face grim as she gets started. Fleet and I stand politely in the viewing area as we watch the bizarre show. Wade's celebrity clogs the air and it seems we're all struggling to breathe around it. It feels almost obscene to watch his deconstruction: his body is so perfect, it creates a sense that the whole procedure should be private. Fleet must feel it too—he jiggles on the spot and can't seem to let his gaze rest in any one place for too long. In contrast, I stand rooted to the floor, staring. Something about the gaping red gash on Wade's chest adds to his godlike status; it makes him seem even more like a leading man, a throwback to the mighty warriors slain in battle.

Mary-Anne's young assistant is obviously trying to manage her emotions but is struggling in the presence of such a high-profile corpse. Her hands shake as she passes Mary-Anne various imple-ments. I can't say I blame her: not too many people will be able to claim the kind of intimacy that she's about to have with the famous actor.

Mary-Anne measures Wade's limbs, reels off his vitals, checks his teeth and his eyes. She examines the wound, measuring its length and using tweezers to pull the edges back. Eventually she cuts him open and starts to handle and weigh his organs. The assis-tant, Lily, hovers around, swabbing parts of Wade's body, bagging hairs and fingernails and taking photos under Mary-Anne's patient instruction. His final photographs, I think, which seems especially sobering considering how photographed Wade was when alive.

I wonder what it would be like being relentlessly documented like Wade was. So known, so *wanted*. Not the instinctive pull that

Ben had toward me as a baby, not the primal maternal cravings I sometimes have for him now. Not even the inexplicable pull of desire that takes over in the first throes of a relationship. Instead Wade experienced a mass, tribal neediness, an expectation that he perform, deliver, and be available to millions of strangers. To be admired so much and to be so familiar to so many—it must do something to your head. I wonder how easy it is to know who you are if everyone else is so busy deciding for you.

'I can't tell you much,' sighs Mary-Anne eventually, with uncharacteristic flatness. 'Aside from the obvious, he's perfect inside and out. He's giving me nothing.' She looks down at Wade with a hint of disapproval.

All pathologists want to find clues on the dead. This is the victim's last chance to talk, to explain what happened, and when something turns up it creates a strange but real bond between pathologist and corpse in an otherwise one-way relationship.

Still looking at Wade's body, she continues, 'Your killer is likely right-handed. I'm fairly certain that the knife collected from the scene is the murder weapon. The blade measurements match this chest wound. We won't get the blood results for at least a week but I expect it's all his. From the lack of prints on the handle, it looks like the killer was wearing gloves. And it's a pretty generic knife. Nothing special. It could have come from an industrial kitchen or from any decently kitted-out domestic kitchen, especially these days with everyone fancying themselves a bloody master chef.'

'Any chance of there being any useful DNA on the body?' I ask.

Mary-Anne frowns. 'Unlikely. That was pretty much a lost cause the second the ambos got to him. But like I said, we'll run everything we can from the weapon, the clothes he went to hospital in and the other props the techs brought in from the immediate area.'

'It still seems weird that our guy just drops the weapon and scrams.' Fleet has produced a toothpick from somewhere and is studiously picking at his teeth as he sits on the bench that runs the length of the room. I catch him throwing a wink at Lily. Her mouth tugs into the start of a smile and there's an extra sway to her hips as she disappears into her office. 'I mean, why do that? It's the main reason we think this wasn't an accident.'

'Maybe he didn't mean to drop it?' I speculate. 'Maybe he panicked?'

'There's a tape, isn't there?' Mary-Anne asks. 'Can you see the attacker drop his weapon on the screen?'

'Nup,' says Fleet, flinging himself off his perch. 'We can't see shit. Honestly, we've scored ourselves a bona-fide snuff film and it tells us nothing. Joke's on us.' His eyes are back on his personal mobile, fingers moving at an impressive speed, and I wonder who he is contacting.

'We'll send you a copy of the footage later today, Mary-Anne,' I say.

'Okay, great. You never know, it may help join some dots. Maybe Wade's attacker wanted to lose the knife as quickly as possible, knowing that people would step on it and compromise the evidence.' She nods to herself. 'Plus, it made it easier for him to disappear into the crowd. Smart.'

'If this was a planned attack then the killer was banking on it being complete chaos both before and after Wade was stabbed.' I think back to the tsunami of people on the tape.

'And very high profile,' comments Fleet. 'If you're into that kind of thing.'

I nod, thinking about this. Aside from acts of terrorism, I can't imagine another crime so public. Maybe we have an obsessive fame-seeker on our hands, someone who wants their fifteen minutes in the spotlight—but if that's the case then surely they'll come forward and take the credit.

'Well, I think that's it in terms of the basics, guys,' says Mary-Anne, cutting into my thoughts. 'There are no defence wounds but I assume that's simply due to the sudden nature of the assault. He looks to be in excellent health aside from the stab wound.' She stands back, flicking the rims of her gloves against her wrists. 'From here we'll run all the standard tests. We won't get the tox screen for a few days but there's nothing to suggest that he had anything in his system. It's just a damn shame, a talented kid like this with everything in front of him.'

I wait for Lily to leave the room before I say, 'Mary-Anne, we have reason to believe that Wade may have been in a same-sex relationship.'

Always the professional, her eyes widen only slightly. 'Okay,' she says slowly.

'Clearly that information stays with you,' Fleet comments from his perch.

'Of course.' Mary-Anne nods and purses her lips.

'I need to ask,' I said, 'is this something you can verify for us pretty quickly? It might lead to motive, so we need to know.'

Mary-Anne sighs. 'That depends. For me to be fairly sure, he'd need to have been having penetrative anal intercourse. And unless this happened recently it won't be absolutely conclusive. But, yes, if it was fairly regular then I should be able to give you an indication. Though, of course,' she adds, 'people get up to all kinds of things, so I can't confirm it's definitely with another man unless there are traces of semen. There are other tests I can run but again, they won't be useful unless the sex was recent. And, of course, I won't be able to confirm if it was consensual, though there are no obvious signs of abuse.'

'Thank you, Mary-Anne,' I say softly.

There is a long beat of silence as the three of us stand there with Wade's butchered body between us.

'My children are devastated by this,' Mary-Anne says. 'Whenever I came home early we'd all watch *The Street* together. Ed Sloan was our favourite character.' She laughs at her own sentimentality and wipes her eye on her shoulder. 'I guess I'm a bit upset too.'

'We're all upset,' says Fleet, picking fluff off his jacket and heading for the door. 'But right now, we just need you to tell us whether this guy was banging Arthur or Martha.'

Thursday, 16 August
8.12 pm

I dig a plastic fork into the oily chicken and shovel what looks like a piece of red capsicum into my mouth. My stomach rolls as it receives the food, the only meal I've consumed all day. Fleet is silent, chewing on a chicken bone, its juices slick on his lips and chin. Dabbing at my own mouth with a napkin, I look around the case room. Tall piles of paper have appeared on the two long tables at the front. Uniforms stream in and out, depositing new information at our feet like dogs fetching sticks. On the TV screen in the corner, a worried-looking news anchor repeats the short string of facts publicly known about the attack on Wade so far. Her words seem to be aimed directly at us: *mystery attack, no clear motive, confusing scene, baffled detectives.*

This afternoon I spoke to Sterling's agent Wendy Ferla while Fleet paid a visit to the Beaufords. Wendy's husky voice breathed down the phone line in between wailing sobs. The Beaufords were more reserved, asking Fleet several considered questions about what had happened on the film set. Amy confirmed that Sterling had come to live with them almost ten years ago when he landed a role on the kid's show *Team Go*. He'd stayed with them for almost six years, though did return home to Karadine for long stretches during that period. Amy mentioned that she and her husband Steve struggled to have more children after they had Jack and that they were keen to have a sibling figure for him. Now twenty, Jack has moved overseas to pursue a career in talent management. Prior to this he was involved in the casting of *Death Is Alive*. Amy and Steve confirmed that they all saw Sterling toward the end of May when he and Lizzie came for dinner.

'He seemed very happy,' Amy told Fleet wistfully. 'It was shaping up to be quite the year for him.'

I informed Wendy that our techs would be at her offices within the hour to review all correspondence she had received on behalf of Sterling and that we would pay her a visit tomorrow. Fleet told the Beaufords that we might need to speak with them again soon, including their son Jack in LA.

'Anything we can do to help,' a teary Amy said to Fleet. She also asked after Matthew and April Wade.

'There's certainly a lot of people who were very invested in Wade's life,' says Fleet after giving me a run-down on the conversation with the Beaufords. 'I still think the attack might not have been intended to kill him,' he says thoughtfully as he skewers a pea. 'Maybe it was supposed to be a warning? He could have survived.'

'You're thinking that Cartwright was pissed at Wade for confronting him about abusing Ava?'

'Maybe,' says Fleet, picking chicken from his teeth. 'Cartwright might not have liked being told off like that.'

'I'm sure he didn't but do you really think that he would derail his own movie? And who would he have hired to do it? It's pretty risky.'

'No idea,' says Fleet. 'But I'm guessing that people like Cartwright have connections and are pretty influential. Maybe he just paid one of the cast or crew members? Or someone in security?'

I think about this. It would certainly have been easiest for one of the cast or crew members to be responsible for the attack. Or someone with an ID pass who knew their way around behind the scenes.

'If that's what happened,' I say, 'there's probably a paper trail. Phone conversations or emails.'

Fleet gulps water from a bottle with a faded football club logo on it. 'Unless they spoke about it on set.'

'We need to get all those interviews done,' I say. 'Maybe someone noticed Cartwright had become close with a cast member recently.' I spot Amir on the other side of the case room. 'Pavlich, how's the cast and crew interview session shaping up?'

'Good,' he replies. 'We're just confirming the last of the cast and crew now. It's going to be huge. I've got thirty-six officers rostered on but I'm pushing for more.'

'Great, thank you.' I give up on my rice, the starch sticking unpleasantly to my teeth. Turning back to Fleet, I say, 'If Ava's telling the truth and Wade did confront Cartwright on Sunday, he reacted pretty quickly to organise a stabbing.'

Fleet seems unfazed. 'No time like the present. Maybe Cartwright was worried that Wade would report him to us—or worse, the Twitter police. That might have been pretty motivating.'

I nod. 'I agree, but he couldn't have known that Ava wouldn't spill the beans herself. I guess we'll see what he has to say for himself tomorrow.'

Fleet stretches his arms high above his head and tips his body from side to side. 'Ms James doesn't have an alibi either, you know.'

'She was in her trailer,' I say, puzzled.

'Sure, about thirty metres from where Wade was stabbed,' he says. 'It wouldn't have been hard for her to slip on a costume and disappear into the crowd. She knew what was going on and how to get close to Wade.'

'But why would she attack him?'

Fleet chews his lip thoughtfully. 'I'm not sure but it's weird that Wade was apparently so righteous on Ava's behalf. How willing he apparently was to rush to her aid. Maybe that's a fantasy she dreamed up. Or maybe they really did have something going on.'

'Or maybe Wade was just a decent guy who stuck up for a friend who was being assaulted,' I retort.

Fleet flutters his eyelashes, controlling himself before a full-blown eye roll takes place. 'It's possible,' he allows.

'And even if they were sleeping together or involved in some way, surely that gives her even less reason to attack him,' I say, confused.

Fleet shrugs. 'Dunno. Maybe she found out about Wade and Kent, or got sick of him having a girlfriend. I sensed a bit of madness in those beautiful eyes.'

'You think all women are crazy,' I say dismissively.

He raises his eyebrows at me. 'Haven't been proven wrong yet,' he quips.

'Look, I agree Ava had access to the scene but I can't see why she'd want him dead. It makes no sense.'

'Maybe she didn't,' he says. 'Like I said before, it could have been a warning that went too far.'

I close my eyes, and then open them to look at the case board. Wade's perfect face stares out at me and I play back the moment when the knife plunged deep into his chest. I shudder. It doesn't feel like a warning to me.

'Ava's pretty tall,' I say. 'Ideally the tech guys will identify the killer on the video and we'll be able to get some basic physical stats. Start to build a profile.'

'Yep,' says Fleet, pushing his fingers through his hair. 'Hopefully we'll be able to put out an alert for a short middle-aged zombie with a stoop.'

'I'm going,' I announce, tired of his negativity. 'I need to get some sleep.'

'Cool,' says Fleet. Then, 'Remind me what exciting agenda you have planned for us tomorrow?'

'Lizzie in the morning. Then Sterling's agent, Wendy Ferla. Isaacs wants us to check in with the Wades again too; hope-fully Sterling's siblings will be here by then. We need to speak to Cartwright as well. I forgot to follow up with the sex assault squad about his response to the formal charge. We can call them from the car after we've seen Lizzie.' I dump all the takeaway containers in the bin and wipe the table with a serviette, feeling overwhelmed with the amount of work we have to do.

'Big day,' comments Fleet. 'I can't wait.'

I walk out past Walter Miller's case room. Two uniforms are still there, quietly sorting through paperwork. I look at the case board, noticing how sparse it is compared to ours. A wave of hopelessness washes over me but in the end I keep walking, knowing that there is not much I can do for Walter now.

◄○►

Outside the chilled air hits my lungs, a shock after the cloying arti-ficial heat of the office. One of the street lamps has blown and I walk briskly through the darkness to get to the pool of white up ahead. A young guy jogs past from behind, startling me as he steps on a stick lying in wait on the ground. In the apartments above, a door slides open and the excited screams of teenagers explode into the night. Just as quickly the door shuts and their screams disappear.

The stars are dull tonight, the upward glow of the city keeping them muted.

I pull out my phone and see a series of missed calls. Dad, Candy, Scott. Annoyed at myself, I vow to call Ben in the morning. Sighing, I skim a text from Josh checking to see if I'm okay; I flick him a quick apology for being so busy. Then I call Candy.

'Gemma! How dare you not call me until now. I am literally *dying* up here.'

'Literally dying, huh?' I smile. 'Well, we can't have that.'

'Can you believe this?' she ploughs on.

'Well, I—'

'I mean it's the most insane story. Just crazy. No one is talking about anything else. I'm also trying to separate my personal feelings here but I'm completely devastated. It's so bloody tragic. Wade was absolutely *gorgeous.*'

'Yes, and—'

'I had a huge crush on him, you know? I told you that, right?'

I smile. 'I think you mentioned it once or twice.'

'So, what can you tell me?'

'*Candy*, you know I can't tell you anything.'

'Oh come *on*. There must be something!'

'All I will say is that it's a total nightmare. Especially with all the journalists getting in the way.'

She ignores my jibe. 'But it was some random psycho, right? Someone in the movie that just flipped?'

'We're not sure,' I say truthfully.

'What's the point of having a fancy detective friend if you won't feed me classified information?' She moans theatrically.

I laugh again. 'Sorry, Candy. But, hey, maybe you can help me. We're seeing Wade's parents again tomorrow so I'm hoping you can tell me more about the money troubles you mentioned.'

'Well, like I said in my message, I hunted down this guy I went to school with who knows the family—he's actually quite cute now, which was a bonus—but anyway, he mentioned to me how he'd heard the Wades are in serious financial strife.'

'But surely if things are that bad then Sterling would have been able to help them out. Loan them money, at least?'

'You'd think so, but maybe they asked and he said no, or maybe they didn't want anyone to know, not even their kids. Of course, I did some more digging. It's definitely bad. They've had a terrible few years with the farm and owe a shitload of money. Their property is huge and it's bleeding cash. It doesn't look like they'll be able to keep it.'

We chat for a bit longer—until Candy starts interrogating me about my love life, and I make excuses to ring off.

I pause at the corner of Collins Street. I suddenly don't want to go to my cold, empty apartment. I look for Macy but she's not in her normal spot, and I hope she's with Lara and safe somewhere.

I know where I'm going before I even let myself admit it. My skin burning, I pass dozens of faces. Hundreds. Melbourne is so full of people compared to Smithson, and is so much more diverse. People here go home to all kinds of different lives, their rituals an alchemic mix of many places. I feel energised by the spectrum of characters who gravitate to the city. It's so much more acceptable to be who you want to be here. There's no set mould to adhere to, no specific life rules laid out to follow.

As I approach the hotel I can almost feel the curve of the wine-glass in my hand. The softness of the velvet lounge chair underneath me. I can imagine running my hands all over a stranger in one of the rooms upstairs. I narrow my eyes at the bellboy as I bear down on the entrance, tossing my hair to one side, pulling off my coat as I step into the warm noisy lobby, the tinkle of glasses joyfully colliding as if announcing my arrival.

Friday, 17 August
7.12 am

I watch the city wake up, my phone pressed against my ear.

'Hey,' I say when Scott answers, my voice still full of last night.

'Hi,' he replies sarcastically. 'This is a nice surprise. I'm sure you saw that we tried to call you last night. Ben wanted to tell you that he lost a tooth.'

'Did you remember to leave him some money?' I ask, without thinking.

There's a long beat of silence down the phone line before Scott replies with exaggerated patience: 'Yes, Gemma. I remembered the tooth fairy money.'

My head throbbing, I close my eyes and picture Scott in the kitchen of my childhood home ready to go to work and take our son to school. 'Can I speak to Ben, please?'

Scott sighs, already exhausted from dealing with me. 'Yes, hang on, I'll get him.' He pauses. 'I assume you were working on the Sterling Wade case last night? We saw you on the news yesterday morning.'

'Yeah. Sorry, I should have let you know not to call yesterday. It's been a bit crazy.'

Scott laughs meanly. 'Gemma, it's always a bit crazy with you. I realise a dead movie star is especially out of the ordinary but don't blame him for you not being available. That's fairly normal.'

'Scott, I don't want to do this now,' I snap. 'Please just let me speak with Ben. I have to leave soon.'

Scott's frustration swirls into my small lounge room. 'Sure thing, Gemma.' Then, 'You know, you've probably never thought about it, but mornings are actually pretty crazy for us these days as well, so just make it quick, okay? We have to leave soon too.'

◄O►

A strange side benefit of being a detective is the voyeuristic glimpses you get into the highs, lows and all the tiny details in between that make a life. Over the years I have seen it all: suburban drug dens, palatial mansions, glossy teenage bedrooms, small dingy homes reeking of human struggle. I've seen garden sheds that double as bedrooms and modest units that sleep several families. I've found shoeboxes filled with sex tapes, read private love notes and scrolled through mind-boggling internet histories. It's an odd thing to be thrust into the intimate life of another human. And because most people don't know they're about to die, when we arrive it's as if someone hit pause on a computer game. Lipstick marks are still on wineglasses, fresh hair clogs the shower drain. The dog is whining for a walk.

It's true what they say, that we are more alike than we are different: the same vices, habits and secrets turning up over and over again. But every now and then something stands out as odd. Something jars. Loose threads that seem to lead nowhere but keep you coming back all the same.

Mostly, I never meet the strangers I come to understand so well. Of the two missing person cases I worked where the presumed dead victims were found alive, it was incredibly disconcerting for the imagined people to appear in the flesh. Usually, however, the dead stay dead, but their ghosts remain in close proximity, fully formed in my mind.

I often sense a victim around me, ushering me toward clues. I feel their cool disappointment when there's no solve; their approval when we make a breakthrough. Murder victims have unfinished business and it is my job to get them the last scrap of justice possible from the world that ejected them so cruelly. The dead people I encounter can be demanding, hijacking my thoughts and putting firm cold fists around my temples. My head can be a crowded place. I wish I knew how to escape it sometimes.

The blare of a horn brings me back to the road in front of us. The traffic has morphed into a long, slow slug and the early morning fog is still stuck to the buildings as if it has something to hide. Next to me Fleet fidgets like a kid.

Speaking with Scott earlier rattled me, and the hours I spent with a strange man last night have both buoyed me and planted a seed of loneliness deep in my soul.

'Are you getting excited about being at home with the stars?' Fleet says as he parks the car in the service vehicle spot outside Wade and Lizzie's apartment complex.

'Yeah, I can't wait,' I reply sarcastically, 'it's totally my thing.'

'Maybe you'll pick up some styling tips,' he says rudely, swinging out of the car.

A flush spreads from my chest to my neck. He's been in a foul mood all morning, barely saying hello and grimacing through our case meeting. I look down at what I'm wearing. My black suit jacket is a size too big and my pants are an unfashionable grey. Fleet, on the other hand, manages to look completely haphazard but cool in faded black jeans and a chunky leather jacket.

'Quickly,' he says as if I'm five years old.

My burning face is slapped by the cold air as I get out of the car.

Wade's apartment complex is one of those old converted redbrick factories—the kind that used to produce shoes or chocolate—now dedicated to the comfort of wealthy young professionals and their expensive things. We enter a painfully stylish lobby with a single globe hanging from the high ceiling on a long rope, burdened with illuminating the whole area. An armchair occupies the far corner and we walk across polished concrete as smooth as ice toward the elevator. A giant mirror reflects our every move—we look tiny, like hobbits creeping toward the edge of the earth.

'Ah, takes me back to my own modest early twenties share house,' quips Fleet.

'Level 3, Apartment A,' I say, pushing the corresponding buttons. Above, someone scans us in. We ride up in silence, transformed into blurry silver shapes on the elevator door. A *ping* announces our arrival and we step out onto aggressively gleaming floorboards.

'Hello,' says Lizzie in a wavering voice, from a doorway a little further up the hall.

Despite the industrial common areas, the apartment is light and airy. The rooms wrap around a circular courtyard that all the apartments in the complex face into. A large tree grows from its centre, giving the impression of a private oasis amid the hustle, bustle and relentless pursuit of progressive cool just metres away in hipster land. My immediate thought is that the design provides excellent stalking conditions. Depending on how security-conscious Sterling, Lizzie and Brodie are, anyone in the surrounding apartments on this level or above could have let their imagination run wild as they watched Wade go about his life. Maybe someone watched him dress in the mornings. Or watched him with Lizzie. Or with Brodie. Maybe they've been watching him for months, fantasising about being closer to him. Harming him.

Lizzie seems lost in thought as she stares at a giant photo board propped on a side table. Dressed in tailored jeans and a neat navy blazer with gold buttons, her brown hair in loose waves, jewellery around her neck and on her fingers, she looks like she's about to go for a job interview.

I always find it fascinating that some grieving people use clothes as a shield from the pain, taking care to put on their best armour as if the better they look, the more likely they'll be able to deflect the moments of crippling agony. Whereas others become incapable of grooming, as if spending even one minute on something so trivial is akin to dancing on the dead person's grave. In contrast to Lizzie, after my mother died I don't think I looked in a mirror for almost a week. My appearance was the last thing on my mind.

'How long have you lived here, Lizzie?' I ask.

'About eighteen months,' she murmurs softly.

I walk over to her and put my hand on her shoulder. I look at the photos too. There must be at least a hundred shots. Sterling and Lizzie are in most of them, surrounded by beautiful faces and perfect bodies dripping in designer clothes and jewellery.

Being a detective has altered how I process a new environment. I've spent enough time around various forensics teams as they rip through a room and upend a life that I now find myself doing the same with my bare eyes. I can almost smell the DNA that drips from the surfaces, sense the smudges of fingerprints, the remnants of sweat and other unsavoury body fluids. No matter the plushness of a room or the quality of the bed linen, we all leave pieces of ourselves everywhere we go. Even my nasty hollow of an apartment would no doubt provide a decent amount of information about me: my skin, hair and tears already lodged deep inside the cheap sheets and worn carpet.

I feel Sterling's presence here. His tanned skin is embedded in the smooth sandy floorboards. His chiselled face is carved into the marble-drenched kitchen. Despite the youth of the occupants, the furniture is straight out of the sixties. A huddle of painfully chic light grey couches is dwarfed by giant copper dome lamps. A curved glass coffee table sits between them and there's a retro record player in the corner. Huge prints of iconic ads from past decades adorn the walls, promoting the virtues of soap, beer and Coca-Cola. A large vase of fading white roses is like a small tree on the kitchen bench. I picture Sterling's long, lean body stretched out on the couch, perhaps Lizzie curved beside him as he strokes her hair. My vision jumps, and now I see Sterling and Brodie locked in a passionate embrace, arms rising as clothes are pulled off. Kissing.

I shake my head and make the couch empty again.

Lizzie sinks back against the cushions. She seems so much older today; not in her schoolgirl gear but still prissy. Despite the symmetry of her face, she's not as pretty as Ava. There's something unremarkable about her: she's more of a blank canvas than a masterpiece. Still, I feel gritty and plain against her glossy cleanness.

'Hello,' says a man's voice from behind me, making me jump slightly.

Lizzie's brother Kit has walked into the kitchen. He pours a glass of water and brings it over to his sister, who gives him the faintest of smiles in response. He sits next to her and gives her hand a squeeze.

Fleet and I lower ourselves onto the couch opposite. Lizzie looks at me, her eyes as unfocused as a baby's. She manages another faint smile. 'Thank you,' she says softly. 'Thank you so much for looking after me the other night. I wouldn't have coped without you being there. You were so kind.'

'It was a terrible shock,' I say. 'How are you feeling now?'

She opens her mouth to reply but the movement turns into a full-body collapse and suddenly her head is in her hands and she is choking on sobs. Kit strokes her back, staring at the top of her head. After a couple of minutes Fleet stands up and fetches a box of tissues from the kitchen bench. He puts it on the coffee table near her, then sits back down beside me.

'Where's Brodie?' he asks, as she clutches at the tissues like a lifeline.

'He's gone out for a walk,' replies Kit.

'He's pretty messed up,' adds Lizzie. 'We both are.'

'We'd like to ask you a few questions, Lizzie,' I say. 'Do you think you can manage that?'

'Yes, I want to do whatever I can to help—sorry,' she says, taking a deep breath to steady herself. 'I'm just struggling to believe this is actually happening.'

'Lizzie, you knew Sterling so well,' I say. 'And we are obviously doing everything we can to work out what happened on Wednesday. We're wondering if there's anything you can think of that we should know about.'

She raises her head, her eyes drowning in tears. She takes a deep, shaky breath. 'I don't think so.'

'Sterling never mentioned getting any strange messages from fans? He never mentioned being scared or uncomfortable about anything?'

'Not really. A lot of people wrote to him online but I don't think they were dangerous.'

'What about the other cast members, or the crew?' I press. 'Was he close to any of them?'

'He was friendly with everyone, but not really friends with them. He was actually kind of shy in a way.'

'He never mentioned being followed?' says Fleet.

Lizzie lifts her head and some life comes into her eyes. 'Well, maybe. Sterling did say something about that.' Her voice breaks a little as she says his name, but she lays her hands out on the coffee table and seems to steady herself. 'I didn't think anything of it then, but maybe now . . .'

I look at her encouragingly. 'What did he say, Lizzie?'

'Well, about a fortnight ago he said he was feeling weirded out because he thought someone was following him.' She brushes more tears from her eyes. 'I kind of laughed it off because he probably *was* being followed. I mean, he was a celebrity. People wanted to talk to him and take photos of him all the time. We both got a bit of that sometimes.'

'But he said this was different?' I say.

'I guess so. Enough that he mentioned it to me.'

'Did he see this person? Describe what they looked like?' asks Fleet. He slouches in his chair as if he's watching TV, and I feel a surge of frustration at his sloppiness.

Lizzie looks at us helplessly. 'No. He just said he thought a guy was following him home one day. Sorry, I wish I had more to tell you. I remember it was the day that he met with Katya March, our producer, about the shooting schedule. They'd been trying to make it work around a trip to LA that Sterling had planned. They met at some bar near our apartment—I don't know the name but I know where it is. I can show you.'

'Was it late when they met? Do you remember what time he got home?' I ask, thinking that we might get lucky and score some CCTV footage from that night, though it's unlikely. Most small businesses only keep footage for a week or two.

'No, I got home just before him, maybe around eight. He walked home. It's less than ten minutes from our place. He's been followed before but it's normally just people wanting his autograph. This time he seemed a bit spooked, which wasn't like him.'

'Is there anything else you can remember about what he said?' I press.

She shakes her head, biting her lip. 'I don't think so.'

'We'll definitely look into it,' says Fleet. 'Can we ask you some other questions?'

Her phone keeps buzzing on the couch next to her, but she ignores it.

She blinks. 'Of course.'

'Let's start with Riley Cartwright. Did you know him before you were cast in the movie?'

'Don't you want to hear how Sterling and I met?' Her fingers clench around the water glass and she looks to be on the brink of tears again.

'Ah, sure,' says Fleet, sounding momentarily thrown. 'That's a good idea, talk us through that.'

'Well, obviously Sterling's on *The Street*, you know, the soap?'

We nod.

'I did heaps of little roles on it when I was a kid, mainly as a hero extra—you know, a line here and there but not an actual part. Before she died, Mum was very serious about me finishing school before I did too much acting or modelling. But I kept in touch with everyone, did a few stage shows with a few cast members over the years, saw them at events, things like that.'

'Right, so did you meet Sterling on set?' I ask.

'No.' Her lip juts out and trembles slightly. 'No, this movie we were shooting was going to be our first job together.'

'Okay, so then how did you meet?' Fleet is firm, clearly not wanting Lizzie to turn back into a sobbing mess.

'Well, one of the girls on *The Street*, Milla Hersham? She played Rose Flightman.' Lizzie looks between us again but we are both blank. 'No? Well, anyway, she had a party at her place about three years ago and I went along. I was so excited to meet Sterling, I mean half the girls there were, but I really wanted to talk to him about work. Acting, I mean. I figured I could really learn from him.'

'But you ended up really hitting it off?' I say.

She smiles and then crumples as reality trumps history. 'Yeah. Not like instantly. We didn't hook up that night or anything but we kept in touch. He offered to put in a good word for me with one of his mates who was directing a short film. Let me know about auditions, stuff like that.'

'Sounds like a nice guy,' I say gently.

'Yeah. He was the best,' Lizzie says, twisting her hands together. 'He was always really generous with his time.'

'So then you did hook up—when was that?' Fleet presses.

'Maybe two, three months later. That September we had our first proper date. I moved in around the start of last year.'

'When did Brodie move in?' I ask.

'Just a couple of months ago. He was going through a rough patch and Sterling wanted to help him out.'

'Did you mind your love nest being crashed?' asks Fleet.

Lizzie blinks vacantly. 'No. We were often home at different times. Sterling worked long days on set and I often worked nights doing plays and short films. It was nice for him to have someone to keep him company.'

I force myself to keep my gaze on Lizzie rather than exchange a look with Fleet. But I notice Kit's gaze darting around, and I wonder if he has suspicions about Sterling and Brodie.

'Right,' Fleet says, crossing and then uncrossing his legs. 'And how did it come about, you two both being in the film?'

'Riley had wanted to work with Sterling since forever. They'd been talking about doing a project for a long time. Riley was signed up to direct the movie about two years ago and suggested Sterling for the lead. It was all falling into place but then the funding was cut. Everyone was gutted. Sterling had been talking about moving to the US and figured that if he didn't have that film shoot to stay here for, then we should just take the chance and go, start auditioning for roles and all that. But then the storylines on *The Street* got better and he scored a film role so he decided to wait out the year.'

Lizzie is talking fast, clearly happy to have her mind busy and distracted by the past. Her hands have stopped gripping each other in her lap and curve around her kneecaps instead.

'And it obviously all got resolved eventually?' Fleet says, leaning forward.

Lizzie moves back slightly in response. 'Yes. By the beginning of this year the shoot was back on and they just picked up where they'd left off.'

'No hard feelings?' Fleet asks.

Lizzie looks puzzled. 'No, there was nothing to be angry about. Funding falls through all the time, it's no big deal. Sterling was just happy to be able to still do the movie. And the money was great, more than he'd ever been paid before. Same for me.' She tugs at her ring again, before saying carefully, 'If I'm honest though, I think that the movie was a bigger deal for Riley than it was for Sterling. He hadn't had a decent project for a while and he wasn't in a great place. I mean, it was huge for all of us but Sterling was starting to get offers from Hollywood. I'd been asked to audition for a few parts too. Nothing was definite but our agents were pretty positive about our chances. I think Riley needed Sterling. Everyone knew that him being cast in the film was why the new investors came on board.'

I take this in. Did Riley Cartwright like being so dependent on his leading man?

'What do you mean that Cartwright wasn't in a great place?' I ask her.

'I think he has some problems,' she says diplomatically. 'There were rumours of drugs and gambling but it might have been just talk. You have to be careful you don't believe everything you hear.'

'Any other rumours about Cartwright?' Fleet asks.

Her forehead wrinkles prettily. 'No. He has a temper sometimes but a lot of directors do. I know some people find him hard to work with but he's always been good to me.'

It seems she hasn't heard about the sexual assault accusation.

Swiftly changing tack, Fleet says brightly, 'Were you and Sterling still planning to move overseas?'

Lizzie looks around the room as if she's worried someone will overhear her. 'Yeah, after Christmas. Sterling wanted to spend it at home with his parents. We hadn't told anyone yet. He was still under contract for *The Street*, and we weren't one hundred per cent sure when we'd go, but we were making plans.'

Kit keeps his gaze on the floor. He and Lizzie are obviously close, and I wonder how he feels about this.

'Okay, cool,' says Fleet smoothly. 'Now let's talk about the past few days.'

Lizzie looks lost again, as if she had temporarily forgotten about Sterling's death. 'The past few days,' she repeats.

'Yes. The movie shoot started on Monday?'

Lizzie leans back in her chair and nods wearily. 'Yes, we'd been doing rehearsals since June but the shoot officially started this week.

We did some inside scenes first, which were kept pretty well on the down low. Wednesday was the first street day and it was always going to be hard to keep it under wraps. We were shooting the main zombie scene on Spring Street when Sterling . . . when it happened. The plan was to film there for three days and cover it all off in one go.' Her voice cuts in and out as she tries to avoid crying.

'And how was Sterling?' Fleet asks. 'Anything out of the ordinary?'

'The whole thing was surreal. I've never been on a production like it. It's been full on. Sterling was more used to it but I think he was still pretty overwhelmed.' Lizzie succumbs to a large, shuddering sob. 'We had so many plans, you know. What am I going to do now?'

Kit rubs her back with renewed purpose. 'It will be okay, Lizzie,' he soothes.

She nods slightly and sniffs, dabbing her eyes with a tissue. 'I'm sorry,' she says, turning back to us, 'I know you're trying to ask me questions.'

'You're doing great, Lizzie,' I reassure her.

She breathes deeply. 'Okay. So, it was a big week but Sterling seemed fine. He was feeling the pressure but he was enjoying the shoot. The rehearsals had gone well and the press was really good. It felt like the start of a new phase.' She briskly brushes fresh tears away.

'And what about you? Were you enjoying the shoot?' Fleet asks.

Lizzie spaces out. She gapes at Fleet without speaking. For a minute, I think she's clammed up but then she says quietly, 'Yes. It was exciting. I liked my character and I was so excited for Sterling. Everything was going well.'

'Did you get along with everyone? What about Ava James?'

Lizzie's lip curls momentarily but then the blank look is back and I think maybe she's just trying to quell the crying. 'Like I said, we all got along. The performances were really coming together. Riley was happy. Everyone was getting along, it was perfect until . . . this.' Her chin wobbles again and her skin flushes a blotchy red.

'We really are sorry, Lizzie,' I say, 'this must be so difficult.'

'Yeah. It is. I feel like I don't have a future.' She sobs.

'Did Sterling ever cheat on you?' asks Fleet.

Lizzie's head snaps up, her face slick with tears. 'No!'

'Did you ever cheat on him?' presses Fleet.

'No,' she says, looking to me for help.

Kit sits up straighter and I fully expect him to tell Fleet where to go, but his mouth remains in a thin line.

'He wasn't jealous,' says Lizzie firmly. 'He just didn't let emotions like that in.'

'He ever get into fights?'

'No. Honestly, he was a really chilled-out guy. He stood up for what he believed in but he didn't have a temper. We trusted each other.'

'So you can't think of anything that makes sense of what happened?' continues Fleet.

Lizzie looks bewildered. 'Only what I told you about him being followed a few weeks ago. I mean, he did have a few intense fans. Mainly when he first joined *The Street* but I think it was pretty normal stuff. People obsessing over him on Facebook and Twitter. Sometimes people would send him emails, or letters to his agent or the TV studio. I don't even know if he read them. It could get pretty full on, especially if he had a movie coming out. Some people were really creepy but Sterling was never worried so I wasn't either. Do you think that some stranger might have done this? Someone who contacted him online?' She sits up urgently, her eyes wide. 'Maybe that's who attacked him. Could they have snuck onto the set somehow?'

'We don't know yet, Lizzie,' I say.

She nods vigorously again but it soon drifts into nothing.

'It sounds like you and Sterling were pretty serious,' I venture. 'Living together, planning a big move, working together.'

'We were very serious.' She looks down at her left hand as the gemstone in her ring catches the gentle sunlight and flickers vividly. Her eyes swim again. 'We were engaged, actually. He proposed last week. We just hadn't told anyone yet.' She shoots an apologetic glance at her brother. 'Not even family.'

'It's a beautiful ring,' I say to fill the silence that would normally be full of congratulations. Even I can tell it is expensive: the gemstone is large and set in a popular vintage style that I've noticed in the windows of designer stores near my apartment.

'Thank you.' Her mouth fumbles a brief smile. Her eyes glaze over as she looks at it. 'I love it. It's so me, the antique style. Sterling surprised me with a romantic meal at home last Wednesday. We were going to announce it once the shoot was over.'

I give her a sympathetic look, then turn to Kit. 'When did you last see Sterling?' I ask.

'Me?' His brow furrows slightly. 'I think it was the weekend before last. I came over on the Sunday morning and we all went out for coffee. I saw Lizzie for dinner this past Sunday but Sterling didn't come.'

'He was busy rehearsing,' she whispers.

'And where were you late Wednesday afternoon?' I ask.

'At the airport. I was just about to get on a plane for a work trip when Lizzie called me. I went straight back to the car park and drove to the hospital.' He glances at his sister. 'I couldn't believe what she was telling me. I still can't.' He speaks softly. In many ways, he reminds me of Brodie—they have a similar gentle vibe, and I wonder if this makes Lizzie more inclined to overlook any doubts she might have had about Sterling's relationship with his friend.

I also wonder whether Sterling told Brodie about his engagement to Lizzie despite their agreement to keep it under wraps. In my experience, secrecy is often sworn but there aren't many things, good or bad, that actually stay sacred.

'Lizzie, we'll leave you alone soon,' I say, 'but do you mind if we quickly take a look around? Sometimes it helps us to see where someone lived.'

'Of course,' she says to me, as her eyes flit doubtfully to Fleet. She pulls a throw rug across her lap and curls into the end of the couch. 'Some other police officers came last night to get Sterling's computer. I think they got his phone and laptop from the lockers on the film set.'

'You will get it all back,' I assure her. 'We just need some time to go through everything in case something that might help the investigation turns up.'

◄○►

Fleet and I enter the main bedroom, and I pull the door shut. It's a large space, with an unmade king-size bed low to the ground against the stark white wall; layers of bed linen lie across its bottom half. The windows run floor to ceiling just like in the main room. I walk over and gaze down into the central courtyard.

'That tree must look incredible in summer,' I comment.

Fleet fingers the spines of books on a large shelf. It's crammed with as many photo frames as books. 'I was just thinking that same thing—stunning,' he says sarcastically.

I give him a withering look as I stand next to him, taking in the beautiful smiling faces in the photographs. Lizzie and Sterling are in most of them, alongside faces I recognise from TV shows. Sterling looks happy. His perfect features are always arranged in a smile and his skin is tanned, unlike the light grey I recall from the autopsy table.

From the other room, I hear the muted sounds of Lizzie answering her phone and immediately crying around a tumble of words as she speaks to a well-wisher.

'The more we hear about this kid, the more perfect he seems,' says Fleet.

'I know. Perfect looks, money, fame and generosity. Even a social conscience.' I point to a certificate from the Royal Children's Hospital thanking Wade for contributing to their fundraising efforts.

'And engaged as well—he wasn't messing around,' muses Fleet.

'Maybe he just wasn't a party boy.'

'Seems like a waste.' Fleet chews on a fingernail. 'Imagine the women he could pull looking like that.'

'I guess he was in love,' I reply. 'Though I wonder what the engagement meant in terms of Brodie. Do you think he knows about it?'

'Maybe. We don't know for sure he's telling the truth. Or even if she is.'

'So maybe Brodie found out about the engagement and flipped.'

'You think he could have attacked Wade?' asks Fleet, seeming to perk up at the idea.

I tap my foot as I look around. 'I really don't know but his alibi is pretty sketchy. Feeling betrayed is a good reason to lash out.' I pick up a throw rug folded across an armchair; it is the softest material I've ever touched in my life.

'Maybe,' says Fleet. 'Or maybe Brodie just got sick of sharing.'

I think about other crimes of passion I've worked on. Mostly jealous men, almost every one discovering that a woman he loved had a mind of her own.

'We might be able to see if their correspondence took a nasty turn,' I suggest. 'Maybe Wade was trying to pull away.'

'Brodie does seem very sensitive,' says Fleet. He picks up a pile of books from a bedside table and drops them back into place one by one, his face screwed up in distaste. 'Poetry,' he drawls. 'I can't believe people read this stuff.'

We head back into the lounge room just as Lizzie ends her call. I hear the rumble of a kettle boiling—Kit is back in the kitchen. Two mugs sit on the bench in front of him with teabag tails hanging out.

'We're just going to take a quick look in Brodie's room while we're here,' I tell her.

Lizzie, puffy faced, looks up with a furrowed brow but nods.

'Do you want a hot drink?' asks Kit and we shake our heads.

Brodie's room is dark compared to the master bedroom. The bed is neatly made but the doona looks worn and the lone built-in shelf is a spray of everyday mess. Rubber bands, lolly wrappers, coins. Several empty cigarette packets litter the bedside table. A large photo of Sterling and Brodie sitting on a Ferris wheel takes pride of place.

'Not very stylish for a gay guy,' comments Fleet as he looks around. 'I reckon I could give him a run for his money.'

I don't say anything. Something about the photo has saddened me; perhaps it's all Brodie has left of Sterling.

'He's only been here a little while,' I say. 'And Lizzie did say he was going through a tough time.'

'Maybe they screwed in Wade's room,' whispers Fleet, wrinkling his nose. 'It's much nicer.'

'Enough,' I say. I'm well over his constant jibes.

I give the room one last scan and we return to the lounge. I look out at the tree, its skinny branches like tiny hands reaching toward the surrounding apartments. I wonder if Sterling felt exposed here.

'Lizzie, we have to go,' I say. 'We'll be in touch but if you find or think of anything else we should know about, please call us straight away.'

'Do you think I'm safe here?' she asks me, her hands gripped around a huge white mug.

'I'm sure you are,' I reply. 'But if anything worries you, please let us know.'

As we exit the apartment building, I look over at a street market stall selling jewellery and handmade cards on the corner. Rugged-up couples with hands in each other's pockets stroll past, pausing to look at the wares.

Fleet shoves a cigarette in his mouth as we near the car, shielding his face from the wind. He smokes hard and fast, flattening it into the ground.

'Gosh, home visits with two beautiful actresses in as many days,' he says with a singsong lilt. 'We are lucky, aren't we? Come on,' he says, yanking the car door open before I can respond, 'mustn't be late for the appointment with our agent.'

Friday, 17 August
11.56 am

Wendy Ferla's crisp white South Yarra office is an overwhelming jumble of paper. Loose sheets, notebooks, Post-its, books and old movie tickets litter the desk, the chairs around the desk and most of the floor.

A large framed black-and-white photo of Sterling is propped on the bottom shelf of a bookcase with a line of tea light candles burning beside it.

'Wendy will just be a moment,' a harried young woman with red-rimmed eyes tells us as she pushes piles of paper out of the way with the butts of two sparkling-water bottles. She cocks her head to the side, causing her long earrings to jingle. 'She's just out there.'

Fleet and I spin around to see a woman through the office's French doors, pacing in a small courtyard and gesturing wildly as she talks on her mobile.

The assistant, who looks too young to be legally employed, flashes us a sad smile. 'Everyone's been calling her. You know, since it happened.' She glances at the photo of Sterling. 'She's been on the phone for hours. Everyone wants to talk to her about him. Like, just saying the same things over and over. It's kind of weird.'

Fleet looks distastefully at the avalanche of papers. 'People are weird,' he says.

'You are *so* right,' the girl says to Fleet as if he's a genius. 'Anyway, she knows you're here so I'm sure she won't be long.'

'Cheers,' says Fleet, admiring her retreating figure.

He looks around and makes a face at the mess. 'Well. Lucky we're happy to stand, huh.' He picks up a shiny gold paperweight shaped like a handgun, turning it over and pretending to aim it at an expensive-looking vase that holds a single white rose.

I feel another jerk of irritation. Fleet and I remain awkward, still frequently bumping into each other. Despite brief flashes of cama-raderie, most of the time we're like two pieces of wood with the grain running in different directions. He's so deliberately obtuse, inexplicably intent on not liking people and in turn giving them zero reasons to like him. And it annoys me more than I can explain that I have no real sense of how he feels about me.

'Jeez, c'mon,' he mutters, tapping at his phone and dropping his fist onto the desk.

Outside, Wendy Ferla is still pacing in an uneven circle as she talks on the phone, emphatically waving a hand in the air.

Fleet is watching her. 'So this chick's been Sterling's agent from the start, right?'

'That's what she said on the phone,' I confirm.

'Wonder if she knows much about his personal life?'

'Agents are normally pretty close to their clients, aren't they?'

'You been watching trashy movies again, Woodstock?' He smirks at me and I notice his fingers are twitching—I can tell he wants a cigarette.

'Just try to be nice for once,' I snap, as Wendy yanks the door open.

A slightly sour floral fragrance wafts into the room as she enters. She is taller than she'd appeared when she was outside, though it's hard to tell where her head ends and her hair starts. Dyed orange curls explode around her face; some are pinned back but several ringlets have escaped and sway loosely past her shoulders and down her back. Her face is heavy with grief but she holds her head high.

'I'm sorry to keep you,' she says. 'Everyone needs to talk about what happened.'

'Detective Sergeant Woodstock,' I say, holding out my hand. 'We spoke yesterday.'

Fleet introduces himself too and then we stand awkwardly, unsure where to sit.

'Come in here,' she says, walking past us into an adjoining room. 'It's much nicer and there's nowhere to sit in there. Billie should have thought of that.'

Fleet bugs his eyes out at me as we follow her into a spacious lounge. It's spotless, with a two-seater couch and two comfortable-looking armchairs. A huge vase of lilies on a side table is made to look even larger due to the mirror behind it. Several bunches of flowers are piled at its base; a large army of sympathy cards stand like soldiers next to them.

'I'm sorry if I'm a bit distracted.' Wendy sits and then abruptly stands, shifting to the other armchair. 'Please sit.' She jiggles her leg up and down. 'I still can't believe this, you know.' She flaps her heavily ringed hands in the air. 'I don't really know what to do with myself.'

'When did you last see Sterling?' I begin.

She puts a hand on her heart as if trying to manually calm it down. 'Ah, well, last week on Tuesday. He's been so busy with rehearsals for *Death Is Alive* that we hadn't caught up properly for ages. We had lunch and discussed his future.' She emits a strange noise and fans at her face. 'Oh, goodness me.'

I catch her eye, trying to get her to focus. 'So you said you've been Sterling's agent since he first began acting?'

She nods. Despite the papery wrinkles around her features, there's a youthful aura about her. 'Yes. I met Sterling when he was twelve. Such a country boy back then. He was just a child but already a beautiful soul.' A crumpled hanky appears from somewhere and she dabs at her eyes. 'I helped place him with the Beaufords. They are an amazing family. Very prominent in the industry. They only had one child, Jack, and they were more than happy to take in Sterling and give Jack some brotherly company. This will hit them very hard too—they really embraced Sterling.' She shudders through a few breaths. 'Truly, this is just devastating. Talking to April and Matthew is breaking me. Good, honest people like them, it's just, well, they shouldn't have to deal with something like this. They barely coped with his success. I just really can't believe it. Sorry.' She closes her eyes, her lips moving as if she's talking to herself. 'Ask me anything,' she says after a few moments. 'I just want you to find out what happened. I can't bear the thought that this was deliberate. But that's why you're here, isn't it?'

'We're investigating all possibilities at the moment,' I tell her.

'You manage all of Wade's business dealings, correct?' says Fleet.

'Yes, that's right. Every dollar he earns goes through me.'

'And all of his publicity and correspondence?'

'Yes.' She nods earnestly. 'I manage all his engagements with my team here.'

'When we spoke on the phone you said that Sterling had admin access to all his social media accounts.'

She nods.

'Is that normal?' I ask.

'Yes. Most of our clients like some level of interaction with fans but leave the news alerts and community management to us.

The young ones do prefer to be hands-on though. It's just their world, I guess.' She leans forward. 'I've been in this business for a really long time and I tell you, it's changed so much in the past few years. It's a completely different ball game now. You have to constantly feed the media beast. Everything is so disposable and you can become irrelevant quickly.' She falls back against the chair and her eyes seem to get stuck on the vase of lilies. 'Sterling was unique in that he understood that world but he didn't let it get him down. He had a good head on his shoulders from a young age. He was very rare. Very special.'

Fleet kicks out his legs and relaxes into his armchair. 'We'll obviously be reviewing everything in due course, but from your perspective was any of the correspondence he received of concern?'

Wendy sighs and toys with the phone in her lap. 'I knew you were going to ask me that. It's hard to know what to tell you and of course I've been driving myself crazy about it ever since . . . this all happened.'

We look at her expectantly.

She holds out her hands as if in surrender. 'I mean, he got everything. Nice messages, obsessive ones, threats. Career advice, criticism and film offers. Marriage proposals, requests for money, voodoo spells. The whole gamut. The world is a weird place full of weird and wonderful people. We don't have any other clients who attracted the kind of attention that Sterling did. He was incredibly popular.' Her voice wobbles dangerously.

I keep talking, trying to pull her away from the sadness. 'When you say "threats", what do you mean?'

Her phone starts buzzing. She looks at the screen and pulls at her lips with her fingers before saying, 'You'll see yourself that some of the stuff is pretty hard to believe but nothing he got was unusual. Even the crazy things. He got far more than our other clients but those types of message are pretty typical of what all our clients receive. From behind a computer screen, anything goes.'

'Were direct threats ever made on his life?' I ask.

'No. A few times people said they were watching him. Following him. Or people described how they'd make love to him. Every now and then there were threats of violence.' She looks between us, seeking our understanding. 'But that is honestly so normal that I wasn't worried. We couldn't possibility report every threat—we'd never get anything else done.' Her eyes brim.

'Well, no doubt we'll be in touch with any questions as we work through it all. We may need access to some of your company bank accounts too. I assume that won't be a problem?' Fleet says, his tone making it clear that it will be a problem if she refuses.

'Of course,' replies Wendy, looking slightly bewildered.

'Wendy,' I say, 'you've known Sterling since he was a kid and you seem to have a good relationship with the Wades. What are they like?'

She clasps her hands together and bows her head solemnly. 'They are a lovely family. Just good decent country folk. April was a teacher for a while, but really she's all about the kids and the farm. Matthew is a lovely man. It's them I can't stop thinking about. They will never get over this.'

'What about their other children?' asks Fleet.

Wendy hesitates. 'I don't know them nearly as well,' she says slowly. 'And it was probably quite hard for them having a brother who was so famous. So *perfect*.' Her eyes glitter as she looks between the two of us. 'He really was, you know. I used to think how bizarre it was that a child with such X factor was born in the middle of this little farming town in Australia. I used to joke that he was the chosen one.'

'Sterling wasn't close to his siblings,' Fleet cuts in.

It's not exactly a question, but Wendy answers it anyway. 'I'm not sure if that's exactly fair. I think it was just hard for them to relate to him. They are so different. Always were. Plus, he moved away at a fairly young age and spent nine months of every year living with another family. A family that, if I'm honest, was more suited to him. Amy and Steve Beauford were very supportive of Sterling—they really understood him. I know April and Matt did everything they could for all their children, but Sterling was cut from a different cloth and they found his passion for acting challenging. He would have made it all the way, you know. There's no doubt in my mind.' Wendy leans forward again. 'Do you know that just last week he was offered a lead role in a US soap and a smaller role in a major Canadian film? He said he wanted some time to think things over before formally committing, but I told him he should accept both offers. Those roles would have been a huge step for him and really put him on the map.'

'I'm surprised he even needed to think about it,' I say. 'It sounds like a dream come true.'

'He had a real homebody streak,' Wendy replies, brushing tears from her eyes. 'He knew that if he left, it might be forever. He just wanted to be sure he was ready.'

'Back to the Wades,' says Fleet. 'Did he ever speak to you about his siblings?'

'Not really,' she says. 'I remember when his sister got married. He went home for a few days then. He felt a bit guilty sometimes—you know, with all the amazing things that came his way. And he was pretty good about keeping in touch with his parents. He spoke to them all the time and made sure they felt included in his life. They were proud of him, of course, even though it wasn't their scene. I always tried to support them when they came to Melbourne, especially when Sterling was younger.'

'And did Sterling stay close to the Beaufords?' I ask.

'They definitely stayed in touch,' replies Wendy, confirming what Amy Beauford told me. 'I know that Sterling continued to seek career advice from them, which made perfect sense. Creatively they have a lot in common.'

'What about Lizzie Short?' asks Fleet.

Wendy purses her lips as if deciding what to say. 'I don't want to speak out of turn,' she says, 'but I personally think Sterling had outgrown that relationship.'

'What makes you say that?' I ask.

Wendy blows out a breath and shrugs. 'Sterling really carried Lizzie. I never understood it but he was incredibly good to her. He seemed to have a real soft spot for that girl. He took her under his wing and was her biggest cheerleader.' She holds her hands up as if silencing us. 'Now don't get me wrong, she's a sweetheart, but Sterling was on another level. It would have come to a natural end over the next year or so.'

Fleet raises his eyebrows. 'Well, that's strange. We've just been speaking with Lizzie and she told us that she and Sterling were engaged. Apparently he proposed last week and they were going to keep it quiet until after the shoot.'

I study Wendy's surprised face.

'The silly kid,' she says finally.

'So you wouldn't have approved?' I say.

She looks down at her hands, curled into a knot in her lap. 'Honestly? No.'

'Did he ever talk to you about proposing to Lizzie?' I ask.

'No,' Wendy replies curtly. 'Not a word.'

'Weird he didn't confide in you,' Fleet comments.

She reels back a little. 'I didn't manage his personal life,' she says pragmatically. 'But engaged or not, I'm not sure it would have lasted. They were both caught up in their own romance sometimes. She's an orphan, you know, and quite needy. She really clung on to Sterling. Their relationship became quite co-dependent. But I guess it doesn't matter now anyway.' She lifts her shoulders in defeat. 'Poor girl,' she says as an afterthought.

'Brodie Kent,' I say.

Wendy straightens and looks warily at me. 'What about him?'

'What was he to Sterling?' I press.

'A leech,' she says bluntly.

I don't let my face show my surprise. 'What makes you say that?'

She lowers her voice conspiratorially. 'Look, that might be a bit harsh, but in this world you get people gravitating toward you for the wrong reasons. Brodie Kent was desperate to make something of himself, and he saw Sterling as a way to jump the queue.'

'An opportunist?' prompts Fleet, sniffing loudly.

'Yes. That's a good way to describe him. He's not particularly talented but he has grand plans. I'm sure he thought he could get famous by association.'

'He does claim to have been very close to Wade,' I venture.

Wendy gives a dismissive laugh. 'Him and everyone else. Honestly, the boy is delusional.' She's becoming more animated, the grief momentarily forgotten as her rant picks up. 'I suspect he had feelings for Sterling. He was obsessed. But it was a one-way street.' She shakes her head. 'I told Sterling that it was a bad idea, Brodie moving in with him and Lizzie. It wasn't healthy. That boy was always giving him bizarre advice about roles he should take and brands he should partner with.'

'It sounds like you don't think Sterling had very good judgement when it came to relationships,' I comment.

Wendy pushes her wild hair to one side as she considers this. 'I've always been pretty protective of him, I admit.' She looks sheepish.

'He was very loyal, like I said. And kind. He wanted to help people. It helped him ease the guilt he felt about his success.'

'So, he liked having a project—someone to help?' I prompt.

'Yes.' Her phone lights up again, and she eyes it for a second. 'That's right. It was like he surrounded himself with people who needed him. He wasn't often dazzled by celebrity. He was confident but very humble. Not arrogant at all.'

'And what about Ava James?' I ask. 'We've heard the rumours. Was something going on there?'

'I have no idea. But she would have been a wonderful match for him.' Wendy gets a faraway look. 'She's an absolute star. Sterling would have learned a lot from her.'

'I can't imagine Lizzie being thrilled with that,' says Fleet darkly.

'Of course not, but their romance was purely puppy love.'

'They were engaged,' I remind her.

Wendy shrugs. 'Engagements end. I'm sure she pressured him into that.'

I find it interesting how dismissive Wendy is about Wade's relationship with Lizzie. 'Did Sterling ever speak about Ava to you?'

'Yes. He loved working with her. This movie was a completely different level for him. Riley Cartwright is a lunatic but he's a talented director. I went to a couple of the rehearsals last month— Ava and Sterling were magnetic.'

'In what way is Cartwright a lunatic?' I ask, raising an eyebrow.

'He's up and down like a yo-yo, the way a lot of directors are. Probably on something, judging from the few times I've met him, but he gets the job done. Or seems to.'

'Did he and Sterling get on?'

'Mostly. Sterling mentioned being frustrated by his moodiness but put up with him well enough.'

'We heard they had a bit of a falling out,' I press. 'An argument last weekend.'

'I don't know anything about that,' says Wendy, looking confused.

'So what will happen with the movie now?' says Fleet, before she can ask us anything.

'I have no idea. I just have to focus on getting through the funeral and supporting the Wades however I can. Everything else can wait.' Her composure wobbles. 'I've never had a client die before.' She bites her lip and combs her fingers through her hair. 'I just don't want to believe it.' Her phone is ringing again, and she glances at the screen and then looks back at us. 'I really should speak to that person. Will we be much longer?'

'We're done,' says Fleet. He gets to his feet, the movement exposing a surprisingly tan torso with thick dark hair.

I'm not quite done yet. 'Wendy,' I say, 'did you ever get an inkling that Sterling was in danger?'

'I worried about him all the time,' she tells us, her grey eyes serious. 'I loved that kid like he was my own.' She swallows around a sob. 'But never in my wildest nightmares did I think something like this would happen. I was more worried about him hitting the big time and leaving me.' She laughs bitterly. 'Even though it was probably inevitable.'

'Had he ever mentioned he might do that?' I ask kindly, recognising that in Sterling's death, this woman has lost her own dreams.

'He always said I'd be his agent forever—but I'm sure it crossed his mind. People would have been in his ear all the time. And it's no secret that I'm not a young woman anymore.' Her forehead creases as her face drops, the hopelessness palpable. 'But he was so loyal. Probably too loyal.' She takes a deep breath and wipes under her eyes, smudging her make-up. 'The kid just always found the good in people. Even if it was invisible to everyone else.'

148

Friday, 17 August
2.27 pm

'So, as well as playing a lead role in a major Hollywood film,' says Fleet, 'Wade was planning world domination while carrying on a secret relationship with his male housemate and a secret engagement with his girlfriend. Plus, he was gallantly confronting a sleazy director about coming on too strong with his secret starlet girlfriend in his spare time.' Fleet whistles. 'Obviously the guy was more organised than me.'

'He did seem to be keeping himself quite busy,' I agree, as I nose the unmarked squad car through a pack of frenetic reporters and direct it toward the St Kilda hotel where Wade's family is staying. 'Though we don't know that Ava was anything more than a friend.'

I can feel Fleet roll his eyes. He must think there's no way Wade wasn't sleeping with the beautiful actress.

'There's quite a lot we don't know,' Fleet mutters. 'Give me the nice and simple homeless man's murder any day.'

I start to say something to challenge Fleet but decide against it. I don't want to increase the tension between us.

Fleet insisted that I drive to the Wades' hotel and is now looking moodily out the window while his personal phone vibrates in his lap with intermittent texts.

'Going to get those?' I ask stiffly.

He grunts in response.

We creep along St Kilda Road, the windscreen wipers working double speed to keep up with the heavy rain. The radio presenters are talking about the Jacoby investigation. They're using the word 'allegedly' a lot and staying just on the right side of the law. The case sounds so glamorous when you listen to it from their point of view—all drama—which is in stark contrast to the piles of paper-work in the case room and Nan's gloomy recount of the dead-end witness statements.

Unfortunately, despite the resources we've thrown at it, we've turned up little hard evidence. Meanwhile the media has delighted in confirming that Sasha, the key witness, is a walking cocktail of substances after years of chronic abuse. The situation hasn't been helped by the revelation that the dead woman, Ginny Frost, attempted suicide at the beginning of the year. Despite the incredible science we can now apply to our cases, so much of it still comes down to who saw what; we desperately need another pair of eyes, ideally more credible ones, to back up what Sasha claims she saw that night.

The young blond man who Sasha says also witnessed Jacoby arguing with Ginny has never come forward. And Jacoby denies having been on the balcony at all that evening. 'She was a very troubled young woman,' he's fond of saying, with a sad expression.

'He said, she said,' I mutter.

'You losing it over there?' grunts Fleet, typing furiously on his phone.

'I was just thinking about the Jacoby case. How it's really just his word against the escort's.'

'Isn't it bloody always in these cases?'

'I guess.'

'Well, I suppose it would help if the mysterious hot man that woman claims she saw hadn't disappeared into thin air.'

Fleet is right. Despite being very drunk and not perceiving his facial features in the dark bedroom, Sasha provided a decent description of the young man—around twenty-five, fair-haired, athletic—but apparently none of the other guests can remember seeing him. Most of them are in their forties and fifties, and there's conveniently no video surveillance on the penthouse level or the lifts. No one fitting the description Sasha provided has shown up on any of the footage secured from the entryway either. Much to Jacoby's delight, the mystery man is increasingly looking like a figment of Sasha's imagination.

I stab at the buttons on the dash, trying to turn up the heat. 'God, it's freezing.'

'Get used to it,' Fleet says ominously. 'They reckon there'll be snow on the mountains this weekend. It's enough to make me miss my home town.'

'You're not from here?' I say, surprised. I tend to assume that I'm the only outsider.

'Nope,' says Fleet, clearly not wanting to elaborate.

I turn my attention back to the road. 'Okay, so where am I going?'

'Some poncy joint off Fitzroy Street,' Fleet says. 'Left up ahead, after that white parked car.'

I steer us awkwardly into a narrow car park. Outside we pass another huddle of reporters, their eyes glued to their phones, and a few cameramen with their lenses trained on the hotel entrance.

'I wonder what Sterling's siblings will be like,' I say.

Fleet shrugs, his fingers on his phone again.

Water runs theatrically down the glass wall behind the reception area, and a woman with a glossy ponytail and a blindingly white smile greets us. 'Checking in?' she inquires.

'No,' I say quickly as Fleet smirks. 'We're here to see the Wade family. We're from the homicide squad.' I show her my ID.

Her smile vanishes. 'Oh, of *course*. Those poor people. Such a tragedy.' She leans forward conspiratorially. 'I just read online that he and his girlfriend got engaged last week too. It's *so* sad.'

Fleet makes an exaggerated coughing sound.

'Well, anyway, it's just awful,' the woman says, seeming to take the hint as she shifts to the other side of the desk and picks up a phone. 'I'll let them know you're here.'

'Engagement news spread quickly,' Fleet comments to me under his breath.

'I guess with no development on the case, the media will snap up everything they can.'

'Like crocodiles,' he agrees. 'But I guess Lizzie told them?'

I think about this. 'She must have. The media have been at her since the attack. Maybe she just decided to put it out in the open. And she probably wants people to know.'

He stretches his neck. 'Sterling might have told someone else and they could have gone to the press?'

'I wonder if the Wades know yet.'

'They're fine for you to go straight in,' says the girl as she hangs up the phone. 'Just through there. Room three, first on the right.'

'Thanks,' says Fleet, treating her to a charming smile. 'I guess we're about to find out,' he says to me.

Walking up the hallway, I feel apprehensive. The Wades have now had time to process their son's death, so they're likely to have shifted into the phase of mourning where their sentences trail off to nothing and they forget to blink. I tend to find parental grief the hardest of all.

Fleet's hand reaches past my hesitation and raps swiftly on the door. After a few moments a round-faced young man opens it, his eyes darting between the two of us before settling steadily on the floor at our feet. He's wearing a faded grey T-shirt that clutches his bulging curves. His hair is the same colour as Sterling's but the consistency is different, fine and limp. He must be Paul Wade, not the son-in-law, Rowan.

Fleet holds out his right hand and introduces himself. Paul shakes Fleet's hand while itching the back of his neck. He doesn't say anything.

'Detective Sergeant Woodstock,' I say, offering my own hand.

'My folks are inside.' Paul's voice is a low rumble. He ignores my gesture and walks away from us along the short hallway.

Fleet forces some air between his teeth as we follow him.

The central room is a combined lounge and kitchen. Stainless steel gleams from the fridge, oven and sink area; the rest of the décor is an expensive-looking modern stone.

The Wades look completely out of place. Matthew is wearing a flannel shirt and high-waisted jeans. He's sitting on a kitchen stool and staring at the bench. His wife is on the couch next to a plump woman who looks about thirty. Melissa, I assume. She's rubbing her hand in rhythmic circles on April's back, looking miserable. April's whole body shakes. Paul sits on the floor near his mother's feet and leans against the front of an armchair, his eyes fixed to the mute television, which is playing a cooking show. I wonder if he's in shock.

A mobile phone starts ringing.

'Excuse me,' mutters Matthew, pulling it out of his pocket as he disappears into another room.

I move to sit next to April. 'How are you, Mrs Wade?'

She doesn't seem to hear me.

'Are these your children?' I ask.

She nods robotically as the woman on the couch says, 'I'm Melissa.'

Matthew reappears. 'Sorry. I've got some neighbours trying to sort out the farm. There's things that can't wait. The animals.'

'Please don't apologise, Mr Wade,' I say.

'Do you have news?' There's a desperate edge to his question that I decide to ignore.

'Nothing concrete yet,' I say calmly, 'but we've committed a large task force to your son's case. We're doing everything we can to find the person who did this.'

Fleet picks up a chair that faces into a small writing desk; he flips it around and straddles it. 'So, what's your name?' he asks the man who is clearly Sterling's brother.

'This is Paul,' says Matthew. 'And this is Melissa. Our other children.'

Paul's expression remains blank. Melissa stands to shake my hand and I realise she is unusually tall.

It always strikes me as odd that people can be made from the same ingredients but each end up being a completely different dish. Sterling's siblings are both blond and have the same colour eyes as the ones I saw staring at the morgue's ceiling yesterday. But the dimensions of their faces are different and somehow their brother's famous wide-eyed gaze looks alien and cold on them. Their skin is tinted from the sun but their bodies are thick and doughy, hinting at booze and overeating.

'Mr Wade,' I say to Matthew, 'this is obviously a very difficult time.' April starts sobbing quietly into her hands. 'Since our talk yesterday, have you thought of anything Sterling said that now seems important—anything he seemed worried about?'

'Wasn't it just some looney fan?' pipes up Paul, his voice carrying the grain of the country. 'That's what all the news stories are saying.'

Melissa blows her nose loudly into a tissue.

'It might have been a stranger,' I allow, 'but we need to consider all options. It's a very unusual situation. We're almost certain it was a planned attack and that does lead us to assume a motive. It may have been someone your brother had aggravated, unknowingly or not.'

'Did he mention anything about his work or personal relationships?' asks Fleet. 'Anything he was worried about?'

Matthew shakes his head. 'I've been going over everything in my head, trying to recall what we spoke about, but you just don't think you're going to need to remember that kind of stuff.' He pounds a fist gently to his chest as if trying to dislodge something. 'We talked about the farm. He always asked, even though he wasn't interested.'

'What about you, Paul? Have you talked to your brother lately?' asks Fleet.

'Me? Nah. We weren't close. Nothin' to talk about.'

'He called a few weeks back when I was at Mum and Dad's,' adds Melissa. 'I spoke to him for a bit. I asked him about the movie. My husband likes that American actress.'

'It can't have been easy having a brother in the spotlight?' I venture.

'You get used to it,' says Paul, shrugging.

'When did you both get here?' I ask, perplexed by Paul's bluntness.

'Yesterday,' says Melissa. 'Dad called me on Wednesday night to tell me what happened. I sorted the kids out so that Rowan, my husband, can look after them for a few days, and then I flew down.' She glances at April. 'I knew Mum'd be a mess.'

'You didn't come together?' I ask lightly.

'No, I live in Karadine, near Mum and Dad,' replies Melissa. 'Paul was in Castlemaine. I called him after I spoke to Mum.'

'Do you live in Castlemaine, Paul?' I ask.

'Nah. I'm just housesitting for a mate. I'm painting his house while he's overseas. I move around a lot, just follow work, you know?'

'What's work for you?' Fleet asks, clearly wanting Paul to corroborate what Matthew has told us.

'Just odd jobs. Painting, building fences—whatever people need.'

'Have you done the, ah, operation yet?' Matthew interjects, gripping the back of the couch.

'Yes,' I reply. 'The preliminary autopsy was conducted yesterday. The coroner will have her final report ready in a few days. You can apply to see the findings if you wish but I have to warn you that family members often find this information distressing.'

April utters a strangled sob. Melissa grips her hand.

'Did you find anything?' asks Matthew. 'Anything that might help?'

'Not at this stage,' says Fleet, and I try not to think about what Mary-Anne might be doing to their son's body as we speak.

They nod and I see the pain flit across their broken faces as the imagined horrors keep coming.

'Are you close to Lizzie Short?' I ask them. 'Or Sterling's housemate, Brodie Kent?'

April's crying has subsided slightly but her shoulders shake alarmingly.

Matthew is giving his wife a helpless look. 'We met Lizzie, of course, a few times when we came down to visit. And Sterling brought her home once.' Matthew clasps his hands together. 'She seems like a nice girl but we barely know her. And we only met Brodie one time. Last year, before he moved in. He seemed very, ah, theatrical.'

Matthew says this in a way that makes his homophobia obvious. I realise that if Sterling was trying to keep his sexual orientation under wraps, perhaps it was to hide it from his family as well as a shrewd career move.

April says quietly, 'Brodie seems a nice enough boy but very different from Sterling. He's very intense. But we always found coming here very overwhelming.'

'What about you two?' Fleet asks the siblings.

'We met her,' says Melissa. 'Lizzie, I mean. Years ago.' She wipes at her red-rimmed eyes. 'She seemed lovely.'

'Paul?' prompts Fleet.

He shrugs. 'She's pretty.'

'And did you meet Brodie?' I ask.

They shake their heads.

'Lizzie told us that she and Sterling had recently decided to get married,' Fleet announces, looking from April to Matthew. 'It's already hit the media. Did you know anything about that?'

Paul mutters something under his breath.

April's head snaps up and her eyes suddenly focus. 'Married?' she says flatly. 'But they were so young.'

Matthew glances worriedly at his wife. 'He never said anything to us.'

'Lizzie told us they hadn't told anyone,' I assure him. 'They were going to wait until the shoot was done to announce it.'

'We thought they would move overseas together,' mumbles April, pinching the end of her thumb over and over. 'Lizzie seemed very ambitious.'

'It certainly seems like Sterling was being offered parts in Hollywood,' I say. 'Can you think of anyone who might have been upset by him leaving?'

'Us,' says April softly.

No one says anything for a few moments. Paul's face has gone red but it's hard to read. His gaze is back on the TV.

Fleet taps his foot as if to fill the silence. 'Have you been in contact with the Beaufords?'

I catch Paul's eyes darkening.

'Well . . .' Matthew falters. 'Not yet. We've had so many other people to speak to.'

'That's understandable.' I assure him.

'We will though. I know Sterling still saw them and they were always very good to him.' He throws a look to his wife as though he's after support, but it's clear from April's vague stare that she's no longer following the conversation.

My work phone comes to life in my pocket. I pull it out enough to see the screen. Isaacs. 'Excuse me,' I say to the family, before slipping into the hallway. 'Sir?'

'Are you still with the Wades?'

'Yes, sir,' I reply, startled by his bluntness.

'Well, wrap it up and head back here. There's been a confession.'

'For real?'

'We're not sure. It's anonymous but we're taking it seriously. The guy seems legitimate. Call me on your way back.'

'Yes, sir,' I say.

As I return to the room my blood is on fire, the anticipation of a possible resolution pounding in my limbs.

'So, what happens now?' Matthew is saying to Fleet.

'We try to find whoever did this, and—'

'We have to go,' I announce, careful to keep the charge that's running through my body out of my voice.

'We'll be in touch,' says Fleet, shooting me a puzzled look. And as he passes by the couch I'm surprised to see him place a reassuring hand on April's shoulder and smile at Melissa. 'Please call us if you think of anything at all that might be useful in solving Sterling's case,' he says softly. April looks up at him gratefully.

'Those reporters were still outside the hotel this morning,' Matthew says as he trails us to the door.

'Yes, they'll probably be there until you leave,' I tell him. 'Remember, if their behaviour crosses the line, we can give them a warning. Just let us know. But Mr Wade, I have to tell you, the media attention around your son's death will be intense for a while yet.'

'We just don't know what to say to them.' He rubs his fists into his eyes like a child. 'Our son was the one who lived in this world. We don't understand it at all.'

'No one is good at this, Mr Wade,' I say, stepping into the hall and turning back to face him. 'It's difficult no matter what.'

'I know you're right. But Sterling, he was always comfortable in front of a camera. He loved the attention. April and I were so scared when all this acting business started. We were so worried we'd lose him. We worried about drugs. About predators. We never thought we'd lose him like this.' Matthew's sun-gnarled hands clench at his sides. 'And now all these people are saying how much they cared about him. It makes me sick. They didn't care about him. Not like we did.'

I think about Mary-Anne almost in tears at the autopsy table.

'I'm very sorry, Mr Wade. It must be awful having all these strangers think they knew your son.' And I find myself meaning it, suddenly furious at the public outpouring of grief, the personal claim that everyone is laying on Wade's death. Standing next to his father, I find it grotesque.

'Thank you,' Matthew says wearily, his decency irrepressible even in grief. 'We're just simple farming people. We never wanted any of this.'

Friday, 17 August

3.44 pm

'Why the speedy exit?' asks Fleet, rushing after me toward the car.

'Someone's confessed,' I say over my shoulder.

Fleet whistles. 'Anyone we know?'

'Apparently not.'

I beep the car open and shove my phone on the speaker dock, pressing Isaacs' number.

'We're in the car now,' I say when he answers.

'Did you say anything to Wade's parents?' he asks.

'No,' I reply. 'They're not in a good way. We made our excuses and got out of there.'

'Good. I want to keep this quiet until we work out how legitimate it is. No point upsetting them even further.'

'What exactly happened?' I demand.

'A man called the hotline about an hour ago claiming to have stabbed Wade.'

'And what makes you think it's legit?' I ask, tapping the brakes to let a young mother run across the road. She's shielding her baby from the rain with a plastic shopping bag. 'I mean, by eight this morning we already had over forty people claiming responsibility, right?'

We get false confessions during every high-profile murder case—everyone is looking for a purpose on this earth, and owning up to a murder is apparently one way to anchor yourself to something hard and real—but the virtual tsunami of confessions the Wade case has stirred up is unlike anything I've seen before. Fleet and I have three teams working on these claims, running names through our systems and tracing IP addresses.

'I know,' says Isaacs, 'but this particular one is detailed enough to take seriously.'

'Did he know Wade?' I press. 'Did this guy have any direct contact?'

'From what we can tell he may have been a cast member but that isn't one hundred per cent confirmed.' There's a heavy dose of frustration in Isaacs' voice.

'What do you think, sir?' I ask, again wanting his opinion. I'm not used to having a boss who holds so much back. Jonesy would always give me his complete assessment of a situation whether I asked for it or not.

Isaacs steps neatly around my question. 'I believe an individual with some kind of mental health issue is the most likely suspect. And this guy has quite a lot of details about the attack. He could be an opportunist dicking us around, but at this stage it's adding up.'

'What details did he mention?' asks Fleet.

'He described the knife used, and what Wade was wearing. He mentioned Lizzie rushing over and her screaming. In fact, he did a pretty good job of overviewing the whole scene. And he seems to have a real issue with Wade. He's aggressive.'

I turn this around in my mind. 'Most of that info could be assumed from the media coverage.'

'Or leaked by any of the hundred people who were there,' says Fleet ominously.

Isaacs cuts in, 'Of course some information has leaked. Lord knows enough people have touched this thing, but it's also possible that this guy really was there, as the attacker or a witness. Either way, we want to speak with him. Our killer may have attacked Wade as a means of gaining a profile and this could be him reaching out to claim his status as a celebrity killer.'

'But we can't tell if this guy is on the footage from the movie set, can we?' I say.

'Not yet,' admits Isaacs gruffly. 'We're still trying to confirm who is who.'

I grip the steering wheel, feeling unsettled at the thought of the answer to this mess being as simple as a random unstable guy.

'We're almost back, sir,' I tell Isaacs. 'We'll see you shortly.'

◀○▶

A few minutes later I turn into the station car park and shut off the engine.

'What do you reckon?' I say to Fleet.

'About this crackpot confession?' He's already fumbling for his cigarettes. 'Who knows? It could be legit but my money is on it being one hundred per cent bullshit.'

'Yeah. Though like Isaacs said, it's the most likely scenario. If this guy turns out to be a cast member, his confession definitely carries more weight.'

While I know it's plausible that a total stranger became so obsessed with Wade that it manifested into something sinister, I still find it hard to get my head around. I'm uneasy about things that don't have logical explanations; I don't like the idea that anything is possible. On one hand, I know that there's a little bit of stalker in all of us—it's why we read the papers, it's why social media has taken off. Gossip, speculation and idol worship are as old as the hills. But I find the psychology of stalking a total stranger difficult to fathom. I've certainly had my share of obsessions, and as a teenager my preoccupations occasionally led to unhealthy behaviour, but I can't imagine having such strong feelings about someone I've never met or met only in passing. Physical attraction, sure. But for me, an emotional connection takes time to develop.

From my perspective, someone who was in Wade's orbit, no matter how peripherally, is more likely to be responsible for his death than a random stranger.

Last year back in Smithson, I was involved in a stalking scenario. A widow fell in love with a detective in a neighbouring town. He'd investigated the accidental death of her husband on their farm, and the kindness he showed the woman and her daughters during that difficult time was enough for her to form strong feelings for him, despite his marital status. It started innocently enough. She called him just a little more often than was comfortable, and drove past his house on her way home from her retail job. But when she started following his wife around town, then watching his family have dinner through their lounge-room window as she sat in her parked car, clearly something was amiss. I read the woman's diary, tentatively handed in to us by her eldest daughter: page after page of deluded fantasy. She was going to make him see. Make him understand that it had all happened for a reason—her dead husband *wanted* them to be together. It was frightening, her fierceness, the force and devotion with which she'd plotted a future with this stranger, but it was sad too. All that energy funnelled into someone who had no inkling of the effect he was having on another human being.

I shift my gaze across to Fleet, who is wrangling a crust of sleep out of the corner of his eye. 'What?' he says, feeling my stare.

'Nothing,' I say automatically.

'The Wades seem like a pretty close family, don't they?'

'I think it's safe to say that Sterling was the odd one out,' I reply.

Fleet is watching a young girl lean into the front window of a station wagon to talk to an officer, her low-cut top revealing a nasty blue bruise at the top of her breast.

'Paul didn't seem especially upset about his brother though,' I add.

'Absolutely not. The green-eyed monster is alive and well in that one. Reminds me of my own brother.'

I wait for him to elaborate but instead he gets out of the car. I follow him to the bottom of the stairwell where he plonks himself down and smokes like a teenager, his hand curled around the cigarette, his lips in a pout as he breathes out grey puffs.

'I was thinking,' I say, 'about what my contact in Smithson told me—that the Wades are having money trouble. I assume that Sterling had a lot of money for a guy his age. If most of his cash goes to his family, that isn't going to be a problem anymore. They'll definitely be able to keep the farm. Maybe even retire, if that's what they want.'

Fleet nods, tapping ash onto the ground.

I add, 'They said they didn't know about Sterling and Lizzie getting engaged, but what if he told them?'

'What, do you think they might have worried that Lizzie would start chipping away at their retirement plan?'

'It's far-fetched,' I acknowledge, 'and I honestly can't see the parents thinking like that, but maybe Paul or even Melissa decided that some of their brother's wealth should be redistributed.'

The smoke mingles with the fresh icy air. Sitting in the cold next to Fleet, I feel an unexpected wave of loneliness.

'Well,' he says, wiping ash dust off the tip of his shoe, 'let's keep you happy and dig around in pretty boy's finances, though I think we'd both be shocked if either of the remaining Wade siblings pulled off something like this. They don't exactly seem to be nailing life like their brother was.' Fleet somehow looks older today, a faint spray of wrinkles fanning from each eye. 'It's probably just normal family bullshit,' he continues, throwing a mint into his mouth and getting to his feet, 'but I agree we should cross them off the list. Clearly Paul's relationship with his brother was strained, and where there is money trouble there is motive.'

'Maybe Paul knows people in the city?' I suggest.

Fleet shrugs agreeably. 'Look, if this mystery caller that Isaacs is so keen on really did kill our celebrity friend, then I'm all for it. I'm missing some really good shit on Netflix. But I have a feeling that our answer is far closer to home—and that we're a long way off yet. Lizzie and Brodie bother me. Paul Wade bothers me. Ava and her harassment claims bother me. Riley Cartwright bothers me. I mean, come on, everyone's revealing these major secrets the second Wade's dead? Something doesn't add up.'

My work phone rings and I jump. Fleet doesn't even seem to register the sound.

'Hi, Mary-Anne,' I answer.

'Detective.' She takes a breath. 'I have information regarding what we discussed yesterday.'

'Yes,' I say, and Fleet's eyes fix on mine, anticipating news.

'Well, I can't tell you who with, or exactly how recently, but in my opinion Wade was regularly engaging in same-sex intercourse.'

◄○►

Simon Joseph Carmichael is a 27-year-old actor and part-time cafe worker. He's been an extra on a range of Australian TV shows and films over the past ten years, scoring a bit part in a comedy sketch show on the ABC late last year. He earns, on average, just over forty thousand dollars annually. He lives in Preston with a 23-year-old housemate who is studying to be a dental nurse. He's Caucasian, with brown hair and brown eyes, and is of average height and average build. Pleasant-looking but completely forgettable. Three months ago, he wrote on Facebook that he was 'pumped' to be a zombie in the new film *Death Is Alive*, calling it his 'big break' and describing the production as 'next level'.

On Wednesday afternoon a fellow cast member took a photo of him with cloudy eyes and blood dripping down his face, gore and insides pushing out of a deep gash in his neck.

After calling our case hotline this morning he went on to post a rant called 'The Moment'—under the alias 'Dark Knight'—to Wade's Facebook page at about 3 pm, describing in detail the attack on Wade. When others questioned the extent of his inside knowledge, he replied, 'I was there, I did this. I saw it all. I made this happen.' He also wrote that Wade was 'untalented' and 'an average actor who got lucky'.

The tech guys traced his computer and picked him up just after 6 pm.

I stare at him now through the one-way glass of the interview room. He sits calmly, hands folded together.

'He doesn't look much like a celebrity killer,' mutters Fleet, joining me. Stale smoke rolls into my nostrils.

'No. But he was there. We've found him on the tape. And he didn't stick around to speak with the uniforms either—he got the hell out of there. He was one of the people in close proximity to Wade, though it's unlikely he was near enough to attack him. Still, he could have a buddy, another cast member. Maybe they worked together and Carmichael has simply decided to go rogue and tell the world.'

Fleet places his hands along the rail below the one-way mirror and drops his body down as if he's about to burst into a series of push-ups. 'Why go to all this trouble though? If he really wanted to harm or kill Wade, surely there would have been easier ways to go about it. On a film set there are lots of ways to make something seem like an accident. This is complicated and headline-grabbing.'

I sigh. 'I know. I feel like we're looking for a narcissist—someone who deliberately did this crazy thing for attention. So based on his behaviour today, maybe this guy does fit the bill. But he wasn't wearing a mask, and surely the killer was one of the masked men right near Wade.'

Two masked men and two hooded men were in the scene around the time Wade was stabbed. Only two gave preliminary statements on Wednesday afternoon. Over the past day or so I've become convinced that one of the other two isn't a cast member and somehow joined the frenzied mass, made his way to Wade and stabbed him before disappearing into the crowd.

'Shall we have a little chat to Mr Carmichael?' says Fleet, pushing away from the rail.

'I want more background first,' I say. 'I want to have a clearer theory. He seems to have no family and not many friends. The guys are trying to pull his financial, phone and medical records right now. Let's wait for those to come in and then talk to him. If he had direct contact with Wade, this might start to make more sense.'

'Suits me,' says Fleet. 'My guess? This guy is just some low-grade hack who's confused life with his sad-arse computer games.'

◄o►

I haven't known Simon Carmichael for long but I'm already sick of him. Further analysis of the footage has revealed that he was a metre or so behind Wade at the moment we believe the attack took place. He also seems to be suffering from extreme delusions. We're almost one hundred per cent sure he's not our guy—he's just a guy who has wasted a whole lot of our time.

Fortunately, the afternoon did turn up some useful information. The mild trouble that Matthew Wade mentioned his son Paul had experienced after high school turns out to be three separate pub fights. In each instance, it seems Paul reacted to some run-of-the-mill taunting with his fists, lashing out at fellow patrons. The injuries he inflicted weren't serious but he was banned from every pub and hotel in the area, which Fleet and I agree is probably the real reason he left Karadine.

Riley Cartwright's phone records show that he called Ava James roughly forty times in the fortnight leading up to the first day of production. Always in the evenings after rehearsals. Ava didn't call him once. Sometimes his calls went unanswered; sometimes they spoke for a few minutes. Often he would call her straight after a call had ended and she didn't answer. Her case against him is strengthening. There are also a few known drug dealers among Cartwright's contacts; he's made several recent calls to them as well.

Sterling's phone records, on the other hand, seem squeaky clean. There are only a handful of placed and received calls that we are following up. Most of his calls were to Lizzie. There was an almost clockwork weekly call to his parents. A few to Wendy Ferla. A handful to Brodie's prepaid mobile. A few sporadic calls to Ava but nothing to substantiate their rumoured affair. Almost all the texts Wade sent were to Lizzie and Brodie, mainly telling them what time he would be home: neither stream of messages was overly affectionate, though he was the kind of modern guy who doles out kisses with abandon. Sterling did call Ava early on Saturday morning, which backs her claim that they met up after Cartwright's unwanted advances last Friday and she told him what happened. I wonder if Wade's meeting with Ava outside of the film schedule may have caused Lizzie or Brodie to feel insecure. Whatever the case, it seems he respected Ava's privacy and didn't tell anyone the details of what happened between her and Cartwright. And so far, her claims haven't reached the media.

I rub my eyes, craving sleep. Fleet's nowhere to be seen. Realising it's late, I figure he must have left already. I decide to call it a night too.

Walking out through the car park, I call Josh, jabbing my fingers roughly at the screen. He answers and I can hear the sounds of Friday night footy in the background. Cheering and the clink of beer glasses.

'Hey, you,' he says over the noise.

'Hey.'

'Don't tell me you're calling to cancel on me tomorrow night?'

'Not yet,' I reply. 'Sorry for the radio silence. It's been pretty nuts.'

'I can't even imagine. This Sterling Wade thing is just insane. I've been watching the news constantly. All the old footage of him they just keep playing over and over from his shows and ads and stuff, it's pretty sad.'

It starts to rain and I square myself against a concrete column. A cold snake of air slithers up my pants leg, causing a chill to run through me.

'Yeah,' I say. 'It's been a total circus.'

'I'll try not to have a late one tonight so that I can look after you tomorrow. I'm thinking some good wine and pasta are in order.'

I smile—his enthusiasm is infectious and the thought of someone going to an effort for me is definitely appealing. 'Sounds great. Hopefully things don't go pear-shaped tomorrow. I'll try to be at yours by seven-thirty. I'll let you know if anything changes.'

A huge cheer roars down the phone and we say goodbye.

I watch as people rush past in the hazy rain. It doesn't look like easing up. An older man holding two identical little boys in matching football beanies runs by making race-car sounds as they squeal in delight. He throws me a withering look, probably envious of my seemingly carefree existence.

I walk on feeling invisible. Insignificant. I marvel for the hundredth time that there is no way for anyone to know that I am a mother, to tell at a glance that Ben exists. I know women who are permanently touched by childbirth, changed by the experience, but not me. I have no scars, no telltale signs on my skin. It's as if pregnancy temporarily hovered over me and then lifted and vanished, leaving no trace of its visit. It was the same when I had the miscarriage. Something was there and then suddenly it wasn't. A possible future was immediately erased. No one knows about it except my old friend Anna—and Felix, although I'm still not sure whether he believed me. I try not to think about it often; I never really let myself consider what I lost to be a baby, another Ben.

Now I have no school lunches to pack, play dates to plan, homework to figure out. I nursed my son, soothed his cries and held his hands as he took his first steps, but time has dulled these primal contributions. They could easily belong to someone else. I feel fraudulent claiming Ben's achievements as my own.

Apart from Macy and Isaacs, no one in Melbourne knows about Ben. As I walk the streets, trudge through the days, my motherhood is a secret. Something that no one would assume. I am too hard. Too empty. Too remote. Too selfish.

But Ben did change me. I feel more fear than I did when I was childless. I am all too familiar with what can go wrong. I have lost so much already and I am not naive enough to think that loss is dealt out in fair portions. Pain and sorrow do not discriminate or show mercy—they can strike at any time. Ever since Ben was born, ever since the moment I was gifted my own precious perfect human, I've counterintuitively held him at arm's-length, terrified that one day I will have to endure him being taken away.

Saturday, 18 August
8.54 am

There is no rain today but the air is heavy with the cold. Coffee-laden onlookers walking along Spring Street slow to watch Fleet and I talk to Cartwright. I suspect they sense we're connected to the tragedy that unfolded here only days ago. Maybe a few of them recognise Riley.

He looks thinner than he did at the hospital. He's agitated and blotchy, pacing around in small circles and repeatedly pushing his stringy hair behind his ears. His eyes are wide and bulge slightly. Not knowing what his normal demeanour is, it's hard to tell whether Ava's accusations and Sterling's death have caused his erratic behaviour or if he always runs at such a high frequency. And from what Wendy said and Lizzie alluded to, Riley is an intense character. The two leads on his assault case told us that he flat out denied Ava's claims when they formally launched their investigation. In just over three weeks he's set to appear in court for the initial hearing, and Ava has said she'll stay in Australia to see this through.

All the film set's security barriers have been removed, while the piles of flowers laid down earlier in the week have been shifted to the lawns of the Treasury Gardens. They're still fresh and vibrant, thanks to the weather. Cars roll past, hurried by the occasional toot of a horn. It's not the kind of place where grief can linger for long; it's too embedded in the cut and thrust of the everyday.

'So we started setting up the scene just before 3 pm,' Cartwright mumbles, stopping in the middle of the path near where the main camera was positioned. 'We'd done some other stuff in the morning, some scenes just with Sterling at his work desk. And we shot the first few cafe scenes with him and Lizzie.'

'Where was that?' I ask.

'In a studio in the Docklands,' says Cartwright. 'We were shooting a lot of scenes there. It was where all the bedroom, kitchen, cafe and office locations were set up.'

'Where else were you shooting?' I ask.

'All over Melbourne,' he replies. 'On the streets, parks and a little bit in regional Victoria. There are a few farm scenes at the end when Ollie and his girlfriend are hiding out from the zombies.'

'Those were Sterling's and Ava James's characters, right?' I confirm, looking at Cartwright pointedly as I say Ava's name.

He breathes in and presses his lips together. 'Yeah, that's right. We were also shooting at a few landmarks. Above Flinders Street Station in the old ballroom space, and in the Botanic Gardens. That's where the zombie lairs are.'

Fleet looks like he's about to comment on the concept of zombie lairs but has a rare moment of maturity and decides to let it go. 'It's a big film, huh,' he says instead.

Cartwright nods. 'Huge. An absolute beast. The planning has been intense. The permits, the insurance. I've never been so busy. The pressure was crazy. And now this, well.' He drops his gaze to the ground and shakes his head. 'It's completely surreal.' He thrusts his hands in and out of his pockets. Pulls at his lips with his teeth.

'Was there anything unusual about Sterling's behaviour?' I ask.

'Nope. He was great.'

'Totally normal then? No outbursts?'

'I don't think so.' Cartwright squints as if he's trying to remember. 'He was a pretty relaxed guy. The crew were loving him. He made an effort with names, remembered things. He was just decent like that.'

'Do you work with the same crew all the time?' asks Fleet, lighting a cigarette.

Cartwright brightens a little. 'Can I have one of those, man?'

'Sure,' says Fleet, sliding one out of his packet.

'Thanks.' Cartwright lights up and sucks deeply, closing his eyes. 'God, this is a nightmare,' he mutters.

'You were about to tell us about the crew?' Fleet presses.

'Yeah, yeah. I've worked with a lot of the guys before. Australia's not that big a place. You always get a few new faces on every shoot though, especially for scenes like the one we were shooting on Wednesday. You need people with certain skills.' He pauses and looks puzzled. 'None of them had anything to do with this. They were nowhere near him.'

'We're just trying to work out if someone could have given the killer details about the shoot,' I say.

Cartwright laughs bitterly. 'Everyone knew everything about this movie. It was impossible to keep things under wraps. Even if one of the fucking make-up artists said something, it wouldn't have made a difference. Our shooting schedule was pretty much in the news every day.'

'What about security?' I ask. 'How easy would it have been for someone to slip into the zombie cast?'

'I don't know. A team of people managed that stuff. That wasn't my area.' He circles his hands around his mouth and blows warm air into them. 'I do know that we had to jump through all the standard hoops. Police checks and all that bullshit.'

'How well did you know the extras appearing in the zombie scenes?' Fleet asks.

Cartwright shrugs. 'Not well. You remember some faces from other shoots but there were so many people. And when they had costumes on, it was pretty impossible.' He squints and looks up at the sky where the sun is doing its best to push through the heavy layer of cloud. 'I really don't think it would have been that easy for anyone to get onto the set. There were barricades everywhere and we had guards.'

'But it's possible,' I say.

'Of course,' he admits, fidgeting. 'I hate the idea of someone in the family doing this.' He itches the side of his face. 'Did the footage we gave you help? Could you see who did it?'

'We're working through the cast list,' says Fleet, neatly stepping around his question.

'So, from your perspective the shoot was going smoothly?' I ask.

'Yeah. It was looking good. The costumes looked amazing and my DOP was pumped about the light. It was exactly what we wanted.' He gestures to the sky. 'Good old bleak Melbourne.'

'DOP?' I ask.

'Director of photography.'

'It's like you had an army to make this movie,' I say.

'This shit doesn't just happen,' he replies. 'It's epic. Expensive. So much work goes into every second of film. People don't get that.'

'How much longer were you planning to shoot for on Wednesday?' I ask.

'Just over an hour,' he replies. 'A couple of kids were in the scene and there are heaps of rules about how long they can be on set, so we didn't have much time.'

'When did you realise something was wrong?' Fleet asks.

Cartwright fixes his eyes on the ground. 'I don't know. I think maybe I've blocked it out or something. I can't really remember. Definitely not for a while. I mean, it was supposed to be a really dramatic scene. You are supposed to feel like you're in there with him, Ollie, pushing through all the zombies. It's desperate, you know? I just thought Sterling was really getting into it.' Cartwright looks haunted. 'But when he fell to the ground I wasn't sure what was going on. I guess I thought he'd tripped or fainted. I remember thinking that I'd give him shit later.' He laughs jerkily. 'Obviously I never imagined that someone had hurt him.'

'Was it planned which of the cast would be close to him?' Fleet asks. 'How structured was the scene?'

'The only real rule was that the A zombies were allowed to be close to Wade—they were what we call "featured extras". All the other zombies were B's or C's. The A's had to be close to the camera and pawing at Wade, but we weren't specific about which of the A's would get nearest to him. We wanted them all grabbling at him, competing with each other so that it looked authentic.'

'Makes it bloody hard to investigate,' says Fleet sarcastically.

Cartwright looks at him wide-eyed. 'It was the right way to make the scene work. We needed it to be genuine.'

Walking us through the plan for Wednesday afternoon's shoot, Cartwright points out where everyone was supposed to be for different parts of the scene. He explains that the rest of the script, which they never got to capture, sees the army of infected humans lift up Wade's character Ollie and take him into the park, not realising that he has a rare immunity to their poison. 'He looks infected but he keeps his mind,' explains Cartwright.

'So he becomes like a zombie mole?' queries Fleet.

'Exactly,' says Cartwright. Yet again his movements are jerky, like his brain is an extra beat behind controlling his muscles. 'It's a cool concept. His character ends up torn, with sympathy for both agendas. He can see that humans are ruining the planet but he wants to protect his loved ones.'

I nod as though taking in the poignant message, then decide I've waited long enough to ask the hard questions.

'What was Sterling's relationship with Ava James like?' I ask.

'Ava?' Cartwright looks at me sharply.

'Yes. We are well aware of the accusations she has made against you but are leaving that in the capable hands of our colleagues. Right now, I'm just keen for your view on her relationship with Sterling.'

Cartwright stares me straight in the eye, raw hostility suddenly steaming off him. I can easily imagine him putting his hands on Ava, her asking him to stop, him ignoring her.

'They hit it off right from the start,' he says. 'Just good mates. I've heard the rumours about them hooking up but they wouldn't have had the time. Even if they had, Sterling wouldn't have cheated on Lizzie. And no doubt Ava thought he was good-looking and nice but not exactly in the same league as some of the Hollywood guys she's starred alongside. He was pretty straight really. He was a bit star-struck by her initially.' Cartwright half laughs. 'We all were.' He twists his hands, pulling each finger in turn and cracking the knuckles. 'That's where she's gotten mixed up. She's angry with me because things didn't work out between us. I'm not very good at relationships and I can be a bit intense, you know? Maybe I came on too strong. But really, I just admired her. And she was into me at first, I swear. Anyway, she and Sterling were great co-stars. A director's dream.'

'Like Woodstock said, we're not going to get into who touched who right now,' says Fleet, waving the assault case away. 'Let's talk about you and Sterling instead.'

'Me and Sterling?'

'Yep.'

'We were good,' says Cartwright, his eyes shifting from left to right. 'You know, mates.'

'We've heard there was a bit of tension between you,' I say.

Cartwright jiggles around on the spot, shaking his head like a kid. 'Nah, not really. Just normal movie shit. It's weird, going from mates to me being his boss. But it was fine, we respected each other.'

'What about the argument you had last Sunday?' I ask.

'Argument? That was nothing. Just a bit of pre-shoot nerves on both sides. Making a movie is stressful, especially with the kind of budget we had.'

'We heard it was really heated,' I press.

Cartwright manages a brief laugh. 'No, it really wasn't. We just had a little misunderstanding about Ava. Sterling seemed to think it was his job to keep the peace on set. I set him straight and we were fine. Ava's obviously still a bit confused, which isn't surprising with all that's happened. I'm sure that will all be sorted out.'

'I like your confidence,' says Fleet in a way that indicates he thinks it is misplaced. 'You say Sterling was a peacemaker. I know from personal experience that do-gooders can really grind my gears. Did his righteous shtick piss you off?'

Cartwright sighs. 'It feels weird to talk about this now.' He pulls his long hair away from his neck and twists it into a straggly ponytail, closing his eyes briefly. 'Look, Sterling was a good guy. A very good guy. Did he have an earnest streak? Sure. But I put that down to his wholesome country upbringing. I really liked him and I figured that a lot of his naivety would be beaten out of him in Hollywood in good time. You don't get to make it in that place without being a bit of an arsehole.'

I look at Cartwright and suddenly see a classic Peter Pan type. An ageing cool guy who is starting to shift into bitter mode.

'Interesting perspective,' I say. 'How much did you know about his Hollywood plans?'

'Not much. Probably about as much as you guys know from reading the news. We used to talk about his career a bit more, but lately it's all been about the film.'

'Ever heard any other rumours about Sterling?' Fleet asks, starting on a fresh cigarette.

Cartwright shrugs again. 'Oh yeah. It's all pretty standard— drugs, cheating, nice, not nice. The news beast must be fed so the journos end up just making shit up. It's easier than doing proper research. And it's not like anyone is ever held accountable.'

'You were getting a lot of good press about the film though,' says Fleet. 'I've seen some interviews you've done. So the media coverage isn't all bad.'

'No,' says Cartwright, sighing. 'It's not. That's the problem. They're parasites but we can't live without them. They are the gate-keepers to the audience. To the money. Gotta make the world go round, I guess.' He taps his foot on the ground and rubs his hands together again. I notice that his lips are tinged with blue. 'Sterling must have wondered what the hell was happening. I keep thinking about that, how confused he must have been when he was stabbed. We were all right there but no one knew to help him.'

'We're interviewing everyone from the set later today,' I say. 'I assume you know about that?'

'Yeah,' says Cartwright. 'A few of the crew called me last night. Everyone is totally freaking out, you know. Dudes who I thought were unbreakable have been crying down the phone to me. It's fucked. My producer, Katya, she's worried about being sued for negligence or trauma. Our legal people are all over it.'

'You might be spending a fair bit of time with lawyers over the next few months,' says Fleet.

Cartwright scowls. 'This whole situation is a nightmare. And who knows what will happen with the film?'

The four of us walk back toward Wellington Parade where our car is parked under a giant leafless tree.

'How is Lizzie doing?' Cartwright asks.

'She's obviously very upset,' I tell him, 'but she's coping.'

'She's a sweet girl. Probably not cut out for this industry but a decent little actress. I don't know what to say to her, but I should call her, shouldn't I?'

'I'm sure she'd appreciate that,' I say. 'She's being bombarded by the media.'

'Yeah, well, she'll need to get used to that,' he says bitterly. 'They absolutely love shit like this. Heartless arseholes.'

'You want a lift anywhere?' asks Fleet.

Cartwright has both hands in his tight jeans pockets. Sunglasses on. He looks up the street. 'Nah. I'll get the tram.'

Out of curiosity, I have to ask him one last question. 'You really have no idea what's going to happen with the film now?'

'Katya tells me we're legitimately insured against stuff like this, believe it or not. But I don't know—I want to finish the film but I can't see anyone except Sterling in the lead role.'

'Maybe you just need some time,' I suggest.

He looks unconvinced. 'All the actors and the crew have other movies to shoot. So no, it's not like we have heaps of time.'

'Do you have another project after this?'

'Not really,' he says stiffly. 'And I doubt this crap with Ms James is going to help my prospects.'

Fleet and I simply look at him.

'Fuck,' he says abruptly, 'I wish she'd just talked to me about it. There was no need to go to the police, for god's sake. We could have cleared it up in a second.'

'Maybe she didn't feel comfortable talking to you about it,' I retort, my anger rising at his lack of insight.

'Yeah, well, it's too late now,' he says cynically. 'I'm really looking forward to the media storm raining down on me. I might just get away for a bit.'

'Well, don't go anywhere without letting us know,' I say. 'We'll probably need to speak to you again.'

He nods and his bony hands shake as he toys with the zip on his coat, pushing it up and down so that it makes a ripping sound. We leave him standing there as we head to the car. 'Hey!' he calls after us. 'Can I have another smoke?'

Saturday, 18 August
11.19 am

We grab an early lunch—an underwhelming sandwich for me, a greasy pie for Fleet—and half-heartedly argue over Cartwright's version of his relationship with Sterling. As we head toward the warehouse for the cast and crew interviews, Chloe calls with more news on Sterling's phone records.

'That landline call he received last Sunday night? It was made from the house Paul Wade was staying at in Castlemaine. The call lasted for over six minutes,' continues Chloe, as Fleet aggressively overtakes a slow-moving Barina.

'And that's it?' I say. 'There are no other calls between Paul and Sterling?'

'Nope,' she says. 'From what we can tell, that is the first phone contact they've had in almost a year. There are no emails or messages on social apps either.'

'Did anything else interesting show up on Paul's phone records?'

'He regularly called sex hotlines but that's it. Mostly he called his parents and his sister. He did get cut off for almost two weeks not paying his bill a few months ago.'

I thank Chloe and hang up, relaying the info to Fleet.

'Sex hotlines?' he says. 'I can't believe anyone with access to the internet would bother with that.'

'Maybe he's an old-fashioned kind of guy.'

'Interesting that he called Sterling last weekend.' Fleet glares at a passing cyclist for no apparent reason. 'Especially since he told us they hadn't spoken in months.'

'Exactly,' I say, picturing Paul's sullen face. 'Also kind of stupid to lie about it. Surely he must know we can pull call info, and that we'd see the Castlemaine number.'

'He doesn't strike me as super bright. And some people can't help lying.'

'True.' I watch the landscape become more industrial as we reach the other side of the city. 'I wonder what they spoke about?'

'Well,' says Fleet, parking the car and yanking on the handbrake, 'once this little adventure is over, I guess we'll ask him.'

We're greeted by a rumble of voices as we push the heavy warehouse door open. Outside it looked almost like an audition call, with a few uniforms milling about, directing attractive people into groups. The surrounding streets are jam-packed with haphazardly parked cars. Inside, it's a zoo. In addition to our case team, there are hundreds of people, most of them tall young men with close-cut beards and trendy haircuts.

I spot Amir and beckon him over. 'How many do we have here?' I ask him.

He wipes his forehead. 'All but twenty. So there are about three sixty-five here. I gotta say, this hasn't been easy. I've never been involved in anything like this.'

'Celebrities are usually a protected species,' quips Fleet. 'They don't die very often.'

'Right,' replies Amir awkwardly, clearly not sure how to take Fleet's comment. His response makes me realise how accustomed

I've become to the sarcasm. 'Anyway,' he continues, 'we're getting there. We're hoping to secure all the primary interviews today but it'll be a late one. Our main priority is obviously ID'ing the people who were in close proximity to Wade during the attack.'

Amir runs us through the plan for the day, explaining the process they will follow.

He leads us to a long table covered in large sheets of paper. Every cast and crew member has been numbered and is being plotted on a detailed map of the crime scene. This will allow us to identify who was close enough to Wade to have attacked him; to establish whether we have someone on the tape who can't be accounted for; and thirdly, to see if anyone on the periphery of the scene remembers an extra going against the grain in the minutes afterwards—a zombie desperate to distance himself from the epicentre.

Once we have all the eye-witness accounts we'll be crosschecking them against the disparate CCTV footage that continues to roll in from the top end of the city. We've already received over seventy hours of tape from the council and surrounding retailers to review.

The high-pitched melody of a phone starts up nearby, the notes lacing through my headache.

I nod as the buzz in the room goes up another notch. 'Good job,' I tell Amir. 'Let us know the second anything comes up.'

'Will do,' he says, visibly bursting with the responsibility of his task.

'Hive of activity, isn't it?' says Fleet, looking bored as he surveys the room.

To my left, a lanky guy with thick black-rimmed glasses is asking one of the constables if he can go somewhere quiet for a few minutes to do a quick Skype audition.

'These people kill me,' mutters Fleet, as the uniform tells the tall guy that he'll need to postpone his audition until after he's been interviewed. 'And a fucking zombie movie to boot. It's like a bad joke.'

I watch another guy attempt a discreet selfie as he pretends to look at something on his phone.

'Let's head back,' I say, as a coffee craving hits me hard. 'The guys have got this and, clearly, finding anything that will prove useful is going to take a while.'

◄○►

On the way back to the station we get a call from Chloe. The team has looked into Sterling's will and the legalities around his assets and have confirmed that his estate will go to his parents.

'Lizzie might be able to argue some of the items in the apartment are hers,' says Chloe, 'but they don't have any joint bank accounts and his will only lists Matthew and April as beneficiaries. Basically his parents are set to inherit a significant amount of money.'

'How much?' I ask.

'We don't know yet but it will be well over half a million dollars.'

'When did he last update his will?' asks Fleet.

'January,' replies Chloe.

'Lizzie was well and truly on the scene by then,' Fleet comments.

'She was,' I agree, 'but I think a lot of young people just put their parents down to receive everything until they are married or have kids.'

Fleet shrugs. 'Maybe. I just wonder if Lizzie knows she didn't make the cut.'

◄○►

There's a sense of restrained excitement when we return to the case room. A few constables are crowded around a desk along the back wall, their eyes glued to a computer screen.

'What's going on?' I ask them, annoyed that Fleet and I haven't been alerted to whatever has caused such interest.

'Sterling Wade's blog,' replies Ravi.

'Why is that so fascinating?' I ask them.

'The techs just found it on his personal computer,' Ravi says, his eyes back on the screen. 'He wrote it on Wednesday, just before he died. It was never published. A few other blog posts on there were never published either.'

Fleet hooks his thumbs into his belt loops. 'I read an interview where he mentioned doing a blog from the movie set. He said he was going to keep a sort of online diary and publish it every week. If I'd been him I would have sold it afterwards, made some quick cash, not given it away for free.'

Ignoring Fleet, I ask Ravi, 'Is there anything interesting in it?'

'We don't think so,' he replies. 'It's not exactly prescient or anything, it's just kind of weird because of the timing. It's odd reading something that someone wrote an hour before he died.'

'You get used to it,' says Fleet, pulling out his lighter. 'I've read many a shopping list penned by the recently deceased. Anyway, I need a smoke,' he says over his shoulder as he walks out.

'Email us the files asap,' I say to Ravi. 'And can you get the techs to give us an update on Wade's social media accounts?'

He nods. 'We also just heard that Wade's funeral will be next week, on Thursday.'

'Was that reported or did you hear it from the family?' I ask.

'Mary-Anne told us. She spoke to the family. Apparently they were considering taking the body back to their home town, but now they've decided to have him cremated here.'

More officers enter the room, their voices low as they discuss whatever parts of the case they've been clawing and picking at over the past few hours.

'Okay, well, add it to the schedule,' I say to Ravi. 'Get on to those social accounts, okay? I'll see you all at the case meeting later.'

I head back to my desk; I want to read Wade's blog away from the rest of the team.

Calvin and Nan are standing near Nan's desk, talking in low voices, their faces drawn.

'Hey!' I call out to them.

Nan shifts her head in mild acknowledgement.

'Hi, Gemma,' says Calvin. 'How's the Wade case going?'

'Slower than I would like,' I say.

'Shame that little prick Carmichael wasn't your guy,' Nan says with a snort.

I shrug. 'Yeah. It sure would have made things easier if he was.'

She snorts again.

Fleet appears, reeking of smoke, his cheeks flushed plum. 'Hey, team. I've missed you guys. What's happening?'

Calvin stretches his skinny arms high above his head. 'Sasha Cryer committed suicide last night. It's just been called in. The story's going to break shortly.'

'Oh god,' I say, thinking about the scared, skinny woman I tried to comfort as she cried about the death of her friend. That was just over a month ago.

'Yep,' confirms Nan. 'She wasn't particularly reliable, but still. If this thing ever goes to trial she certainly would have been useful. She was the only person who saw Jacoby arguing with Ginny Frost on the balcony that night. Apart from her alleged mystery man, of course.'

'Are you sure it's a suicide?' I ask.

Nan laughs bleakly. 'We're sure, which is a shame. I would have loved for Jacoby to have gone all *Godfather* and had her killed. Another chance for us to nail his arse to a jail cell.' She juts out her ample hip. 'But unfortunately, this was a run-of-the-mill cry for help. Bathtub style.' She cracks her gum loudly and smiles at us. 'Annoying.'

'At least you have her statements, right?' says Fleet, clearing his throat. Nan's bluntness is too much sometimes, even for him.

'Of course. But with her gone, Jacoby's defence will be more likely to weasel their way out of it. And it will make it even harder to ID the missing witness—assuming he really was there. This mess seems pretty similar to the shit you two are trying to *wade* through,' she smiles smugly and adds, 'pun intended.' She tosses a mint into her mouth. 'At least we're keeping the journos happy,' she continues drily. 'They couldn't make this shit up. Movie stars, homeless guys, escorts. They get to use all their favourite words.'

Feeling flat, I ease into my chair and log onto my computer. I see the email from Ravi that contains Wade's posthumous blog posts.

Nan pulls her coat on. 'Well, we're off to look at a dead girl,' she announces cheerily.

Calvin looks at me apologetically, transforming into Inspector Gadget as he dons a tan trench coat. 'See you guys later.'

'Hopefully one of us gets a break soon,' says Nan ominously, looking over at Isaacs' office.

Our boss is on the phone, his arm making a sharp triangle as it bends to his hip, his jaw locked as he talks, his feet rooted to the ground.

'I think he's copping some heat,' she adds as she walks past.

Blinking hard in an attempt to freshen my eyes, I open the Word file dated last Wednesday.

Writing just before the zombie street scene from his mobile trailer, Sterling details his pre-shoot nerves and some of the techniques he employs to overcome them. He mentions how stressful the week has been and references 'some difficult decisions' and a 'falling out with a good mate'. He says he can't wait to share some 'massive news' with all of his fans 'really soon'. He signs off with, 'This is shaping up to be the best year of my life. I feel so lucky.'

<o>

The terrifying truth about every case we work on is that no matter what, the answers are out there somewhere. Whether we stumble across them or not is due to an uneven mix of luck, experience and sheer bloody-mindedness. For this reason, part of leading a case involves monitoring how deeply to go into the detail. While it's tempting to latch onto a thread and pull hard, it's just as critical to step back and look at the big picture, to weave all the threads together. Fleet and I are the conductors and we need to be careful we don't get stuck playing the instruments. But, of course, no matter how good you are, things are always missed. Sometimes I think about all those clues scattered around, hiding in paperwork, stuck onto case boards—a telling sentence filed away in a taped interview, a critical strand of hair that blew away in the wind— and feel overwhelmed. Every cold case is a box of evidence that a bunch of frustrated detectives just couldn't quite make sense of. And the brutal truth is, there are as many sliding door moments when working a case as there are in any average day at the office. It's just that our mistakes and oversights sometimes mean that people get away with murder.

I come back from the bathroom trying to shake the soft buzz in my ears, which seems to be directly feeding off the pressure of my growing tension headache. Ralph Myers is walking in front of me, his arse wobbling in its self-important way.

'Hey, Ralph!' I call out as I catch up with him. 'How's the Miller case going?'

I follow him into the case room, where a couple of uniforms are doling out slices of pizza. I look at my watch, surprised to see that it's already 6 pm. I need to get out of here, go home and throw myself in the shower if I want to get to Josh's place for dinner on time.

'All going well, thanks, Woodstock,' says Ralph breezily. 'It's just a tough one with the site and the victim being so isolated. Unlike your case, where you have witness statements coming out of your ears.'

I smile politely and nod, glancing up at Miller's autopsy photos: his sagging skin resting loosely on his sharp bones, the dark ugly slash where his soul leaked out.

'Well, I hope you get out of here relatively early tonight,' I say distractedly, the buzz in my head turning up a notch.

Ralph rubs his ample stomach. 'I certainly plan to—just refuelling before another hour of power and then we're done for the day. You're welcome to join us if you're hungry.'

Thanking him but declining the offer, I head out of the room, away from the smell of hot cheese, to the Wade case room, kneading the back of my neck.

'Hi,' I say to Ravi who is seated at the back of the room. I quickly review the hotline call log and the case sheets. 'Anything I need to be across?'

'Not really,' he replies, standing up nervously as if I'm royalty. 'More CCTV footage from the city has come in. And we've received all of Wade's financial info now.'

'Great, thanks,' I say, making it clear he should sit down again.

'Did you want to look at Paul Wade's phone records?' he asks casually. 'I know you guys are planning to speak to him about the call he made to his brother last Sunday. We don't think there's anything else worth looking at except for the occasional call to a sex hotline.'

I squeeze my eyes shut, rubbing them for a few seconds. A swirl of colour explodes behind my eyelids.

I blink at Ravi, who is holding a sheet of paper over one of the open case folders, ready to file it if I say no. 'Um, yeah,' I reply vaguely. 'I'll have a quick look.'

He hands the printout to me.

Half an hour later I'm packing up my things at my desk when I quickly scan the document. For a guy in his late twenties, Paul's mobile call history was oddly sparse, telling the story of a loner life. The call he made to Sterling last Sunday was from the landline of the Castlemaine house, so it isn't on this record. The outgoing calls are mainly to the Wades' farmhouse, while the incoming calls are mainly from the same number and another that I know is Melissa's.

Lizzie claims to know nothing about the Sunday conversation between Sterling and Paul—Fleet spoke to her earlier about it. I make a mental note to find out if Wade said anything about the call to Brodie.

I head back to the case room to file the call summary with the other reports, when I notice the last line on the sheet: Melissa's incoming call to Paul on Wednesday in the late afternoon, following the attack on their brother. A jolt goes through my body as I realise that when Paul spoke to his sister, he was already in Melbourne.

Saturday, 18 August
7.44 pm

I've been at Josh's apartment for less than twenty minutes and my brain is struggling to let go of work and embrace the domestic scene before me. Phrases from Sterling's blog post tease the corners of my mind. I wonder what he meant by 'massive news'. Was it his engagement to Lizzie? The role in the US soap that his agent told us about? The Canadian film? Or something else? And why was Paul Wade lying about being in Melbourne on Wednesday? Is it connected? As much as I found Paul's lack of empathy off-putting, I doubt he knew enough about the workings of the film to orchestrate this attack—unless someone was feeding him information. Though he does have a history of violence, I remind myself. I press my fingers to my head, trying to quiet the rattle of thoughts.

Josh is in the kitchen flitting around like a moth: cracking eggs and boiling water, pouring wine and adjusting the volume of music that blasts from an invisible speaker system. I have no idea what he's thinking but I would hazard a guess that his mind isn't jumping between alibis and violence.

'Can I help?' I ask, thinking that at least if I'm occupied with a task, I won't have to watch him fussing.

'Absolutely not!' He points a finger at me, commanding me to stay where I am. I sip my wine obediently and he nods in approval. 'You've had a terrible week,' he says. 'You need to relax.'

Feeling tense, I look around the room reminding myself it's not his fault that his thoughts aren't fixed on death.

Josh's apartment is beautiful. It's not particularly big but it's a lot larger than mine. Candy would describe it as luxe. I'm pretty sure his parents are helping with the rent. It's been freshly painted; I detect the faint scent of recently refreshed walls. The light bounces off kitchen surfaces and is absorbed into the cushiony lounge. Gauzy curtains float gently over subtle heating ducts, and fresh flowers explode out of the crystal vase on the table. Jazz music flows from the speaker system, making an odd dance partner for my grim thoughts. Josh is twenty-nine, three years younger than me. I think about my own life at twenty-nine—hell, my life now—and marvel at the differences.

'So, Sterling Wade,' Josh says, whistling between his teeth as he assembles a fancy-looking salad. 'Wow, huh?'

'Yeah,' I say warily. 'You know I can't say too much about it, Josh.'

'I know, I know,' he says good-naturedly. He tops up my wine. 'Hey, so, when a case like Wade's comes out of nowhere, how many detectives work on it?'

I smile. 'You do realise that all our cases come out of nowhere, right? We don't tend to get a heads-up.'

He laughs. 'You know what I mean.'

'A case like this definitely demands a big team and puts us under pressure,' I tell him. 'We don't neglect other cases or anything but certain things are prioritised. For example, I've been pulled off the homeless man's case. Some of the old cases get downgraded. We obviously can't get to everything. We just don't have the people.'

I think briefly about Walter Miller slumped in the freezing tunnel, sitting alone in his own blood, and can't help feeling like I have abandoned him.

Josh doesn't say anything for a few minutes, and the room fills with the sounds of vegetables being chopped and then sizzling in a frypan. He starts humming along to the music.

This could be my life, I think. I could spend my evenings sitting here with Josh as he cooks delicious meals and asks me about work. We could make plans, talk about restaurants we want to go to, movies we want to see. Maybe we would even travel: I've never been out of Australia. Everything in Josh's body language, the way he engages with me, indicates that's what he wants. A normal relationship where a joint future is happily mapped out and navigated.

Before I even have the chance to picture Ben, an icy fist grips my insides and I cross and uncross my legs, thinking about those nights I've spent in the hotels. How I don't want to stop.

Josh's voice breaks into my thoughts. 'Are you really stressed?'

I finish my drink and pour another glass, blowing air out of my cheeks. It's hot in the apartment, cosy, and I'm flushed from the heat, the forced relaxation, the wine.

'The whole squad is under pressure,' I reply. 'This case is as high profile as you get. And then there's the homeless man's killing on top of that—people don't like it when the vulnerable are attacked, so there's a lot of political pressure. And, of course, the Jacoby case still isn't resolved. My boss is determined to give that one last big push.' I swallow a large mouthful of wine. 'Everyone is on edge.'

Even as I'm talking, my mind continues to churn, reviewing pieces of information. The knot of disparate threads is loosened by the alcohol, and they rejoin and begin to braid together. Something is trying to make itself clear but I can't seem to see it.

I'm also unsure about what Josh wants from me tonight—whether he sees this as a significant step in our relationship. So far, he hasn't pushed things between us physically, but we've barely been alone together in private, and I'm conscious of where things might go without the noise and buffer of others.

I look over at him, waiting for his response, but he doesn't say anything. He's focused on the meal preparations. But he seems a bit more distracted than usual tonight, and I wonder if he's nervous too.

I top up my glass and get up to look out the window. The view of the city is so different from this side of the river. It looks less overwhelming, calmer. I reach out and trace one of the office towers through the glass before my eyes shift back to my shadowy reflection.

For the hundredth time, I wonder what Josh sees in me.

When we met a month or so ago, I'd come from the Jacoby press conference and was bracing myself for a court appearance with a strong coffee at the cafe next to the courthouse. Josh appeared in my line of sight, his casual gesture indicating that he wanted to sit on the spare seat next to mine. I shuffled along and smiled up at him that it was fine. We got talking. He seemed both impressed and a little intimidated when I told him I was a homicide detective. He insisted we exchange numbers but I assumed I'd never hear from him again. But he sent me a message that night asking me out to dinner.

I enjoyed his company from the start. Not only is he extremely good-looking but he is easily the most uncomplicated person I have ever been involved with. Texts flowed and dates were suggested. He is keen but never pushy, and from the start has seemed to understand that my apartment is off limits. Most importantly he appreciates that my job comes first. I suspect he thinks I am damaged goods, worn down from past relationships, but he doesn't pry. He seems comfortable with being stuck at first base. I've no doubt Josh could have his pick of dates but maybe he thinks I am interesting, unlike the women who usually cross his path. Perhaps I am an experiment. Perhaps he likes me. I have no idea.

Even if Ben didn't exist, and setting aside my inability to settle into something and invest in it, we are so different. Josh has seen so much more of the world than I have but in so many ways he is blinkered. His existence is one of privilege, his smooth path into adulthood generously lubricated with a steady flow of money. He hasn't had to battle for anything. He is all soft edges and optimism. I am hard and my settings default to cynicism and doubt.

Josh expertly dishes up two generous bowls of pasta and the fancy salad, placing them proudly on the table, and gestures for me to sit. It's been days since I've eaten a proper meal and I hoe into my serving enthusiastically.

Josh declares that we should talk about something else before launching effortlessly into a steady stream of conversation about his sister, her new boyfriend, a new guy at work, his impressive Qantas Frequent Flyer Points balance and his new gym routine. I marvel at his ability to propel the conversation forward, appreciating that it means I can remain a passenger with only minimal contributions required.

Finishing my food, I go to the fridge to retrieve the wine. On the way back to the table, I notice a small stack of manila folders on the kitchen bench: 'bills paid' and 'bills yet to pay' reads Josh's neat handwriting on the tabs. I top up his wineglass. An automated air freshener lets out a little puff of fragrance from its perch on the wall as I walk past the table and sink onto the couch, toying with the tassel of a throw rug. I've eaten too quickly and feel queasy. Josh finishes his meal and settles into the armchair opposite me. He tilts his head back to drink some wine and then sweeps his hair to one side, resting his chin on his hand. For a moment, he looks so much like a boy band member on an album cover that I almost laugh.

'Is it strange working on a case where the victim is so famous?' he asks me.

'I thought we weren't going to talk about my work,' I reply, smiling.

I lie back against an oversized cushion and look at the row of photo frames on the side table. Shots from family holidays when Josh was much younger. Shots of him with his mates. They remind me of the array of photos on display at Wade's apartment. Josh's evolution from cute young boy to handsome young man is charmingly documented. There are a few shots of him in rowing gear with other clean-cut boys. A photo of him in university robes graduating. Josh beaming as he cuts a large birthday cake while a group of happy tanned people clap. I pause briefly at an image—one of the older women in the background looks familiar, but I can't place where I've seen her.

I realise Josh is waiting for me to respond.

'Yeah,' I say, 'it's definitely weird working a case where everyone knows the victim. Or thinks they know him anyway.'

'It must be totally bizarre,' marvels Josh. 'I mean, the whole thing is. I still can't get my head around it. Hey, so what happens if you don't get a lead? How long do you work on it until it goes cold or whatever?'

I stifle a yawn as I reply. 'It depends. There's so much to process with a case like this. And there are so many witnesses. That's the good thing about the cases here in the city,' I add, 'there's normally lots of people around.' I stretch out my legs. 'Though witnesses can bring their own problems. People haven't always seen what they think they've seen.'

Josh joins me on the couch, and I shift to the end so we are facing each other. He slides his legs between mine and launches into a longwinded story about a fraud case his law firm is working on at the moment.

I start to feel sick and wish he would stop talking. My stomach is struggling to process the large injection of food, while my over-worked brain continues to sift through the leftovers of the past few days. How does it all fit together? Is any of it relevant?

I begin to wish Josh would disappear so I could close my eyes and sleep right here on his couch in peace.

'You seem pretty tired,' he says. 'I'm guessing you don't want to meet up with my friends?'

I look at him through half-shut eyes, fixing on his smooth face.

He flashes his dimples at me shyly. 'It's cool if you want to stay here.' He swallows, his Adam's apple bobbing nervously as he throws back some wine.

Underneath the tinkling music, I hear a clock ticking somewhere in the apartment.

Josh shifts closer to me and rests his hand lightly on my upper thigh. 'Do you want any dessert?' he asks, his voice lower. 'I have ice cream.'

'I actually don't feel very well,' I say, sitting up as a knot of panic steadily works its way through my body.

I want it to be like it is with the men at the hotels. Where I don't have to think and I don't need to worry about anyone's feelings. Where my thoughts disappear and I achieve primal, blissful noth-ingness. But in those instances, sex is the end. With Josh it might be the beginning, and it terrifies me.

I don't want to talk anymore. I don't want to be here.

Josh leans forward and kisses me. It's tentative, as if he's asking for permission after the fact. I'm still sitting upright and can't bring myself to do what I'm supposed to: pull him close and rearrange myself so we're lying side by side. Instead, my hands hang loosely at my sides. My body has shut down.

'I'm sorry,' I say as I pull away, 'but I really don't feel well. You should go out, meet up with your friends. We should do this another time.'

He studies me carefully but I have no idea what he's thinking.

'When I'm feeling better and not so tired,' I add, trying to explain.

'I hope it wasn't my cooking,' he says and laughs awkwardly.

'I think I'm just completely exhausted, you know? I'm sorry I'm not much fun to be around at the moment.'

I can't tell if Josh is disappointed, but I sense some relief from him too. Maybe he's not sure if we are more than friends either. I gather my things and reassure him I don't need to be escorted home. I hug him goodbye, thanking him for dinner, and repeat that he should go out and meet his friends.

━◀○▶━

Bundled into a cab, I head back toward the city, electricity sparking up and down my limbs.

I pay the driver and get out. I'm teetering on the brink of being sober and feel wide awake. I pause at the bottom of my apartment building, already knowing I don't want to go home.

I glance at my reflection in the window. My hair is wild from the wind. A few metres away, a man sitting on a bench drinks from a paper bag, his eyes clouded with a milky haze. I avert my gaze and walk on, the cold wind prompting tears. I have no plan but it's not late, just past 10 pm, and restaurants and bars are cosy blazes of orange, laughter pouring out, switching places with the cold every time a door is opened. I walk for maybe ten minutes, pushing past loved-up couples, groups of noisy young boys reeking of smoke, harried-looking parents carrying sleepy children, and a homeless man and his dog, their white puffs of breath mingling in the night.

Maybe I should call Josh and tell him I want to come out after all. But no, that's definitely not what I want. I want to be alone. I want a drink. It starts to rain, a hazy half-hearted release from the sky. A door swings open a few metres from me and a giggling threesome of girls exits a busy bar.

'Can you *believe* he said that?'

'I know!'

'Seriously, what the fuck?'

They fall quiet as they light cigarettes before they revert to their collective disbelief over whatever *he* said. I sense them watching me as I step toward them, heading to the bar's door, and the blonde gives me a polite smile as they shuffle over to let me past. 'Fuck, it's cold!' one of them exclaims.

When I push inside, my frozen face is hit with a blast of heat. I smell alcohol and sweat. An open fire. Hot chips. I look around the small room, the music running through the floor and up my legs. My ears buzz with chatter as I weave my way to the bar and shed my coat. The bartender throws me a smile while he shakes a silver canister around his ears.

The couple next to me are talking in low, serious voices and I catch pieces of their conversation. *Your fault. Not fair. So unreasonable.*

'Sorry,' a voice says in my ear as a man pushes his body into me.

'Are you waiting for someone?' the bartender asks, appearing in front of me.

I shake my head. 'No, I just want a drink.'

He lifts his brows. 'Can do. What do you fancy?'

'Whisky,' I say and watch his brows lift a little higher.

Thirty minutes later I'm on my second drink and my thoughts are drifting past me. I decide to stop trying to catch them.

No one has spoken to me aside from the bartender. In Smithson, I could barely go anywhere without bumping into someone I knew. The familiarity was suffocating. The inane small talk. The constant observation. This invisibility suits me much better.

'Good night?' The bartender is slicing some limes a little way along the bench, and for a moment I'm not sure whether he spoke or I imagined it.

He glances up at me, clearly waiting for an answer.

'Yep,' I say.

'Excellent,' he replies.

A girl leans across the bar to order a drink. Her forehead almost touches his. He starts to mix more drinks for the insatiable crowd of revellers and I am left alone again.

Sterling Wade would never have had moments like this, I think as I look around. Moments where he could just fade into nothing. Everywhere he went he was known. Like the entire world was a small nosey town. He was always noticed. Watched. Followed. I wonder what that would be like, the relentless recognition. He would rarely have met someone without suspecting they liked the package more than the person.

But then maybe that's always the case. I'm sure Scott was initially drawn to my work as a detective; he found it intriguing and appealing, until it gradually became the thing about me he hated the most. No doubt Josh will be the same.

A hazy slideshow plays in my head. Sterling getting stabbed, the shock on his face raw and real, the surge of zombies, Lizzie's screams. I wonder what was really going on in their relationship. Was the engagement a cover for his relationship with Brodie? Or had Sterling perhaps called things off with Brodie? Would that have made Brodie resentful, even dangerous? Or is it possible that Lizzie is lying about the proposal and trying to claim the highest status of grief that she can? The timing of the engagement does seem odd— at the beginning of a gruelling film shoot—but maybe Sterling got carried away in the excitement of it all. They were making plans to move overseas; everything points to their relationship being serious. Still, I'm struggling to believe that Lizzie was unaware of Sterling and Brodie's relationship. Surely living in the same house would make it impossible to avoid. Perhaps she just didn't want to see it. And was Sterling gay or was he bisexual, or simply in love with Brodie? Is it possible that Lizzie and Brodie were closer than they have led us to believe? Did they perhaps both feel betrayed by Sterling?

The young actor was so much more complex than his light-hearted interviews suggest. He was on the cusp of so many things. A new level of fame, a possible move overseas. Who would want to cut that short?

In my mind, I thumb through more pictures: the autopsy, the angry dark wound near his heart. His perfect face. His parents' heartbreak. His siblings' seeming indifference. Cartwright's dumbfounded shock. Lizzie's tears. Brodie's passionate grief.

My glass is empty. I should go. I feel hot, my underarms are damp and my feet are on fire inside my boots. The other women here are dressed in skimpy tops and narrow jeans with strappy heels. Their painted faces are layered like mountains with peaks and dips that I'm sure I don't have. I don't know how to be like them. On the rare occasions that I dress up and wear make-up I feel public and exposed, as if my face is a beacon. The scrutiny it prompts makes me uncomfortable. I much prefer the comfort of hiding in plain sight.

'Another?' asks the bartender, standing right in front of me.

'I'm not sure I should.'

'It's on the house,' he says, his voice suddenly low and full of meaning.

We make eye contact and a jolt of pleasure surges straight to my core.

'Well, okay then. I'll be back, I just need to go to the bathroom.'

'Sure,' he says, his eyes lingering on me.

I wait in the short queue in the dim corridor, flat against the wall, as swaying men and women walk past. One man eyes me appreciatively. 'Having a good night?' he asks and I shrug, looking at the floor to ward off further conversation.

Back at the bar I sip my fresh drink as a loud voice in my head tells me to leave. I pull out my phone to see that it's past midnight. There's a text from Josh saying he hopes I feel better when I wake up. With a start, I realise that Josh is the closest thing I have to a friend in Melbourne. Seeing how terrible I am at staying in touch with my small collection of friends in Smithson, he's becoming the closest thing I have to a friend anywhere.

'You okay?' asks the bartender, who is starting to clean up. He is rhythmically placing dirty glasses over a small tap that shoots a burst of water up into their guts.

I look at him and wonder how to answer.

'I think so,' I say.

'What do you do?'

Sterling's dead body flashes into my thoughts. 'I'm a teacher,' I reply.

'I always wanted to be a teacher.'

I smile back at him, pushing the ice in my glass with my finger so that it keeps bobbing back up. It's like a tiny swimmer choking for air and I force it under again, holding it down for longer. I keep seeing the deep black line across Wade's chest, just under his rib cage where his life leaked out.

'What grade do you teach?'

I blink, looking into his eager face. 'Uh, Year Ten.'

His mouth pulls into a mock grimace. 'Teenagers, huh. Must be exhausting.'

'Yeah. It is.'

'So how come you're here alone tonight?'

'Why do you think I'm here alone?' I say automatically.

He leans in, encouraged, and looks deep into my eyes, pretending to try to figure it out. 'You deal drugs on the side? A Tinder date that went bad? You're a Russian spy?'

I laugh in spite of myself. 'All of the above.'

'Yeah, it was pretty obvious in the end.' He serves a group of tattoo-covered guys as I keep drinking.

A thought desperately tries to find its place in my mind. Sterling's corpse flares again, that angry final legacy carved into it. The image won't leave me alone.

'Hey,' the bartender says, 'so we shut in about fifteen minutes.'

I hold his look but can't bear it for too long, so I pretend to search for something in my bag. 'That's fine,' I tell him. 'I need to get going anyway.'

'Cool,' he says. He disappears out a side door as I knock back the last of my drink. My throat burns and my skin feels loose on my bones. I'm very tired but my brain continues to flit erratically around the gory pictures.

The bartender returns carrying a tray of clean glasses, a dish-cloth on his shoulder.

'I'm Zac,' he says, reaching across the bar to shake my hand.

'Zoe,' I say quickly. I know what is coming next.

'I'm not closing up tonight. Do you want to go somewhere else for a nightcap? My shout.' He looks at the bar, then the last group of people at the table behind me, his eyes roaming anywhere but my face as he waits for my answer.

'Sure. Why not.'

He looks toward the back room. 'I reckon I'll be done in about ten or so.'

'Okay. I have to make a quick call, so I'll just wait outside.'

The night air shrinks my lungs and I lean against a lamppost. There are fewer people around now and they are quieter, walking with heads down, pushing through the cold.

Stay or go, I think. Stay or leave.

Minutes later Zac emerges from the bar, giving me a soft smile as he zips up his jacket.

'Where do you want to go?' he asks.

'Your place,' I say without hesitation.

Zac lives in a scruffy loft apartment in Collingwood. In the tiny kitchen a tap drips loudly into a metal sink, and I find myself counting along to its steady beat. I sip my gin and tonic as I watch him scroll through an endless list of alternative music tracks.

Before the first song is over, Zac leads me into his room, pulls off his jumper and pushes me onto the bed. He's rough and I want it, want him inside me. I want all the thoughts to stop, to have some peace.

With every thrust I breathe in sharply, my eyes fixed on an abstract painting, the colours slashing across the canvas. In my mind knives plunge into skin, opening wounds; faces are twisted in pain. Panic rises in my chest as I'm trapped under Zac's weight. Completely helpless. He holds my face and kisses me. I feel desire and guilt meet in the middle, as I get closer to the point of nothing.

After our frenzied blur of sex is over, Zac slides down next to me and I turn to face the wall, my skin damp and flushed, my heartbeat slowing as I will him to fall asleep. I'm desperate to escape but his arm rests heavily on me and I shift away from its weight, emitting a sleepy-sounding mumble.

'That was amazing,' Zac whispers as he softly pulls his fingers through my tangled hair, lifting it off my face. 'I'm glad you picked my bar to have a drink at tonight.'

He gets out of the bed and I hear the sound of a drink being poured. Returning, he sits propped up next to me sipping his whisky and humming to the music, his fingers playing piano along the top of the blanket. After a few moments, he pulls the covers up around us and turns the lamp off. I smell booze, faded after-shave and the mild musk of our sweat. I feel his body sink into sleep and I lie awake next to him for what feels like hours, willing myself to sleep but seeing knives stabbing into flesh every time I close my eyes.

Sunday, 19 August
6.32 am

Upon waking, the night before feels like a dream but the sharp pain through my forehead tells another story. I dress quickly, creep out of Zac's place and walk to the end of Smith Street. Curious fingers of morning light prod at me. I pause against a brick wall thinking I'm going to be sick but the moment passes.

I hail a cab and make it back to my apartment where I lie in bed, my eyes on the grey sky through my window as I wonder what Ben is doing. He's probably watching cartoons. Or maybe he's in bed with Scott. I let my thoughts drift from Ben and Scott curled up together to Ben snuggling with Scott and a woman, a stranger. I cry out loud and haul myself upright. My thoughts won't be tamed when I am in this headspace and I look around the apartment for a distraction. Catching my reflection in the mirror I see that I look terrible: cracked lips, sallow skin, my hair a ratty dark cloud.

In the shower, I pray that the alcohol will work its way out of me quickly, taking its pain with it. As awful as I feel, one thought continues to pulse in tandem with my aching head. I need to get to the station to look at those autopsy pictures again.

◄○►

After pacing around the case room for over thirty minutes, my theory circling in my head until I hear sounds that I know aren't really there, I call Fleet.

His voice is clogged with sleep. 'Woodstock? What is it?'

With a start, I realise it's only just after 8.30 am on a Sunday.

'Hey,' I stutter, suddenly feeling very foolish. I clear my throat. 'I think I've got something worth going to Isaacs with.'

There's a pause as Fleet covers the phone to talk to someone, surely a girl, and embarrassment snakes through my insides.

'Look, sorry, I didn't realise it was so early—we can talk about this later?' I suggest, wanting to end the conversation I've been desperate to have all morning.

'No, no,' he says, more awake. 'Now is fine. Gotta get moving anyway. Who wants to sleep in on a Sunday? Not me.'

His voice is typically wry but carries an unusual flatness. I can't get a handle on his mood or whether he is annoyed to hear from me or not.

'Okay, I'm upright now,' he says. 'Hit me.'

'Right, well.' I force some strength into my voice. 'After our meeting yesterday I was here last night, just wrapping up a few things. I was talking to Ralph and I noticed the Miller case board. Something stuck in my head about it. And then last night I realised that the autopsy photos are almost identical to Wade's. I mean the injury looks exactly the same.'

Fleet doesn't say anything for a few moments and I experience an excruciating twist of impatience mixed with the fear of potential ridicule.

'What about the reports?' he asks finally. 'Do they suggest we're looking at the same killer? What does my favourite pathologist say?'

'I haven't spoken to Mary-Anne yet,' I admit. 'I wanted to talk to you first. But that's the other thing—she didn't do Walter Miller's post-mortem. She was away, remember?'

Fleet makes an indecipherable sound. I hear a muffled female voice and the phone turns to white noise again before scuffling back to Fleet as he stifles a yawn.

'Okay, Woodstock, let's meet. I could use a coffee. Give me, say, half an hour and then I suggest we make like the kids and spend stupid amounts of cash on eggs and bacon, and maybe some avocado toast.'

◄○►

Fleet looks worse than I do. His hair is in desperate need of taming and thick stubble creeps across his face like a fog. His eyes are hidden behind dark glasses but I suspect they are at least as blood-shot as mine. We sit outside so he can smoke. For a few minutes, I simply watch as he rhythmically alternates between sucking on a cigarette and slurping his coffee.

'Big night?' I say sarcastically.

'You betcha,' he says, clearly not bothered by his shabby state. 'You?'

'Big enough.'

He nods approvingly. 'Well, us young ones can't be all work and no play.'

We are surrounded by perky people decked out in cosy winter workout wear and drinking wholesome smoothies from recycled jars. Instead of chairs there are milk crates and each table has a little bonsai on it. I take a tentative sip of my own coffee: the smell alone makes me gag.

I tell him about the question marks around Paul Wade's alibi on Wednesday.

'This combined with the pub fights in Karadine are making him seem like someone we need to look into,' I say.

Fleet sighs, prodding his forehead with his fingers. 'You really think Paul's up to masterminding something like this? The guy struck me as someone who struggles with basic life tasks.'

'I know, but then why lie about being in town? Maybe someone else was the mastermind and he was just the muscle.'

Fleet stretches his arms above his head, squeezes his eyes shut and then nods again. 'Interesting. Well, I guess we'll see if big brother Wade has a reasonable explanation for his trip to the city. And for lying about it.' He coughs and clears his throat. 'God, I feel like arse,' he mutters. 'Alright. Show me these photos before I order some food.'

I remove them from the envelope and lay them out in front of him, while I block prying eyes with the menu.

'So, these are obviously Wade's,' I point at the taut, tanned chest marred by the angry dark line, 'and these are Miller's.' Fleet holds them side by side. 'They were almost the same height,' I add, eagerly watching his face as he studies the photos. 'It's not just that the wounds look the same—there's the proximity and the similar MO. The tunnel where Walter was attacked is less than a kilometre from the top of Spring Street. And both were unexpected, unprovoked attacks. Well, not heat-of-the-moment attacks anyway.'

Fleet is nodding slowly, and I can't tell if he is agreeing or thinks I'm nuts and is trying to work out how to tell me.

I rush to keep talking. 'I mean really, there are a lot of similarities.'

Fleet coughs again, a nasty guttural sound that's fleshy with smoke. 'Yeah. Except that one victim was a mega-star and one was a complete nobody.'

'I admit that part doesn't seem to make sense. Unless there is something linking them that we can't see yet.'

'Come on, Woodstock, as much as we both want an HBO thriller to land on our lap, it's pretty unlikely.'

I roll my eyes. 'I'm not looking for drama, I'm just saying that there might be a link.'

A petite waitress with striking green eyes and serpent tattoos on both hands appears at his side. I swiftly gather up the photos and shove them back into the envelope as he orders.

'You think they knew each other?' he asks.

'I don't know,' I say. 'It doesn't seem likely. But maybe the killer knew them both?'

'The homeless man's murder could be completely random,' says Fleet. 'I obviously haven't been across it since that first night but that's where I thought it was headed. Just some opportunistic nut getting his jollies, or a psych case. Or maybe someone who had a problem with homeless people and thought he was doing society a favour. But Wade's murder can't be random.'

'I know,' I say, trying to work through the possibilities in my mind.

'I think you're right about the wounds though,' Fleet says, peering at the photos again. 'They definitely look similar and the attacks were, what, less than two days apart? How did this not get picked up?'

'Two different pathologists, for a start. And I guess Sterling's death just eclipsed everything else. I mean, you're right, there's no obvious link from a profile perspective.'

'I guess it's lucky you were snooping around in Ralph's case room.' Fleet smirks.

'I wasn't snooping,' I say defensively, but the banter between us feels good. 'Anyway, imgaine if there really is a link.'

'Game changer,' Fleet declares as his breakfast arrives. A steaming mountain of bacon and eggs on a square wooden board. 'Want anything?' he asks as he shakes a generous snowstorm of salt onto his meal.

'No thanks.'

I feel worse now than when I woke up but I'm grateful that Fleet is taking me seriously.

'Why don't you call Isaacs while I eat?' He spears a piece of bacon with his fork and waves it at me. 'Let's get some meat on the bones of your theory.'

Monday, 20 August
8.05 am

'So what do we think we're looking at here?' Isaacs is the only one in the room not seated, and he looks as wired today as he did when he came into the station at lunchtime yesterday to hear my theory. 'Well?' He places his hands on the back of a chair and drops his shoulders, settling his gaze on each of us in turn.

Based on the pointed looks that Ralph and Billy give me, they clearly think I'm the one who should respond.

I open my mouth but Fleet swoops in before I can say anything. 'We spoke to Mary-Anne. She thinks it's possible that Woodstock is right, that the two crimes were committed by the same person.'

I look at him, surprised by this public backing. 'Yes,' I continue, 'Mary-Anne thinks that the Wade murder weapon could have been the same as the one used on Walter Miller. The wounds match but we're still waiting on the bloods. As to what it means if it *was* the same guy, we don't know yet.'

Isaacs lifts his shoulders up and down as if they are sore. 'And we can't get the bloods any earlier?'

'We've asked. Hopefully we'll get the report in the next few days,' Fleet replies.

Isaacs closes his eyes briefly and makes a polite grunting sound. 'Okay, but in the meantime, there's no hard evidence to suggest that the crimes are linked, is there?'

I realise that my heart is racing. My skin blooms with sweat, there isn't enough oxygen in the room, and everyone's eyes fix on me, making it hard for me to find the right words. I sit up straight and visualise pushing my nerves away. 'No, sir, no hard evidence, just the things we spoke about yesterday. The proximity and timing, mainly. And the brazen, unprovoked nature of the crimes.' Isaacs draws a breath, about to interrupt, so I continue quickly, my voice strong. 'I appreciate that the Wade case is different, but both crimes were carried out in very public places. The victims were caught off guard. Almost like executions. Maybe there is commonality in that.'

I am desperate for my theory to be true, for us to make some significant progress. I hope no one else can hear the mild pleading in my voice.

'It could be a serial,' says Chloe, the light catching her hair as she shifts in her chair.

Isaacs seems annoyed by her comment. 'We have nothing to suggest that,' he says firmly.

'I do wonder about the stark differences between Walter Miller and Sterling Wade,' I say to the group. 'I mean, they seem about as unlike each other as you can get. I don't really have an explanation for that unless the killer somehow knew them both.'

'Maybe we have a collector killer,' says Calvin. 'Maybe it's a deranged challenge to attack different kinds of people. Could be an internet thing.' He looks around the room for approval. 'You know—homeless person, celebrity, priest, kid.' He swallows. 'The randomness could be the strategy?'

Even though I don't buy Calvin's theory, I had briefly pondered a similar scenario. But I catch Ralph swallowing a smirk, and I decide not to say anything.

'Are we sure there's no link between Wade and Miller?' asks Nan. 'Wade didn't do charity work with the homeless at some point or something like that?'

'We need to look further into it,' I reply, 'but nothing has turned up so far. Of course, it's possible they met at some point and there's no trail.'

'Forgetting all this for a minute,' says Isaacs, waving my inconvenient theory away, 'where are we at on everything else?'

All eyes shift back to me. 'We're working through a huge amount of information. Alibis, mainly. Admittedly, we don't know if the perpetrator is on our radar but in terms of known persons of interest we still can't confirm the exact whereabouts of Brodie Kent or Paul Wade at the time of the attack. Fleet and I think Paul is worth looking into more seriously even though we have doubts about him as a suspect. We'd like to interview him formally and go at him pretty hard to see what falls out. Even some of the people who were present can't be completely crossed off the list. Ava James, for example, claims to have been alone in her nearby trailer. And we're still considering the possibility that Wade was being followed weeks before his death.' I pause and look around the room. 'There's also the argument Wade had with Riley Cartwright on the Sunday. We're unsure if that's relevant.'

Fleet chimes in. 'We're getting nowhere with the broader cast and crew. Based on the interviews it does look like there was an extra unidentifiable person in Wade's proximity but we can't ID them from the video footage. We've got a shitload of witness statements that tell us absolutely zilch. The security company maintains that there were no breaches that afternoon—but then, they would say that. Everyone did scan in and out so it would have been difficult but not impossible. And the background checks have only turned up minor past offences. If our guy had an insider helping him, it's not going to be obvious.'

I sigh inwardly, thinking about the mountain of data we still need to work through.

'Alright, alright,' says Isaacs, holding up a hand as if to block out our incompetence. He cups the lower half of his face with his hand, pulling the skin downwards. 'Ralph and Billy, keep working the Miller case as you were. I know you've got limited bodies on it now anyway and I don't want to lose focus. If nothing else comes of this new theory, then we'll need to reduce your team next week.' His eyes settle on me before shifting across to the other side of the room. 'Nan, Calvin, I want you to look into this possible link. Give Woodstock and Fleet the headspace to work other angles on the Wade case without any distractions. Chloe, you continue to support on Wade.'

My head jerks before I've fully processed what Isaacs said.

'We're still pretty deep in the Jacoby mess,' says Nan darkly. 'Sasha Cryer's family has joined forces with the Frosts, and they're pushing for an inquest—which we think they'll get, following her suicide.'

'Well, I want you to juggle both,' retorts Isaacs. 'We're tight for resources and I've been told from above in no uncertain terms to make what we have work.'

Nan nods briskly, her expression indicating that she is resigned to the general hopelessness of the force, its poor funding and our gloomy lives.

'Right,' says Isaacs. 'You should all keep me updated on new information that comes in. And not a word of this to the media— I do not want to see any more news reports questioning the safety of the city.'

The others get up and I quickly rise too, my fists curling in frustration. Fleet's hand is on my shoulder, guiding me out of the room away from the others. He shepherds me all the way to the car park. The cold air is like a blast from a hose. It grabs my rib cage, forcing the warm air out in a burst.

'What?' I hiss. 'Why are we out here?'

Fleet is tapping a cigarette from a packet. 'Because I need a smoke after our special pep talk. And you need to cool down.'

My arms fold involuntarily. I'm freezing out here without a jacket. The wind has found entry points through my clothes and is needling into my pores.

'I'm fine,' I tell him, stamping my feet on the spot.

'Sure you are,' says Fleet, disappearing behind a cloud of smoke. 'You're absolutely thrilled that Isaacs has thrown your lead to Nan and her obedient labrador to follow up.'

'Why doesn't he trust us?' I say, hating the whine in my voice.

'Maybe because we haven't given him a reason to yet,' says Fleet bluntly, but with a kind smile. After a moment, a smile tugs at the corners of my own mouth and I roll my eyes at my own childishness.

Fleet winks at me. 'Come on, Woodstock, you're new here and the jury is out on me, so we've got everything to prove.' He squints as he sucks the last of the smoke out of the cigarette butt. 'On the upside, we haven't got much to lose.'

'We're going to work the Miller angle anyway, right?' I say tentatively.

'Sure. It can be our side hustle,' he says with a laugh.

'Can I have one of those?' I ask, after a moment.

He nods, not quite hiding a smile when he hands it over. 'By the way,' he says as I light it, 'don't you think it's weird that the Wades want to have the funeral here?'

'Yeah, I would have thought they'd want to farewell their son in their home town, but I guess his whole life was in Melbourne. Plus, they must want to get this over and done with and then go back to Karadine in peace. They probably don't want this shitstorm following them home.'

Fleet scratches his guts through his shirt. 'I guess. I wonder how they'll deal with his foster family being there.'

'It can't be easy sharing your kids,' I say. My heart twists as I think about Ben replacing me, which is entirely possible based on the situation I've created.

'No, I guess not,' Fleet says and looks at his phone. 'Jesus, thirty-one calls to the hotline since yesterday!'

'It's crazy, isn't it?' I reply, shifting my weight to ward off the cold.

'Sure is,' he says. 'Did you see the boxes in the case room?'

'No.'

'The techs printed out all of Sterling's social media feeds from the past six months. And all his private messages. And all the emails that were sent to Wendy. Plus the physical letters sent by snail mail. I've never seen so much shit in my life.'

I picture all those people sitting in bedrooms or offices, on trams or in classrooms declaring their love, hate and everything in between for a man they've never met.

'Full on,' I mutter.

'Yeah,' says Fleet. 'And I didn't even get one Christmas card last year.' He clears his throat and spits neatly onto the ground. 'Sorry,' he says, shrugging unapologetically as he heads back inside.

I fall into step behind him, conscious of keeping pace with his long strides and noticing the way his hair curls naughtily into the top of his shirt collar. The Wade case might be all over the place, but for the first time in a long time I feel like I have an ally.

Monday, 20 August
2.01 pm

Paul Wade toys with his watchband. Through the wall of the small conference room the hotel has loaned us, I hear the tinkling of the water feature in the lobby. It's making me feel on edge.

'So,' I say, leaning forward across the table to eyeball him. 'How about you tell us what you were really doing last Wednesday afternoon?'

Paul lifts his head sullenly. A large pimple is brewing over his left eyebrow.

'My family will want to know why you needed to talk to me today,' he says, sounding like a little kid.

'Feel free to tell them,' I say, without sympathy.

'I was in Castlemaine,' he says.

'Try again,' I say. 'We know you were in Melbourne.'

He looks at the ground. 'I didn't do anything,' he offers lamely.

When Fleet and I arrived at the hotel, the Wades were talking to a puckered-looking funeral director and his attractive young assistant about Sterling's funeral service. Lizzie and Wendy Ferla were there too, but from what I could tell it had fallen on Melissa to make most of the decisions. April and Matthew sat on either side of her, looking defeated. Apologising for interrupting, we asked to speak with Paul, which seemed to rouse only mild concern from his broken parents. Lizzie, on the other hand, watched wide-eyed as Paul left the room and I wondered what she was thinking.

'We're not saying you did anything bad, Paul,' says Fleet, 'but you sure as shit weren't painting your mate's house in Castlemaine either, which is a problem. We like things to be neat around here. So. Let's try this again: where were you on Wednesday afternoon?'

Paul squeezes his eyes shut before saying, 'I always planned to come to Melbourne this weekend. Go to the footy.'

'Yep, we're not disputing that,' Fleet replies with artificial patience.

We found football ticket purchases for both Friday night and Saturday afternoon on Paul's maxed-out credit card.

'But why did you come into town on Wednesday?' Fleet presses. 'And why did you lie about it?'

'I was with a woman,' he eventually mutters.

'What woman?' I snap.

'A prostitute,' he says so quietly it's almost a whisper.

'Very convenient,' sighs Fleet. 'Manage to grab her name? Phone number?'

'No.' He reddens. 'I picked her up. It wasn't like, at a place or anything.'

'You were with a street sex worker?' I say, not quite able to keep the surprise out of my voice.

He nods and squirms in his chair. 'Yeah. Look, I didn't want to say anything. I don't want Mum to know. Or Dad. But it's got nothing to do with Sterling.'

'Yes, well, we don't need to shout it from the rooftops but we need a bit more detail so we can verify it. This is serious, Mr Wade. We can't account for your whereabouts at the time your brother was fatally attacked. We're going to need to find this woman and confirm your alibi.'

Paul reddens more deeply. 'Well, I don't know her name but I was with her in my van. I picked her up then I took her to an underground car park. Um, on St Kilda Road. No one's around there during the day. I dropped her back in St Kilda and headed to the city. I was about to go to a pub, just play the pokies or whatever, when Mel called me.' He makes eye contact with me for the first time. 'I know it doesn't look good, 'specially as my brother and I weren't mates, but I swear I had nothing to do with what happened.'

'Is meeting up with sex workers on the street something you do regularly?' Fleet asks.

Paul lifts his shoulders and mumbles, 'Just sometimes when I come to the city. I don't like going to the places. Everyone looking at me and stuff.'

'Where do you usually stay when you come here?' asks Fleet.

'Dunno. Just cheap places. Sometimes I sleep in my van.'

'Why did you call your brother on the Sunday before he died?' I ask.

Paul looks like he's about to deny it before he takes a deep breath and lifts his shoulders in defeat. 'Mum was at me about it. Thought we should talk more.'

'So it was a duty call?' says Fleet sceptically.

Paul grunts. 'Yeah.'

'Did the chat go well?'

'Not really. Sterling started going on about all the fancy shit he was doing. He didn't give a toss about me and my life.'

'How did the call end?' I ask.

'Dunno. I was pissed off but it was just . . . normal, I guess. We hung up. I hated talking to him. We had nothing in common. Never have, really. He just didn't get it, how hard it is for normal people.'

Paul is getting worked up, his jaw clenching repeatedly as he rocks forward on his chair.

'I don't know,' says Fleet, 'it seems like your brother did a lot of charity work and donated money to causes. He seemed to have a caring side.'

'It was total bullshit!' explodes Paul. 'All that effort he put into bloody strangers while his family is struggling to make ends meet. I fucking hated it.'

I let his charged words fade from the room before I ask, 'Did Sterling know how much trouble your parents were in financially?'

'He must have known. Last time he came up it would have been obvious. My parents are proud people and they don't like to make a fuss, but he would have known.' Waves of fury cross his face as he tries to keep a lid on his emotions.

'It must be tough watching your folks struggle like that,' says Fleet.

'It's tougher on Mel. She lives up the road from Mum and Dad. She and her husband help out on the farm but they've got their own problems. One of their kids needs special care so they have a hard time of it.'

'But Sterling didn't have to worry about any of it,' I say.

'Nope,' says Paul indignantly, his eyes shining. 'He left Karadine when he was a kid and barely came back. Got himself a fancy new family and that was it.'

'He visited though, right? And he stayed in touch with your parents. They told us he called them every week.'

'Yeah, well, he probably felt guilty or something, I guess.' Paul slumps back into his seat. 'He only visits once a year. Mum and Dad don't let on but they hated all his TV and movie stuff. They just wanted him home. But he thought he was too good for the farm. Too good for us.' Paul rubs a meaty fist over his eye. 'Mum is pretty upset about him getting engaged and not telling anyone. I know that everyone thought he was a superstar but he was a selfish little prick.'

Fleet and I don't respond.

After a moment Paul feels the need to substantiate his statement. 'He was. He was so ungrateful, especially to Mum and Dad, seeing how they did so much for him, and letting him move to Melbourne as a kid.'

'Well, at least he can be generous now,' says Fleet. 'He hadn't lived with Lizzie for very long and his last-known will directs all of his assets to your parents. So even if she can claim some of them, I doubt your family will have to worry about the farm anymore.'

Paul grunts and stares rudely at the wall.

'But maybe you already knew that,' adds Fleet.

Paul remains silent, his large arms crossed in front of him.

'Okay,' I say, sighing, 'why don't you describe the woman you say you spent last Wednesday afternoon with?'

Tuesday, 21 August
11.06 am

Even in our modern, digital world, alibis aren't always as easy to confirm as you might expect. Sometimes we luck out and deal with people who have highly scheduled lives, like lawyers or doctors. And anyone who has a personal assistant is a godsend when it comes to piecing together daily movements. People who work in labour jobs are handy too: a factory worker usually turns out to be exactly where they said they were and this can be confirmed by several others. It's the unemployed, the students, the single, the stay-at-home parents and the elderly who cause us the most trouble. And some people can simply be vague about their movements. Sometimes this is deliberate, but often it's because they drift through their lives without taking much notice of what they're doing at any given time. When you have nowhere particular to be, you can end up being everywhere.

Soon after my arrival in Melbourne I worked a case in which one of the main suspects was an older man, a widower, who spent most of his days catching the train to the end of the line and back again. He liked the feeling of going on a journey, and as a pensioner this daily joy cost him only a few dollars. Trying to nail down his whereabouts in the lead-up to an assault became a very time-consuming CCTV puzzle.

One of the biggest issues with the Wade case is that we don't know whose alibi we need. Most of the cast and crew can now be accounted for, but the additional masked person remains a mystery. We don't know if they are known to us or a complete stranger. We can't work back from where they were supposed to be at the time of the attack.

To that end, we've settled on a spray and pray approach and are just ticking off the whereabouts of everyone in our sights.

We now have a team of uniforms trying to verify Paul Wade's alleged afternoon dalliance last Wednesday. They are slowly working their way up and down the streets of St Kilda as they search for the dark-haired lady in question. So far no one remembers seeing Paul or his van and our team certainly hasn't happened upon the lucky woman. Because his phone was off for most of the afternoon we have no way of knowing if he's telling the truth about being in St Kilda between 3 and 5 pm. All we know is that he was near Flinders Street Station by the time Melissa called him just after 5.30 pm on Wednesday.

We've confirmed the Beaufords' statement that they were both in Adelaide on the day of the attack. Their son Jack was at home with his girlfriend. All the communications we've found between Wade and the Beaufords, and Wade and Jack, are extremely positive. He was more intimate with them than with his parents. 'Hell, I considered asking them to adopt *me*,' Fleet told me. 'They are so charming it's ridiculous. I can see why Wade was smitten.'

Frustratingly, no one can confirm that Ava James was in her trailer during Wade's attack. There's no CCTV footage from the areas around the three makeshift trailers that were positioned at the top of the park, and because the entire area was under a security lockdown she didn't have a personal guard with her. One of the cast mentioned that just before the zombie scene began, they saw Ava outside a trailer talking on her mobile; she claims she never left her trailer and watched the whole scene play out on a split-screen. We're trying to confirm if she made or received a call during that timeframe but her overseas phone company is making local access to her records difficult. While we know it would have been easy enough for her to slip on a costume and join the seething mass, we're not convinced that she could have made it back to one of the costume trailers without raising any suspicion. All we can be certain of is that Ava didn't leave the set until she demanded one of the security guards take her to the hospital about twenty minutes after the attack—her hysterics were witnessed by many.

Brodie Kent maintains he spent the day just 'wandering around the city'. We've managed to verify his presence at one cafe where he had a coffee at 11 am, but aside from that he was just one of thousands of bodies walking the streets and taking in the sights.

We decide to ask him to come in for further questioning.

—◀O▶—

Brodie answers breathlessly when I call, immediately wanting to know if there's a development. He is disappointed when I tell him I can't share any information but says he's nearby and will come in straight away.

Looking pale and haunted, he sits nervously opposite us in the same interview room as last time. We grill him for more detail about what he was doing on the day Sterling died. 'I was just thinking,' he insists. 'I was working on my screenplay and I find it helps when I walk around, taking in all the different types of people. I stopped a few times for coffee and I used the bathroom in David Jones, but aside from that I was just walking and listening to music.'

Brodie admits being near Spring Street at various points throughout the day. He can't remember exactly where he was when Wade was attacked but says he deliberately avoided the crowds. His phone died sometime in the afternoon, and he claims he didn't find out about Sterling's death until he saw the news when he got home around six-thirty.

I sigh, frustrated that, just like Brodie's walk that day, we are simply looping in pointless circles.

'Tell me, Brodie,' I say, deciding to change the subject, 'did Sterling mention anything about a phone call he received last Sunday?'

He scrunches up his face as he thinks. 'On Sunday?' he repeats.

'Yes, later in the afternoon, maybe around four-thirty.'

'He spoke to his brother on Sunday,' says Brodie. 'I got home from a dance class and he was pretty upset about it.'

'Did he say what they talked about?'

'Not really. He just said that his brother called and that almost straight away Paul picked a fight with him. The guy's a homophobic jerk.'

'Do you know what the argument was about?' I press.

'No, he didn't say. He wasn't close to his family. They never really understood him.'

'Do you think Sterling's brother knew about you and him?' asks Fleet.

'No way. Definitely not.'

'How do you know he's homophobic then?' asks Fleet.

'Just from what Sterling told me. His parents, they seem like nice people, but they're very old-fashioned. My parents are kind of the same. But his brother has no excuse. I think he was jealous of Sterling even though he would have done anything for his family.

He was amazing like that. Paul was a big part of Sterling not feeling like he could be his true self. You should see some of the stuff Paul posts on Facebook. It's really disturbing.'

'It doesn't seem like Sterling had much contact with his siblings,' I say.

'I don't think he did. Especially not Paul. It made him really sad, the way his family didn't accept so much about him.' Brodie's mouth pulls into a bizarre shape as he tries to stifle a sob. 'I'm dreading the funeral. Do you know how weird it will be for me?'

'It must be very difficult,' I say gently, trying to imagine being in Brodie's position.

He nods, tears spilling from his eyes. 'I'm so lonely without him,' he says, his body trembling through a contained sob. 'I'm not close to my family, I don't have that many friends. I wish so badly he was still here.'

'You have Lizzie,' I say tentatively.

His dark eyes glisten. 'I like Lizzie, I do, and she's good to me . . . but, well, I know this sounds weird but Sterling was the one who held us all together. Without him around it feels unnatural. Plus, she has her brother and a ton of friends anyway. They're at the apartment all the time. Especially now. I don't want all that *noise*.'

'Did you feel bad about lying to her like that?' Fleet questions, implying that he should have. 'It's pretty rough carrying on with her boyfriend under the same roof.'

Brodie sighs and briefly puts his head in his hands. 'I know it wasn't right but I believed in what Sterling and I had so much, I guess I just figured it would all work out somehow. I didn't want to hurt Lizzie and neither did Sterling. I think I convinced myself that they would break up. And when she'd moved on, we could make our relationship official.'

'Are you certain she didn't know?' I ask.

'I really don't think so. We were super careful. Sterling was still affectionate to her.'

'Brodie,' I say, 'we don't doubt what you've told us—that you had a sexual relationship with Sterling—but it doesn't help that there was so little communication between the two of you.' I stare at him until he meets my eyes.

'Like I said, we were very careful,' says Brodie flatly. 'He was really paranoid about people finding out. Especially Lizzie.'

'Over the past few weeks there were minimal texts and private messages between you, and barely any calls,' Fleet jumps in. 'That makes it impossible for us to know exactly what kind of relation-ship you had, especially recently.'

Brodie tilts his chin in that defiant way only the young can. 'I know what we had. Me moving in with him made it obvious just how right we were for each other.' His eyes fill with tears. 'When Lizzie wasn't around it was perfect, like we were a real couple.' He wipes at the wetness on his cheeks. 'But you're right, I have nothing to prove it all now. I never thought I would have to. Now I feel like *I'm* dying.' He waves his hands in front of him theatrically before letting them settle in prayer on his chest.

Next to me I can feel Fleet actively rejecting Brodie's drama before he bluntly says, 'I guess from where I sit I'm just struggling to understand why you came forward with all of this. I appreciate that you didn't go to the media, but if no one knew then it has no bearing on the case. Sterling isn't here to verify it. What's the point of us knowing?'

Brodie looks pleadingly at us. 'I just wanted someone to know. I can't tell my parents, I can't tell Lizzie. I wanted someone to know how much I care. I hope he knew. And I want to know who did this to him.'

'I can understand that,' I say, offering a counterpoint to Fleet's harshness. 'It must be hard to keep the level of your pain secret.'

'Exactly,' he says, shuddering. 'It is a nightmare.'

'The problem is,' says Fleet, 'close relationships are the first place we tend to find motive. And we still don't know where you were when Sterling was attacked.'

'I didn't hurt him,' says Brodie firmly. 'I'm not a violent person. I could never do something like that to anyone. Let alone someone I loved so much.'

Fleet looks at him, unblinking. I roll my neck from side to side, stretching out the sore muscles while I keep my eyes on Brodie.

I'm about to speak when Brodie caves under Fleet's stare and says quietly but firmly, 'all I can say is that everything I've told you is true.'

'Do you think Sterling was as serious about your relationship as you were?' I ask gently. 'Is that something you worried about?'

An edge creeps back into his voice. 'I don't know much about anything anymore but I know how we felt about each other.'

'Why do you think he proposed to Lizzie then?' I press.

His jaw hardens as he grits his teeth. 'I'm not sure he did. I think Lizzie's lying.'

Tuesday, 21 August

5.43 pm

I look up from my paperwork and shake my head, trying to get my exhausted eyes to focus. I miss Ben, I realise, identifying the specific ache of want that passes over me. I miss our easy intimacy. I miss his stream of questions and soft smooth skin. I miss holding his small body in my arms. I let my mind wander for a moment, and picture being back in my old lounge room with Ben playing at my feet. But the image won't hold. A cramp forms in my calf. I miss my son but I can't see myself returning to live in Smithson. I shake my head and circle my shoulders in their sockets. Going backwards isn't an option, I think for the millionth time. I need to make this life I've chosen work.

Following Brodie's accusation, we reviewed the reports that the case team had already pulled on Sterling's and Lizzie's credit cards and bank records. There are no transactions that indicate the purchase of an engagement ring. April Wade confirmed that it isn't a family heirloom, and Lizzie says she has no idea where or when Sterling got it. Yesterday afternoon Lizzie agreed to have the ring valued and Chloe accompanied her to a jeweller. While the gemmologist confirmed the high value of the stone in the popular vintage setting, the origins of the ring remain a mystery.

After our review of this material, Fleet called Lizzie and had her describe Sterling's proposal to us again. She detailed a bended knee over a romantic home-cooked meal at their apartment the week before he died. Sure enough, Wade purchased an expensive bottle of champagne and spent over a hundred dollars at a gourmet food wholesaler in the early evening of the night she claims he proposed. And his credit card records show a purchase of flowers for good measure. I remember a vase of fading white roses wilting on Lizzie's kitchen bench the day we visited. Brodie was on a night shoot that evening, a TV commercial set in a supermarket, so Sterling and Lizzie had the place to themselves.

I keep playing our conversation with Wendy Ferla over in my mind—the part when we told her about Sterling's engagement. And the look on April's face when we told her. Clearly, neither woman knew as much about Wade's life as they would have liked. It seems that, despite his open and friendly nature, he kept things from a lot of people.

'Quite the home bloody cook, wasn't he?' says Fleet, reviewing the receipt from the gourmet food and wine store: a range of cheeses, a fillet of salmon along with fresh herbs and a side of white asparagus.

'He was a total catch,' I agree.

'Yeah. Apart from the secret gay relationship,' Fleet says, fetching some water from the cooler and placing a cup in front of me. 'And the possible affair with his co-star.'

I smile in thanks and take a large gulp.

We seem to have retained our easy rhythm since my call to him on Sunday morning. I think we both know that any leeway we had with Isaacs is gone now—the clock is well and truly ticking, and we're both feeling it. It makes sense that we buckle down and work closely together, and get the best out of our team.

'Christ, all these interviews,' Fleet mutters, scrolling aggressively down the screen with his battered computer mouse. When he came in this morning, I noticed that he was looking better than I've ever seen him. He has shaved, revealing creamy skin, and there's product in his hair. He probably figures he'll be on the news at some point soon. It's a good bet: Wade's looming funeral is like blood in sea water and the sharks are going mad.

'I don't know how Wade had time to do the TV show,' Fleet says, 'let alone anything else. I swear to god the guy was just chatting up journos the whole time.'

'I know, the publicity alone seems like a full-time job.'

Even though I know that Sterling was a big-name celebrity, I'm still surprised by the amount of recent content available about him. In the past month alone, he features in over forty interviews, and hundreds of fresh pictures are available online. I click on another article, 'Wade Wades In', and am treated to photos of Sterling in sky-blue board shorts swimming in the ocean with a male friend and a border collie at St Kilda Beach.

'God, I hate the internet,' I sigh.

Fleet snorts but I can't tell whether it's in agreement or derision.

'Maybe it's like a kind of therapy?' I continue.

'What is?'

'The interviews. Seriously, I mean, he's done, what, at least three hundred interviews in the past few years. That's a lot of self-reflection. A lot of time talking about yourself. Some people pay big dollars to psychologists for that.'

Fleet snorts again. 'Well, it obviously doesn't work. Aren't most actors in permanent therapy?'

'I guess.' I get up and walk out into the main part of the office to stretch my legs. It's quiet here this evening. There are only the soft murmurs of conversations and the intermittent tapping of computer keys. The mechanical hum of the heater forms a steady backing track.

I fetch a Monte Carlo from the tearoom and grab one for Fleet.

'Thanks,' he mutters, shoving it into his mouth as he scratches at the side of his face.

I go back to reviewing Sterling's financial records. For a man in his early twenties he was making an impressive living. He definitely could have afforded to buy that ring for Lizzie, and it's pissing me off that we can't find any trace of its purchase. I wonder if he had a secret bank account. Or a stash of cash squirrelled away somewhere.

'Sterling must not have realised how bad his parents' financial position was,' I say, looking at the steady deposits of cash into his account. 'He certainly had the ability to help them out.'

'Children don't always behave in the way you would expect, I guess,' Fleet says, his eyes on case reports.

'I suppose not, but still. I'm inclined to think that he just didn't know. If he did know then his brother's right, it seems pretty selfish.'

Fleet makes a non-committal sound. 'Maybe his folks aren't as sweet as they seem. Maybe he offered and they declined. Parents can be stubborn.' Fleet says this last part with feeling.

'Look at all these calls,' I say a few minutes later, flicking through the latest hotline summary. Another generous mix of fantasy and facts for us to follow up. The thump of my headache intensifies.

'So, this is pretty different from working a case in a small town, huh,' Fleet says.

I look up in surprise. It's probably the most conversational thing he's ever said to me.

'Same, same but different,' I say.

'Plan on getting back home much?'

I'm about to reply—some smartarse remark about how I wouldn't want to leave him now that we're such good friends—when Isaacs' head appears in the doorway.

'In here, you two,' he barks.

We exchange a look before getting up and making our way across the room. Nan is at her desk, in the row adjacent to ours, her wide frame aligned with her oversized computer screen as she types aggressively on her keyboard. She appears to take no interest in us but I know she misses nothing. She's like a sly old tabby and I don't doubt for a second that she knows exactly what's what in her alleyway.

We enter Isaacs' office.

'Sir,' I say, in greeting.

'Boss,' says Fleet.

'Sit,' says Isaacs.

We sit. He cracks his knuckles and moves back behind his desk, standing there for a moment before he settles into his worn leather chair. I start to think through what we might have done wrong; the room carries the distinct aura of punishment.

'We have a problem,' he states, his nostrils flaring slightly.

Fleet and I remain silent.

'Wade's blog posts, the ones that were found on his personal computer, have somehow made their way to the media.'

'A leak?' I say.

'It looks that way. We don't think that Wade ever uploaded the files.'

'I just can't believe that anyone on the squad would put the case in jeopardy like that,' I venture.

'Well, you're very naive then,' snaps Isaacs.

I reel back slightly, blood making a beeline to my cheeks.

'Look,' says Isaacs, his voice firm, 'you're both young.'

My hands form fists, which I unreasonably want to use to punch Nan's smug face. Fleet remains erect and stony-eyed, but a little pulse is beating in his neck. He's mad as hell too.

'You're young,' says Isaacs again, in case we missed it the first time, 'and this case is very high profile. It's much more complicated than I first thought. In my experience, when leaks occur it tends to suggest a lack of respect for the case leads.'

I recall all of the faces looking up at us in our meetings, the sense of shared determination in the room, and just can't believe that one of them would put us in this position.

I can virtually hear Fleet begging me to keep quiet but I speak anyway. 'It's a tight group, sir. Considering the hours and the intensity, things have been running smoothly.'

'I don't like having to explain information leaving this office without authorisation,' says Isaacs as if I haven't spoken. 'I've been fairly impressed with how you've both handled things so far but the scrutiny is only getting worse. I've just had word that there will be a story on Wade's blog post running on the news tonight. Leaks are unacceptable and I need to ensure that you two are demanding respect from the team. I want you at one hundred per cent when working together, and I expect rigour in terms of security. Understood?'

I nod and Fleet nods, and for a few seconds the two of us are just sitting there, nodding like idiots.

'The Jacoby case is slowing down,' Isaacs says. 'Nan and Calvin will be freed up soon, and I want them brought across this when they have the capacity. Nan can help manage the younger officers.'

Rage floods through me. The timing of this dressing-down, just as Fleet and I are getting on the same page, seems so unfair.

'Is there anything else, sir?' I ask tentatively, after a few moments.

'I won't bore you with the half of it,' he says, somewhat wearily. 'But suffice to say if we can't put this one to bed it's not good news for any of us.'

Tuesday, 21 August
8.34 pm

Ben is telling me about his football club's end of season award event. His little face fills my phone screen and is lit up with excitement as he asks if I'm coming.

'I'm not sure, sweetheart,' I say, struggling to keep smiling. 'When is it?'

'On Sunday, I think. Dad knows.'

'Well, I'll have to see. My work is pretty busy at the moment.'

'Yeah, that's what Dad said you would say,' he replies.

My hand clenches the phone but I force a little laugh. 'Your dad's a clever guy,' I manage.

'It's going to be so much fun,' Ben continues, and launches into a detailed overview of what a school friend told him happened at last year's function, his right-hand waving in the air as he talks. His two budding adult teeth have given him a slight lisp and my throat constricts as I watch him talk.

We do our star-watching routine, my voice slightly choked up as he exclaims over a rabbit he's convinced he can see in the sky.

Afterwards I'm restless. I pace around the apartment trying to decide what to do. I was supposed to catch up with Josh but he cancelled on me, claiming a hectic workload. I feel a twist of unease in my stomach and wonder if our aborted date on Saturday is the real reason behind his reluctance to meet. If I were him, I wouldn't bother with me either.

In the end, I call Dad. He tells me about a shed that he's building at his friend's place and the new library being built in Smithson.

'It's a beautiful structure, Gemma,' he says. 'Very modern. Like some of the places I saw when we were in Melbourne. You would probably like it.'

'Sounds great,' I reply, realising that Dad still doesn't understand that the reason I left Smithson has nothing to do with the aesthetics of the architecture and everything to do with my constricting throat and racing heart.

'Are you coming home on Sunday for Ben's award night?' he ventures.

I work hard to keep the irritation out of my voice. 'You know how hard work makes it for me to get back, Dad.'

'Of course, of course,' he says quickly. 'I just wondered. Rebecca and I will go, so I'll make sure I take some photos for you.'

I'm annoyed that Rebecca will be there watching my son and I won't. 'Thanks, Dad,' I say after a pause.

'When do you think you'll be coming for a visit?' he asks.

'I'm not sure,' I say stiffly. 'I was thinking that maybe you might bring Ben again in the school holidays. I probably won't have too much time off until much later in the year.'

'Oh well,' says Dad, clearly not keen on the idea. 'Yes, that's something we can think about. It would be good to spend some proper time with you, Gemma.'

We speak for a few minutes longer and then we hang up.

Grabbing my cigarettes from my bedroom drawer I open the sliding door, stepping out onto my tiny balcony. The freezing air rages against the exposed skin on my face and hands as I plonk myself on the upside-down plastic crate under the bathroom window. When I light up, I realise I can no longer deny that I'm smoking again, seeing as this is at least the fifth packet of cigarettes that I've purchased since moving here. A fifteen-year-old habit that I can't afford—either financially or health-wise—but that comforts me. My dad and Scott would kill me if they knew, and based on the rant about all the people smoking that Ben went on when he was here, I don't think he'd be too impressed either. I hear a cough not far away and lean forward to spot the glow of a cigarette tail and the shadowy outline of a guy a few apartments down. I think of all the lonely people sitting on their balconies close by—smoking, freezing their arses off and looking out into the night—and feel a strange little flutter of fondness for my neighbours. The vice-like grip of lonely panic that coursed through me when I lived in the cottage in Smithson has gone, replaced by a steadily growing camaraderie with hundreds of strangers.

I inhale hard and almost gag as the smoke grips my throat. A car's horn blasts on the road below and I'm rewarded with a jolt of vertigo as I look down. The wispy grey clouds I've created brush into my eyes, causing them to water. God, I think, I really shouldn't be smoking.

I've been spending too much money lately—it seems to flit in and out of my bank account like a slippery fish. Even though I earn slightly more now than I used to, things are tight. Rent here is expensive. And Scott hasn't had a great run with work this year: with all the uncertainty around the potential closure of the cannery, there's not a lot of commercial development in Smithson.

I take a final drag and then crush the cigarette into the crowded flowerpot, reuniting it with its yellowing brothers. I think about Isaacs lecturing us earlier and my anger charges back. I get why he believes Fleet and I are a risk—hell, *I* think we're a risk—but I hate the way the skin between his eyebrows creased, and then there was that little moment when I sensed *pity* in his eyes. Pity always drives me spare.

I light another cigarette, just as my work phone rings in my jacket pocket.

'Hey,' I say a little breathlessly, after fumbling to retrieve it.

'Good evening,' says Fleet. 'Got you at a good time?'

I work to calm my racing pulse.

'Of course.'

'What are you up to?'

I take a drag. 'Sitting on my balcony, smoking.'

Fleet emits a healthy belly laugh and I find myself laughing as well. 'Good for you,' he says, still chuckling. 'And a perfectly reasonable response to a pep talk with Mr Fun.'

'I'm so angry,' I say.

'Don't worry, Woodstock,' says Fleet. 'It says more about him than us. He's stressed and worried about his rep. No point getting carried away in his drama.'

'I'm not getting carried away. It just pissed me off.' I suck hard on the cigarette.

'Good,' says Fleet. 'I think you're a better detective when the chips are down. Hey, so, I didn't actually call you to check on your mood, I just thought you would be interested to hear this straight away.'

'What is it?'

'The team working on Ava James's assault claims have picked up another charge that was made against him a few years ago. It was dropped.'

'Interesting,' I say.

Repeat sex offenders make up more than half the criminals reported to the police in Australia so this isn't altogether surprising.

It's also not uncommon for claims to be dropped. Often people, particularly women, can read the unjust writing on the wall, and they decide it's best to try to block out the bad memories and get on with their lives.

'Was it a similar situation?' I ask. 'Another actress?'

'No,' says Fleet, 'but we do know this person. It was Katya Marsh, the film's producer.'

Wednesday, 22 August
7.12 am

Macy is back in her usual spot. Her dark hair curls out from under the heavy woollen loops of her beanie and she is surveying the scene in front of her blankly.

I'm feeling wide awake from an unexpectedly solid night's sleep and the hottest shower I could handle. I place a steaming coffee down in front of her. 'Good morning.'

She shifts her gaze up to settle on my face, shrugs and mumbles her thanks as she takes a sip.

I let a few beats go by. 'I've missed talking to you this week,' I tell her. 'Are you okay?'

'Can't complain,' she says, her voice lacking its usual wry tone.

'Where have you been?' I venture, unsure if she wants to talk to me.

She has more coffee. Wipes her mouth. Shifts into an upright position. 'I been moving around a bit with Lara. She's still not doing very well. I'm trying to look after her but we're both pretty spooked about what happened to Walter.'

I don't say anything, knowing that there's no real comfort I can offer. I imagine what it would be like not having anywhere safe to go. In many ways Macy is invisible but she is also permanently exposed.

'Plus, my back's been playing up,' she continues. 'We went to a shelter for a few nights and slept in a bed. I hate it there with all the people all over the place, but you know,' she shrugs, 'this beautiful body isn't as tough as it used to be.' She flashes me a smile and for a moment the old Macy is back.

'Well, I was worried about you,' I say, feeling utterly useless. 'Is your back better now?'

'It's better than it was,' she says, staring out at the road again before her almost black eyes land on me. 'You worked out who killed that movie star yet?'

'No,' I tell her. 'But we're trying.'

'Humph,' she mumbles. 'You'd want to hurry up. You don't want the rich folk ending up as paranoid as us poor fellas.'

◄O►

The police gym is dark and empty; the line of TVs along the ceiling give it an eerie glow.

I sit astride one of the bikes and pedal up to a steady speed, the burn surging quickly and filling my thighs. When I tune in to the news, the breakfast show hosts are discussing Sterling's funeral tomorrow. They cut to a reporter standing outside the city cathedral who launches into an enthusiastic overview of where all the action will take place.

'Do we know how the family is holding up?' asks the pretty lady in the studio, her taut brow furrowed.

'They're living an absolute nightmare right now,' replies the reporter, his voice running over recent footage of Matthew and April Wade outside their St Kilda hotel, looking scared and disoriented.

'And what about his fiancée, Lizzie Short?' presses the anchor.

'Well, in what should be the happiest time of her life, she is about to farewell the man she was set to spend the rest of her life with,' says the reporter grimly, as a montage of pictures fills the screen, all of the happy couple together.

'And we're hearing that Lizzie had more exciting news to reveal before this tragedy, is that right?' chimes in the male host.

'Yes, that's right, Phil,' says the reporter. 'The production company behind Wade's hit soap, *The Street*, has revealed that Lizzie is set to join the cast later this year. News that is now surely bittersweet for fans who would have loved to see the pair acting opposite each other.'

'In the light of what's happened, will she still be taking the role?' asks Phil.

'It's unclear at this stage. The entire production was shut down after Wade's death last Wednesday but we've been told that filming is set to resume next week. We should know more about how they plan to manage the departure of Wade's character then.'

'Well, one thing is for sure,' murmurs the female host, 'tomorrow is sure to be an incredibly sad day.'

They both make little tutting sounds before moving on to a story about hormones in meat, and I ease into cool-down mode.

Jumping in the shower, I think about how odd it will be for Lizzie to work with Sterling's old cast without him being there. Or maybe it will make her feel closer to him?

I dress and head back into the office, falling into step with Brenton Cardona just as he ends a call.

'Detective Woodstock,' he says, tipping his head.

'Hello, Mr Crime Scene Cardona,' I say, smiling at him.

'Feels like ages since we've met over a pool of blood or a lifeless body.'

'At least a week,' I reply.

'Well, certainly my tweenage daughters have spoken of nothing but Sterling Wade since then. I feel like I know everything there is to know about the poor guy.'

'How are they taking the news?' I ask him as we approach the tearoom.

'Not well,' he replies wryly. 'Though the young are resilient. You'll be pleased to know my eldest asked if I could sneak into the morgue and cut off a piece of Wade's hair to bring home to her. Reckons she could sell it on eBay for thousands.'

'Very opportunistic,' I say, laughing as he shakes his head in mock horror.

'How's it all going?' he asks, his voice suddenly serious.

'Okay,' I say and meet his kind eyes. 'Not as well as we would like though.'

He nods and says goodbye as I step into the case room.

Fleet is leaning over one of the juniors, their eyes trained on her screen. He lifts his head and his dark eyes bore into mine. I shift my gaze, feeling slightly uneasy.

'Anything interesting, guys?' I ask.

Fleet shrugs. 'Not so far.' He straightens up. 'I'm still finding it hard to get a read on Paul Wade. I can't work out if he's as dumb as dog shit or hiding an incredible intellect under that stupid face.'

'Yeah,' I say, scanning the latest in the logbook. 'There's a lot that isn't clear. And I guess we need to talk to Katya March today too.'

Fleet closes his eyes as if in deep thought. He doesn't open them for a long time.

'Are you okay?' I prompt, perplexed at his odd behaviour.

'Yes, yes,' he says. 'Sorry, I'm just thinking. I do that sometimes, you know.'

I roll my eyes. 'Well, maybe save it until the case meeting is over. You can think when we're on the way to find out what Ms March has to say.'

'Aren't you all business today?' he mutters, but his tone is friendly. 'I'll round up the troops.'

I finish scanning the logbook as our uniforms file in, looking at me expectantly. I try to banish the negative thoughts that have me doubting their commitment to the case. Doubting their commitment to me. Surely if one of them leaked the blog post it was down to foolishness, not malice.

'Right, we're one week into this thing and Wade's funeral is tomorrow,' I say to the panel of eager faces. 'It's time to get this done.'

I reel off our areas of focus, then inform the team that Fleet and I are seeing if there is any relevance in the historical charge against Cartwright that was dropped.

Heads nod and notes are made. Surely, I think, looking at them all, we will solve this thing. I clench my jaw, riding a pleasant surge of confidence that we will nail this guy.

'I want Wade's finances looked into again,' I say. 'I want to review anything that doesn't add up. Maybe he was being blackmailed, or perhaps he was mixed up in a business deal that went bad. Maybe he had funds stashed away somewhere. And we still need to work out where that engagement ring came from.'

Fleet and I have agreed that Brodie's doubt about Wade's proposal was an obvious reaction for him to have, but it still bothers us that we can't trace the origins of the ring. Where did Sterling get it from? Could it have been stolen? Given to him?

And I still think it's possible that Sterling told Brodie about the engagement—maybe even broke up with him at some point during that week. If so, in terms of motive, Brodie moves to the top of the list alongside Paul.

'I also want to be alerted if anything pops up on the CCTV as the analysis comes in,' adds Fleet. 'Especially if it looks like someone was fleeing the scene.'

'Lastly,' I say, my voice strong, 'I want to be sure that nothing goes any further than this group. Unfortunately, it seems some information was leaked recently. This is inexcusable. A full internal investigation will be carried out. We need to be a tight team on this. Our ability and professionalism is not to be the focus of news reports, am I clear?'

There is a rumble of agreement as the group rises. I eyeball each of them while they file out. One of the techs pops her head into the room just as the last uniform exits. I raise my eyebrows at her expectantly as she walks over.

'We might have something,' she begins.

'We're taking anything you can give us,' says Fleet.

'Well, we're doing searches on all of Wade's computers, as you know. And we've seized all the shoot tapes from the film and the production company. We've also done a search on one of the film company's computers about their insurance policy. You know, to find out exactly what was covered and what wasn't.' She impatiently pushes her unruly hair behind her ear. 'So, I called the insurance company to get a copy of the policy, and they said that Katya March, Cartwright's executive producer, called them last week, two days before the attack on Sterling, asking that the full policy be sent to her as well.'

Wednesday, 22 August
1.28 pm

Katya March crosses and then uncrosses her long legs. Her knitted black jumper has a large blue embroidered eye, adorned with sequins and pieces of loose thread, on the front. She is wearing an aqua beret and her lips are the brightest shade of red I have ever seen. She looks like a piece of art.

Loud pop music blares from the speakers hanging on the wall in the cafe and blends with the rock song a busker positioned outside the main door is playing on his guitar. A waitress with a tear-drop tattoo on her cheek takes our order, swaying to the music as she scribbles on her notebook.

'I was worried about the production,' Katya says. 'I just wanted to ensure I covered all our bases.'

'What were you worried about in particular?' I ask.

Katya looks at us, clearly weighing up what to reveal.

'He was using again,' she says, after we've ordered.

'Sterling?' Fleet asks.

'No!' she snaps, then lowers her voice. 'Cartwright.'

'Drugs?' I ask.

'Of course, drugs. Anything he can find, generally.'

The waitress deposits coffees in front of us and I wait for her to walk off before I ask, 'Did you see him using?'

'Believe me, you can tell. When he's on it, he's bouncing off the walls.'

'Tell us about the sexual assault charge you filed against Cartwright a few years ago,' I say.

She purses her lips as she loads a teaspoon of sugar into her drink. 'That's in the past.'

'Take us on a trip down memory lane,' says Fleet.

She sighs. 'Look, it was a big misunderstanding. Riley is an intense guy. We were working together around the clock on a film and there was a lot of pressure. I didn't get how the industry worked back then. I was young and I freaked out. Reacted too quickly. After a while I realised that Riley has his issues but isn't a bad guy. I dropped all the charges and we've worked together ever since.' She sips her drink, leaving kisses of red around the rim of the glass. 'He's a genius and I look after him. Or at least I try to.'

'We've heard rumours of gambling,' I venture. 'Do you think . . . ?'

'Yep,' she cuts me off. 'It's all linked. Drugs, booze, money. Like a game of dominoes. He's an all-or-nothing kind of guy.'

'Was that how it was with you?' asks Fleet, noisily slurping his drink. 'He wanted it all?'

'Like I said, I was young back then,' she says firmly. 'I misunderstood the situation. He didn't mean anything by it at all.' She drops more sugar into her coffee and gives it a forceful stir as if to change the subject. 'The worst part is that I really fought for him to do this film. I thought he was ready.' She takes a sip. 'That's why I was so fucked off when I could tell he'd started to slip.'

'Let's talk about Ava James for a minute,' I say.

Katya rolls her eyes.

'I'm assuming you're aware that Ms James has made a formal complaint about Cartwright, which we're looking into.'

Katya gives a tiny nod.

'We know Sterling was pretty protective of Ava,' I continue. 'And that he confronted Cartwright about his inappropriate behaviour toward her last week. Do you think Cartwright was pissed off that he was getting in the way? If he thought they were hooking up in secret, he might have been pretty jealous.'

'Look, I heard all the rumours about Sterling and Ava but I don't know.' She pushes her hair away from her face and it stands up tall in a little quiff. 'Maybe they were screwing, maybe they weren't. Sterling was protective of her though, that's for sure.'

'Protective enough to make Cartwright feel threatened?' Fleet presses.

Katya shrugs. 'He was annoyed at being lectured about it. He was always calling Ava, pretending he wanted to talk about the movie but really just trying to hook up with her. Ava seemed fine with it at first. I think it was Sterling who made her think it was a big deal. She's a total drama queen. To be honest I think she liked the attention until she didn't.'

I tilt my head, disappointed in her flippant dismissal of Ava's claims.

'Were you there when Cartwright and Wade argued?' Fleet asks.

'Yeah. It was just Sterling being Sterling. He had a real righteous streak.'

'How heated was it?' I ask.

She shrugs. 'Heated enough.'

'Did they kiss and make up?' asks Fleet.

'Sort of. I think Cartwright was shocked at being called out on the thing with Ava. People don't normally stand up to him like that. But he and Sterling spoke on the first day of filming and they were fine.

The whole situation wasn't ideal but, like I told you, Cartwright's not rational when he's like this.'

'Do you think he had anything to do with what happened to Sterling?' I ask, trying to ignore the gaze of the huge staring eye on her jumper.

She looks at us like we're mad. 'No way,' she says. 'Cartwright's a good guy, he's just a bit of a mess. He mixes with some shitty people, sure, but he doesn't benefit from Sterling's death. No one does.' She fiddles with her watch, an oversized wooden panel with black hands and markings. 'Believe me, this is beyond a disaster to manage. No one knows how to deal with it.'

'Well, he doesn't have to do the film now,' I point out. 'but he still gets paid, right? He can sit around at home out of his mind. Maybe he was looking for an out and thought this was it. Maybe he was pissed off after that argument and just figured to hell with the whole thing. Maybe he didn't want to have anything to do with Ava after her rejection and was worried that she might report him. Could he have called on one of his drug-dealing mates to deal with Wade?'

Katya looks at me, eyes wide as if it's just sinking in that Cartwright might be in serious trouble. 'No way, I can't see it. He's not malicious. Plus, and maybe you don't get this, but it doesn't matter how fucked up he is, he would always want to make the film. Movies are his passion. In a way, that's all he's got.'

Wednesday, 22 August

3 pm

Wiry bristles have sprouted on Cartwright's cheeks and chin since we saw him on Saturday morning. It seems he's slept very little during that time. His eyes are carved into his face and his movements are small and jerky, the ticking of his thoughts seeming to echo around the room.

'Ah, sorry,' he says, gesturing at his messy loungeroom, 'I was going to tidy up a bit this morning but we had a fire evacuation, if you can believe it. Um, maybe sit here.' He sweeps a pile of newspapers and clothes along a small futon to clear a space, clapping his hands as he looks at us expectantly.

'Thank you,' I say, plonking myself down firmly.

Riley's apartment seems to match him perfectly. It's haphazard and seems to transcend eras. It's a bit rock, a bit pop and very eclectic. I'm tempted to water some neglected-looking indoor plants that run along the wall under the mounted flatscreen TV.

'I'll stand,' says Fleet, his eyes on a fresh newspaper that rests on a slab of beer. Sterling's perfect face stares up at the ceiling with the words 'FINAL ACT' in giant letters next to it.

Riley hovers for a second, looking between the two of us, and then sits on a small stool across from me. 'It's just so bad,' he says, seemingly to himself. 'I just keep playing that moment over and over in my mind.' He puts his head in his hands. 'Do you think it would have made a difference? If I'd realised earlier?'

'Doubt it,' says Fleet bluntly, 'the knife went straight through his heart.'

'God,' Riley chokes out.

'We've been hearing that you haven't been in the best state of mind lately,' says Fleet, flicking dirt from under his fingernails. 'Even before the attack on Wade.'

Riley jerks his eyes away from Fleet's hand and meets his gaze. 'I told you, it's always stressful shooting a big film. Making movies isn't just about the art anymore, I can tell you that for sure. It's about the big fat executives getting bigger and fatter.'

'Nah, that's not what I'm talking about.' Fleet obnoxiously clicks his tongue. 'We hear you've been a bit of a mess. Maybe taking things you shouldn't.'

Riley scowls but then his jaw wobbles and he looks around the room as if he's hoping someone will appear and distract us. 'I've not been in a good place.'

'How's your drinking?' I look pointedly at the kitchen bench where empty brown glass bottles are scattered.

'Fine, thanks.'

'That's not what we've heard,' I press.

'Okay, I drink a lot, but so what? Who doesn't these days?'

'Wade didn't,' I respond. 'It seems like he was quite the kale-eating fitness freak.'

'Yeah, well. Mr Perfect was on the other side of the camera. It's different for actors. They just turn up and get all the glory.' Riley's snort turns into a bitter laugh.

'We've also heard that Ava James isn't the only woman you've had a bit of hassle with over the years,' Fleet adds. 'Katya filed a complaint a few years ago.'

Cartwright itches at his wrists. 'That was nothing. Katya and I are mates now. She overreacted to some friendly attention, but we sorted it out. Ava's the same—if I could just talk to her about it, we'd be fine.' He looks toward the kitchen and his face shakes with a small tic. I notice the tremors in his hand as he scratches his face.

'That is not a good idea,' I say. 'I strongly suggest that you leave Ms James alone.'

His gaze drifts to the floor and I'm not sure he's even listening to us.

'Were you committed to this movie?' asks Fleet.

'One hundred per cent,' says Cartwright. 'This year was all about this movie for me. If I'm honest, it was keeping me going. I'd waited a long time for it to happen. I don't know what I'm going to do now.'

'Maybe the answer is in that pile of mail,' says Fleet, gesturing toward two large stacks of unopened envelopes resting on a fat leather ottoman. He pushes away from the wall and walks toward the door, fingering framed photos as he passes. 'Unless it's just a load of bills.'

'Mr Cartwright,' I say, 'the issue we have is that through our investigations it's become clear that you've had regular communication with several people we happen to know quite well.'

'I don't know what you mean,' says Cartwright, shifting his weight from one foot to another.

Fleet sighs exasperatedly. 'What we're trying to say is that while you obviously didn't attack Wade yourself, you certainly know people who wouldn't have blinked an eye at doing something like this. Are you understanding us now?'

'I had nothing to do with this,' says Cartwright, his eyes huge. 'I swear.'

'Good,' I say. 'You have nothing to worry about then.'

Riley licks his lips. 'What are you going to do? Will you go through my bank accounts and stuff like that?'

A message appears on my phone: the team think they've located Paul Wade's mystery sex worker. I look at Fleet who is reading his phone too, clearly having received the same message.

'Don't worry, Mr Cartwright,' he says, glancing up at Riley. 'We'll be in touch if we discover anything else we need to talk to you about. In the meantime, you just focus on keeping your nose out of trouble. We're watching.' Fleet looks pointedly at the small mirror on one of the kitchen stools and wipes at his nostrils.

I stand and Riley shifts forward, about to do the same.

'It's fine,' I say to him. 'Don't get up.'

We turn around at the door. Cartwright is standing in the middle of the room, his brow furrowed as if he's trying to figure out what to do next.

'Maybe get some sleep,' suggests Fleet. 'It's a big day tomorrow.'

Thursday, 23 August

10.19 am

'Listen to this,' I say to Fleet, reading from an online article as we head in the direction of the church. '*A select group of mourners will bid popular actor Sterling Wade farewell today in a private funeral in Melbourne. His family members have asked for privacy and respect as they remember the murdered star. Homicide detectives are still baffled by the bizarre attack on Wade just over a week ago, which took place on the set of his latest film* Death Is Alive, *and will not confirm if they are actively pursuing any suspects.*'

'Well, they would know,' says Fleet, sounding annoyed.

'They go on to talk about how Ava hasn't been invited to the funeral and how it's basically going to be a who's who of the Australian film industry.' I keep scrolling. 'There's also a link to an exclusive Sterling Wade photo gallery, including never-before-seen family photos.'

'Just what his parents will want today, I'm sure,' says Fleet, lighting a cigarette. 'Here, show me.' He gestures for me to give him my phone, smoking furiously as he scrolls. 'God, would you look at the comments?' he says, smirking. 'Who are these people?' He glares at random passers-by as if they might be responsible for the words he's reading on my phone. 'I mean, come on, we have someone called *Sterling's Wife* pledging to name her first-born child after him.' His thumb flicks across the screen. 'Plus there's a whole lot of people who think we're doing a shit job—in their expert opinion, of course.' He hands back my phone and bins his cigarette. 'Let's get a coffee before the sideshow,' he says, already walking off.

We stop at the cafe where we met for breakfast on Sunday and order coffees. Fleet remains moody, stretching his legs out under the table and texting on his personal phone.

I look at him and wonder what's going on in his world.

'Pretty rough on Lizzie having rumours of Wade's affair with Ava splashed all over the news on the day of his funeral,' I say, trying to get him to talk to me.

'I'm sure she has other things to worry about,' he replies, not looking up from his screen, 'like what lipstick shade is mourning appropriate.'

Our coffees finished, we head toward the church. The service isn't due to start for thirty minutes but already it looks like the red carpet of a daytime awards show. Alongside the glamorous crowd there's a cluster of camera lenses, their shiny unblinking eyes pointing at the guests like rifles.

'Private funeral, my arse,' mutters Fleet, throwing gum into his mouth.

The scene is an assault on the senses: beautiful women teetering on high heels gush loudly as they greet each other, hugging and kissing as if they're returning from war, but I can also feel the desperation of the media, the hope that those gathered to farewell Sterling Wade will display some unguarded moments of emotion to be captured and beamed around the globe.

Near the tall church doors, I spot two blond heads: Sterling's siblings. Their pale hair is slicked back unattractively. Paul looks particularly sullen. I can't see Matthew or April but I can see Amy and Steve Beauford, the epitome of glamorous grief, standing with a young blond man—probably their son, Jack, who looks a lot more like Sterling than either of his biological siblings do.

I look again at Paul, who appears to be kicking some rubbish off the top step. He alternates between adjusting his tie and rubbing his hands together.

Joanne Scanlon, a tall skinny girl with fine threads of long brown hair, has provided Paul with an alibi for just over an hour last Wednesday afternoon. She says he picked her up in St Kilda and drove her to a corporate car park. She gave him a blow job in the back of his van, then some time later they had sex. He then dropped her back where he'd found her. She knows this all happened after 2.30 pm but can't be sure of the exact time.

'He didn't say much,' Joanne told us. 'He was kind of a silent type. But he handed over the money no problems, which is all I ask for.'

'You wouldn't guess that Paul could go twice in an hour, would you?' says Fleet, still fidgeting next to me.

I don't respond but watch as batches of handsome people make their way toward the huge doors, pausing to show ID and be crossed off the guest list. I watch as a woman passes her large handbag to a guard so he can riffle through its contents before lifting her arms to be scanned. The cameras pick up their pace, a chorus of clicks ringing in my ears.

I feel apprehensive, and removed from the whole thing as if someone is about to call out 'Cut!' and everyone will laugh and snap out of the sombre mood.

Several reporters talk earnestly into video cameras, gesturing to the stars behind them as they smooth windswept hair. Despite the oversized sunglasses worn by most guests, I can see a lot of familiar faces: it's as if Sterling Wade's funeral exists in a parallel universe, with some of Australia's most loved characters stepping outside their worlds, blurring into reality and coming together in the name of grief.

A pack of skinny young men with carefully trimmed beards appears from around the corner, and the journalists roll toward them like a wave. I give Fleet a questioning look. 'The puppy pack,' he explains. 'Those kids are all hot stuff, earning a crap load more than you or I ever will, just by standing around and looking pretty.'

'Speak for yourself,' I joke, straightening my bulky shirt and fluffing my hair.

'Come on,' Fleet says, looking up at the church. 'Time to go in.'

As the mourners continue to file into the church, the clouds seem to lift as if they're trying to get as far away from the sadness as they can. I shiver when a gust of wind charges around us, and I make eye contact with a square-jawed man I'm pretty sure stars as a cop in a TV series. We exchange polite smiles and I wonder if Sterling Wade's killer is here somewhere, watching.

◀○▶

The service feels perfunctory, as if the Wades just want the whole thing done with. Matthew reads out a short religious passage and talks briefly about Sterling as a child. His commentary stops short of Sterling's teenage years. April's sobbing echoes around the church as he talks. The minister takes over after that, detailing the remaining decade of Wade's life like he's reciting his résumé. Then Lizzie briefly rises, flanked by Kit and a girlfriend. Looking frail in a long black lace dress, she declares her eternal love for Sterling, promising to do all the things they had planned to do together. 'I promise I will make you so proud of me,' she says, looking at Sterling's coffin, her chin wobbling.

After this, a diverse symphony of sobs provides a soundtrack, their echoes creating a whirlpool in the high ceiling. Shapely arms heavy with jewels are lifted to wipe teary eyes. A tiny old lady, almost hidden beneath an oversized hat, moans intermittently as a stunning young man pats her back reassurringly.

I watch April shuffling along behind her son's coffin, her elbow linked with Wendy Ferla's as if they're schoolgirls. April seems shrunken and confused. At one point she looks my way, but there is no recognition in her gaze. Medicated, I think, recognising the cloudy stare.

Lizzie cries neatly into a black handkerchief, the reassuring arms of her brother and friend around her. She gives the Wades cursory embraces outside the church before being pulled into a circle of young women who paw at her, stroking her hands and hugging her tight.

'It's all very polite, isn't it?' says Fleet, picking at some fluff on his jacket.

I spot Brodie, pale and ethereal, hovering like a ghost just to the left of the action, clearly unsure of his place. He seems to gravitate toward an oblivious Lizzie, whom he follows around like a timid dog.

In contrast, Cartwright leans against the wall of the church beside Katya, observing the scene from behind Ray-Bans as he smokes aggressively.

The journalists are still breathless as they fuss around the tear-stained clusters of stars, doling out condolences and begging for sound bites that can be wrangled into headlines.

Fleet coughs noisily and looks across the busy street. The stream of cars is at a standstill, all eyes trained on the action outside the church rather than on the road ahead. On the footpath a guy wearing earphones is so distracted by the sight of a high-profile newsreader that he walks into a bin.

'Well, this has been fun, despite not prompting a public confession,' says Fleet. 'Should we grab something tasty and head back to the office?'

'Sure,' I say, throwing one last glance at the Wades. Melissa and Paul look stiff in their ill-fitting clothes, and Melissa is deep in discussion with the funeral director and a man I assume is the head of security; she points to the media scrum, indicating that she wants them kept at bay. Matthew and April have eyes only for their dead son's coffin, which rests in the back of the hearse. Several security guards in suits roam the area and two flank the rear of the hearse, forcing mourners to give it a wide berth.

I tear my eyes from the familiar faces and fall into line with Fleet. Lizzie stands a few metres away from Sterling's family, gripping Kit's hand and talking earnestly to a serious-faced journalist with a microphone, her gaze continually drawn back to Sterling's coffin.

'No Ava,' I comment.

'Nope,' says Fleet, squinting into the white winter light. 'I guess she really wasn't invited.'

We cross the rain-slick road.

'It does seem odd she wasn't welcome,' I say. 'She and Sterling were friends and the service didn't seem that exclusive, despite the media beat-up.'

'Maybe the family didn't want even more of a scene than it actually was. With Ava would have come more media and security. Lizzie probably didn't want to deal with it and got in Melissa's ear.' He slows outside a greasy-looking hole in the wall that promises chips, gravy and hotdogs. I wrinkle my nose. 'You can get a salad next door,' he says helpfully.

'I wonder what she's doing right now,' I say.

'You mean Ava?' he asks.

'Yeah. It would be weird not to be invited to the funeral of someone you care about. It seems pretty petty.'

'Come on, Woodstock. You know as well as I do that death makes people even pettier than life does.'

'True,' I say, watching a huddle of sparrows fight over the remains of a meat pie.

'But you've got me thinking about what lovely Ava might be up to in that huge hotel room.' He makes his voice all dreamy. 'Assuming she's not sticking pins in a Riley Cartwright voodoo doll, maybe she's trying to distract herself from her grief. A nice bubble bath, maybe? Some scented candles. Maybe a sneaky glass of bubbles and a good cry. And then, if it all gets too much, perhaps a hand might drift to her creamy thighs—'

'Order me some chips,' I snap, stomping off before he can reply.

I walk up to Swanston Street, just wanting to get away from him for a moment. A homeless man lurches into my shoulder, asking me for money. Some young girls run past, knocking him out of the way and forcing me to step into the gutter.

A dusting of rain begins to fall and I join a cluster of people under the awning of a shoe shop. I lean forward to look along the street and see if Fleet is approaching. Damned if I'm going back to get him. I smile at a round-faced little girl as I exhale warm air into the chill. Finally I spot Fleet making his way through the crowd, carrying two paper bags.

Just then Mary-Anne calls, confirming that the lab has found traces of Walter Miller's blood on the knife used to stab Sterling Wade.

Thursday, 23 August
3.37 pm

A breakthrough can drive a case forward, unblock a jam and provide a clearer pathway—or it can bring everything to a grinding halt. I'm now worried that linking the Wade case to Walter's death will result in the latter.

'Right, everyone,' I say. 'Sit down, please. We have news.'

The case room zips into immediate silence, the air flush with anticipation.

'So,' says Fleet laconically, scratching his back and lifting his shirt in the process, 'it seems that two of our cases have come together.'

Eyes widen and foreheads rumple.

'The blood work suggests that the knife used to kill Sterling Wade was used less than forty-eight hours earlier in the stabbing death of Walter Miller, the 62-year-old homeless man killed in Carlton,' I inform them.

'Now, there is more than one explanation for this,' I continue calmly. 'It's possible that Miller's killer dumped the knife somewhere and that Wade's killer found it before using it. However, this is highly unlikely as the wounds are so similar, almost identical.

Based on the evidence we currently have, we think we're looking for the same perpetrator.'

Everyone is nodding, clearly doing what we've been doing these past few days—trying different theories, seeing what fits.

'I want to be very clear: we do not think that this necessarily means our perpetrator will kill again, but it's a possibility. We also don't know if this means our victims were connected to each other. Nothing has turned up so far.'

'From here,' Fleet says, 'we'll merge the two investigations. Current work on all live leads should continue, but we need to shift the focus to any links to Miller and actively check alibis for both crimes. We obviously know more about Wade's network than Miller's, so we'll start there, but we need to work from the other direction too.'

'We must find out if Miller was in contact with anyone involved in the movie—perhaps a crew member who volunteered with the homeless,' I say. 'We think it's possible Miller came across some information that became problematic for our attacker.'

Fleet details an action plan for the next forty-eight hours, and we reinforce the need for absolute diligence with all case information. Ralph, who is in the final stages of handing over the reins of the Miller case, watches on gracefully, his world-weary expression indicating that he's happy to let the kids have a turn in the driver's seat.

◄◦►

'Right, let's Cluedo,' says Fleet, pretending to make a magnifying glass with his fingers.

'Don't be an idiot,' I retort. Earlier I told him that my old partner Felix and I used to joke about playing Cluedo when we were trying to figure out a case, and Fleet rolled his eyes and made a sarcastic jibe about my country ways.

'Nah, come on,' he says, 'I'm serious. I think it will help loosen up my theories. Like a board game enema.'

He gives me a sweet look and I soften. It's so much easier when we're getting along.

'Okay, Colonel Mustard, let's play.'

We're alone in the case room, the last of the uniforms having left five minutes ago. The finality of Wade's funeral lingers and I feel the pressure of a solve more sharply than before. It's always better to nail a case before a body is farewelled—the closure is much neater for everyone.

'Both attacks were aggressive,' I begin, looking at the enlarged autopsy photos.

'But precise,' suggests Fleet. 'One clean wound. The person was in complete control, even if they were a tad insane. They can manage their emotions.'

I push off from my chair and stretch out my aching back. 'Maybe it's one of those mental illnesses where you think someone is asking you to do something. Like voices in the head. Apparently that's how a lot of stalking cases start out. People think they are being instructed to follow certain people.' I pause to chew the edge of a corn chip. 'Did you read that stuff on celebrity stalkers that the psych in Sydney sent us?'

'Yep,' says Fleet cheerfully. 'That was some fucked-up shit.'

'We can't discount it.'

'No, we can't. It's still very likely that our guy is some deranged loner who isn't on our radar yet. So let's leave that fine specimen at the top of the list. Suspect number one: a nameless, crazy, right-handed stalker with delusions of power, on the movie set with a sharp knife, and who wasn't known to Wade, Miller or us.' Fleet looks at the board.

I let a beat slide by. 'You still don't think that's right though, do you?'

'Not really,' he says. 'Do you?'

'I'm not sure. I still feel like our other suspects hold a lot of promise. Especially based on all the other things that were going on in Wade's life.'

'I agree,' says Fleet, pointing at Paul Wade's licence photo.

'Suspect two,' I say. 'A jealous, lying older brother with a weak alibi and a history of violence who worried that his parents were facing bankruptcy and saw a way to put things right. Thoughts?'

Fleet yawns. 'I find sibling rivalry so tedious. I mean, why can't everyone just be happy for their ridiculously successful sibling and enjoy the expensive Christmas presents?'

A young woman walks past our open door, notices us and circles back. 'Do you guys want a coffee?'

'No thanks,' we say, holding up our tepid mugs in unison.

'Tedious or not,' I say to Fleet, facing the board again, 'that sibling thing might gnaw away at you. Feeling inferior all those years, watching Sterling's star rise and rise. The relentless narrative of the golden child—whereas from Paul's perspective, he's just the brother who shirked his duty. Then your parents hit hard times, and you and your sister are the ones left to pick up the pieces, so it seems even more unfair. Paul and Sterling spoke that Sunday night for the first time in ages. Paul says he was pissed off, and Brodie says they argued. Maybe Paul just flipped.'

Fleet blinks a few times and then squints at the picture. 'They barely look like brothers, do they?'

I look up at Paul's round face, dull gaze and limp yellow hair. 'No, not really.'

Fleet tips his head to the ceiling, causing his neck to crack. 'Okay, so Paul comes to Melbourne sometime between Sunday night and Wednesday morning. He could have killed Miller, although why? We know he gets his rocks off in the back of his van with a prostitute between 2.30 and 4 pm on Wednesday. And then what, he goes to the film set, whips on a zombie costume and stabs his brother? It doesn't play for me.'

'I agree,' I say. 'But then, where was he for those missing few hours?'

'Dunno,' says Fleet. 'Maybe doing something else he doesn't want us to know about.'

I glance back at Paul's photo.

'Maybe,' I say. 'Okay, well, next we have the secret lover who was sick of being a secret.'

'I definitely think Kent's hiding something,' says Fleet. 'There's something off about him.'

I look at Brodie's photo. 'Really? I just think he seems completely broken. Like he's still in shock. Plus, I still don't see motive. Maybe he found out about the engagement and was upset, but attacking Wade in response like that? It doesn't add up. And can you imagine him killing Walter Miller?'

'Obsession and love are good friends though, right?' says Fleet. 'Maybe he lost his mind at the thought of losing Wade. He went into a rage. It's happened before.'

I meet Fleet's eyes, thinking. 'True. But Brodie seems genuinely devastated.'

'His alibi is a total piece of shit. For both of the murders.'

'Also true,' I agree with a sigh.

Fleet stands up and points at two photos on the board in quick succession. 'Unlike the newly engaged Lizzie Short.'

'Lizzie might be involved,' I say, as images of Brodie and Sterling embracing push into my mind. 'She might have found out about Wade's infidelity and convinced Brodie that he was being used too. Maybe they teamed up.'

'Jesus, Woodstock, this isn't *The First Wives Club*.'

'Think about it,' I say. 'It makes sense. Whether he had bad intentions or not, Sterling was using them both.'

'Sure, it sucks. But there is no benefit in having him dead, is there?'

'Unless they just wanted him gone? They were humiliated and wanted to punish him?'

Fleet slaps either side of his face gently, probably struggling to stay alert. 'Ava might have wanted her knight in shining armour out of the way as well,' he points out. 'She could be lying about Cartwright, or exaggerating.'

'Dangerous territory,' I warn, 'accusing a woman of making a false harassment claim.'

'I know, I know,' he says, lifting his arms in the air, 'but hear me out. What if Ava wanted Sterling to think Cartwright was hassling her? She might have been trying to cause trouble between the two of them.'

'It's possible,' I allow, 'but then look at the calls Cartwright made to her and the fact that Katya made a claim in the past. It's pretty clear he has a problem with women. I bet there are others.'

'Maybe Ava didn't like Sterling treating her like a damsel in distress. Or maybe she thought it would lead to a romantic relationship and he shut her down.'

'There's still nothing but rumour to suggest they were involved,' I remind him.

'Yeah, and attacking him or getting someone else to seems like a pretty extreme response to being rejected,' he admits.

'These people *are* extreme though,' I muse, 'and used to getting their own way. But I think Ava is a long shot. And what about Miller—why would she kill him?'

'Okay, but Cartwright clearly had stuff going on,' says Fleet. 'He argued with Wade on Sunday. He probably felt like things were unravelling. He's under a ton of pressure, he's back on the drugs, and then his picture-perfect leading man is lecturing him about how to behave. Maybe he imploded.'

'Maybe,' I say, trying to think, 'but once again, how does it link to the Miller case?'

Fleet shrugs. 'Clearly he didn't commit either of the crimes himself. Maybe one of his drug buddies was booked twice that week?'

I press my fists against my head. 'It doesn't make sense. Why would a hit man drop his knife?'

'It all makes sense if the killer is some nutter,' points out Fleet. 'Perhaps we're looking for logic where there is none.'

'I know, I know.' I sigh, standing up, hands on my hips, barely seeing the case board anymore as my eyes stare through it. 'And then we're back to the random stranger again.'

Fleet cuffs me lightly on the shoulder. 'We aren't going to finish this game of Cluedo tonight. Come on, Miss Scarlet. It's time to get some shut-eye.'

Friday, 24 August
10.52 am

My phone buzzes in my pocket as we're grilling Brodie Kent. We've discovered he volunteered at a large city homeless shelter when he first moved to Melbourne from Adelaide, and we're trying to establish if he crossed paths with Walter Miller. Frustratingly, the paperwork on file at the shelter is as vague as Brodie about his time there. Since Sterling's funeral, the little light he had left inside seems to have disappeared and he speaks in a flat monotone. I fantasise about parting his thick hair and splitting his head down the middle, peeling back his scalp and seeing the truth that lies within. As much as I sense his grief is genuine, his inability to be definite about his whereabouts is making me uneasy.

Brodie says that last Monday evening he was watching TV at the apartment with Sterling and Lizzie until about 9 pm. Then he went into the city and had a few drinks, before buying a ticket to a late movie session at Melbourne Central. He says he walked home just after midnight, getting there sometime after 1 am. Circumstantially, he is shaping up to be our strongest suspect.

'Will Lizzie be able to confirm you were watching TV and the time you were out last Monday?' I ask him.

He blinks. 'Yes. But they were both asleep when I got home.'

'Tell us who you remember from the shelter,' I say.

'I don't really remember specific people, more just how working there made me feel,' he says, looking at the table. 'It was very special, helping people like that.' After a minute or so, his eyes widen. 'Do you think someone from the shelter hurt Sterling? Someone who lives on the street?'

'Just try to answer our questions, please,' I reply.

'I was on a lot of drugs back then,' Brodie admits quietly. 'I went to the shelter high quite a lot, so things are hazy. I wish I could help more.'

'And you're certain you went to the movies by yourself last Monday?' I ask, my phone buzzing again.

He nods tiredly. 'Yes, I often go on my own. I used to go to the movies when Sterling was busy with Lizzie. It was a good way to distract myself.'

'Do you have the ticket?' Fleet asks.

'I doubt it. It might be in a pocket somewhere.'

'What about a credit-card record?' I suggest.

'My credit cards are all maxed out,' says Brodie, a little defensively. 'Why are you asking me about where I was that night? Sterling was fine then, he was at home with Lizzie. I don't understand—what is going on?'

Fleet mutters something under his breath before saying, 'The problem is, Brodie, we're having trouble pinning down your whereabouts. You're always on your own and you seem to spend a lot of time just walking around.' Fleet gets up and paces the room in a little circle, stretching his back. 'Don't you have any friends?'

Brodie's eyes flash and he bares his teeth. When he speaks his voice is like a blade cutting across the small table. 'Don't you get it? My entire life was on hold because of him. He swanned around

SARAH BAILEY

with Lizzie, making plans to move overseas, telling me he loved me, to be patient.' The skin on his neck is stretched as he spits out the words. 'And I was just waiting like an idiot, always waiting!' He slams a fist onto the table and bursts into tears.

The room crackles with his outburst. My heart roars into gear and thumps loudly.

Fleet lifts an eyebrow and clears his throat. 'Settle down, mate.'

Brodie's eyes are still full of fury, his hands balled at his sides.

'Does the name Walter Miller mean anything to you?' I ask.

'No!'

I soften my voice. 'Did you know Sterling had been offered a major role overseas?'

Brodie is breathing heavily, as if he's been running. He pushes away from the table and folds his arms, his eyes now completely clear. 'He was always getting offered roles. We talked about it sometimes. I said it would be a good time for him to break up with Lizzie.'

'Did he agree?' I press.

'I think so.'

'Would you have gone with him?' asks Fleet.

'That was the plan, wasn't it?' replies Brodie tersely.

'We don't know, Brodie,' says Fleet, 'was it?'

Brodie scowls and his voice is full of venom as he hisses, 'I don't fucking know either, do I? Maybe he really did propose to her, and I was being fed a bunch of lies. I don't know what to believe anymore.'

We go around in circles with Brodie for a few minutes longer, but he has shut down again. His alibis remain vague and we can't confirm a direct link to Walter Miller despite the shelter connection.

'It's good to see that our apparently spineless friend has at least a tiny bit of backbone,' says Fleet when I return from walking Brodie out.

272

'Yes.' I recall the fury in the young man's eyes. 'He's clearly much closer to the edge than we realised.'

'And more capable of violence than we realised, perhaps?'

'Well, his little blow-up was interesting, but I don't know if it means—' My phone buzzes. 'Yes,' I answer impatiently.

'Hi,' says Chloe. 'Sorry to interrupt, but I wanted to update you on something. Two things actually, both about Paul Wade. Firstly the tech guys have found a money transfer that Sterling scheduled before he died. Five thousand dollars is set to hit Paul's bank account this weekend.'

'Does it have a description?'

'It just says "for dad",' Chloe replies.

'Okay, what else?' I ask, having no idea what the money transfer means.

'Paul has turned up on some city CCTV footage from last Wednesday afternoon. A retail store handed it in this morning.'

'Where was he?' I ask, locking eyes with Fleet, who is obviously desperate to know what is going on.

'Just near the corner of Collins and Spring. It looks like he was walking away from the film shoot just after the attack on Wade took place.'

Saturday, 25 August
11.17 am

The trees close in on me as I steer the hire car nearer to Smithson. I pull the sun visor down in an attempt to block out the unfiltered light. I don't seem to be able to get enough air into the car and I fiddle with the controls again. I decided to come the back way from the airport; it takes the same amount of time but the road is winding and tends to be less popular. Sure enough, I have it all to myself. For one crazy moment, I think that perhaps I'm completely alone, that maybe there is no one else left out there, that everyone has just disappeared. I am achingly tired, the result of a sleepless night paired with an early start. I clutch the steering wheel, my pale hands threaded with fine veins. They don't look like the hands of a mother, or the kind of hands that can take on a killer.

The Wades have been out of contact since the funeral. Paul Wade's mobile has been off since Wednesday; the messages we've left on his phone and with his parents haven't been returned. Melissa's husband Rowan answered his mobile yesterday afternoon but swiftly hung up when we identified ourselves. Sterling's family has gone into lockdown.

'We need to speak with Paul Wade,' I told Isaacs after Fleet and I cornered him in his office yesterday afternoon. 'He lied to us three times—we now have evidence he was in proximity to the crime scene at the time of the attack. Plus, we don't know when he came to Melbourne. He said he sleeps in his van sometimes so it could have been any time from Sunday night onwards. Maybe he arrived earlier in the week when Miller was attacked.'

Isaacs tipped forward and gripped the edges of his desk. 'Is there anything to indicate that Paul Wade knew Walter Miller?'

'Not that we know of. But it does look like the guy spent quite a bit of time in Melbourne for no apparent reason. He's a bit of a drifter so it seems feasible that they came into contact.'

'And you know for sure that Paul went back to Karadine with his family?' Isaacs said.

'We're pretty sure,' Fleet replied. 'We're still waiting on the airlines to get back to us. We had the local cops go around to his mate's address in Castlemaine and he's definitely not there.'

'Alright,' said Isaacs. 'Send an officer up there to speak to him. And find out why the family isn't talking.'

'I was thinking I'd go,' I said, raising my hand like a kid in class. 'It's a short drive from my home town and there's a family matter I need to attend to this weekend anyway.'

There was a short silence. I kept my eyes down and gathered my notebook, standing up as if the decision had already been made.

'Okay,' said Isaacs, 'go to Karadine tomorrow. When can you be back?'

'Monday, sir,' I replied, already wrestling with a bubble of unease at the thought of going home.

I slow down as I reach the familiar T-intersection. Tall grass crowds the bases of the fence posts. In the middle of the road ahead, a large crow feasts on the insides of a dead kangaroo. To the right is Smithson and, a little further along, Karadine. Left leads to the centre of the country. To red desert. To nothing. I look back and forth between the roads, letting the car hum on the spot even though no one is coming.

◄〇►

I pull over a few kilometres from Smithson and call the Wade farmhouse again. I try Paul's mobile, then Melissa's. Still no answer.

I bypass Smithson's main street—I want to get my visit to the Wades out of the way before I surprise Dad and Ben. I think about how happy Ben will be that I can come to his soccer event tomorrow. My body aches to hold him but there's something intoxicating about dragging it out for a few more hours.

About thirty minutes later, a sign informs me that I have reached Karadine. I have only been here a handful of times: it's a tiny farming community that consists of a cluster of shops and a few wineries. I pass the evidence of minor civilisation until the road thins and turns to dirt.

A stream of dust flies out behind me like a smoke signal. Huge gums line both sides of the road, and the fields are dotted with cows and horses. I pass several tired-looking letterboxes, lonely at the tops of driveways that trail off into the distance.

I reach the Wades' property which, unlike the other residences I've passed, has its gate shut. A few bouquets rest near the wooden stumps at either side. Just before I turn the car into the driveway, I pull on the handbrake and quickly jump out, pushing the gate open and collecting the flowers. After stacking them carefully on the passenger seat, I slowly steer the car along the ruler-straight driveway until a ring of vibrant green appears like an oasis. As I draw closer I see a squat stone house nestled on dense lawn among several trees. To my left are acres of picturesque, albeit dry farmland. Beyond the house is a steady climb of mountains.

Parking behind an ageing ute, I study the house. It looks exactly how a farmhouse should look, with fecund herb gardens bursting from under the protection of the eaves and a flourish of wildflowers forming a haphazard barrier along the front.

Before I have the chance to exit the car, the front door swings open and Melissa steps out, her face twisted into a scowl. 'No,' she says, shaking an outstretched hand at me, her whole body leaning forward. 'No.'

'Hi, Melissa,' I say evenly, shielding my face from the sun.

'Please,' she says. 'We've had enough.'

'I need to speak with Paul.'

'No. No speaking about Sterling anymore.' She runs her fingers through her limp hair, pushing it away from her red face. 'Do you know what this is like for people like my parents? They don't deserve this.'

'I need to speak with Paul,' I repeat. 'If he doesn't agree to speak with me here, I'll have to take him back to Melbourne.'

'Why?'

'Can you get him, please? Or I can come with you?'

She huffs air through her nose for a few moments. 'Wait here.'

I slip on my sunglasses and gather up the bouquets, placing them on a patch of lawn out of the sun. Leaning against the car, I breathe in air that is jarringly pure and lightly scented with flowers and grass. Snippets of conversation drift my way before the door swings open again and Melissa heads back toward me with Paul following feebly.

'Hi, Paul,' I say. 'We just need to have a quick chat.' I look around. 'Let's sit over there.' I point to a wooden bench near the side of the house. 'Melissa, you don't need to be here.'

'I better go and be with Mum anyway,' she replies, looking worriedly at Paul. 'Let me know if you, um, need anything.'

After she leaves, I look squarely at Paul, who seems to be having trouble swallowing.

'We know you were in the city when your brother was attacked, Paul. Right near the crime scene.'

'No, I wasn't,' he says sullenly.

'Yes, you were. We have you on tape.'

He twists his hands in his lap, his eyes fixed on the grass in front of us.

'Why do you keep lying to us, Paul?' I say.

'Do I need a lawyer?' he finally asks.

'Up to you,' I reply. 'I'd like to think we can straighten this out but, if you prefer, we can do this formally and you can arrange legal counsel.'

'I don't want to go back to Melbourne.'

'That's fine,' I say. 'But you need to tell me what you were doing in the city on Wednesday, 15 August. We know you were with Joanne until around 4 pm but we have a recording of you walking away from the crime scene about fifteen minutes after your brother was stabbed. What were you doing there, Paul?'

He smacks his hands on the wooden bench either side of him. 'I don't *know*.'

'Were you trying to get close to Sterling, Paul?' I prompt. 'Was there something you wanted to tell him?'

'I don't know,' he repeats.

'Were you angry at him?'

'Sort of.' He kicks at the ground. 'But it wasn't about that. It won't make sense if I try to explain it.'

'Well, let's just start with what you were doing there?' He doesn't reply. I sigh. 'Okay, so we know you and Sterling spoke on the

Sunday evening before he died. Is that why you came to Melbourne? Did he say something during the call that upset you?'

Paul draws a line in the dust with the tip of his boot, throwing a quick glance at the farmhouse. Then he erupts, jolting to his feet. 'We needed money, okay! Mel's kid needs to go to a special school ages away from here.' He gestures around us. 'Mum and Dad won't admit it but their house is falling down around them and the farm's a mess. Sterling brings us some fancy shit we don't need when he visits and thinks it's job done. It was a joke, an absolute joke.'

I don't say anything for a moment, letting his rage fade into the country air.

Then I speak calmly. 'So you called Sterling to ask for money?'

Paul looks surprised to be standing up and doesn't seem to know what to do with his hands. 'It's Dad's sixtieth soon. I thought that maybe if we said we needed money for his birthday, we could use it to help with a few things.'

'Why didn't you just ask him directly? Explain what was going on with the farm. Surely he would have understood.'

'He already thought he was so much better than us. We don't want his bloody handouts.'

'I can understand you didn't want pity, but he was family.'

'Don't you get it? We didn't *want* his help,' hisses Paul, fury bursting from him, 'but we really needed it.' He leans toward me menacingly. 'Do you know how hard it is to make a life like this work?'

'I'm sure it's very tough,' I say.

'Tough!' he spits. 'A farming life is hell on earth and Sterling bailed on us right from the start! He never lifted a finger on the farm but he sure liked bringing it up in every bloody interview. It was good for his image when it suited him.' The blue rings of Paul's eyes are on fire.

'What did he say when you asked him for money?'

'I said we wanted to plan a party for Dad and that we needed a deposit for the hire place, and he started talking about all this stuff we should do, basically taking over and I just lost it. He had no idea. I said that he just needed to give us the money and that Mel and I would sort everything else out, and he got really upset, saying we always left him out and that he wanted to come up with ideas too. As if it was all about him.'

'Did he agree to give you the money?'

'Yeah,' admits Paul. 'He said he'd transfer it to me.'

'How much are we talking?'

'Five grand.'

'Okay, so Sterling agreed to give you some money. I still don't get why you were in the city, Paul.'

He paces on the spot and grabs at his hair. 'I don't know! I don't know why I do half the things I do.' He smacks himself on the forehead with open palms and makes a primal grunting noise. 'I'm an idiot.'

I look at his puffy face and can't help feeling a bit sorry for him.

A tractor starts up in the adjacent field and the roar of its engine drifts across the paddocks. The sun is high above us and I'm clammy inside my jacket. All the open space is making me feel uneasy.

'I just wanted to see the movie being made,' he says to me finally.

'You wanted to watch the film shoot?'

'Yeah.'

'Why?'

'I don't know!' He looks at me, pleading. 'I just wanted to see it, I guess. My brother is a famous movie star and I'm earning less than twenty bucks an hour doing shitty odd jobs.' He wipes his sleeve across his forehead before sitting down heavily and burying his head in his hands. 'Everyone always asks me about what Sterling's doing, and I thought for once it would be cool to say I was there. That I had a VIP pass and watched it live. Sounds fucking stupid now.'

'Tell me where you went,' I say.

'I parked my van near the MCG then I walked up to the corner of Spring and Flinders to where all the barricades were.' He licks his cracked lips. 'People were everywhere but I pushed in to the front, and I could see the director—he was sitting up high on a machine and he had a little screen so you could kind of see what the movie would look like.'

'Did you see Sterling get attacked?'

'Yeah, sort of. I didn't know what was going on until everyone started screaming. I could hear Lizzie mostly and then people were going crazy but I didn't really know what had happened.'

'Why didn't you stay? If you thought your brother was hurt, didn't you want to make sure he was okay?'

Paul looks at me and shrugs. 'Dunno. I just didn't. We're not like normal brothers.'

'You came to Melbourne quite a lot, Paul, didn't you?'

'Sometimes.'

'Did you ever see Sterling, maybe without him realising?'

'I knew where he lived,' replies Paul.

'Is that a yes?' I press.

'I saw him sometimes.'

'When did you come to Melbourne last week, Paul?'

'I drove down on Monday,' he admits. 'I like going there. It's like I'm alone even though there's so many people. Around here every-one's always asking about Sterling—you can't get away from it. Even in Castlemaine people know who I am. In Melbourne I can sort of just disappear.'

I sense a movement at the farmhouse door and I can make out Melissa's silhouette behind the flyscreen.

'Did you ever speak to your brother when you went to Melbourne, Paul?' I ask.

'No,' he shakes his head vigorously. 'I didn't.'

'Why spy on him then?' I press. 'Why seek him out?'

'I dunno,' he says, looking at me desperately. 'I guess I just wanted to see it for myself. You know, his life. I always felt like it could have been me.'

Saturday, 25 August

2.18 pm

I pull up on the street outside Dad's place. It looks exactly the same—with the exception of a large orange pot bursting with flowers, right next to the front door. The colour is jarring against the neutral colours of the house.

I quickly call Fleet and update him on my chat with Paul.

'So he just happens to be in the city metres from where his brother was attacked but had absolutely nothing to do with it?' says Fleet, noisily chewing into the phone.

'That's what he says,' I say.

'You believe him?'

I sigh. 'I think I do.'

'You don't think he got a taste for the idea of having some cash and the potential of a huge payday pushed him over the edge?'

'It's possible. He's definitely angry. He's intensely bitter about Sterling's lot in life compared to his own. And he's a pretty lonely guy.'

'But?'

I try to articulate the hopelessness that Paul Wade had omitted. 'He's confused. He wasn't cut out for farming, clearly he couldn't cope, which made him feel even more directionless. He was supposed to be the son who inherits the farm and does the right thing, so now he's dealing with a big dose of failure. He isn't in a relationship and I'm guessing he doesn't have a good track record with women. Matthew and April are quite dependent on him and Melissa, which has led him to feel even more resentful of Sterling. I think his little escapes to the city are his way of being anonymous.'

'I don't know, Woodstock,' says Fleet. 'Lurking around the city, hitting up sex workers and spying on his brother? He sounds totally looney tunes.'

'I think he honestly believes all of his bad luck was somehow due to his brother's success.'

'But why follow him around?' presses Fleet. 'It's fucking creepy being watched by your own family.'

'I think he just wanted to see for himself the amazing life that Sterling had. In a weird way it justified his resentment.'

'I guess we all have our secrets,' says Fleet, muffling a burp.

'I guess so.'

'Are you going to speak with him again?' he asks.

'My gut feeling is that he wasn't involved but I suppose it depends on the tapes. Has anything else turned up showing him closer to the scene?'

'No. And I tend to agree with you—angry or not, I can't see Paul pulling this off. It had to be planned and he couldn't have planned it, at least not on his own.'

'Motive, but without the means.'

'Creepy, but with no clue.'

I laugh. 'I should go.'

'You still back on Monday?' he asks.

'Yep. Monday afternoon, hopefully. There's just some stuff I gotta do here.'

For a second I think he'll ask me to elaborate but he just coughs into the phone.

'Let me know if anything else turns up on Paul,' I say. 'I can easily swing past the farmhouse again if I need to.'

'Will do, Woodstock,' replies Fleet before hanging up.

Throwing my work phone into my bag, I check my personal phone and see a missed call from Josh. I realise I haven't even let him know that I'm away. Surely whatever relationship we have is becoming more tenuous by the day due to my rampant neglect.

Bird calls whip through the warm air as I get out of the car. On closer inspection, Dad's house looks neater than usual: the lawn is trimmed short and there's a new doormat.

I press on the buzzer and hear the sound dance through the house.

'Gemma!' says Rebecca, clad in an apron, her neat bob swinging as she pulls open the door. 'My goodness, this is a surprise.'

I smile stiffly, intensely annoyed to find her here.

'Ned!' she calls out behind her. 'It's Gemma!' She beams at me, clasping her hands together. 'Your dad is going to be *thrilled.*'

Dad appears and wraps me in a hug. 'Gemma, sweetheart! What are you doing here?'

'I had a lead to follow up on one of my cases nearby, so I thought I'd call in.'

'The Wade case,' says Rebecca knowingly. 'His folks don't live far from here. Remember I told you that, Ned?'

'Can you stay for Ben's soccer presentation on Sunday?' asks Dad. 'He will be so excited.'

I nod, wishing Rebecca would disappear.

'I can't believe they make you work on the weekend,' she says, patting me awkwardly on the arm.

'It's not really a nine-to-five job,' I retort.

Dad clears his throat. 'Come in, sweetheart. You look tired. Rebecca has been baking—you can probably smell it. Come in, come in,' he fusses.

Stepping inside, I can immediately smell Rebecca's homemaking efforts. Dropping my bag next to the couch, I take in a vase of flowers on the bench and a floral throw rug across the couch.

'Now let me just cut you a slice of this cake,' Rebecca says, holding up a knife. 'It's still warm.'

'I'm not really a cake person,' I say.

'Gemma . . .' says Dad.

'What? I'm not.'

'That's fine,' exclaims Rebecca. 'What else would you like instead? I have some lovely homemade soup, or I can make you a sandwich?'

'Just a water is fine,' I say.

Dad eyes me as he settles on the couch. 'So, when do you go home?'

'Monday,' I say. 'I've got to get back. It's been a pretty full-on few weeks.'

Dad shakes his head in sympathetic disbelief. 'It all sounds very bizarre, darling. I hope you're being careful.'

I wave his concern away. 'It's fine, Dad.'

Rebecca hands me a large glass of water and places a plate boasting a huge slice of fruit cake on the arm of the couch.

'Thanks, Bec,' says Dad, giving her a smile.

'Thanks,' I mutter, sipping too quickly on my water and spluttering.

Dad and Rebecca chat about the latest Smithson news, jumping in and out of each other's sentences. I grip the water glass. I'd forgotten how high-pitched her voice is.

'So are you both coming to the soccer thing tomorrow?' I ask.

Dad holds Rebecca's hand and nods. 'We sure are. Ben formally invited us. He wrote us a little card—it's around here somewhere.'

'Cute,' I say, irritated but trying to hide it. 'I'm obviously going to go and see Ben this arvo and hang out with him for a while. But then I thought that you and I could have a late dinner tonight, Dad, after Ben goes down?'

He smiles at me before exchanging a look with Rebecca. 'Well, sweetheart, we already have plans but you're welcome to join us.'

'We're having the neighbours over for dinner,' adds Rebecca. 'Do you know the Parsons? No? Well, anyway, it would be lovely to have you come along.'

Something is building inside me and I find myself getting to my feet just like Paul Wade did earlier. 'Is there any way you can postpone the dinner?' I swallow. 'It would be good to just hang out with you here, Dad, and catch up properly.'

'Gemma.' He shifts so that he's more upright. 'Sit down, sweetheart.'

I'm about to protest but something in his look makes me reconsider. I sit. 'What?' I say stiffly.

'Darling, I wanted to tell you this earlier but I didn't because, well, I wanted to tell you in person.' He removes his glasses and rubs each eye in turn before putting them back on. 'And now I guess it's as good a time as any.'

'What is it?' I ask, my eyes fixed firmly on him.

'Well,' his voice wavers, 'Rebecca was spending so much time here that we thought it made sense for her to move in.'

All the saliva in my mouth disappears. 'Right,' I manage to choke out after a few beats. 'When did that happen?'

'About three weeks ago,' says Rebecca. 'I'm just getting a few bits and pieces done to my old place, painting the fence, and then I'll be popping it on the market.'

Dad squeezes her hand and then looks at me again. 'It's all going so well, Gemma,' he says softly. 'So well, in fact, that we've also decided to get married.'

'Married?' I blurt.

'Yes. There are no firm plans or anything. Who knows, we might never get around to it, but at some stage hopefully we'll make it all official.'

My chest stretches and I feel like I'm going to pass out. 'Married,' I say again.

Rebecca holds out her hand. 'We got my mother's old ring reset,' she says, showing me a gold band featuring a row of sapphires. 'It's beautiful, isn't it?'

'Where are Mum's rings?' I ask suddenly, realising I have no idea.

Dad looks alarmed, shooting a quick glance at Rebecca, who is still admiring her ring.

'She was buried with it, sweetheart,' he says. 'She only wore a wedding band.'

'Well,' I say, aware that I need to keep speaking, to fill this moment with words. 'Congratulations.'

'I did mean to tell you sooner, Gemma,' says Dad. 'I just didn't want to tell you on the phone. That didn't seem right.'

'It's fine,' I say, springing to my feet. 'It's great.'

'Yes,' says Dad nervously. 'Well, we certainly think so.'

I look at my watch, overwhelmed by the smallness of the room. The smell of cake. 'I have to go. I should get over to Scott's.'

Dad scrambles to his feet. 'Will you come back for dinner?'

'I'll set up the spare room,' says Rebecca, glancing back and forth between us.

'No, no,' I babble, 'I think I'll just hang with Ben.'

'Let me give you some keys so you can get in later,' says Dad.

'No need,' I say. 'I'll stay at Scott's.'

With Dad and Rebecca watching me, I grab my bag and back away from them, a smile plastered on my face. 'Have a nice night. And congratulations, like I said. I'll see you at Ben's soccer thing.'

Saturday, 25 August
2.59 pm

My heart refuses to calm down as I drive the short distance to my old house. I feel high, every skin cell on edge, my brain whirring so rapidly that I'm actually thinking about nothing at all.

Turning sharply into my old street, I breathe around an unexpected sob as I pull up a few metres from what's now Scott's house. I put my hand over my mouth, looking at myself in the rear-view mirror, riding out the surge of emotion. I know this is childish, ridiculous. Mum has been dead for years and Dad has a right to be happy. I don't even live here anymore. What is wrong with me? I run through this internal dialogue, listing all the reasons why this marriage is a good thing, but my hands won't stop shaking and I teeter dangerously on the brink of tears.

Behind me, Scott's car turns into the street. For some reason I hadn't even considered the possibility that they would be out. He parks the car in the driveway before jumping out to retrieve Ben from the back seat. Ben emerges holding a football and kicks his short legs in the air, making Scott laugh until he puts him down. He runs across the front lawn before turning around and yelling something to Scott.

Scott yells something back then swipes his phone on, scrolling the screen with his thumb and pressing it off again. He looks like a nice man. A nice guy. There's still a kindness about him, a friendliness, even after all I've done to him. His hair is sweetly scruffy. He's average height, average build, average-looking. He's a way better person than me.

He bends down, gesturing for Ben to kick the ball to him.

I get out of the car, squinting into the sun as Scott runs forward to catch it. They both turn around when I slam the car door. Scott's eyes slide into mine and he brings his head back to my level. His eyebrows raise slightly while he snaps his limbs into action.

I lift my hand as if I'm visiting a distant relative. I drop it again and it slaps my side and I have to scramble to keep my bag on my shoulder. I don't know how to do this.

'Gem,' says Scott, and the years of our closeness are concentrated into that one familiar sound.

'Mum!' yells Ben, racing across the lawn and jumping into my arms. As I hold him, Scott's eyes crease and I can't tell if it's in fondness or frustration. I could never really tell.

Scott walks over and puts an arm around me in a distinctly brotherly manner. 'This is a surprise,' he says neutrally.

'Mum, Mum, Mum,' Ben is saying over and over. 'We didn't know you were coming.'

'I barely knew I was coming,' I tell him.

'What are you doing here?' Scott asks.

I place Ben back on the ground and hold his small head in my hands. I feel such an intense desire for him that I don't quite know what to do next.

'I had to speak with someone who lives up this way, so I thought I'd come to visit. And apparently, someone has a special soccer presentation tomorrow afternoon.'

'Are you coming to the awards, Mum?'

I smile and kiss the tip of his nose. 'Yes, darling, if that's okay with you.'

'Yes, definitely,' says Ben and my insides start to slowly untwist. He wriggles to get down. 'Let me show you how I kick the ball, Mum,' he says, racing off across the lawn.

Scott and I stand side by side, watching our little boy.

'Are you heading back to Melbourne on Monday?'

'Yep.'

'Ben will love you being there tomorrow, you know.'

'Yeah. It's lucky how this worked out.'

'You should have told me you were coming though. You can't just turn up, Gem.'

'Sorry.'

Ben scores a goal in the game he has created and yells as he runs in a circle.

'Are you going to go and see your dad?' Scott asks.

'I just came from there,' I say, the anxiety knotting inside me again. 'He told me that he and Rebecca are engaged and that she's moved in.'

'Ah,' says Scott, ducking his head.

'You already knew!' I exclaim, hurt.

'I noticed her ring,' says Scott sheepishly.

'Aren't you a bloody detective,' I say bitterly.

Scott looks like he's about to say something then decides against it. His eyes still on Ben, he says, 'I've actually got some work stuff to catch up on, so why don't you hang with Ben and then we can all go out for dinner if you're not busy? We were just going to the pub anyway.'

'That sounds great,' I say, relieved that he is making this so easy.

'Okay, good.' We stand there awkwardly until Scott shouts out to Ben, 'Hey, kiddo, Mum's going to have a kick with you for a bit. I've got some stuff to do.'

Ben nods happily. 'Mum, you stand at the letterbox and I'll show you how far I can kick.'

Pushing everything else out of my mind, I nod and jog over to my position, for once happy to be told what to do.

Saturday, 25 August
6.12 pm

'Ready to go?' asks Scott, his hair still wet from the shower as he pulls on a jumper.

'Yep,' I say, ruffling Ben's hair while he rolls the dice. 'We might need to finish our game another time,' I tell him, pulling my shoes on.

After carefully moving the board game to the desk in Ben's room, we head outside.

'Aren't you going to drive your rental?' Scott says as I walk over to his car.

I look at him, confused. 'No, why would I?'

'The pub is closer to your dad's place so there's no point in you coming back here and then driving all the way back again.'

'I thought I might stay here tonight,' I say quietly.

'Gemma, you can't stay here.' Scott pulls open the back door and straps Ben into his car seat.

'Oh,' I reply stupidly. 'Why not?'

'It's just not a good idea,' he says firmly, over the roof of the car.

I look out into the street. A trail of fairy lights flicks on across Sheri Faber's veranda. Sheri always was a show-off, desperate for attention.

'Are you seeing someone?' I ask Scott.

He follows my line of sight and turns back to me with a withering look. 'Gemma. I promise you, I'm not seeing Sheri Faber. Never have, never will.' He shakes his head. 'God, you're unbelievable.'

'Well, why can't I stay with you then?'

He sighs—the deep, exhausted sigh of someone who has big responsibilities. 'Because, Gemma. You just can't, okay?'

'Why?'

'Because I don't want to confuse Ben. Because I don't want to go backwards. Because I *am* seeing someone and I don't want to stuff it up. Because of all those reasons, Gem.'

'You're seeing someone?' I repeat.

'Yes, Gemma. I am. You don't know her.' Scott talks slowly, as if I'm a child.

'But you just said you don't want to confuse Ben, so explain to me how that works if you're seeing someone?'

'We'll meet you there,' Scott says, getting in the car and slamming the door.

◄o►

Bronte's Bar and Grill is a half-decent pub on the western edge of Smithson. My rental car rattles along the uneven roads. I know this town back to front but in the fading light I notice little changes, as if someone has added brushstrokes to a painting. My childhood whips past. I'm going too fast and just for a moment I wonder what would happen if I put my foot to the floor and closed my eyes and completely let go. Let the universe decide what should happen to me. Instead, I grip the wheel and breathe through the madness until I enter the dimly lit car park.

'We're going to get a dog,' Ben says, after we've been shown to our table and served drinks. I can't stop breathing in his clean earthy smell. He smells like home. Like memories. I clutch his small hand under the table as we order food—I hope it takes a while to come so that I can keep holding his hand.

'We're going to *think* about getting a dog,' Scott clarifies.

'Well, that's exciting,' I say, smiling at Ben.

As Scott sips his beer, I watch him, trying to work out if he seems different, trying to work out if he loves this new woman.

'What?' he says to me and I shake my head.

Ben's head whips back and forth between the two of us, his hands wrapped around his glass of water.

'If you're not leaving until a bit later on Monday, maybe Ben can stay home from school for the morning.' Scott is talking slowly. He doesn't usually talk like that. 'Can you manage to get him back to school before you head off?'

I bristle, he sounds so condescending. 'I don't know if I can manage that,' I reply sarcastically.

Scott takes a long sip of his beer before letting his eyes settle on me. 'Gemma,' he warns, like I'm a misbehaving pet.

'Another drink?' asks a perky waitress, her eyes flicking over Scott and then to our ring-less fingers.

'No,' I say rudely, even though I'm desperate for another glass of wine.

'Yes, please,' says Scott, smiling at her and indicating his almost empty beer.

'Can I please have a lemonade?' asks Ben politely.

'Of course,' we say at the same time.

'Are you sure you don't want a drink, Gem?' Scott asks.

'No, thanks,' I reply. 'I don't really drink these days.'

He raises an eyebrow at me.

The waitress shoves her pen and notepad back into her apron pocket. 'One Sprite and one beer coming right up!' she says, her voice tinkling like a bell.

'So, the Sterling Wade case must be pretty interesting.' Scott says it sincerely but I know he hates everything to do with my job. To him, death—especially of the suspicious kind—has always simply meant my mind is absent, closely followed by my body. He's never understood my instinctive need to solve a puzzle. Over time, I swear he could smell my cases on me; he would scrunch up his face when I walked in the door as if the evil had followed me home. But I suppose even Scott isn't completely immune to celebrity.

'It's like nothing I've ever known,' I say. 'The media coverage is insane.'

'Yeah, we saw you on the news a few times. Mum sent me an email about it. It was the first time I'd heard from her in ages.' Scott's parents live in the UK and are essentially hermits. I can picture his large docile mother firmly embedded in her floral lounge suite, enthusiastically watching episodes of *The Street*.

'Did he really just get attacked by some stranger in broad daylight?' continues Scott.

'Pretty much. You know I can't say too much but there's a lot of weird stuff underneath the surface. It's pretty frustrating.'

'But you're the lead on it, right? That's good.'

'I am. Well, Fleet and I are. And Isaacs, my boss, is obviously overseeing everything. I don't think he trusts us yet,' I add.

'Fleet's another detective?'

'Yep.'

'Is he a nice guy?' asks Scott mildly.

'He's a weird guy,' I say.

Scott nods and then smiles at Ben before picking up a napkin and wiping the corners of his mouth. I wonder if Scott is thinking about my relationship with my old partner Felix. Scott and I never talked about it, not really, but I think he suspects something was going on. I blink an avalanche of Felix memories away. I have no idea where he is now, though I assume he's still in Sydney with his wife and daughters.

'Are you staying at our place, Mum?' asks Ben, interrupting my thoughts. He has a sip of his drink as he pushes his fringe out of his eyes.

'Come on, mate, I already told you that Mum is going to stay at Grandad and Rebecca's,' says Scott lightly. 'She needs to keep Rebecca company.'

I roll my eyes just as our food arrives.

'She's not that bad, Gem,' says Scott. 'I know it's all been pretty quick but your dad seems really happy. She obviously cares about him. It's good for him to have someone like that in his life.'

'Well, she's certainly made her mark on the house,' I say gloomily, as I saw into my rare steak. 'There are bloody plants and flowers everywhere.'

'I like Rebecca,' Ben declares as he shoves chips into his mouth.

'Sure, well, she's a nice lady,' I say diplomatically, keeping my eyes on my plate as I eat another corner of meat. We all chew in silence and then Scott bursts out laughing. Ben starts laughing too and eventually so do I.

After the meal, we all order hot chocolates and Ben really warms up, chatting to me about his schoolmates and the play he has a small role in. Scott talks a little about the new retail strip his company is developing, the sharp line of stress that slices into his brow deepening. I can tell he's worried about money.

Outside, the still warm air is thick and creamy. The sky blinks with stars.

'Bye, Mum,' says Ben, holding on to me with his strong little arms.

I close my eyes and breathe him in. 'Bye, sweetheart. I'll see you tomorrow, okay?'

He gives me a tiny wave as he climbs into his car seat.

'So how serious is it? With the woman?' I ask Scott, after he settles Ben in, slams the car door shut and leans against it.

'God, Gemma, you are unbelievable. You really are.' He laughs nastily and shoves his hands in his pockets.

'I'm just interested,' I say. 'Come on, tell me.' I start to shift on the spot; my limbs feel itchy. 'Do you have her over to our place? Does she know about me?'

'Know what about you, Gem?'

'I don't know. Everything, I guess. Tell me. Do you screw her when Ben's there?'

'Seriously, Gemma, you're out of line. I know you're upset about your dad and Rebecca but I'm not doing this with you.' His face relaxes and suddenly it's more worried than angry. 'Look, Ben stays at your dad's once a week. Sometimes I see her then. Ben has met her a few times. Sometimes we go out for dinner. My behaviour is definitely not something you need to worry about. She's nice. Ben is fine. He's a happy little boy.'

'Lovely. So you have cosy little dinners just like the one we just had. And when my son is at my dad's, you fuck some girl's brains out. That's just great.'

A couple exit the restaurant and shoot us curious looks as they walk quickly to their car. I see Ben's face, a slice of white in the shadowy back seat.

'Our son lives with you,' I go on. 'I have a right to know who he's exposed to.'

'Right. And what are you exposing yourself to down in Melbourne? No, no, come on, tell me,' Scott says, as I throw my eyes skyward. 'What kind of wonderful role models are you mixing with?' He slaps his hand comically against his forehead. 'Oh, that's right. It doesn't matter. You can do whatever you like.'

'You want Ben to live here with you, right?' I ask, scared for a moment what his answer will be.

Scott sighs and I remember him doing that a lot before I left. 'Of course I want him here with me. I definitely don't want him in the city with you. But still, Gem, it's not easy. Even you must get that?'

I nod absently, thinking about Ben's visit to Melbourne. The unrelenting responsibility of looking after him, of *worrying*, had been overwhelming. My days in Melbourne are still anchored by him, but they don't have the forceful pull of his wellbeing tugging at me all the time. I am, despite my anxiety, essentially free.

'I guess I just don't want him to forget me. That's all.' I whisper the words because saying them too loud is terrifying.

Scott rubs at his eyes. 'Oh, Gemma. He *worships* you. Can't you see that? It's probably the thing I worry about the most.'

'You used to worship me too,' I point out.

'True,' Scott agrees. 'But now I know better. That little guy, on the other hand, will never get over you.'

I look at Ben, his head tipped to the side as he cruises toward sleep. 'I don't know about that,' I say.

'Well, I do.' Scott yanks open the driver's door. 'You're welcome to come over tomorrow before the soccer presentation. Otherwise we'll see you there.'

'Okay.' I wish we were just arriving at the pub so we could go inside and have dinner all over again.

The door slams and Scott waves as he turns out of the car park. Two glowing red eyes bob along in the dark before disappearing into nothing.

I stand completely still, letting the loose breeze circle around me. Then I spin around and find myself accosted by a wave of disorientation as it takes me a few seconds to remember I have a rental car. Standing next to it, I fish out my cigarettes and light one. There is no one around and the leaves of the gum trees paw at the lamp lights, turning the ground into a flickering ocean. I smoke hard and fast, scenes from the day encoring in my head. Stomping on the cigarette I beep open the car. Inside the air is hollow and fake, the smell of newness jarring in a place like Smithson.

I drive back into town and head to Main Street. Parking the car, I shut off the lights and look at the bar. Music pulses and the silhouettes laugh and talk and drink through the windows. I picture myself walking in, ordering a drink. Laughing, flirting. Getting lost in time and not worrying about tomorrow.

I get out my phone.

'Gemma!'

'Hey, Candy,' I say, trying to keep my voice steady. 'Are you home? I'm in Smithson and I need somewhere to stay.'

Monday, 27 August

2.14 pm

Melbourne's skyline comes into view as the taxi creeps along the freeway. I raise my eyes to the road as we slam to a halt. A horn blares.

'Arsehole!' yells the cabbie. 'Sorry,' he mutters to me.

More horns join the chorus, blending with the eighties song on the radio.

I shift in my seat. My legs have twisted with cramps the entire way home. My ankles are itchy and so is the back of my neck. I lean forward to see past the line of cars.

'What's going on?' I ask.

The driver shrugs. 'No one in this city knows how to drive anymore.'

We inch forward again. I resume scanning my emails. A few minutes later my ears prick up as the radio host announces that he is about to interview Lizzie Short to find out how she's dealing with the tragic death of her fiancé.

'Can you please turn up the volume?' I ask the driver as I try to decide how to reply to a text from Dad. He is clearly beside himself about my reaction to his engagement news and while part of me feels guilty at marring his happiness, every other part of my being hates the idea so much that I simply can't be rational about it.

The ad break ends and the radio host introduces Lizzie solemnly, recapping Sterling's brutal death. Her voice fills the car, and I picture her pale face and glossy long hair. She sounds older, weary. She speaks cautiously; there's a beat between each question and her answer.

'The whole country is mourning with you, Lizzie,' says the host earnestly. 'Tell us, how are you coping?'

'Thank you,' she says. 'I'm not sure I am coping really, I'm just trying to get through each hour, each minute sometimes. It's so, so hard.'

'I can't imagine,' murmurs the host. 'It must have been such a shock?'

'It was. I still wake up every morning almost not remembering what's happened. It's so awful realising all over again that he's gone.' Lizzie makes a muffled sound. 'Sorry, sorry.'

'It's fine, cry if you need to,' says the host, as we turn into Collins Street.

Lizzie draws a deep breath. 'I know that losing someone is always awful but when it's so sudden it's especially devastating.'

'Absolutely. And these circumstances are just, well, unfathomable really. It's certainly impacted everyone I know. And I know that you are no stranger to tragedy. You lost your mother at a young age too, didn't you?'

'I did. Dad walked out when I was five so it was always just me, Mum and my little brother. We didn't have much money but we were super close. It was such a happy childhood. And then when I was fourteen, Mum died in a house fire. Kit and I lived with our aunt until I was eighteen and then we moved to Melbourne together. It was really tough but it has made us even closer.'

'Just here, please,' I tell the driver, pointing to the police station's car-park entrance.

'Terrible, this Sterling Wade business, isn't it?' he says, pulling over and shutting off the meter. 'Being killed in broad daylight like that.'

'Being murdered in the dark isn't much fun either,' I reply, handing him the fare.

◄O►

'She's back,' says Fleet loudly, drawing out the words like a game-show host when I walk in. 'Tell us, Detective Woodstock, how was your little jaunt to the country?'

'Lovely, thanks,' I say quietly, dumping my bag on my desk and flicking on my computer. 'Lots of fresh air.'

His voice drops as he says, 'You sure you're okay to be here?'

I see real concern in his eyes. 'All good, thanks.'

He gives me a long look. 'Right then. Well, back to work, I guess.'

'Exactly,' I say, then: 'I was just listening to Lizzie Short on the radio.'

'Oh yeah?' says Fleet. 'And what did our grieving widow have to say for herself?'

'Not much. I think it was mainly just an opportunity for the radio host to fawn over her tragic life.'

'We've definitely reached peak trauma culture,' he says, biting into a muesli bar. 'Warhol would be proud.'

'I know,' I say, rubbing my eyes. I can't believe it's only three-thirty. 'So, where are we at with everything?'

Fleet wriggles in his chair. The leather of his jacket squeaks as he stretches from side to side. Faded cigarette smoke summons thoughts of dingy bars and loud music.

304

'Well, we found our blog leaker,' he says.

'We did? Who?'

'Some poor junior called Kate Joosten who wanted cred with her hipster housemate,' he replies. 'The silly girl took a photo of the printout in the case room and showed him. He texted it to himself and the rest is literally yesterday's news. Idiot.'

'At least it wasn't malicious,' I say, picturing the unremarkable dark-haired girl and thinking about how bad she must be feeling.

Fleet shrugs. 'Just fucking stupid.'

'Well, I guess it's good to have it resolved,' I say. 'Anything else?'

'Yes. Brodie's missing.'

'Where has he gone?' I ask distractedly.

'Do you not understand the definition of missing?' Fleet says, laughing. 'We have no idea.'

'Lizzie doesn't know where he is?'

'Nope.' Fleet yawns. 'She hasn't seen him since he came home after that little chat we had on Friday. His phone is off and he hasn't touched his bank accounts.'

'Did you actually go around there?' I ask Fleet. 'Maybe he's told Lizzie to cover for him.'

Fleet seems to think about this. 'Yep. I'll get on to it.'

The white buzz of the office lights is making my vision jump. I look at Fleet, talking on the phone, then slide my eyes over to Nan and Calvin who are locked in a heated discussion near the tearoom. Who are these people? What am I doing here?

Ben and I met my old boss Jonesy for a coffee this morning. I hadn't wanted to go to the station so we met at Reggie's, one of my favourite cafes.

Jonesy delighted in grilling me about the ins and outs of police life in Melbourne before embarking on an enthusiastic run-down of the latest Smithson cases. Listening to his familiar prattle, with Ben pressed against my side and drawing circles on my hand with a pen, I felt a wave of intense homesickness despite, oddly, being home.

'And you're okay, Woodstock?' Jonesy said to me as we parted, ducking his head so that I was forced to look into his eyes.

'Are you okay, Woodstock?' asks Fleet now, pulling me from my looping thoughts.

'What?' There's a throbbing pressure behind my eyes. Ben loved me being at his soccer presentation but I felt like I was under a giant spotlight yesterday afternoon. I'm still reeling from the constant questions. The stares. Dad and Rebecca. Scott. Plus, I still haven't called Josh back, so that is probably another relationship I can kiss goodbye.

'It's weird going home sometimes, huh?' Fleet says.

I look at him, surprised. I shrug. 'It's okay.'

'I'm sure it's a nice little place, your home town. Doesn't mean it's not a headfuck.'

He stabs at his keyboard for a few moments. Scrawls something on his notepad.

I venture, 'Do you go back home often?'

'Not really,' he says evenly, underlining so many words it seems unnecessary.

'Do you miss it?' I press.

He snorts but his eyes are kind. 'Let's not turn this into a lie-back-on-the-couch session. Come on, my part-time friend,' he says, jumping up. He holds a pen like a cigarette between his fingers and taps its end on the side of his desk. 'We've got shit to do.'

◄○►

Just as we're about to head into the afternoon case meeting, Ravi Franks comes up to us, holding out his phone.

'Check this out,' he says. 'Ava James just recorded a panel interview talking about the attack on Wade but she also mentions having issues with Cartwright.'

I look at Ava's face underneath the play button on Ravi's phone. 'Does she mention the assault?'

'Not explicitly. She alludes to his arrogance and sense of entitlement. I think she uses the words "inappropriate" and "predatory".'

Standing in the corridor, we watch the interview and I marvel at the desire these people have to share so much of their lives with strangers.

While Ava isn't overt in taking down Cartwright, the message is still clear: she's fighting back. She also does a good job of making her relationship with Sterling seem very intimate, and I wonder if it's an up yours to Lizzie for not being invited to the funeral.

Fleet and I go into the case room and open the meeting. 'Any updates?' I ask the team, more aggressively than I'd intended.

I'm annoyed by Ava's media appearance. Even though nothing she said presents a problem for us specifically, it just feels like another example of this case having a mind of its own. I'm frustrated that we're watching parts of the story unfold just like everyone else.

As the team members run through their reports it reminds me of a big, sprawling game of hot and cold with the person in charge yelling us into dead ends, causing us to trip over each other and land back where we started.

'We might have something,' says Ravi tentatively. 'We've been going through the details on the film production, the security planning, contracts, checking the guards, stuff like that. In the process, we've been given access to the film budget and salaries, and it seems Katya March is getting paid almost double the going rate for a film like this.'

'Is that something she would have negotiated?' I ask.

'We're not sure. But we spoke to a few industry people and it's certainly a figure that stands out.'

'Okay,' I say. 'Good. We'll check it out.'

'There are a few other witness statements to follow up: a young woman claims a man in a hoodie almost knocked her over when she was walking home through Carlton just after Walter Miller was killed,' says Chloe.

I relay my doubts about Paul Wade's involvement to the group. 'But we still need to clear him. Is there any more CCTV to go through?' I ask the constables who are managing all the footage. 'Ideally I'd like to have him on tape at the time of the attack.'

'Some stores are still handing tapes in,' one of them confirms. 'But all the city council footage is in and we can only find him on that one file.'

'Keep looking,' I say.

As everyone files out of the room, I try to call Brodie but his phone is still off. I shove my own phone back in my pocket.

Fleet looks at me, a question.

'Still no answer from Brodie,' I reply, lifting my hair away from my neck.

'I think it's time to make our missing person official,' he says.

Tuesday, 28 August
10.35 am

Katya eyes us warily as she sits across from us in the interview room. Today she wears a bright red blouse under a navy faux fur shrug, her black hair piled on top of her head.

'Riley and I have an agreement,' she explains after we query her inflated pay cheque.

'Like a you-drop-the-harassment-claim-if-he-pays-you-a-stack-of-cash-now-and-forevermore kind of agreement?' asks Fleet.

She purses her lips. 'Something like that,' she says.

'Did Cartwright assault you three years ago?' I ask.

'Like I told you,' she says, spreading her fingers on the table, 'he's a good guy but he acts like a jerk sometimes. Back then I didn't know how to handle him.'

'But you do now?' says Fleet sceptically.

'I know how this world works now,' she says. 'People like Riley are never going to change so you just have to work around them.'

'Okay,' I say, 'so you agreed to drop the charges if he gave you more money?'

'Pretty much. When he first came on to me I wanted to show him who was boss, you know, do the feminist thing, make a formal complaint, stand up for myself. But I quickly realised how inconvenient that made me. No one wanted to hear about it and I was the problem, not Riley. Getting another job would have been impossible.' She shrugs, tilting her chin at us. 'He offered me some money to shut up and I decided to negotiate an even better deal.'

'How exactly does it work?' I ask her.

'It's simple. I keep my mouth shut about what he did and choose to ignore a few of his other *weaknesses*, and I am guaranteed an executive producer role on every film he does at an extremely high salary.' She crosses her arms. 'Based on all the extra shit I do to manage him, believe me, it's more than fair.'

Her cool confidence radiates around the room and I can't help feeling a little bit impressed by her conviction.

'He doesn't really learn his lesson that way though, does he?'

She sighs. 'The saying about leopards changing spots springs to mind. At least this way I get the career I deserve out of it. I'm a good producer.'

'Do you know if he's assaulted other women?'

Her gaze is defiant. 'I couldn't say.'

'But you could guess,' says Fleet.

'I would assume so, yes.'

'Like Ava James,' I say.

'I'm sure Ms James will be absolutely fine,' says Katya, narrowing her eyes and avoiding the question.

'Is there anything else you know about Cartwright that you haven't shared with us?' I ask.

'No.'

'You're sure? There's no other large payment coming your way in exchange for keeping quiet about something?'

'I told you, I'm positive Riley had nothing to do with what happened to Sterling. He can be a creep but he's not a killer.'

'Maybe he got desperate. Wade had dirt on him too but obviously wasn't interested in being paid off to keep quiet,' suggests Fleet.

She looks amused. 'Sterling didn't threaten Cartwright. He wasn't that kind of guy. His little confrontation was more the old-fashioned, do-the-right-thing type. Cartwright was annoyed but to be honest I think he was more pissed off at Ava for running to Wade for help.'

'Will you keep working with Cartwright?' I ask.

'If the price is right, sure. But to be honest I'm not sure if he'll be able to take on another project for a while. He's checked into rehab. Did you know that?'

'No,' Fleet says wryly. 'We must have been left off the group text.'

'He's a real mess this time,' she says. 'I saw him yesterday. So who knows what will happen now?'

'You don't seem that worried,' I say.

'My reputation isn't the one in tatters,' she replies confidently, but I detect real fear in her eyes.

◄○►

'At least we know where Cartwright is,' I say to Fleet, as we walk back to the case room after Katya leaves. 'Unlike Brodie.'

Earlier we spoke to Brodie's parents in Adelaide, an elderly Greek couple with broken English, who told us they haven't seen their son since Christmas and haven't heard from him in over a month. His father's strong accent filled the tiny meeting room as he told us, with a sort of resigned judgement, that his son has a habit of disappearing.

On the day of the funeral Brodie posted a farewell message to Wade's Facebook wall. It was one of over 450,000 goodbye messages that Wade's social platforms attracted that day, the outpouring of grief ranging from the short and sweet to the laboured and passionate. Brodie also uploaded an image to his Instagram of a ferocious ocean with the caption: 'Thank you for everything. Now you are part of the earth, sky and sea.'

A friend commented on his post later that day, asking if he was okay. Twenty-three people liked this comment, and over the past few days three other people have responded, expressing concern about him and offering to help. But Brodie never replied.

He seems to have disappeared into thin air. He has no car registered in his name and his bank accounts haven't been touched for over a week—though seeing as the balances total less than thirty dollars, this doesn't mean much. His credit cards are maxed out. His phone remains off.

'Let's go and make sure he's really not at Lizzie's,' I say to Fleet. 'Maybe he's like the Wades and just wants to shut the world out for a while. And told her to cover for him.'

We make our way across town, which takes twice as long as it should due to all the stretches of roadworks.

'I swear the traffic here is getting worse,' I complain. But Fleet has his eyes glued to his personal phone.

At the apartment, we're greeted by a made-up Lizzie who is about to go out.

'I have a TV interview this afternoon,' she tells us. 'I'm joining *The Street* later this year and so it's part of my publicity obligations.' She takes a deep breath and draws herself tall. 'Keeping busy helps. It's a good distraction from—' She waves a hand at the empty apartment.

Lizzie confirms she hasn't seen Brodie since the day of Sterling's funeral.

We ask to take a quick look in his room. 'Of course,' she says.

It looks exactly as it did the other day.

'You have no idea where he might have gone?' I ask her when we return to the lounge.

'No idea, and I wish he'd told me where he was going. I'm getting pretty worried. I don't think he has many friends. Maybe he went home to see his parents? I think he's from Adelaide.'

I look out the window behind her, noticing little buds forming on the huge tree.

'Well,' I say, 'if he comes home or you hear from him, you need to let us know straight away, okay?'

'Of course,' she murmurs.

As she walks into the kitchen I notice the dark rings under her eyes that the make-up can't hide.

'Are you looking after yourself?' I ask.

'I'm just trying to get through each day,' she says. 'The funeral was awful. I'm so glad it's over.' She smooths her hair. 'Like I said, there's been a lot going on. The media is relentless and I've done lots of interviews. But it's good, it keeps me going.' She looks toward Brodie's bedroom. 'Kit has been staying here most nights because I'm too scared to go to sleep on my own. Do you think Brodie's okay?'

'I'm sure he is,' I tell her. 'He probably just needs some time out.'

Fleet and I don't talk on the way back to the station. I notice he keeps staring out the window and I wonder what he's thinking about.

◄○►

A few hours later I'm making my way through a mug of instant soup that says it's chicken-flavoured despite its distinct beef vibe while reviewing Brodie's patchy income streams over the past few years.

'He's not very good at being an adult, is he?' I comment to Fleet.

'Some of us never quite get the hang of it,' he replies, as he lifts his feet onto the corner of a table and leans back into his chair, stretching his arms above his head and revealing a small tear in his shirt seam.

'Wade must have let Brodie stay at the apartment rent-free,' I say. 'There's no way he could afford a third of the rent unless he was getting money off the books.'

'Clearly Brodie was paying him in other ways,' suggests Fleet.

I roll my eyes and say nothing, wondering why straight guys are always so obsessed with commenting on sexual activity between men.

'Maybe he wanted to be with his boyfriend in heaven and jumped dramatically off a cliff,' muses Fleet, voicing one of my many fears for Brodie. 'Or,' he continues, 'he's as guilty as all get-out and has disappeared into the wilderness, never to be seen again.'

My eyes are starting to burn; even blinking hurts. 'I think I need to go for a walk,' I tell Fleet, pulling at my cheeks and trying to wake myself up. 'I'm falling asleep.'

'Yeah, I'm knackered too,' he says.

I scan the last few rows of Brodie's financials. 'Hey,' I say, as two words suddenly stand out from the others on the page. 'Isn't that Riley Cartwright's company?' I jab at the name: Blood Productions. The company paid Brodie Kent almost six thousand dollars about two years ago. It's one of the largest amounts on the ramshackle list of sporadic payments we've managed to track down.

Fleet comes around to my side of the table and leans down next to me, peering at the paper. I feel his breath on the side of my face. 'Yes,' he says, a thread of excitement in his voice, 'I think you are one hundred per cent correct, Miss Scarlet.'

Tuesday, 28 August
2.59 pm

We locate Cartwright's room in the small private hospital on the edge of the city. He's sitting in an armchair having a foot spa. He looks up when we enter but seems to barely register our presence, his fidgeting hands continuing their mad dance. Similarly, the tiny ball of a nurse crouched in front of him misses only the slightest of beats in her rhythmic kneading of his feet and ankles in the steaming water.

I begin. 'Mr Cartwright—'

'Sit, sit.' He waves us in.

'How are you feeling?' I ask, lowering myself onto a chair. Fleet leans against the wall and gently kicks a heel against the running board. Cartwright's gaze jumps across to the spot where Fleet's foot connects; he blinks every time it makes a beat.

He laughs but the sound carries no emotion. 'Not very well.'

'We need to talk to you,' says Fleet. 'Is this a good time?'

There's a little splash as the nurse's hands keep working in the water. Cartwright looks down at her affectionately. 'Sure. Why not?'

'Alone,' I say, glancing at the nurse.

Cartwright grimaces and pulls his feet out. The nurse immediately grabs the towel next to her and begins to rub them dry.

'Yes, yes, thank you,' says Cartwright, clearly dismissing her. 'That's fine, thanks.'

She bobs her head and lifts the tub, waddling from the room, her tiny muscles bulging.

'Nice place,' comments Fleet wryly, plonking himself onto the queen-sized bed. It's not dressed with the standard hospital linen, instead made up with a soft grey and white patterned doona.

'It's okay,' says Cartwright evenly.

'Do you know Brodie Kent?' I ask, like a punch.

Cartwright doesn't blink but a bead of light wobbles in his pupils. 'Do I? I'm not sure. I know a lot of people.'

'Brodie Kent,' I repeat. 'A young actor and dancer. He was cast in one of your films about two years ago. You attended a five-week shoot with him in New Zealand. Ringing any bells?' My voice is mean and I realise just how tired I am of these people.

Cartwright tips his head back against the chair and rolls it from side to side, stretching his neck. 'Maybe,' he says finally. 'Dark hair?'

'Very dark,' says Fleet. 'He was also Sterling Wade's housemate.'

Cartwright straightens up, more alert now. 'I didn't know that,' he says warily. 'I thought it was just Sterling and Lizzie.'

'So you do know him then,' I say with sarcasm.

'Vaguely. He bugged me for that role, almost drove me mad. I ended up casting him but he wasn't very good.'

'Seen him since?' I ask.

'I went to some drinks earlier this year—one of the casting places put them on—and he was there. But aside from that, I don't think so.' Cartwright bends his long legs and sits cross-legged on the chair.

'Did you speak to him at the drinks?' asks Fleet.

'Nope. Once I recognised him, I avoided him. He's a pain in the arse and I didn't want to have him bug me about another role again.'

'And you're sure you haven't seen him since?' I press.

Cartwright shakes his head. 'Don't think so.'

'He was at Sterling's funeral,' I say.

'I didn't notice. I was pretty out of it that day, in case you haven't heard.' He gestures at our surrounds. 'Landed myself here.'

'Okay,' says Fleet, with zero sympathy, 'and you definitely haven't had any contact with him since?'

'No way. I've been either stoned out of my head or in here. I've barely had contact with anyone.'

'What happened?' asks Fleet. 'The funeral push you over the edge?'

'Something like that,' Cartwright mumbles.

'Alright,' says Fleet, 'so you've had no contact with Brodie Kent since a party earlier this year, correct?'

'That's right. To be honest, he's not someone I've ever thought about. Apart from being annoying, he's completely generic. It seems odd to me that he was part of Wade's crew.'

'So if we check your phone records and emails, there will be no contact between the two of you?' I snap.

He looks steadily at me. 'I would be very surprised if something came up.'

'How long will you be in here?' asks Fleet.

'Dunno. Probably a while. I've had what my psychiatrist calls a "major crash".'

'Does your psychiatrist also say experiencing a major crash is beneficial for someone facing assault charges?' I ask.

Cartwright meets my stare head-on but says nothing.

'Look, mate, we obviously know that you weren't the one to attack Wade,' says Fleet. 'We're just trying to make sure you didn't have a partner in crime to do the dirty work while you watched on.'

Cartwright shakes his head in disbelief. 'You really think I had something to do with this? It has ruined me. I can't sleep, I can't eat. I see Sterling's face as he went down over and over. I'm a mess.'

'Maybe the pressure of carrying a film just isn't for you,' Fleet suggests. 'Perhaps the idea of a large cash payout is far more appealing. You can sit around in this joint with someone rubbing your feet. Maybe pass some money along to your hit-man buddy.'

'No way,' retorts Cartwright, struggling to pull himself up straight in the chair. 'Sterling was my friend and I had no idea about the insurance money until Katya told me. This is just some lunatic who flipped out.' He leans forward menacingly, pointing his finger at me. 'Believe me, being in a place like this you see just how crazy people are. It's not hard to see how someone who was obsessed with Sterling could have taken it too far.'

Fleet and I stand up wordlessly.

'Whatever,' Cartwright mumbles. Then: 'Do you really think that Brodie kid has something to do with this? He always seemed kind of pathetic to me.'

Fleet eases his hands into his pockets as he heads to the door; his fingers must already be on his cigarette packet. 'Brodie may be pathetic but right now he's also missing, so do let us know if he drops in for a visit, won't you?'

Wednesday, 29 August
12.03 am

The buzz of my phone yanks me out of sleep.

'It's Ava James,' breathes Chloe. 'She's been attacked.'

'Is she okay?' I ask, scrambling upright.

'We think so,' replies Chloe. 'She's just been taken to the hospital. Shock and minor abrasions.'

I swap my tracksuit for jeans and a jacket and rub my face with a hot wet flannel before I walk the short distance from my apartment to Southbank.

The Yarra River is a bed of pewter, rumpled with white moonlight. I look across to the other side of the water and see the silhouettes of people walking home, or heading out to bars or the casino to piss away more of their money. Next to me Fleet is smoking steadily, his eyes slits. The forensics team has fenced off the area with tape. Two giant spotlights are aimed at the concrete path as they trawl through every square inch. A curious, eclectic crowd has started to form.

Despite my thick jacket, I feel ice in the air and I can only imagine the temperature of the murky water. We speak to Ava's quick-thinking rescuer: a small wiry arts student who just so happened to be carrying a skipping rope in his backpack. Unfortunately he saw nothing, just heard a splash followed by screams before he rushed over to find a desperate Ava flailing in the freezing water about a metre below.

I open my mouth to speak to Fleet but the cold air steals my voice. I swallow and try again. 'This just keeps getting more and more complicated, doesn't it?'

'Conveniently so,' he replies.

'I don't buy that this was a random attack.'

'Nope.' He blows air into his bunched fists and stamps his feet for warmth. 'If it was, surely the bloke would have mugged her or felt her up or something.'

'Yeah.' That has been bothering me too. 'The guys are checking but there's no CCTV along this stretch of the path apparently. At least we'll probably be able to see who came up and down the walkway unless they climbed the wall somehow.'

'You think she could have faked it?' asks Fleet, just as the thought crosses my mind.

I breathe out a cloud of white air and march on the spot too, willing my blood to keep moving. 'God, I don't know. It seems pretty extreme, but I guess it's possible.' I look up at the moon, a veiny sphere of white light. Tonight it's almost as bright as the sun. 'Maybe she was upset about the media coverage after her interview and wanted the spotlight back on her in a good way,' I muse. 'The press has pitted her against Lizzie, right? The poor grieving widow. Maybe she's looking for some sympathy.'

'Maybe,' says Fleet, gazing out at the water.

We watch as one of the techs shines a flashlight down the side of the stone wall into the water and shakes his head.

'Or maybe this case is just fucking with my mind,' I say, 'and making me think that Agatha Christie plots are coming to life.'

Fleet drops his cigarette unceremoniously and twists his foot, killing the last of its glow. 'These people are all batshit crazy. I know we weren't lucky enough to meet young Mr Wade in the flesh but he's starting to seem like the most normal of them all.'

'I know. My truth radar is all over the place.'

Fleet smirks but he cuffs me gently on the shoulder. 'Truth radar. We don't have those in the big smoke, champ. We just assume everyone is lying. Statistically it's more likely.'

I smile at him and feel like we've hit an even better groove since I've been back from Smithson. I realise how much I want his approval and hate myself for it.

We walk a little further up the path. I nod at a few of the techs and scan the collection of faces behind the police tape in the dim light. Who are all these people? What are they all doing? What secrets are they hiding? I stare for a second too long and their features blur together, my mind creating a bizarre montage of melted faces.

'Yeah, well,' I say, snapping my eyes into focus and banishing the image, 'all I know for sure is that it's becoming increasingly important that we find Brodie Kent.'

◄O►

Ava James sits bolt upright in her hospital bed, eyes wide open as if she is possessed. Her bright blue irises follow us as we walk in but she doesn't say anything. Her hair is no longer red, but a rich dark brown and cut much shorter. It is combed back from her face, still damp, though I assume it's from a hot shower and not the fall in the river. Her right temple is grazed and there's some light bruising on her collarbone. She doesn't blink.

'Ms James?' says Fleet gently, and I can tell that even he is spooked by her vacant stare. 'We'd like to ask you some questions. Is that okay?'

'Yes,' she whispers.

'We're very sorry that this happened to you,' I begin.

She nods, her face a mask.

'What did you do earlier tonight,' Fleet says, 'before all this happened?'

She speaks slowly, her voice even and flat. 'I met some friends for a drink. One of them is staying at a hotel at the other end of the city. I walked there. I wanted some fresh air. I've been walking a lot since everything happened . . .'

I wonder whether she realises we're still here. It's like she's talking to herself.

'Okay,' I say. 'What's your friend's hotel called?'

'The Spence.'

'Did you go anywhere else?' I ask.

'No. My friends wanted to go out but I didn't feel like it. I walked with them about a block to a tapas bar and then I kept going. I've really struggled to be around crowds since Sterling's . . . attack.' She pulls at the bedding with her hands.

'What time was this?' Fleet presses.

'I think just after 10 pm.'

'Was the bar near the river?'

'No.' She's still staring up at me, her eyes hollow. 'The restaurant was near the corner of Spencer and Bourke. I walked to the river afterwards. I didn't want to go back to my hotel room.' A bitter laugh escapes her lips. 'Can't be around crowds, can't be alone. I'm turning into a complete head case.'

'I thought you had full-time security?' says Fleet, clearly trying to keep her to the story.

'I do.' She drops her gaze for the first time, watching her manic fingers. 'I told them I was going to stay at my friend's hotel for the evening.' She looks back up with a flash of her trademark defiance.

'Seems pretty stupid now, but sometimes I just need a break. I like walking at night. People don't tend to recognise me. You probably don't understand.'

'Everyone needs some time out,' says Fleet.

'Yes,' she says, her glassy stare returning. 'Anyway, I walked around for maybe an hour. I had my headphones on, listening to music. I wasn't paying attention to the time, I was just walking.'

I look at Ava and think how impossible it seems that such a beautiful woman can be so lost and lonely. With her legs wrapped in the hospital sheet and her hair waved and damp, she looks like a fantasy mermaid.

'Why did you go to the river?' I ask her.

She doesn't appear to move but a lock of hair slips over her shoulder. She picks it up and toys with it. 'I don't know,' she finally says in the same spooky monotone. 'I decided to walk back to my hotel along the water. I've been walking along there early most mornings this past week.'

'With your security guard?' asks Fleet.

She nods. 'Yes. Tonight is the first time I've gone alone.'

'Are you still staying at the hotel where we visited you?' he asks.

'Yes.'

'Bit out of your way, to walk along the river,' he comments.

'I wasn't in a hurry to get anywhere. I was only going to go home and lie in bed for hours, trying to sleep.'

'Okay,' I jump in, 'so you cut down to the river and walked along the path. Were you planning to come out through the station to the corner of Flinders and Swanston?'

She nods again. 'Yes. And then along Flinders Street up to the hotel on Spring.' Her piercing gaze burns through me. 'You must live around there,' she says suddenly. 'I've seen you walking early some mornings too.'

Ignoring the curious look Fleet gives me, I say, 'Tell us what happened next, Ava. What do you remember?'

Her hands flutter across the blanket. 'I don't really know. I was just walking. I stopped to look at something on my phone. And then it happened so fast. Hands around my neck, grabbing me—like, choking me. I didn't even fight back, I just thought I was going to die.' Her voice drops to a mist. 'Just like Sterling.'

'Have you felt like you were being followed before tonight?' Fleet asks.

'I don't think so. And I'm pretty aware of stuff like that, especially lately.'

'Did you see your attacker at all?' I ask. 'Remember anything distinctive?'

'I was just freaking out waiting for him to stab me. For a moment, I thought he had.'

'You're sure it was a man?' asks Fleet, rocking back and forth on his heels.

'I'm pretty sure,' she says, urgency entering her voice. 'He was so strong.'

Tears well in her eyes, threatening to spill over.

'After he grabbed me I heard breathing in my ear, then he let go of my throat.' She looks at us like a frightened animal. 'I dropped to the ground, my legs stopped working, I couldn't move but I was so relieved. I thought it was over. I got up—I wanted to make a run for it in case he tried to rape me—and then I felt pressure under my armpits.' She squeezes her eyes shut, her perfect hands twisting madly around each other, her nails a beautiful pearly purple. 'He grabbed me one more time, and then I was flying. I couldn't see anything. I didn't really know what was happening until I hit the river.' Her mouth twists as she tries to quell the sobs. 'It was so cold. I tried to scream but I thought the water might be toxic so I was panicking. A man in dark clothes was walking past on the path and his face was covered. He didn't stop even though I was screaming, but I don't know if he was the one who attacked me. I could barely think, it was so cold.'

She shudders and curls her legs up as she tilts forward into a ball. I can tell there is still ice in her veins.

She begins to cry. Deep sobs rack her body. 'I just want to go home.'

Wednesday, 29 August
9.49 am

The case room smells like burnt toast. Fleet and I both look terrible, as if we've aged a decade overnight. He clears his throat and it catches roughly on the beginning of a cold.

After we left the hospital I got a cab home and tried to sleep. I think I finally drifted off around four and woke to my alarm just before seven. The weight of my exhausted eyes is putting pressure on my whole face, and the rhythmic pounding in my head feels like it's counting down to an explosion.

I fan my fingers then lift them up and down one by one. 'What is this guy trying to prove?' I ask Fleet.

He coughs before wheezing into a sigh. 'Fucked if I know.' Yawning, he rotates his head in a slow circle. 'I know we said it seems like it's linked, but maybe it's just a run-of-the-mill late-night psycho.'

'It has to be linked though, doesn't it?' I say, looking at the board along the back wall, the beautiful faces staring back at me.

'Someone *could* have just been following her,' says Fleet. 'Maybe she caught someone's eye at the bar and they trailed her as she went on her late-night stroll? Perhaps they were going to rob her or assault her, but they got spooked at the last minute and pushed her instead.'

I think this over and nod. He's right. Ava wouldn't be as recognisable late at night and out of context; her hair had been tucked under a woollen hat and she'd worn a bulky coat. But at the bar she would surely have caught the eyes of fellow drinkers. Maybe someone followed her, eventually realising she was alone.

Silly girl, I think, before chastising myself.

'It is sort of odd that the one night she doesn't have security trailing her, she's attacked,' I say.

'Yes, I know. She might be being stalked. But we can't rule out the possibility that she's screwing us around.'

'We should pull CCTV from the bar. See if anyone was watching her or left around the same time she did.'

'Yep,' he says, rubbing his eyes. 'I'll get someone on it.'

'It's two weeks today since Wade was killed,' I say after a minute. 'Maybe whoever did this doesn't want Ava sticking around. Maybe she knows something about what happened to Sterling and it was a warning.'

'Pretty dramatic way to say fuck off,' Fleet comments.

'It's worked though. You heard her last night—she'll be on the first plane out of here as soon as she's released from hospital.'

'Well, we know Lizzie hates her, but physically attacking her seems a bit of a stretch. Maybe our friend Brodie has gone all fugitive, hiding in the shadows and only coming out in the dead of night to attack people?'

'Cartwright probably has the most reason to want her out of here but it obviously wasn't him. He hasn't left the rehab centre since he checked in.'

'True,' Fleet says. 'But like we keep saying, if Cartwright's involved in this mess, he's not getting physical. He's working with someone.'

'Yeah.' I'm frustrated that our attempt to discover a connection between Brodie and Cartwright has hit a brick wall—we can't find any contact between them. 'Maybe Ava was originally involved in the attack on Wade but whoever did this just wants her to shut up now and go back to the US.'

'If that's true then it means this is the same guy. Do we really think that's likely? That he's hunting down people close to Wade like in a teen horror flick?'

'Do you really think it could be Brodie?' I ask.

'Dunno. It's not a huge stretch to imagine him pounding the streets at night thinking up weird shit to do. And then there's Walter Miller—Brodie's still the only person we can even vaguely link to both victims.'

I scratch my ankle underneath my thick sock. The skin on my legs is rough, with prickly hairs pushing through. 'Yeah, he volunteered at a homeless shelter years ago. It's not exactly a hot lead.'

'No,' Fleet admits. 'It's not. But we don't have anything else.' He kicks at the floor, making me jump. Glancing at the clock, he says, 'This case is such bullshit.' He pushes his fingers against his temples and bends forward onto the table, and I think that this is the first time he has been so vulnerable in front of me.

'You okay?' I ask after a minute.

He ignores my question and looks at his watch. 'The troops will be here soon, so we'll be able to tell them the good news about Ava. Another celebrity for them all to jizz over and then chat about with their nearest and dearest tonight.' He curls his lip in disgust. 'I need another coffee.' Then he pulls himself to his feet, yawning. 'Do you want one?'

'Sure,' I say, 'thanks.'

He smiles at me as he walks past, the buzz of the real world rolling in as he opens the door.

Wednesday, 29 August

11.02 pm

Trapped in the deepest of sleeps, I dream of fingers and toes. Close-ups of unseeing eyes. My mind flutters around the edges of old cases. Terrified children. Dead children. Ben's sleeping face. So peaceful. Too peaceful? I start to panic that Ben is actually not asleep at all. I step closer to him, lines of moonlight resting on his perfect face. He is so still. I can't think; I don't want to believe what I'm seeing. I step closer, already crying. Ben isn't moving and I'm saying his name over and over and he's still not moving. I touch his face. My hand connects with cold skin and then he disappears. I paw at the empty bed, desperate to find my little boy, pulling bedclothes onto the floor, my cries ringing around the room. He's gone.

My leg kicks out, jerking me awake. A car alarm curls through the night.

Damp and anxious, I lie looking at the ceiling as my body adjusts to wakefulness.

Josh and I met for a drink earlier this evening, seated side by side on uncomfortably tall stools. I filled him in on my week and surprised myself by telling him about Dad and Rebecca's engagement; I even talked about Mum dying. Despite my assumption that he would be dismissive with me since our aborted romantic evening, he was more attentive than ever and seemed to understand my complicated feelings. It felt good to unload on someone who isn't directly involved. He played with my hand as I talked and made me laugh with stories about his entitled co-workers. Looking at him, I felt a rush of affection. I did what I always do and promised myself that when the Wade case is over I'll make more of an effort. Give this a real shot. Men like Josh don't turn up regularly and I need to stop being so careless with him.

Ben called as I was walking home and I forced myself not to ask him about Scott's girlfriend. We talked about school, and I took a photo of the sky over the city and sent it to him. After we hung up, I got home and crawled into bed, tumbling into a restless few hours of broken sleep.

Turning to the clock, I see it's not even midnight. I listen to the various heaves and grunts of the night for a bit longer before hauling myself up and heading into the kitchen. Gritty and irritable, I'm annoyed at my failed attempts to sleep while I have the chance. I run the tap until the water turns hot and then stand at the window as I sip it.

My glass soon empty, I toy with the idea of alcohol but I know I should try to get more sleep. I walk through the apartment, running my fingers along the walls, and climb back into bed, shutting my eyes and willing the next day to appear in front of me.

I must have drifted off because suddenly my eyes are springing open. My work phone, which has somehow ended up under my pillow, is pulling me out of unconsciousness. The name 'Nick Fleet' fills the screen and I feel a sense of dread as I answer.

'What is it?' I ask.

'Woodstock? That you?' He's somewhere noisy—I hear shrieks and laughter in the background. 'Gemma?' The acoustics change like he's stepped into a stairwell.

'Yes? What is it?'

'I need you to come meet me.'

'Now?' For a second I wonder if I'm dreaming this. 'Where are you?' I say as I roll out of bed.

'The casino,' he replies. 'Come now. There's been a development.'

—◄O►—

I toss a ten-dollar note at the cab driver and rush the short distance into the heat of the casino foyer. I call Fleet as I push my way past a steady flow of people. Tall glamorous women in strappy dresses clutch the arms of portly men; drunk teens move in packs, slapping and groping one another, shrieking and giggling. A family who could easily have stepped out of an ad for Ralph Lauren stand together looking disoriented, each holding the handle of a plush-looking suitcase. A young woman dances solo across the foyer with her eyes closed. Unblinking security guards appear to see none of this, only coming to life to ID a group of girls with thick eyeliner.

Before I left my apartment I pulled on a grey jumper and a pair of jeans, covering both with an oversized navy coat. For a moment I think that the guard is going to ID me but he waves me through into the gaming area. The plastic beeping sounds make me feel like I'm in the bowels of a computer game. Everywhere I look people are glued to the illuminated screens, robotically lifting their arms to farewell more money. Fleet's not answering and I scan the aisles of machines, half expecting to see him.

My phone rings and I startle. I am only half present—the other half of me is still asleep in bed.

'Are you here yet?' asks Fleet.

'Yes, I'm here. Somewhere. I have no idea where to go though.'

'I'm at the Solar Bar, near the main tables.' He hangs up.

'Great,' I mutter through gritted teeth, as I walk back to the security guards.

'Hey, sweetheart,' leers a short man in a shiny jacket. He grabs at my waist as I go past.

'Fuck off,' I say and he laughs, his hands in the air.

'Just trying to be friendly.'

'Where's the Solar Bar?' I ask one of the guards, who had watched this exchange with zero reaction.

He blinks slowly and shifts his empty stare in my direction, then lifts his hand to point. 'Down that way, to the left. Follow the chandeliers.'

I soon see Fleet sitting in a booth, a half-drunk martini in front of him, tapping at his phone.

'I'm here,' I announce, sinking into the seat in front of him.

'Gemma Woodstock,' he says. 'Wow. You really are here.'

'You're drunk,' I say, my heart sinking as my embarrassment rises, closely followed by rage. 'What happened?'

'You know, I don't even really know why I called you.' He throws back the last of his drink, sucks the olive off the stick, and then uses the stick to pick his teeth. 'I'm used to having you around, I guess.'

'If this was just you wanting to chat, I'm leaving.' My anger has quickly shifted to a deep sadness and all I want is to be in bed. 'We can talk tomorrow.'

I stand and he grabs my wrist. 'Hey. Come on, Gemma. Don't go, please.'

'Let go of me, Nick,' I say, his first name awkward in my mouth.

'Sorry,' he mutters, dropping his grip. He pushes the glass away and puts his head in his hands and moans.

I look down at the top of his head, his unruly tangles of hair unable to agree on a direction. I notice a few strands of grey at the crown.

Suddenly he launches forward, his head between his knees.

'Are you alright?' I ask.

His laugh is like a slap. 'Am I *alright*?' he repeats, laughing rudely again.

'Okay, fine.' I turn around and start back toward the entrance.

'Gemma!' The chair scrapes the floor as he roughly pushes it back. One of the guards eyes us and his look asks if I'm okay. I nod—I can handle this.

'I can't believe you,' I hiss at Fleet. 'Dragging me out here in the middle of the night because you're pissed. Or have you lost all your money? You need a ride home?'

He closes his eyes as if he's trying to disappear. 'That's not what it was like,' he mumbles.

'I'll see you tomorrow,' I say and turn around again.

'Gemma, I'm sorry. Please stay and have a drink with me.'

I pause, hating myself for it. There's a sadness in his voice. Regret. I don't want to leave angry—our partnership is so important—but I hate that I'm here at his beckoning.

'Please Gemma. I'm not . . . good. I didn't know who else to call.'

I feel myself relenting. Part of me is glad he's reached out to me. 'One drink,' I acquiesce.

'Not here,' he says, taking my arm and guiding me across the room.

Ten minutes later we're tucked into the corner of a small wine bar attached to the casino. Hot air is blasting my face from a vent in the ceiling as I glance at the drinks menu. We order and our drinks arrive almost immediately.

'So do you come here often?' I say sarcastically, sipping my vodka soda. My body is confused at the taste of alcohol, having already been to bed twice. But I'm not tired anymore, I'm wired.

'I'm not a gambler,' says Fleet out of nowhere.

'Not my business if you are,' I say, the liquid warming a trail to my stomach.

'I'm not.' He tips more beer into his mouth. His face is flushed pink and his lips are ruby red. His eyes have a sheen from the booze. 'It's one vice I don't have.'

'Okay.' I have more of my drink and wonder if I'm finally going to find out more about the elusive Nick Fleet.

Creatures of the night surround us. Loners. Tentative couples. Bored-looking bar staff. I think about the bartender from last weekend and wonder if I've been added to his folklore, whether he told his mates about the girl who came to the bar alone, went back to his house, then screwed his brains out before disappearing at the break of dawn.

Fleet laughs hollowly. 'Do you know what I did tonight?' He looks at me, his eyes all over the place. 'I went on a date. This woman has been bugging me for weeks and I'm like, okay, cool, sure, let's go out. Why not? Not getting anywhere on this piece-of-shit case anyway. May as well blow off some steam.' He pulls at his collar. Presses the insides of his wrists to his forehead.

I watch him silently, unsure why he's so angry. I can feel the energy pulsing from inside his body, his blood running hot.

'So I'm on this date. We have dinner. Drinks. It's going well. It's nice. And then I say we should go somewhere else, have a cocktail. And she says, nah. Reckons I have a bad vibe. So she thanks me for dinner and then says she has to leave.'

'Well,' I say slowly, 'I'm sorry you had a shitty date but I'm sure you'll have no trouble getting another one. A better one, I mean.'

He waves my comment away. 'You should have seen the way she looked at me. Like there was something wrong with me. She said I seemed aggressive.' His lips twist into a sneer. 'It's fucked up that I'm the one hunting down the wife beaters and thugs but this chick thinks *I'm* aggressive.'

'You do seem kind of worked up,' I say carefully. 'We've both been under a lot of pressure. Maybe going on a date tonight wasn't the best idea.'

'Inspector Gemma, the relationship detective.' He slumps back into his seat and laughs. 'Ah well, her loss.' He sips his drink. 'Are you seeing anyone?'

'Not really,' I say, not wanting to discuss Josh with Fleet.

Fleet puts on a dreamy voice. 'Don't worry, he's out there somewhere.'

'Whatever.' I'm keen to move this conversation away from me. 'What time did all this happen? Have you just been roaming around here ever since, feeling sorry for yourself?'

He tips back the last of his beer and waves the waitress over for another. I slip a look at the clock, wondering if I'm going to get any more sleep tonight.

'I got pretty wasted,' he says. 'Went to the tables. I meant it when I said I don't gamble but I like to watch. The guys who know what they're doing—it's cool, you know.'

His beer arrives and the waitress raises her eyebrows at me, but I indicate that I'm fine with the drink I have.

'Anyway, then I saw Jacoby,' he says, 'and shit got interesting.'

I put down my drink. 'You saw Frank Jacoby?'

'Yeah. It was weird. He sat down next to me and started playing the tables. He was with his usual cronies.'

'Please tell me you didn't speak to him,' I say, imagining Fleet's drunken aggression and the trouble it might land him in. Land us all in.

'Nah. Don't worry, you can untwist your undies. I just watched them. Like a good little detective.'

'Right,' I say, relieved. As I look at Fleet, I try to think what to say next. There's a madness in his eyes and I can't work out if it's self-loathing or rage. Or both.

'Jacoby was with his crew. A real wolf-pack vibe. There were lots of whispered chats. No doubt some dodgy deals going on. Escorts to be arranged.' Fleet's voice is part TV reporter and part sarcastic comedian. He takes another slug of beer and wipes his mouth roughly. 'Anyhow, I recognised one of the guys he was with from somewhere. I think we pulled him in last year about a suicide—some guy hung himself in the dunny of a law firm, and this guy was a partner or some shit.' Fleet taps his finger to the side of his nose. 'These guys, you know, they're always neck-deep in shit. They can't help themselves.'

'Well, if it was a suicide, that's not necessarily suspicious,' I say, reluctant to get into a discussion about it.

'Maybe. Maybe. But you know, the dead guy's wife reckoned he was being bullied, that he'd been blamed for a whole heap of stuff that he hadn't been involved in, so I don't know.' Fleet shakes a cigarette out of its packet and starts flicking it between his fingers. 'Jacoby and his mates, they think they're untouchable. It fucking pisses me off.'

'So why did you call me?' I ask. 'To talk about Jacoby? Or your shitty date?'

'I dunno. Dunno. Just felt like it, I guess.'

I sigh. 'We should make a move.'

'You know best, boss,' he says, executing a sloppy salute as he tips back the last of his beer.

I take care of the bill and we head out of the bar.

'Where was Jacoby?' I ask, my curiosity getting the better of me.

'At the tables,' says Fleet, 'just through there.'

'I want to see him,' I say, guiding Fleet through the maze of machines.

He's unsteady on his feet as we make our way to the tables. Sure enough, I see Jacoby and his mates backslapping each other and looking incredibly smug. They are clearly also about to leave, pulling on coats and shaking hands with the croupier. I wait until they've started toward the main entrance before pulling Fleet along after them. One of the men with Jacoby is talking loudly into a phone, describing where to pick them up.

Exiting the casino, we're blasted with a last gust of warm air before being thrust into the night. Fleet stumbles and lurches toward a concrete pillar; bent over, he looks as if he's about to vomit. I bend down next to him and speak into his ear. 'Are you alright?'

He squeezes his eyes shut and coughs toward the ground.

I glance at Jacoby and his friends again. They're preoccupied with a loud recollection of one of their wins from the evening.

Dropping my head back down, I whisper to Fleet, 'Come on, let me help you get into a cab.'

He moans as I pull him up and along to the cab rank. I yank open the back door of the first taxi and try to encourage him to get inside.

'If you're not coming, I'm not taking him,' says the cabbie, looking at Fleet with disdain.

'I don't know where he lives,' I tell him.

'Not my problem, love,' he replies. 'You getting in?'

Fleet's weight is now heavy on my left side as he edges closer to sleep.

A sleek silver Audi turns into the casino's curved driveway and parallel parks next to the taxi. Jacoby's crew lets out a little cheer and ambles over to it.

Jacoby opens the front door of the car, and suddenly I'm looking straight into the face of Josh Evans, *my* Josh, a beanie on his head, his eyes shifting from the driveway to the road as Jacoby and his drunk mates clamber in.

I lean forward so that my head is hidden behind Fleet's, but before I can sneak another look into the car Jacoby pulls the door shut and they all disappear behind the tinted windows.

Thursday, 30 August

2.33 am

With the exception of Ben, Dad and Rebecca, no one has been in my apartment since I moved in. As Fleet and I make our way up the creaky stairs I feel an overwhelming sense of panic at letting him into this part of my life. In the taxi, as we left the casino, my mind reeling from the sight of Josh, I prodded Fleet first on the shoulder and then on the face, asking him for his address. I even shoved my hands into his pockets trying to locate his wallet. After a few minutes of this awkward fishing expedition, and a frustrated glare from the taxi driver, I reluctantly gave him my address.

Fleet's head rolls against mine as we reach my apartment door. His thick hair tickles the side of my face.

'I'm sorry,' he mumbles into my hair, 'I'm a mess.'

I ignore him, already dreading the awkwardness waiting for us in the morning. My exhausted mind is struggling to keep up as I lurch between the Wade case, Josh's pale face in the 4WD and the bizarre babysitting role I've found myself in.

I push the heavy door open with my shoulder, then Fleet and I do a strange little dance as I help him to the couch. When I've deposited him as gently as I can, I rush to my room to get a spare blanket, hoping he won't wake up and start talking again. When I return, his head is firmly entrenched on a cushion and his breathing is steady. I pull off his shoes and cover him with the blanket, fetching a glass of water and placing it on the coffee table. He doesn't move.

I grab the photo of Ben from the bookshelf and hide it in a cupboard. I pull the curtain across his little nook room. Then I go to my bedroom, my arms aching from supporting Fleet. I undress quickly. My body prickles with goose bumps so sharp they're like needles in my legs and arms. I slide in between the covers in my underwear and almost cry with relief as my head hits the pillow. Grabbing my phone, I shoot a message to Isaacs saying that we've had a late night and will continue to follow up a lead on the Wade case first thing. That should buy us a bit more time. What state will Fleet be in when he wakes?

Josh's face appears in my mind but I grimly shove it aside. I'll work out how to deal with that tomorrow.

Minutes later, or maybe it's hours, the bed shifts and I'm jolted back into reality. My eyes are still shut and for a moment I think it must be Ben crawling into bed with me. I eagerly drift back into a dream.

A large hand clasps my hip, and I freeze.

The hand circles my thigh, fingers pushing beneath the thin material of my underwear. A moan creeps into my ear.

Fleet.

'No,' I whisper, squeezing my eyes shut.

There is an ache all over me—especially in my throat, which feels as if it has closed over. His hand grips my leg more firmly, then moves to my waist, just above my hip, rough and demanding. I can smell him, alcohol fumes and man. For just a moment I consider letting this happen. His skin is hot on mine, his need thick in the air. He moves against me. My body surges in response to his closeness, but I can't tell if it's danger or desire. I think about turning toward him and letting him touch me. Letting him be inside me. It would almost be easier than turning him away. But it's not what I want.

Suddenly my impulse to be anywhere but living this moment is overwhelming. I curl myself into a ball, willing him to go away.

'I want you, Gemma.' His voice is thick, more animal than human, and comes from the darkness behind me and hovers in the black in front of me. I feel afraid of what he might do to me.

'No,' I say again, louder, forcing the words past the ache pulling at my jaw. I won't cry now, no way.

'Come on,' he says, still grabbing me, trying to put his fingers inside me.

'Don't touch me,' I say, and it's almost a scream.

After an eternity, he releases his grip and the bed moves under me as he shifts his weight to the other side.

Wheezing, I try to calm my flying heart. I stare straight ahead and wish I could somehow turn myself off. Shut myself down. I can't believe he has done this. That I have to deal with this. I turn silently to look at him, trying to think of something to say that will erase what just happened. I can only make out the thin white line of his profile; his fist is pressing into the centre of his forehead. I can't tell if his eyes are open or closed but I can still feel something toxic radiating from his body. I turn back toward the wall, willing for this whole night to be over and wiped from our memories. And then impossibly, despite the racing of my heart and the mad whirl of my thoughts, I fall into sleep.

Thursday, 30 August
7.58 am

It's quiet in my bedroom, the faint sounds of a new day far away. The remnants of a bad dream choke and die, leaving my skin crawling. Emerging from my bedroom, I see that Fleet is gone: the blanket I placed over him a lifetime ago is neatly folded on the arm of the couch; a rinsed water glass is upside down in the drying rack beside the sink. Recalling the scene that played out in my bedroom just a few hours ago makes me feel desperately ill. I should never have gone to meet him, let alone brought him into my home.

I get in the shower and relish the burn of the scalding water down my spine. I scrub all the places he touched, wanting to cry but finding that I can't. Lifting my head, I let the water run down my face and into my mouth. If I could walk out into the ocean right now and let it sweep me away, I would.

I shut off the tap and just stand there, paralysed by the unavoidable interactions in front of me. I'll have to talk to Josh and work out what the hell is going on. Why was he picking up Jacoby and his mates from the casino in the middle of the night? Does it have something to do with one of his fraud cases? The irritating reliability of Josh, the dull but solid rock he has formed in my world, has suddenly turned into a dangerous gaping hole. Who the hell is he really?

And Fleet. I can't bear the thought of seeing him.

I force myself through the motions of getting ready, regret and anger chasing each other around my head like rabid dogs. I pull on a shirt and cover it with a jumper. I comb out my wet hair and tug it into a low ponytail. I drink a large glass of water. A ragged sob blurts out of me and I clench my fists in an attempt to push it back inside. I catch myself in the mirror and wonder what Fleet sees. A lonely woman past her prime? A pushover? A friend? A conquest? A victim? Nothing? Ben's image rises up above the thoughts of Fleet, and the sobs rally again. I can't break now.

I wipe my tears away, sniff hard and take a deep breath. Then I punch a fist hard into the doorframe and walk out, my hand throbbing.

◄o►

'Fleet has called in sick,' Isaacs tells me casually as he walks past. 'Some kind of gastro, or food poisoning. Hopefully you don't catch it, Woodstock. I'd like a case update when you have a moment. I'm keen to know what was keeping you busy last night.'

'Probably a good thing he's stayed away,' says Nan darkly. 'He's been looking terrible all week. You both do.'

With only a few minutes until the case meeting, I smile thinly at Nan before darting to the disabled toilets where I snap the door shut behind me and retch dramatically over the bowl. Red-faced and heaving I stare at myself in the mirror, blanching at the smell. I would strangle Fleet with my bare hands if I had the chance. How dare he bail on me after this? I worked myself up to be in a position to deal with him, to have the inevitable first interaction. The idea of having to ready myself for it all over again feels impossible. His betrayal continues to wash over me. Splashing water on my face, I wait for the colour to fade before I blot my skin on the grit of a paper towel, and head to the case room.

We've lost two of the team to a violent rape that was called in late last night, three to the suspicious death of a shopkeeper in Balaclava, and two others to a hit-and-run. But the eighteen remaining faces that stare up at me as I pace in front of the board still look as resolute as they did two weeks ago—and a lot less tired than I feel.

I kick off the meeting and feel myself begin to calm. I hold on to my notebook, shift papers between my hands, run my eyes over lines of notes. The familiar dance plays out in front of us. Brodie is still missing. We still don't know exactly where Paul Wade was at the time of his brother's attack, or whether he was in Melbourne when Miller was killed. There doesn't appear to be any communication between Cartwright and Brodie, and we have no idea if either of them had something to do with the attack on Ava. The only real development is that our confessor Simon Carmichael has gone to the media claiming to have spoken to Wade's ghost, who supposedly told him he was killed by a loved one.

I look at the magnified photo of the masked zombie on the case board as the team members give their updates. It's beyond frustrating to know that I'm looking at Sterling Wade's killer but we're still no closer to the answers.

In some ways, it's easier to do all of this without Fleet. Without his cool judgement, I don't think about what I'm saying, I just say it. Despite my spinning brain, I'm feeling a renewed sense of purpose. 'Where are we with the footage from the restaurant Ava James was at the other night? I want that checked off today.'

Eyebrows lift at my blunt manner and suddenly I feel myself

getting defensive. How else am I supposed to behave after the night I've had?

'Where's Detective Fleet today?' Chloe asks, approaching me as the team starts to leave the room.

'Oh, sorry,' I tell her, 'I should have said something. He's unwell. I'm sure he'll be back on board tomorrow. Is there something I can help you with?'

'No. No.' She ducks her head, goes to leave and then changes her mind. 'I've been meaning to say that it's really inspiring having a case like this led by a woman. I feel like I've learned a lot.' She runs a hand along her pregnant belly absently.

'Oh,' I say, my face growing warm. 'Well, thank you but it's an equal partnership with Detective Fleet.'

'I know that,' she says, 'but still, you know what I mean.'

I nod and she throws me a little wave and leaves, and I watch her go and wonder what exactly she does mean.

After returning to my desk I call the hospital and am informed that Ava will be discharged later this afternoon. 'She says she's leaving for the US first thing tomorrow morning,' the doctor tells me. 'She is very upset.'

I put the phone down and flip through interview transcripts that detail the accounts of the featured extras who were facing Wade when he was attacked.

We were running toward him like wild beasts.

I was totally lost in the moment.

It was such a high.

Then I panicked.

Something was wrong.

I didn't know what was happening.

I have no idea who would do this.

No, nothing seemed out of the ordinary during the shoot.

I can't think about anything else.

One minute everything was great.

I was going to be in a Hollywood movie, with real stars.

The next minute everything changed.

It was so awful, seeing him lying there like that.

It's funny, really, commented one extra, *how absolutely every-thing can be totally fine and then turn into a complete nightmare in a single moment.*

—◄○►—

At around 3 pm I call Josh, my insides like stone.

'Hey, Gemma,' he answers happily. Before last night I would have found his easy joy mildly saccharine; now my stomach flips.

'Are you busy tonight?' I ask, shutting my eyes. I don't really want to see him—in fact, if I could erase him from the planet I would—but I need to get this done. I feel oddly empowered at the thought of closing out something properly for once.

There is a beat of silence. Josh is probably trying to read my tone. 'Not really,' he says. 'I'm pretty tired though—I ended up having to work last night. But I can catch up if you want to chat. How are you? Is everything okay with the case?'

'It's fine,' I reply. 'I was thinking we could get a drink or something.'

'Sure,' he says. 'Great!' He's clearly injecting some enthusiasm into his voice that he's hoping will rub off on me. 'I should be done by seven.'

'Good,' I reply, my voice firm. 'Let's meet at that bar we went to a while back, the place near the casino.'

Another pause. 'Sure, Gemma, sounds good.' Nerves are creeping into his voice, and I wonder if he'll actually be there.

'See you soon,' I say, and hang up.

Thursday, 30 August
7.03 pm

I check my work phone. Then my personal phone. There's a text from Dad but still nothing from Fleet. My emotions circle like a fussy cat, incapable of settling. Does he even remember what he did? Is he awake right now worrying about how to approach me? Is he angry at me, or ashamed? I can't shake the feeling that this has ruined everything, and it's tearing me apart.

The bar is well-heated but I've left my jacket on: there is nothing relaxed about this meeting. I sip at my gin and tonic. Soft conversations filter through my mind, as do the layers of the Wade case. Laughter erupts from a table near the window just as Josh walks in. A twist of cold air strokes my skin when he bends forward to kiss me before tugging off his scarf and shrugging his bulky coat onto the back of his chair.

'Sorry I'm a bit late—Jesus, what a day!' he says, enthusiastic as always. He rubs his hands together. 'Well, this is nice. Two nights in a row.' He scans the drinks menu. 'How was your day? Any interesting case updates?'

I wait for him to order a drink and then say, 'Why were you at the casino last night, Josh?'

His mouth drops open and his eyes bulge. 'Huh?'

'Why were you at the casino last night?' I repeat calmly.

'I wasn't at the casino.' His wine arrives and he takes a gulp, looking around the room before tossing me a casual smile. 'Why, does one of your friends think they saw me there or something?'

'You were there early this morning in a silver Audi picking up Frank Jacoby and his mates,' I reply, not smiling back. 'Why?'

He shifts in his seat, obviously filtering through options in his mind. He looks directly into my eyes, almost as if he's pleading for me to understand.

'I was just doing them a favour,' he mumbles.

'What the hell is going on, Josh?'

He pales and squirms in his seat. 'Look. Frank's a family friend. My uncle's mate. My uncle asks me to do things for them some-times.' He laughs nervously and has a sip of wine that turns into a splutter.

'How do you know him?' I demand.

'His wife is my uncle's cousin.'

'Ivy Strachan?' I ask, finally putting a name to the face of the woman in the photograph at his apartment.

'Yeah.' Josh has shrunk into his chair now; his shoulders slump and his head dips forward.

'Was your uncle there last night?' I ask.

He nods.

'Jacoby got you the job at the law firm, didn't he?' I say.

Josh nods slowly. I'm hot, warm under my arms and on my chest and neck. My pulse is on the run and does bizarre laps around my body. We both know what's coming next.

'You were at Jacoby's apartment that night,' I say, somehow feeling even more tired than I did before. 'You saw Jacoby arguing with Ginny Frost on that balcony. You're the missing witness.'

Josh looks me straight in the eye, in silent confirmation, before he leans forward and grabs my hand. 'I'm sorry,' he says simply. 'I never meant for any of this to happen.'

◄○►

Hours later I'm still at the bar, my stomach full of burger and chips. Josh is long gone. The day is cruising toward its finish line but my mind is far from winding down. The fury I felt at his deception has drifted into an apathetic numbness. I keep replaying our first meeting at the courthouse cafe over in my mind, feeling beyond foolish at not somehow sensing he held the key to a case that at the time was consuming so much of my life.

In between nervous hand-wringing, Josh told me the whole story. He managed to evade our meticulous investigation more by chance than clever design, as is often the case. His uncle had arranged for him to stay at Jacoby's apartment for several days; his own place was being painted, and he was cramming for his exams. He'd fallen behind during the semester and knew he was in danger of failing, and so he disappeared into an intense study bubble, not leaving the apartment in the three days leading up to Jacoby's Christmas-in-July party—hence completely avoiding the CCTV footage from the entryway that was processed and analysed.

Jacoby had completely forgotten Josh would be there when he arranged his winter get-together. He and his closest friends arrived at 6 pm to get things set up, and found an exhausted, caffeine-addled Josh. He started to leave but his uncle convinced him to stay, insisting that he deserved some time out after so much study. After three days of cramming and virtually no sleep, Josh had a few drinks early in the evening with his uncle and Jacoby's other mates, and then snuck off before most of the guests arrived. He took a sleeping pill and put himself to bed in the guestroom at the far end of the apartment.

Hours later he woke up to see a woman sleeping on the couch near the window. Jacoby was on the balcony arguing with another woman; their fight was heated and Jacoby sounded furious. After a few minutes Josh crept over to the window where he saw Jacoby holding the woman aggressively against the wall as she cried. This was around the time that Sasha Cryer woke from her spot on the couch, and Josh quickly returned to the bed. He feared the worst when he heard Ginny screaming a few seconds later but despite this decided that confronting Jacoby wasn't an option. Hoping the woman on the couch was too drunk to remember anything, he pretended to go back to sleep while trying to decide what to do. Eventually Sasha left the room.

Just before 3 am, his uncle sought him out, telling him they had to leave—there had been a terrible accident and they needed to get Josh out of the apartment. He got dressed as his uncle stripped and remade the bed. Jacoby, Josh's uncle and a male friend accompanied Josh down the fire escape to avoid the security cameras. They drove him to his uncle's place where he hid in the garage until late the following day.

Jacoby told him to keep his mouth shut or kiss his career goodbye.

Josh knew who I was from the beginning, having recognised me from the press conference shown on the news the morning of the day we met at the courthouse. He figured if he could befriend me, he might be able to find out how the case was progressing—and put himself back in Jacoby's good books. He got my number. Did a bit of research and realised I was new in town; he assumed that I'd be open to a new friend. His uncle encouraged the idea.

'But the thing is, I really like you, Gemma. I didn't expect to but I do. You're so different to the people I normally hang out with.

I've stuffed everything up. I should have gone to the police from the beginning.'

Pushing his hand away, I told him that if he didn't go to the police by 9 am tomorrow and tell them what he saw that night in July, then I would turn him in. Apologising over and over, Josh promised he would. We agreed that he won't mention me to begin with, but I know my link to him will become apparent fairly quickly.

I haul myself to my feet, winding my scarf around my neck. As I walk toward home, every step matches the beat of my headache. I feel used by Josh, used by Fleet, and beyond stupid.

A tram rattles past as I make my way up Bourke Street. Giant signs scream at me from shop windows, promising savings and discounts. A jeweller advertises the resetting of old gemstones for new love, which reminds me of Dad and Rebecca's engagement. My jaw clenches and I keep my head down while I cross Swanston Street. Gusts of chilled wind seem to come up from the ground. I pull out my cigarettes, ducking into a laneway to shield the flame from the wind as I attempt to light one. I flick the lighter a few times without success. I turn my back on the main street, trying to escape the wind.

I hear a noise behind me but before I can think anything more than that, I'm slammed against the brick wall with such force that for an instant I think there's been an earthquake. The sting across my face comes a second after the impact, followed quickly by a dull pain that seems to be holding my brain hostage. I try to think, to process what's happening, but there is only an endless ringing.

A large hand shifts its grip on the back of my head and the weight of a body pins me to the wall. Hands run up and down the length of my body. I'm trapped. I breathe out slowly, too shocked to cry.

'Please,' I whisper.

'You stupid bitch,' hisses a voice as the hand releases my head slightly before smacking it into the wall again.

My legs fold in on themselves and I drop to the ground, cigarettes scattered around me as the sound of retreating footsteps rings in my ears.

Friday, 31 August
7.16 am

I am roused by an eager beeping sound and open my eyes to a bright white wall. The pain has attached itself to my head but the excruciating throb from last night has been wrestled into submission by the handful of pills I was encouraged to take.

The pale blue curtain at the end of the bed rustles and the smiling face of a nurse appears. 'Oh good, you're already awake. How's the head?' Her voice is familiar and I recall that she woke me at various intervals during the night, saying my name and shining a light in my eyes.

I swallow, trying to force saliva into my dry mouth. 'It's okay.'

'You poor thing,' she says cheerily.

It all comes flooding back: Fleet's alcohol-ridden breath as he grabbed at me, Josh's confession. The grip around the back of my head before it was slammed into the wall.

'What time is it?' I ask the nurse.

'A quarter past seven,' she says.

Gingerly I sit up. Pinpricks of white form a snowstorm across my vision, but it doesn't seem to make too much difference to the pain.

'I have to go,' I tell her, stifling a yawn and shifting my weight to the other side of the bed.

Her brows dip together and she bites her lip. 'You really should stay for a few more hours. We like to keep an eye on people who've had nasty falls and bumped their heads.'

'I'll be fine,' I assure her, getting to my feet.

'Well, do you have a partner? Someone who can look after you?'

'Yep,' I say, throwing her a quick smile.

After she checks me over, she bustles off to tend to someone else. I get dressed, pressing the side of my head experimentally. I pull back the curtain and walk through the ward. I sign myself out and jump into a cab.

Entering my apartment, I'm surprised to find it exactly how I left it yesterday morning. The blanket I gave Fleet is still folded on the end of the couch. Frodo gapes stupidly, hoping food will find its way into his mouth. Studying myself in the bathroom mirror, I inspect the sprawling bruise that clouds the edge of my face. Fortunately most of the damage is to the side of my head and covered by my hair, though a sharp cut runs along my hairline just above my ear, and the faint rings of a black eye are forming. I wash the area gently in a lukewarm shower and then cover the smudges of blue and purple with make-up as best I can.

I let myself consider what happened. Was it a random attack or some kind of warning? Was it the same person who attacked Ava? Is any of it linked? I carefully comb my hair and stare at my face in the mirror, considering the possibility that it perhaps had something to do with Jacoby. I swallow, feeling foolish all over again. That voice was unrecognisable—I don't want to seriously consider that it might have been Josh.

Josh. The burn of humiliation surges again as I think about the way I was duped. I wonder if he's already at the station. Will he really come forward? My ultimatum was clear and he seemed almost relieved that I'd confronted him, desperate to end the whole sorry saga. Part of me believes he was caught in the wrong place at the wrong time. But I don't know him. I don't know how deep his deception runs, how much influence his uncle and Jacoby have over him.

The one thing I do know is that without Josh's confession, there's very little evidence that Jacoby pushed Ginny Frost over the balcony. Maybe he spoke to his uncle last night; maybe they've formed a plan for how to deal with me.

In the midst of my panic, a text pings onto my work phone: Fleet asking if I'm coming to the case meeting. It's exactly the kind of text he would have sent me two days ago. Before he crossed the clearest of lines.

My breathing quickens and I think maybe I'm having an anxiety attack. But as I clutch the bathroom cabinet, the wave of terror peaks and then quickly recedes.

Not knowing what Josh is going to do makes it difficult for me to decide how to approach things. Should I confess our relationship to Isaacs and risk looking like an idiot, or plead ignorance? If Josh doesn't come forward I'll need to lead the charge, force a tidal wave of action, potentially send myself straight back to Smithson in disgrace.

And that's before giving myself the headspace to consider what to do about Fleet.

Fingers shaking, I text back that I'm on my way. I blow-dry my hair but leave it loose to help hide the evidence of last night's attack. I shrug on my coat and walk out the door, gritting my teeth and swallowing past the lingering sensation of the hand on the back of my head and the terror that took over when I thought I was going to die.

◄O►

'Jeez, what happened to you, Woodstock?' remarks Fleet, looking at me in alarm and I wonder if he thinks that perhaps he might have done this to me.

'I fell,' I say tersely.

My body is out of control, reacting to his presence like he's radiating electricity. All moisture leaves my mouth. Flashes of the minutes in my bedroom flit through my mind.

He's about to say something else when a rumble of excitement erupts behind us. Nan and Calvin are summoned into Isaacs' office. Josh, I think. Isaacs throws me a cool look and I see my career flash before my eyes as his door clicks shut.

'Wonder what that's all about?' Fleet says as he stands up, stretching. 'God! I feel about a million times better today than I did yesterday.' He smiles sheepishly at me. 'I'm getting too old for midweek benders.' He steps toward our case room. 'Are you coming?'

My limbs are like lead as I grab my notebook and follow a few paces behind, struggling to make sense of his nonchalance. Does he remember what he did? And, I think wildly, does that matter?

'Perk up,' he calls over his shoulder, and I stare at the back of his head, fantasising about slamming it against a wall.

No one comments on my swollen face but several glances make it clear that I haven't covered up the bruises as well as I thought.

'Right,' I say, with far more enthusiasm than I feel. 'Because Detective Fleet was absent yesterday, let's quickly get him up to speed. Ravi, please run us through the case log, and then I want updates on alibis and footage.'

I tune out a little as Ravi talks; my vision blurs slightly as I stare into the dark weave of the carpet. I can already tell there's no new information of note, not like the breakthrough that Nan and Calvin are probably about to be gifted.

Fleet cuts Chloe off, barking questions at the team, clearly pissed off that there's still no sign of Brodie. He's hated him from the start, I realise, remembering his discomfort with Brodie's easy declarations of love and unchecked grief.

Fleet gives out instructions for the day before everyone rises. I walk over to the case board, staring at the two dead men, and a wave of guilt hits me square in the middle. There's something we're not seeing. I stand there with heat flooding to my face, reactivating the throb in my broken head, as I think about Wade and Miller collapsing to the ground in pools of their own blood. It could so easily have been me last night; it takes such a short amount of time to kill a person.

I jump a mile when Chloe brushes the side of my arm as she reaches up to pin a CCTV frame of the crowd: they're looking on as Wade is bundled into the ambulance.

'Sorry,' Chloe says.

'Don't apologise. I spaced out for a minute there.'

I look at the picture. It's like an ancient battle scene, with Wade the slain war hero at the front.

'How are you doing?' I ask Chloe, my eyes drifting to her swollen belly.

Clearly pleased to be asked, she puffs out her cheeks. 'Not too bad. It's getting a bit hard to move around as easily as I usually do but I'm fine. I want to keep working as long as I can.'

She attaches another photo to the board and her wedding rings pass in front of my face. I remember the loving gaze Rebecca gave her engagement ring last weekend and the wistful sadness in Lizzie's expression when she'd looked at hers. Through the fuzzy jabs of pain down the side of my face, tendrils of thoughts join together.

'Lovely rings,' I say to Chloe.

'Oh. Thank you. Yes, they are beautiful.'

I recall the jeweller I walked by last night, all the gemstones turned away from the window with just the advertising left in place.

'Chloe,' I say, 'I want you to do something for me.'

'Of course.' She pushes her hair back from her face and squints at me. 'Excuse me if this is inappropriate, but are you sure you're okay? I noticed your injury.' Her eyes are full of concern and I marvel at the ease with which she expresses care.

'I'm fine,' I say dismissively, stepping back. 'I want you to look into an old case—a house fire that killed a woman down the coast about eight years ago.'

—◀〇▶—

Sick with worry over Josh's confession, I take the stairs to the car park on Level 2 and cut through the rows of cars to the tiny platform that looks out over the street. Sheltered from both the wind and prying eyes, I light a cigarette and lean back against the wall. Brodie's pale pleading face won't leave me alone. Every instinct I have is telling me he's in danger.

'Fancy finding you out here,' booms Fleet.

I drop my cigarette. For some reason, this puts me on the brink of tears.

'Things must be bad if you're smoking at work,' he says.

I don't say anything but edge into the corner, wanting to be as far from him as possible.

'You sure you're alright?' he asks, lighting a smoke and peering into my face.

'I'm fine.'

'I don't believe for a second you fell over.' His dark eyes are kind as he says this, his voice full of concern.

Something bursts inside me and to my horror my face collapses, the tears unstoppable.

'Woodstock, what is it?' He comes to me and awkwardly puts his hand on my shoulder.

'Don't touch me,' I say, lurching sideways.

He steps back, holding his hands up. Ash snows down around him. 'Okay, okay.'

For a moment neither of us says anything. The wind whistles around the concrete pillars as though waiting to see what will happen next.

'Will you at least tell me what's wrong?' Fleet asks. 'Or do you just want me to leave?'

'I know who the missing Jacoby witness is,' I say, no longer able to hold it in and knowing that it's all about to come out anyway.

His eyebrows shoot up comically. 'You do?'

I look at the tip of the burning cigarette. 'It's a guy I've been seeing. I think he's going to come forward today. I think he's here right now.'

Fleet seems to think about this for a moment. 'Did you know?'

I meet his eyes and then quickly look away, feeling more stupid than I can remember. 'No, not until yesterday.' I wipe off the last of my tears. 'But it's not going to look good. I'll be all over his phone records.'

'Will he say anything about you?' asks Fleet. 'Did you acciden-tally feed him any information?'

'I don't think so. He said he wouldn't say anything but I'm obvi-ously going to need to deal with it.' I make a strangled sound. 'I feel like such an idiot.'

Fleet nods, still taking it all in. Suddenly his mouth curls in a snarl. 'Did this guy hurt you?' He gestures toward my head. 'I'll fucking kill him if he did.'

I picture Fleet pushing his body against me, his hot boozy breath on my cheek, his fingers digging into my arse. I feel the grip of the hand on the back of my head last night, followed by the shock of connecting with the wall.

I just want them all to go away. I shake my head and push past Fleet. 'I need to go home,' I say, as the sky opens.

—◄O►—

No one is around when I grab my things from my desk and head out into the storm. Rain falls in jagged sheets, filling the gutters and giving new life to old rubbish. I'm quickly saturated, numb to the centre. I'm exhausted. I need sleep.

At home I wrap my wet hair in a towel, swallow a couple of pain-killers with water and crawl into bed, welcoming the soothing buzz of unconsciousness.

I wake just after 3.30 pm in the exact position I curled up in. My head throbs but I feel more rested than I have in a long time. Outside a swirl of rain hovers above the city.

I drink more water and sit near the window, wondering what will happen to me. The investigation into Josh could well see me lose my job. Or at least see a severe black mark chalked against my name. Maybe what I said to Fleet is true—maybe I really should go home, back to Smithson, and stop pretending that I can make this life here work.

Lightning cracks across the sky followed closely by a chilling rumble of thunder. My work phone rings as if triggered by the madness of the weather.

'Detective Woodstock,' I answer, seeing that it's a station number.

'It's me—Chloe.'

'Yes?' I'm relieved that it's not Isaacs but note the charge in her voice.

'I looked into the old fire death. I'm not sure what you were hoping for but it was definitely not a cut-and-dried case.'

'Tell me everything,' I say, wanting to think about anything other than Josh's perfect face.

'Well, arson was never ruled out but the investigation was inconclusive. Lizzie Short's mother died, as you know. She couldn't get out of her bedroom. Her son Kit, however, managed to get out with just minor injuries.'

'Where was Lizzie?'

'Staying at a friend's place.'

'Why couldn't they rule out arson?'

'It wasn't clear if inflammables had been used. The carport was off to the side of the house near Jenny Short's bedroom and investigators found traces of chemicals in there. The place was pretty run-down so it's possible that something caught alight and spread— or that someone snuck into the carport and started the fire. Jenny had a boyfriend at the time who was known to the police. There was a history of abuse and his alibi was never substantiated.'

I play this over in my mind, my eyes still on the dark grey clouds.

'At the time, did the police peg the boyfriend for starting the fire?' I ask.

'It seems like it but they obviously weren't able to make an arrest,' Chloe says. 'Also, there had been another fire the week prior. An old shed a few streets away from the Shorts' place was torched when the family was out of town and the circumstances were similar, so it had them wondering if a firebug was in the area.'

I remember Kit Short's protective grip on his sister's hunched shoulders at the hospital. The unmade bed that day we went to Lizzie's apartment, both sides slept in.

'Chloe,' I say abruptly, 'you definitely never found anything in Lizzie's finances that could have been a payment for that engagement ring, did you?'

'Not as far back as two years. We checked all her accounts. It certainly didn't come from the Wades either—we checked with his parents. Or the Beaufords. He must have paid cash for it. Unless it was stolen.' She emits a little laugh.

'Or it was a gift,' I say.

'A gift,' she repeats, trying to work out what I'm saying.

'You have a picture of the ring, don't you?'

'Yes. Lizzie was happy to help, though she obviously didn't understand what it had to do with Sterling's murder.'

'I'm not certain that it does,' I tell her, 'or that she's done anything wrong, but I want you to dig up everything you can on Jenny Short, especially photos in which her hands are visible.'

◄○►

The rain stops as abruptly as it started. I shower and dress, desperate to get out of the apartment. The air is ice-cold and damp, and people in suits making the transition from the week to the weekend cast nervous looks skyward. The homeless have shifted to the main thoroughfares, taking refuge under the larger shop awnings where they join the stoic buskers. Reaching the lobby of the hotel I frequent, I order a drink and lean back into the blissful softness of an armchair.

Scenes from yesterday sift through my mind, culminating with my head hard against the brick wall. But as the wine goes down I push the memories away and focus on my steadily firming theories.

I remember Kit Short exclaiming that he'd come straight from the airport when he reached the hospital, but I can't recall this being substantiated. Was that for our benefit? I realise that every time I've seen Kit he's been touching his sister. Is their closeness sinister or am I reading too much into it? Is he obsessed with Lizzie, feeling bonded to her by their tragic adolescence?

I wonder if Sterling mentioned his proposal plans to Kit. Maybe Kit gave his mother's engagement ring to Sterling for him to pop the question. Did Kit then discover what his sister hadn't—that Sterling was involved with Brodie? Did he kill Sterling?

Has he done something to Brodie?

I finish my wine and order another. The pounding ache in my temples urges me on. I get out my notebook and scribble down the timeline.

Was the engagement the trigger to this whole thing? But how would the attack on Walter Miller fit in? Maybe Sterling was somehow involved. Could he and Kit be in cahoots? Lizzie says she was home with Sterling the night Miller was attacked, but what if she's lying and covering for her boyfriend and her brother? Or maybe Sterling and Brodie were involved in something and she's protecting them. We might have been looking at this all wrong— Sterling might have attacked Miller. Could that be why someone killed him?

I press the pen into the page of my notebook, looking at the list of names and dates. Murder is always about upside. Who benefits from Sterling's death? It's all there, I know it—I just don't quite see how it fits together.

'Is this seat taken?'

I look up to see a man with neat auburn hair and a sweet fan of crinkles on either side of his blue eyes.

'Ah, no,' I say.

'You look busy,' he says. 'Don't worry, I have work to do too. I just didn't want to be stuck in my room all night.'

I nod politely, keeping my eyes on my notebook.

'That's the shitty thing about travelling alone,' he adds a few minutes later. 'It sounds so great when you're young but it ends up being pretty lonely sometimes.' He takes a sip of his drink and looks up at me, smiling.

I return his smile.

He gets out his laptop and spends the next fifteen minutes tapping away, his brow furrowed.

I relax back into my thoughts, trying the puzzle pieces one by one.

'Do you have to work all night?' asks the stranger.

'Pretty much,' I say.

My phone rings. Isaacs.

I give the stranger an apologetic look. 'Hello,' I say, my voice cracking.

'Woodstock. Fleet tells me you went home sick today?'

'Yes, sir.'

'I need you in here tomorrow,' he continues, his voice firm. 'Let's meet at 11 am. There are a few things we need to discuss. I assume you will be feeling up to it?'

'Yes, sir,' I say as he hangs up.

This is it, I think. An icy terror fills me from the feet upwards.

'Everything okay?' asks the man.

'What?' I reply. I'd forgotten he was there.

'You look like you need a drink.' He puts his laptop on the coffee table and leans forward, his intent clear. 'Let me get you one. Maybe we can take a break from work for a while.'

'I don't want a drink,' I hiss, grabbing my notebook and standing up.

'Fuck, lady,' he says, reeling backwards, his mouth in a nasty sneer. 'I just wanted to buy you a drink. There's no need to turn into a frigid cow.'

As I walk away, he mutters, 'Stupid bitch.'

Saturday, 1 September
10.32 am

The online news is abuzz with the break in the Jacoby case. Josh's face fills TV screens, his head down as he exits the station the day before. Shots of Jacoby outside his Toorak mansion shooing away the press are also played on a loop. Washed clean, the city welcomes the looming scandal, with Ginny's death apparently considered a worthwhile exchange for the salacious events.

Another article details Lizzie's new part in *The Street*. 'The Most Challenging Role of Her Life' reads the headline, with a picture of her at Wade's funeral, crying as his coffin is carried past.

Sitting down at my desk, I stare straight ahead at my reflection in the black of the computer screen. I feel oddly calm.

In contrast, Nan is like a hungry spider, ready to pounce on Jacoby and devour him whole at the first opportunity. Her phone is glued to her ear as she paces the carpet outside Isaacs' office, her eyes gleaming. Calvin is also on the phone and sits at his desk radiating a similar inner glow despite his pale complexion. It's the special shine you get when you're close to solving a case and holding the last few puzzle pieces in your hand.

Fleet is nowhere to be seen, for which I am grateful.

The time is dragging. I just want to get my confrontation with Isaacs over with.

Chloe appears around the corridor and rushes toward me, hands on her belly. 'Do you have a moment?' she asks.

'Just a few minutes,' I say, glancing at Isaacs' closed office door.

We head to the case room and she shuts the door behind us. 'I think it's the same ring,' she says excitedly. 'I found three photos of Jenny Short where you can see her hands. Look.' She lays them out.

Jenny was a nice-looking woman with an enthusiastic eighties haircut. In two of the photos, she has her arms around two toddlers and I recognise Lizzie and her brother. Both images are grainy, lifted from a newspaper article about her seaside-based artworks. It's hard to see her ring.

'That's when she was still married to Lizzie's dad, before he walked out on the family,' Chloe explains. 'And look at this one.' She points to the third photo, this one in colour: Jenny is on a community stage receiving some kind of prize. Clearly visible is the engagement ring that Sterling gave Lizzie Short.

I breathe out air from deep in my lungs and lock eyes with Chloe.

'Take this to Detective Fleet,' I say to her.

She looks confused. 'Don't you want to tell him?'

I hesitate before saying, 'I'm tied up with something else right now. You help him out today. See if you can check Kit Short's alibi for the Wade attack—he told us he was about to get on a plane for a work trip, but I don't know if this was ever confirmed. Find out if there's any evidence that he had tickets or was at the airport.'

'Okay.' She nods, pulling herself tall. 'Leave it with me.'

'Thanks, Chloe,' I say with a genuine smile. 'I appreciate your help.'

Alone in the case room, I feel annoyed that I never looked into Kit's alibi, but there's nothing that can be done about that now. I take a few deep breaths before I turn my back on the photos of the dead men and head toward Isaacs' office.

'Come in!' he barks after I knock.

I take a seat and place my hands neatly in my lap.

'Well, Woodstock, this is less than ideal.'

'I know,' I say.

'I admire your gumption but I'm sure you know this wasn't the best way to go about it.'

I fix my eyes on his face and try to understand. 'No, sir,' I say.

He comes around his desk and leans back against it, folding his arms across his chest. 'Fleet explained the situation, said you'd made yourself sick with worry over it. Now, there are a few ways we can spin this, which we're still working through. But I want to be clear: I am not comfortable with your vigilante efforts. You should have shared your suspicions and the information you had on the Jacoby witness with Nan and Calvin. They were the leads. And you put yourself in danger, which I'm not pleased about either.'

I nod, trying to breathe. Fleet has somehow made it look like I was onto Josh the whole time and had taken it upon myself to go undercover, to placate him into a confession.

'This obviously won't be the last of it,' Isaacs continues, 'but, as you know, the physical evidence is extremely poor, so Josh Evans's statement is critical. It's a good outcome, Woodstock, despite the method.'

'Thank you, sir,' I say, feeling dazed.

'For now I suggest you keep your head down and focus on Wade. Find that missing Kent kid. And look after yourself. There are a lot of people around here who can help you if you need it. You need to get better at knowing your limits.' He gives me a meaningful look. 'Just something to think about.'

Leaving his office, I feel disconnected from everyone around me and so overwhelmed with rage that I think for a moment I will be sick.

How dare Fleet confuse everything like this?

I sit at my desk for over an hour doing little more than stare at the screen. Restless, I stand up with a flourish and then pause, unsure what to do next. There's no case meeting today. I look over at Fleet's desk, which is crowded with mugs and half-drunk water bottles. A folded newspaper lies across the keyboard, a sliver of a photo showing. From this angle, I can't tell whether the blond head in the image belongs to Sterling or Josh.

I head into the tearoom to make a coffee. I flick through the latest news updates as the kettle boils. 'Ava James Returns Home from Nightmare Film Shoot' screams a headline. When I click the link, a video pops up of several burly men trying to keep a huddle of reporters at bay as Ava leaves LAX, dark sunglasses wrapped around her face. 'A total nightmare,' she says in response to being asked about her time in Australia. In the article the journalist notes that James fell out with the film director after Wade's death and accused him of assault, a charge that the actress has now decided to drop. 'It was a big misunderstanding,' she's quoted as saying. 'I just want to get on with my life.'

I stir sugar into my coffee while I think, giving my brain the chance to play with all the pieces of information dangling in front of my eyes.

I rinse the mug then head back to my desk to pull everything I can on Kit Short. I study his driver's licence photo. He definitely looks like Lizzie, but without her glossy long hair he is plain. Forgettable.

I wander back into the case room and check the latest hotline calls, which have dropped to fewer than ten a day. Scanning the log, I see that one of the zombie cast members was arrested for assault last night. Brodie's phone and bank accounts remain untouched.

The attack on Ava is bothering me. What motivated it? Is it linked to Wade's death?

Touching the side of my head, I trace the bruise as I recall the hands sliding down my body in the laneway. I shudder, knowing it could have been a lot worse. Did that have anything to do with Wade or was I just in the wrong place at the wrong time? I'm not sure why it seems so important to keep it a secret—perhaps I feel like enough of a victim already.

Just as I go back to my desk and sit down, my phone rings.

'Woodstock,' I answer, seeing that it's Chloe.

'Hey,' replies Fleet.

I pause. 'Hi,' I say stiffly. 'You're with Chloe?'

'I sure am,' he says cheerily. 'She's driving right now. She's a better driver than you, I think, at least so far. Anyway, I'm liking your ring theory. Makes sense.'

I don't respond.

'So . . .'

'So what?' I reply, refusing to thank him for what he said to Isaacs.

He clears his throat awkwardly. 'Well, we looked into Kit Short's travel plans based on his little airport clue. He definitely bought a return ticket to Sydney and checked into the flight online, but there's no evidence that he was there that day.'

'What about taxi receipts? Uber transactions? SkyBus?'

'Still waiting on those,' says Fleet. 'But we did track down his boss, some big shot in IT at the security firm he works at. He says Kit didn't apply for any annual leave that week and has no idea why he would have gone to Sydney. So it wasn't anything to do with work. Kit finished his night shift at eight that morning.'

My pulse quickens. 'What do you think?' I ask Fleet.

'I'm not sure, I just wanted to get you across it all,' he replies, and the way he says it makes me wish so badly that we could go back in time. 'On paper he could be our guy, especially if he found out Sterling was screwing around on his sister. Problem is, he was working the nights when Miller was murdered and Miss Ava was shoved into the Yarra.'

'Could he have left his workplace unnoticed?' I ask. 'How many people work that shift?'

Fleet sighs. 'Possibly. We need to look into it.'

'Or maybe the incidents aren't linked. He might just have found the knife that was used on Miller, and the attack on Ava was random like we originally thought.'

'Dunno,' says Fleet and I can tell he's running his fingers through his hair. 'Anyway, it doesn't look like we're about to find out. He's not home.'

'You're at his house?'

'Yep. There's a bike out the front but no answer. He's not at work today either but I'm thinking we might swing past his office and have a proper chat with his boss.'

'Did you try Lizzie?' I ask. 'Maybe he's with her. She mentioned he's been staying at the apartment a lot lately.'

'Lizzie's not answering her phone but we'll swing past her place after this. I think it's time to bring her into the station. We've got more than enough evidence.'

'Good idea,' I say, readying myself for the awkwardness of the unavoidable goodbye.

'Gemma?' he says.

'What?' I snap.

I hear him breathing. Picture him sitting in the passenger seat, legs spread, as he tries to work out what to say. 'I was just wondering if you'll be around later today.'

'Probably.'

'Okay. Well, maybe we can catch up?'

'I'll be around,' I repeat. 'I've got to go.'

I hang up before he can say anything else.

Trying to shake the excruciating discomfort I now feel every time I interact with him, I flick through Ava's original statement about Cartwright. I google the TV interview she did on the day she was attacked and watch it through twice. She seems so confident and assured, nothing like the shell of a woman we spoke to at the hospital.

I get up and go to the video suite. 'Edo?' I say, pushing open the door.

'Yo, boss lady,' he replies.

'Did you get all that footage from around the Yarra the other night, when Ava James was attacked?'

'Sure. Did.' He drags the words out with an American drawl. 'We've gone through it already. It doesn't look like any dudes were following her. There's just the guy in the hoodie—I sent you the freeze-frame of him already. He was hanging around the river when she was attacked. And there's a chick and a couple who pop up a few times along the route Ava took. But I doubt they're good for this.'

'Can you see the woman's face?' I ask him.

'Not really. She has a scarf wrapped around her head. Not religious or anything—I think she was just freezing her arse off that night.'

'Send it all to me, please,' I say.

'Your wish is my command.' He snaps his fingers before they fly over his keyboard at an impressive speed.

Saturday, 1 September
3.37 pm

Hours of footage and two coffees later, I am fairly certain: Katya March pushed Ava into the river. On the tape provided by the restaurant where Ava met her friends, I spotted Katya and a friend drinking cocktails at the bar. Katya was tucked away behind a large column but she knew Ava was there—she kept throwing looks her way. Katya left long before Ava. The sharp jut of her hips is recognisable on the shadowy figure watching from a doorway opposite the restaurant as Ava exits with her friends at around 10.15 pm. The same figure appears on another stretch of footage recorded about twenty minutes later, walking a block behind her. The woman's face is obscured by the scarf Edo mentioned, but I'm almost positive it's Katya.

Emerging from the small meeting room I've been holed up in, I go to the case room to see if Chloe and Fleet are back but I can't find them anywhere.

Knowing I don't have the energy to deal with Katya today, I tell two uniforms to arrange to bring her in first thing tomorrow.

Feeling aimless, I go to the Miller case room.

'Hey, Ralph,' I say, standing in the doorway.

'Woodstock,' he says with a nod. He watches as I look around the room. 'We're almost done wrapping things up here,' he tells me. 'Miller will be yours one hundred per cent as of tomorrow. Isaacs just assigned Billy and me to help on a new case.' His thick fingers wrestle with the waistband of his trousers, yanking them up a few centimetres. 'Ah well, no rest for the wicked I guess.'

I nod. 'What's the new case?'

'A few women have been attacked in the city over the past few nights, and we've just arrested a guy. Three reports of assault so far. One women was knocked up pretty bad last night— she's critical.'

I swallow. 'Rape?'

'Fortunately not,' he says grimly. 'Our guy just wants to scare the shit out of women.' He has a sip of Coke. 'Honestly, if I had a daughter I wouldn't let her walk around in the city at night.'

I'm about to explain that's not the way it should work but am hit with an intense wave of exhaustion. 'Well, I hope you have enough to put him away,' I say instead.

Shaking, I jump in one of the squad cars and inch my way through the traffic, not clear on where I'm going until I reach the top of Spring Street. Sliding the car into a vacant spot, I leave the indicator on as I call Chloe and then, reluctantly, Fleet. Neither answers. Annoyed, I call Chloe again and leave a message explaining what I think Katya has done, asking her or Fleet to call me with an update on Kit. Shoving my sunglasses on, I get out of the car and walk a short distance to sit on a park bench. Looking up and down the busy street, I remember back to that Wednesday night when it was empty in the wake of the attack. The pool of blood that Sterling left behind marring the ground.

I assume Katya attacked Ava in a twisted defence of Cartwright. Somehow over the years she has become oddly fused to him; she seems to take great pride in the way she feels she rose above his abuse and made it work in her favour. No doubt there are other women whom Cartwright abused but Ava was the only one who threatened the order of things. Katya lied the other day: being so closely entwined with Cartwright means that her reputation is on the line too, and I suspect this uncertainty pushed her over the edge. Begrudgingly I acknowledge that her strategy has worked— Ava has retreated like a turtle into her shell.

A bike bell dings a warning, forcing an ambitious pedestrian back to the curb. I spend a few minutes watching the parade of people. Taxis, cars, trams.

I'm convinced Katya had nothing to do with the attack on Sterling. At that point, from her perspective, killing or threatening him wouldn't have made any sense. Ava was yet to formally accuse Cartwright of anything. Although Wade had confronted him, by that Wednesday the matter was essentially sorted out.

I check my phone: still nothing from either Chloe or Fleet.

I think about going home—at least I should be able to get some sleep, knowing that my job is safe—but something about the idea of being alone is incredibly unappealing. I think about how likely it is that I will never see Josh again. I add up the number of times we met and realise it's probably less than twenty, and yet he had become a part of my life. Despite the reliance that I'd started to have on him, I have a feeling I won't find it hard to fill in the hole he leaves. To me, our relationship was more about the potential of a certain kind of life than a true connection.

I walk a little further down the path to the corner of Flinders and Spring. Huge droplets begin to fall from the sky, their size almost comical as they splatter onto the ground. I ease myself into the car just as lightning splits the sky.

Safely sealed away from the weather, I blast the demister to clear the fog from the windows. I edge my way into the traffic, heading up Spring Street, onto Nicholson and past the museum. The traffic isn't nearly as busy here and I speed along in my warm bubble, trying to think. Bizarrely the sun emerges, pushing through the clouds and shining through the rain.

I'm convinced that Kit Short started the house fire that killed his mother and was also involved in killing Wade, but whether Lizzie knows any of this I'm not sure. How has she not recognised her mother's ring? If Jenny Short stopped wearing it after her husband left, I suppose it's possible; Lizzie would only have been about five at the time. I couldn't even remember that my mother had an engagement ring, and I was a lot older than that when I last saw her wearing it.

Considering I'm not that far from Lizzie's apartment, I cut through some side streets to get to Brunswick Street. I try Lizzie's phone but there's no answer. The rain gone, people now crowd the footpaths, their eyes concealed behind variously shaped lenses as they hurry along sipping pre-wine lattes, their arms weighed down with shopping bags. The shopfront mannequins are already in their summer best: skimpy dresses and retro shorts. I approach Lizzie's apartment complex. Scanning the streets for a park, I pull over with my indicator on.

I'm just about to call her again when a black 4WD exits the underground car park and sails past. It's the same car that Kit Short brought to the hospital that first night. I stare through my tinted rear window as the car drives off. Without really thinking, I pull out into the street and fall in line behind the 4WD.

A message from Fleet appears on my work phone and I glance down when I'm stopped at a red light.

Still no sign of Kit anywhere. We're going to call it a day. See you tomorrow.

Relieved that I don't have to talk to him, I wonder if he and Chloe spoke to Lizzie as I keep following the 4WD. It turns away from the city. Where is Kit headed? Was he just with Lizzie or was he home on his own? I jam my phone into the console and hit Lizzie's number. It rings out again.

In the thick traffic, I lose track of the car for a few moments but manage to keep it in my sights until it takes a right into a suburban street. I vaguely remember from his ID that Kit lives in Coburg and figure he must be going home. I pause at the corner, the day rapidly fading away, and watch as the 4WD turns into a driveway about halfway up the street. I park under a large tree around fifty metres away. Staring at the modest-looking weatherboard house in the dim light, I'm surprised to catch the swish of a long ponytail as Lizzie disappears inside.

I'm just about to call Fleet and tell him to get back here when I realise that parked in front of the 4WD is an unmarked squad car. My insides roll. Are Fleet and Chloe still here? Surely not—I spoke to Fleet hours ago. I reread his text and try to call him but it goes straight to voicemail.

I yank on the handbrake, slip out of the car and make my way toward the house.

Music blares from the property next door and smells of dinner waft through the air. I peer over the fence at the end of the driveway but the house is silent. Nothing moves.

I slip past the 4WD and reach the vacant squad car. A jacket I recognise as Chloe's is on the back seat.

The curtains across the front of the house are drawn. I notice a side path that runs in between the house and the garage, into the backyard.

My eyes on the front door, I call Isaacs just as I hear raised voices coming from inside. I leave him a voicemail telling him to send backup to Kit Short's house.

The yelling continues. A female voice and a male voice. I crouch down and make my way further down the path.

My heart thumps as I sift through a thousand scenarios. I don't know what Kit is capable of, or if he might hurt Lizzie, but clearly he sent me the text from Fleet's phone. Where are Chloe and Fleet? Are they here too or did they leave their car here for some reason?

Creeping under the house windows, I make it to the corner of a small deck. I glance around the yard. There are no plants or trees, just a run-down shed and a few square metres of patchy lawn.

Night is starting to muscle in. The last notes of a rock song carry over the fence.

'You idiot,' says a sharp voice, muffled by the glass. 'This is bad, Kit, real bad.'

A strange animal sound curls into the night.

'Shut up!' yells a voice that I think is Kit's. There's a loud *smack*.

After straightening my legs until I'm standing, I lean forward so that I can see inside. Chloe is seated on a kitchen chair, her arms pulled behind her, her swollen belly straining against her shirt, her face blotchy and streaked with tears. Thick tape is wrapped around her mouth and head.

Lizzie and Kit Short are locked in an intense stand-off about a metre from her, their identical blue eyes burning.

Fleet is nowhere to be seen.

'What the fuck are we going to do now?' hisses Lizzie.

Kit's eyes flit around as if looking for answers.

Lizzie makes a furious sound and kicks floor.

'I'm sorry,' Kit whines. 'They were talking about you. I heard them saying that they knew the ring was Mum's, that they were going to go and get you. Take you to the station. I panicked.'

'I could have handled it,' says Lizzie. 'Fuck. I knew you should have kept staying with me. I can't trust you on your own. Dropping that knife was bad enough but this is a disaster. You need to fix this, Kit.'

Madness flares in his eyes. 'We could leave them in here, start a fire.'

'Fuck, you're stupid,' snaps Lizzie. 'How do you think that would look?'

'What about the park out back?' he says. 'We could take them to the creek. No one goes there.'

Lizzie nods, her mind clearly racing. 'Well, we can't stay here. Let's go. We'll have to sort out their car later.'

My fingers barely work as I pull my phone out of my pocket. A missed call from Isaacs. I turn away from the window and start texting him when a glass door slides open.

I shove my phone back into my pocket and drop to the ground, curling myself into a ball.

All the lights in the house snap off and Fleet stumbles onto the deck followed by Kit, who is nervously pointing a gun at his head. Fleet's hands are tied together with rope and there's a red mark above his right eyebrow. Thick tape is wrapped around his mouth and head.

Chloe appears next, a knife glinting at the side of her face.

'Come on,' says Lizzie. 'Let's not make this harder than it needs to be.'

The odd foursome make their way across the lawn to the back gate, which swings open into the creeping darkness. I run beside the side fence and cut along the back, reaching the gate just as it pulls shut behind them. I wait for a minute before carefully pushing it open. It doesn't creak and I let out the breath I have been holding in. I can just make them ahead of me, shadowy figures already halfway down the gentle slope of the hill. Darting from tree to tree, I hope I'm not imagining the faint ring of a doorbell echoing behind me.

Saturday, 1 September
6.24 pm

The wind tosses the arms of the trees around in a wild dance. It's freezing, all traces of warmth from the winter sun sucked back into the sky and chased away by the rising moon. Possums run across their wooden corridors high above, their staccato chatter shrieking into the night. Sticking to the grass, I make my way soundlessly toward the group as they head to the base of the hill. I grip my gun, holding it out in front of me, feeling the repeated buzz of my phone in my pocket. I assure myself that the uniforms will soon see the open gate and know to follow us down here. I just don't know how long it will take.

Lizzie? I think, still trying to understand. I remember her on the couch at the hospital, her tidal wave of grief crashing through the room, and the way she visibly deflated with the news of Sterling's death. Was that relief? Relief that her monstrous plan had worked? But why would she want Sterling dead? Access to his wealth wasn't guaranteed. She's lost her chance at a Hollywood lifestyle. It must have been his affair with Brodie. Or maybe she believed the rumours about Ava? Nothing else makes sense.

Ahead of me, at the base of the hill, the four silhouettes have stopped. I pause too and see a soft glow a little further along. Someone is holding out a phone screen to light up the ground in front of them. There's a rustling as bodies crash forcefully into bushes and bracken. In the faint moonlight, I see two pale faces low to the ground, eyes huge above the shiny tape that covers their mouths.

Pieces of conversation drift towards me in the wind as Kit and Lizzie argue.

I creep closer, trying to avoid standing on any sticks.

'You have to shoot them,' Lizzie says.

'Yeah, I know, I know,' says Kit, turning on the spot in an odd little circle, the gun resting against the side of his head, pointed at the sky.

'The water is deep at the moment,' she says. 'If we fill their clothes with stones or something, no one will find them for ages. Maybe never. We'll get their phones and take them somewhere else so they can't be tracked here.'

'Yeah, yeah,' Kit mutters.

'Well, what are you waiting for?' snaps Lizzie, whirling around with the knife in her hand.

'It's just that she's pregnant,' says Kit.

Lizzie's eyes flit to Chloe and then back to Kit. 'Yeah well, that doesn't change the fact that she can ruin everything. This is your fault, Kit, not mine. Everything was fine before you lost your head. Everyone wants me now. I'm getting offered so many roles and interviews. It's finally happening.'

'I know, I'm sorry.' His lip trembles and he presses the flat of the gun against his head again. 'Idiot,' he whispers, seemingly to himself.

Fleet has his back to the base of a tree. Chloe is a few metres to his left, propped against a large rock; her face is disturbingly white. Kit keeps his eyes on the ground and steps toward Chloe.

I hear the trickle of water. High up in the sky I see tiny flashes of a plane flying overhead. Lizzie is only metres from me, her long ponytail gleaming as it catches the moonlight. 'Hurry up, Kit,' she hisses. 'We still need to get rid of their car.'

Kit lifts his arm, aiming the gun at Chloe. He appears to take a deep breath as if preparing himself.

I pounce out of the shadows, no longer able to wait for the backup that I'm sure will come. 'Don't do it, Kit,' I say, pressing the tip of my gun against the side of Lizzie's head.

He doesn't drop his arm but he shifts his gaze to his sister. 'No, no,' he whimpers. 'Don't touch her.'

Lizzie doesn't speak but moves her eyes across to look at me. In them I see a hollowness that I had mistaken for grief.

I look at Chloe a few metres away, bruised and terrified. I meet Fleet's stare and see unchecked terror marred with relief.

'Where's Brodie?' I ask.

Kit doesn't move his arm, the gun still trained on Chloe, but he now looks at his sister. 'Brodie?'

'We don't know where Brodie is,' snaps Lizzie.

I nudge the gun into her hair just above her ear. 'You're lying.'

She looks at me and smiles. 'I don't care if you don't believe us.'

I think about the shed in Kit's backyard. Or even the creek in front of us. They could easily have gotten rid of the body.

'Why, Lizzie?' I ask.

She sighs. 'Why what?'

'Why attack Sterling?' I say. 'Why all of this?'

'Because,' she says, her voice low, 'it's never been about me!'

'It's never been about you,' I repeat.

'No!'

'I don't understand,' I say.

'He was going to leave me,' she says, her voice eerily calm. 'He was going to move overseas and treat me like a piece of dirt.'

'I thought you were both going overseas?'

'That's what he said!' screams Lizzie. 'We were always supposed to go together, and then he said that because I got the role on *The Street* I should stay.'

I nod. My eyes are still on Kit, who is looking between Fleet, Chloe and Lizzie. 'I'm sure he was just trying to support you.'

'No,' whispers Lizzie. 'He got me that role because he was trying to get away from me. He said he thought I would make a good soap actress—that it was my big break. Do you know how humiliating it was going to be when he dumped me to move to Hollywood?'

'He never proposed to you, did he, Lizzie? That romantic dinner he organised, that was him telling you about the overseas roles.'

'I have been *so* patient,' she says, her voice like a blade through the air. 'It was my turn.' Her mouth pulls into a smile as she turns her head into my gun. 'But then I figured out a way to have all the attention on me. Have you seen how since the attack, everyone wants to talk to me? I'm the grieving widow. I'll be more famous than I ever could have been as Sterling Wade's girlfriend.' She smiles slightly. 'I have been offered so many roles. I knew it would be like this. Everyone loves tragedy.'

With my gun, I push her head back to face the other way. 'What about Walter Miller, Kit? Did you kill him too?'

'Walter Miller?' says Lizzie, puzzled.

'She means the homeless man.' Kit's face is flushed and blotchy and he shifts his weight from foot to foot. 'I used to see him when I walked home from night shifts. He was always alone, sleeping in that tunnel.'

'We needed to be sure it would work,' Lizzie says without emotion. 'I wasn't sure Kit could do it. Sterling couldn't be the first one, it was too risky.'

'So you killed a man as practice?' I say with disbelieving horror. I imagine telling Tammy Miller that her father was treated like a disposable prop.

'Everything had to be certain,' stammers Kit. He's begun to shake from head to toe.

'Just like with the fire, right?' I guess. 'You lit the fire that killed your mother, didn't you?'

He starts to shuffle on the spot, shooting desperate looks at his sister. 'No,' he says uncertainly.

'Kit and I needed a fresh start,' says Lizzie, her voice lifting in volume with her frustration. 'Our mother was pathetic. Dad left us because of her. She almost ruined everything.'

'She didn't want Lizzie to be an actress,' adds Kit.

'She wouldn't let me audition for anything,' spits Lizzie. 'She was jealous of me.'

'Lizzie,' I say, before I realise there's nothing to say. 'It didn't have to be like this.'

'He was going to leave me,' she repeats softly, her jaw clenched. 'I couldn't have that.'

'How did you get onto the set that day, Kit?' I ask.

Lizzie rolls her eyes and answers for him. 'Too easy. I got a spare ID pass weeks ago when I said I lost mine.'

'You just walked right in there,' I say, and picture it. Kit looking out from behind his mask. No one having a clue that a killer was in their midst. Sterling caught up in the moment and then being struck by unthinkable pain. No one helping. Lizzie's distraught face. Pawing hands. Blood draining onto the street as Kit quietly and slowly disappeared into the crowd.

I look at Lizzie and see a monster.

A voice threads through the darkness at the top of the hill and white spots of light circle madly through the trees. Kit startles and steadies his arm again.

Chloe sobs and draws in a sharp breath.

'Kit,' I say, 'put the gun down. You know this is over. I can help you. Don't make it worse.'

'Now, Kit!' screams Lizzie, dropping to the ground and rolling aggressively toward Fleet.

I move at the same time Fleet does. He bucks his body, throwing himself into the air and landing on his feet, before ramming heavily into Kit, headbutting him.

A *crack* twists though the darkness, followed by a loud shot.

I slam into Lizzie, pushing her into the trunk of a giant tree, before smashing into the ground. My mouth full of dirt, I scramble to Chloe and use my body to shield her bulging stomach from whatever danger is behind us.

'Chloe!' I say urgently.

Her eyes are full of panic. She moans. Blood, sticky and wet, spreads down one side of her white shirt.

Kit makes a horrible sound where he has fallen.

There is a flash of silver in the moonlight as Lizzie reels toward Fleet and then back again so quickly I don't realise what's happened at first. She backs into another large tree, breathing like a wild beast and holding a knife out in front of her before she turns and disappears into the night.

The red line seems to split Fleet's face in half. Stunned, he rolls onto his side, squeezing his eyes shut. Blood streams down his neck and into the dirt.

'Over here!' I yell up the hill. 'Help. Please!'

Kit isn't moving. Fleet coughs and splutters.

Turning back to Chloe, I force myself to breathe. 'It's okay,' I say automatically. 'You're going to be fine.'

I pull off my jacket, frantically trying to work out where the blood is coming from. I push the material against her shoulder. She has grown even paler and strains her arms against the tape, kicking her legs in vain.

'Shhhh, shhhhh, don't move,' I soothe, tears sprouting into my eyes.

I place a hand on the top of her belly, thinking that she's only here because of me. She is boiling up, and underneath my hand I feel the flutter of movement. Swirling torches light up the night around us and I hold her close, telling her it's going to be okay and praying that I am right.

Monday, 17 September
10.55 am

The chatter of tourists blends with beeps from electronic devices as Fleet and I sit in the sun on the sand-coloured steps at Federation Square, sipping takeaway coffees.

His scar is covered by a row of fine beige bandages. It starts at the centre of his forehead, cutting diagonally down his face, across his nose and ending at his chin. I can't stop looking at it. He taps out a cigarette with his left hand, lights it and sucks hard, wincing. Chunky black sunglasses shield his eyes. He flicks the ash from his smoke distractedly, shifting his weight and cursing under his breath.

The air between us buzzes, thick with unsaid things, though the toxic energy that crackled after that night at my apartment has dulled, replaced by something flatter.

'So, you're feeling okay?' he asks finally, looking across the road to Flinders Street Station.

'I'm fine—it's just this that's holding me back.' I lift my bandaged arm in its sling, grimacing slightly.

My elbow was sprained when I threw myself against Lizzie, though it wasn't until afterwards, when Chloe was taken to hospital, that I realised how much it hurt.

'What about you?' I ask Fleet. 'Are you . . . doing alright?'

'I'm fine,' he replies dismissively, his gaze on the parade of cars.

It's almost midday and the traffic is relentless, ferrying people to lunches and meetings, shifting slowly past the line of cabs and noisy buskers.

I'm so used to the constant sound now. I'm not sure I could go back to the quiet.

Ben, Dad and Rebecca returned to Smithson three days ago. They arrived the day after our showdown with the Short siblings.

'You must stop doing this to me, my girl,' Dad said, pressing his lips into my forehead as he took in my bruised face and arm.

'You're in all the papers,' Ben told me, an edge of pride in his voice.

'You really are,' Rebecca agreed excitedly. She indicated her bulging canvas bag. 'I bought copies of all of them.'

At Rebecca's suggestion, the two of us had a coffee together the day after they arrived. Summoning what I could tell was rare strength, she sat me down and gave me a talking-to. Told me how much she loved my dad. Told me my attitude toward her has been immature and unfair and that she wants us to get along for Dad's sake. Deeply ashamed, I agreed and apologised.

Even beyond that, their trip was different from last time. Once they were assured that my physical wounds were fairly superficial, they embraced the opportunity to explore the city, discovering its hidden gems. Come September, Melbourne was eager to shed its winter coat. Buds blossomed on spindly branches. Bulbs broke through the rich brown soil. Sunlight wove in and out of the city laneways, timid at first and then with confidence, enticing people to go outside.

I've emerged from my own kind of chrysalis: reborn, or at least awakened. My head is clearer than it has been in a long time.

A nearby family has ambitiously ordered ice creams and I smile as I watch the youngest boy struggle to keep his cone upright.

'Jeez, it's not that hot,' says Fleet, frowning at the family.

'Oh, lighten up,' I admonish, 'they're happy.'

He grunts and sucks on his cigarette again. 'Thank god Chloe is going to be okay.'

'I know.'

'Do you think she'll come back to work?' he asks me.

'I don't know. It's too early to say.'

He nods. 'Isaacs won't tell me anything, says he wanted me to have a complete break, but when I asked about the baby he said she's doing okay.'

'I can't get a straight answer from anyone. But I think she's doing as well as can be expected.'

In the end, the doctors decided it was safer for Chloe's baby to be born early rather than stay inside her traumatised body. The bullet had lodged in the flesh just below her collarbone and she had taken several hard knocks to the stomach. At just over twenty-eight weeks, her baby was born by caesarean: a tiny girl called Olive.

Visiting Chloe in hospital, I apologised over and over for sending her out in my place that day. She wasn't buying it. 'No one could have known that Kit would flip out like that,' she assured me.

It seems that Kit Short did indeed panic that afternoon. As soon as Fleet and Chloe turned up he knew we were onto him. He grabbed his unlicensed gun—a weapon he'd stolen from his mum's boyfriend almost ten years ago—and slipped out the back door to hide down the side of the house. He listened to Fleet on the phone to me, heard him detail our suspicions about his involvement, and then say they were about to go to Lizzie's house to question her. This apparent threat against Lizzie set him off and, without warning, he sprang out from the side of the house, holding a gun against Chloe's head. He herded them both to the kitchen where he tied them up, pacing around the room as he switched between crying and frantically calling his sister.

'He was all over the place,' Fleet says. 'Without Lizzie telling him what to do he was like a five-year-old. Albeit an armed dangerous one.'

'Did you think he was going to kill you?' I ask quietly.

Fleet lights another cigarette and smokes robotically before answering. 'I didn't think it was looking good,' he replies eventually, running his hand along the tip of the scar. 'I was worried about Chloe and the baby.' He stubs his cigarette into the crease of a stone. 'Have you seen Lizzie?' he asks, shifting to lean back against the step.

'Yes,' I confirm, 'I've seen her.'

Lizzie had been tracked down in the early hours of the morning about two kilometres along the creek. She was sitting in the dark. I observed her being interviewed at the station a few hours later— she refused to speak then and has barely said a word since.

'She's one messed-up young woman,' I say.

The papers have reported that Lizzie suffers from a personality disorder that has manifested into an obsession with fame. Her defence team is certainly embracing this theory, having engaged several high-profile psychologists. It seems that her desire to be known, to be successful at all costs, has played a role in her unhealthy relationship with the media and her own celebrity status.

'They both are,' says Fleet. 'Kit's dependency on his sister was something else.'

'I'm sure their lawyers will use their mental health issues to put forward a strong case.'

'It's bullshit,' he mutters.

'Well,' I say, thinking as I often do about Walter Miller, the truest collateral damage I have ever known, 'they clearly both need help.

Whether they end up in jail or a clinic, it will be for an extremely long time.'

'Any word on Brodie?'

'I spoke to Calvin yesterday,' I say. 'Apparently Brodie called his parents earlier this week. He told them he's been staying in New Farm. A suburb in Brisbane.'

'So he really did just run away?'

I shrug. 'His dad has no reason to lie. Kit and Lizzie maintain they have no idea what happened to him. I still think Kit found out about Sterling and Brodie but I wonder if he was too scared to tell his sister. Maybe he was embarrassed on her behalf.'

Fleet seems to think about this. 'I guess after everything that happened I can sort of see why Brodie would want to disappear.'

I picture Brodie breathing in nature, trying to ground himself amidst his grief. I assume the place he is in has vast open spaces like Karadine and Smithson. I watch all the people around us right now, the hundreds of faces, the relentless activity, and can see why Brodie wanted to run away and disappear into a new life. To get some quiet after what happened. Ironically, the noisy place he has run away from is where I have finally been able to find some peace.

'I noticed there are quite a few weirdos on the net declaring their love for Lizzie,' Fleet says. 'She seems to have some real fans. Her brother too.'

'Maybe she'll end up getting the adoration and fame she wanted. I did hear that a publisher wants to offer her a book deal after the trial.'

'Fuck,' he says, shaking his head. 'The depressing thing is, it will probably be a bestseller.'

I nod and smile wryly. 'Have you heard about Ava James's big tell-all interview?' I ask.

'No.'

'Apparently she's doing a two-part interview on American TV about Sterling's murder and Cartwright's abuse.'

'Including the part about Katya attacking her?'

'Well, it's getting a bit complicated,' I say feeling a sharp stab of discomfort talking to him about this. 'Isaacs told me that Katya is now claiming that Cartwright and Ava had a consensual relationship when she first signed on to the film. But when he started coming on to a make-up artist in front of her, she decided that he needed to be taught a lesson. Katya claims Ava exaggerated the incident with Cartwright and manipulated Sterling to come to her defence.'

Fleet keeps his gaze on the passersby. 'But if that was true, why did Ava come forward after Wade died?'

'Katya thinks she wanted an out. She wasn't sure what would happen with the film but she was contracted to finish it no matter what. Obviously she wouldn't have been expected to work along-side Cartwright if he abused her.'

Fleet doesn't respond and I wonder what he's thinking. My brain flits to us in my bed, his hands gripping my skin.

'In her interviews Katya admitted she followed Ava to the river that night but swears she just wanted to talk to her. She says she was trying to convince her to drop the charges but Ava wouldn't have any of it and they argued, and Ava fell into the river.'

'But why didn't Ava just tell us that Katya attacked her?' asks Fleet, puzzled.

'I think Katya was pretty threatening that night,' I reply. 'She claimed to have people ready to back up her claims that initially, at least, Ava was into Cartwright and that his flirting was welcomed by her. I think Ava felt her case against Cartwright getting flimsier and flimsier and, after Katya actually attacked her, she just shut down and decided it would be easier to forget the whole thing and leave Australia.'

'Unbelievable,' says Fleet, shaking his head again.

We sit in silence for a few moments. I shift my arm because it's aching again.

'When do you think you'll be back at work?' I ask.

'Same as you—next week. Just not in the field for a while. Don't want to scare the kiddies.' He laughs, but he lifts a hand to his bandage again and I see a flash of emotion across his features. 'I saw you the other day,' he blurts out.

I turn to him. 'What do you mean?'

'I was having a coffee the day I got out of hospital. At that cafe we've been to a few times. You were with your family.'

I swallow and look at my lap, not sure what to say, my heart racing as if I've been caught somewhere I shouldn't be.

He's staring at me. 'Your son looks like you. I could tell he was yours straight away.'

'Yes, that's Ben,' I say simply, even though my feelings for Ben are anything but. Or perhaps they are just the simplest of all feelings.

'He doesn't live with you, does he?' Fleet asks.

'No.' My voice comes out in a whisper.

'Why not?'

'I'm not sure.'

Fleet seems to accept this. We sit for a moment longer, my insides twisting.

'We shouldn't work together anymore,' I tell him. 'I'm going to speak to Isaacs about it when I get back.'

A trio of seagulls argue at our feet and Fleet kicks his foot out to shoo them away.

'Makes sense,' he says eventually, still facing straight ahead.

'I didn't want any of this, you know. I'm so angry at you.' My words come out in a tumble and they aren't quite right but they are better than nothing.

'I get it, Gemma,' he says, kicking at the seagulls again. 'You gotta do what you gotta do.'

My hands have curled into tight balls, the nails cutting into my palms. I have to get out of here before I start crying. It's clear he's never going to give me what I want; he can't or won't say the words.

'I have to go,' I say stiffly, getting to my feet.

'Bye.' He looks across at the train station again.

I walk up the wide stairs away from him, my face collapsing. I think I hear my name and reluctantly turn around, but Fleet hasn't moved. He's still hunched over, his hair beginning to grow into a messy tail, a fresh cloud of smoke reaching into the air above him.

Monday, 24 September
7.22 am

Holding my hand above my brows, I squint into the sun as I make my way toward the rumble of noise in the middle of the Treasury Gardens. I keep to the edges of the crowd, breathing in air thick with pollen as I bounce along the emerald grass. Pausing, I stand on an exposed tree root and take in the scene. There must be over three hundred people here already: elegant business types sipping coffee, intricately tattooed men and women with cigarettes hanging out the sides of their mouths, young families with kids sucking on yoghurt pouches in prams, elderly couples holding hands and looking around expectantly.

Through the sea of faces, I spot Macy at the front, near a row of signs. She's wearing a rumpled sky-blue jacket and her arm is around a young girl with a scruffy ponytail. Someone taps on a glass bottle as if they are about to make a speech, just as a man hands me a pamphlet: a young Walter Miller smiles out at me. It looks like the photo was taken at a restaurant or bar. His haircut is all eighties, and he's wearing a suit and a colourful tie.

The conversations fade when Tammy Miller makes her way to the front of the crowd. She flashes a nervous smile at someone in the audience as she brushes her curly blonde hair away from her face. Her shoulders rise and fall as she takes a deep breath. She welcomes everyone and thanks us for coming. Then she tells the story of her father's life. After this obituary, she recounts her own childhood memories and tells us that, when she was a young girl, Walter was her hero. Next, two of Walter's homeless friends talk of his kindness. His decency. I look down at his picture again and my eyes prickle with tears.

At the end, everyone is asked to sing his favourite show tune from *Brigadoon*. People smile at each other through their tears as they sing.

After the service, I weave through the clusters of people to a park bench. I catch Macy's eye and gesture at her to join me. 'Morning,' I say as she approaches.

Her face cracks into a giant smile. 'You came.'

'Of course.'

The warmer weather has her even chattier than usual. She tells me about seeing an old friend here this morning she lost contact with over ten years ago, and how one of the retailers got in touch with Tammy Miller and said she wanted to donate all of her old clothing stock for the homeless to wear to this service—and to keep, of course.

'It suits you,' I say, touching the cuff of Macy's jacket.

She looks down at herself proudly, running her hands along the material. 'Thanks. I quite like it.' She purses her lips, catching herself. 'How's it going with your fancy psychologist?'

'Good,' I admit. 'I don't actually mind going.'

Macy makes a soft sound of approval. She smiles at me and gives my hand a firm squeeze.

Then she's accosted by Lara, so I say goodbye to them and walk the few blocks to work. I'm listening to classical music, something that my psychologist has suggested. Stepping to the beat, I slot comfortably into the stream of people diving into a new week.

When I get to work I feel like a new kid on my first day at school. I swipe into the main office and self-consciously head to my desk. I took great care with my appearance this morning, painstakingly blow-drying my freshly cut hair with my good arm and applying a little bit of make-up. I'm trying to make more of an effort, to look after myself.

Isaacs' door is shut, but the light is on in his office. The whir of the air con and the steady beat of someone typing are the only sounds I can hear. A bunch of flowers in a plastic water jug has been put on my desk; a few curling brown petals litter my keyboard. There is a nasty-looking pile of paperwork in my in-tray.

Nan leans out from her desk to peer at me. 'Well, welcome back then,' she says curtly, before turning back to her screen.

I keep my smile to myself. 'Thanks, Nan.'

Calvin appears from the kitchen, carefully holding out an over-filled coffee cup. 'Gemma,' he exclaims warmly, 'good to see you. You look lovely.'

'Thanks, Calvin.'

'Woodstock,' says Isaacs, appearing in his office doorway.

'Hello, sir,' I say, standing up.

'Welcome back. Please, come in here for a moment.'

I go into his office, inexplicably nervous. I've spoken to Isaacs three times since the showdown in the park behind Kit Short's house. Immediately after the shooting we had an intense discussion at the hospital when Chloe was in surgery, and I was beside myself with guilt and worry. The next day he called and told me that I was to start a treatment plan with the squad psychologist, insisting that I take some time off. We spoke again early last Monday morning. He gave me an update on the case and we agreed that I would return to work today. He has been brisk and professional through-out all this, and I'm not quite sure where I stand now that the dust has settled.

I perch on the chair opposite him.

'How are you feeling?' he asks kindly.

'Good, thank you. I'm glad to be back. My arm's feeling much better and I should be ready to hit the gym in a few weeks.'

'Just see how you go. There's no rush.' He toys with a pen, putting it down and then picking it up again. 'And you're seeing the psychologist?'

'I am,' I say, my voice strong. 'It was a good idea. It's probably long overdue.' I pause and clear my throat. 'I think I found the winter here especially difficult, plus being away from my family was hard. But I have some strategies to work with now.'

Isaacs nods and then surprises me with a smile. 'Well, that's good to hear.' His face settles and he crosses his arms. 'I know we've been over this already, but what happened to Chloe wasn't your fault.'

'Thank you, sir. I'm just glad she's going to be alright.'

'Yes, thank god for that.' He forms a pyramid with his hands. 'Now, in terms of this week, I wanted to let you know that Fleet won't be in. He probably won't be in next week either. So I was thinking that you can work with Nan and Calvin while you get up to speed and finalise everything on the Wade case.'

I feel a strange combination of relief and frustration at this news. Part of me wants to tackle Fleet's presence head on, work out how to navigate it. See if I can cope with it.

'But Fleet told me he'd been given the all-clear to come back,' I reply.

'This doesn't have anything to do with his injuries. He decided to go back home for a few days. His daughter is having some issues again. Anorexia and substance abuse this time, I believe.'

I stare stupidly at Isaacs, my mind trying to process the word 'daughter'.

'Fleet wants her to finish high school but she's threatening to drop out, so he decided he needs to spend some time with her. He's worried she's a suicide risk. I understand his ex-wife has her own issues at the moment so can't look after her. No doubt you know a lot of this.'

I tip my head forward in a nod, mute.

Isaacs is clearly waiting for me to respond.

'Sir,' I say, the nerves I've been keeping at bay suddenly overflowing and flooding my body, 'there's actually something I want to talk to you about.'

'Yes?' he says expectantly.

Briefly I imagine telling him everything, imagine saying the words and all that would come with them, but I'm just not ready.

'Going forward, it isn't a good idea that Fleet and I work as leads together,' I say.

Isaacs' grey gaze bores into mine.

'Our styles are very different,' I add, 'and it isn't healthy for either of us, or good for the cases.'

'Well,' he says, 'it's no issue from my perspective and it's something we can easily accommodate.' He taps the tips of his fingers together. Looks at them briefly before looking back at me. 'Is there anything specific I need to know about, Woodstock?'

Blood gallops through my veins. 'I'm not sure yet.'

'But maybe?'

'Yes, maybe.'

He moistens his lips and nods, hands on hips. 'I'm here if you ever need to tell me anything, Gemma. I'm always interested to hear anything you think is important for me to be aware of. I hope you feel you can talk to me.'

'Thank you, sir. I appreciate that. I think I just need some time.'

'No problem,' he says smoothly, and I wonder whether he can somehow read my scrambled thoughts. 'You've had a challenging few months, Woodstock, and I'm not just talking about work. My advice is that you look after yourself and stay focused. Keep your head down and get into a solid routine. Learn from Nan and Calvin—they're good detectives.'

'Yes, I will. Thank you, sir.' I stand up and inch backwards toward the door.

'My door is always open Woodstock, even when it's shut,' he replies.

I bob my head in a strange little girl gesture and float to my desk. My mind is reeling and my limbs feel floppy as the adrenaline drains out of them.

Nick Fleet has a daughter? A *teenage* daughter? I remember all those times he was on his phone, fingers flying madly across the screen. His frequent mood swings. And the time in his car when he refused to tell me what was wrong. And then I'm back in my bed, his hand on my thigh, and the familiar shame returns. The irony of my own split world, half of it locked away from common view, isn't lost on me but I still feel the burn of his secrecy. I think about his failure to own up to what he did to me. His inability to apologise.

I look over at his empty desk and think how nice it would be to go back to the start. But I know better than most that you can't undo what has been done. Whatever we were to each other, he ruined it. Part of me hates him for that.

I try to picture his daughter. Does she look like him? I remember what Fleet said about knowing that Ben is my son. I feel a pulse of pride at the thought of the blueprint of our faces linking us together no matter what, no matter how far away he is from me.

I turn back to my own desk and look at the stack of paperwork. I need to push Fleet out of my mind. That conversation with Isaacs was step one, I tell myself. I will speak to him about what Fleet did, but I was being honest when I said I need more time. Last week I told the psychologist about Fleet and the random attack that night in the city, and I know I'll want to keep talking about what happened to me.

My phone announces a text: Ben is using Scott's phone. When he was visiting I taught him about star signs, and he's started sending me my daily reading from Smithson's local news website. Candy thinks it's hilarious, seeing as she knows the young intern who manages the astrology section with the help of his grandma and Google.

New beginnings beckon, but make sure you stay true to yourself.

I roll my eyes and put the phone down.

I watch Nan and Calvin talking to each other, their trademark awkwardness as obvious as ever. I feel alone but not lonely. I feel determined.

Through the windows the sun is elbowing past the clouds, the light swirl of morning mist disappearing like a magic trick. The office is starting to fill; individual voices thread together and form a reassuring buzz. Phones ring. Paperwork is stapled. Things are getting done. I really am glad to be back. I'm still apprehensive about the future but I'm also looking forward to it.

Rebecca called me last night, wanting to make plans for Christmas. She seems to have officially taken on the role of family matriarch. 'You will come home, won't you, Gemma?' she asked tentatively. 'Ned would love that, I know. And Ben, of course.'

'Yes,' I assured her, 'maybe just for a few days, but I will come home.' As I said it I realised the dread I'd felt about spending Christmas in Smithson has mainly faded away. Rebecca babbled on about Ben and my dad, selling her house, and I felt an unexpected wave of fondness toward her. She isn't my mother, she isn't even my friend, but she makes my dad happy and that's something I can be grateful for. On one of the televisions mounted on the far wall, a photo of Lizzie and Sterling appears behind a news anchor. The screen cuts to a montage of footage from various TV shows and films, and then to old photos of Kit and Lizzie. Lizzie's trial looms in the not-too-distant future, then Kit's. I'll need to give evidence. Frank Jacoby's trial is set to begin in January.

We'll all do the required dance. Go through the motions. Hope like hell that justice will be served.

I'm reading through a DNA report I requested over six weeks ago when I sense movement behind me. Two dark-suited men enter Isaacs' office. Both have the bleak look of having witnessed a fresh death. Isaacs' door closes.

I look over at Nan and Calvin. Nan raises a bushy eyebrow at me.

Not five minutes later, the door swings open and Isaacs steps out.

'In here, please,' he says to us, his voice low and clipped.

Hooking my hair behind my ears, I fall into step with Nan and Calvin, shoulders back and head high, blood coursing through my veins, ready for whatever is about to happen next.

Acknowledgements

Writing a book requires me to constantly deep-dive into another world, which means I'm absent from the real one for large chunks of time. Therefore, I would like to thank all the people who keep my earthly life ticking along, especially during the intense editing phases. These people include Tom, my parents Susan and Kevin, my sister Jane, my work family at Mr Smith, and an amazing bunch of people I am lucky to call friends.

I want to particularly acknowledge my beautiful and increasingly interesting sons, Oxford and Linus, who are (relatively) patient during the boring hours that Mummy spends 'making a book.' Oxford in particular is becoming an asset when it comes to naming characters, and the defensive passion he displays as he analyses reader reviews, particularly negative ones, is endlessly entertaining. Their unique ability to help me keep things in perspective is invaluable.

As with *The Dark Lake*, this book was a team effort and I have many people to thank for helping me turn the initial jumble of ideas and words into a book.

To Lyn Tranter at Australian Literary Management, thank you for always pushing me and for your thoughtful feedback.

I appreciate your perspective, your high expectations and your passion for the character of Gemma. Thanks also to Sarah Minns and Kirsten Tranter for reviewing the manuscript and providing several wonderful suggestions which made their way into the finished product.

To the awesome team at Allen & Unwin, thank you for your support, guidance and professionalism. In particular, I would like to call out Tom Gilliatt, Louise Cornegé, Tami Rex, Christa Munns and Sarah Baker, who helped the book get safely off to print and successfully onto shelves. And I'd like to direct an extra loud shout out to the incredible Jane Palfreyman, my publisher: I feel very lucky to have found myself in your orbit.

To Kate Goldsworthy, editor and proofreader extraordinaire, I am in awe of your brain and appreciate your meticulous feedback, your curiosity, your funny side notes and love for my characters. It has been an absolute pleasure working with you.

To all the individuals who provided technical information and insights into the world of a homicide detective, thank you. Thanks also to the medical professionals who patiently answered my tricky questions. All errors are mine, and I am solely responsible for any moments where the suspension of belief is required.

Into the Night is predominantly set in Melbourne and I loved having the chance to bring my hometown to life through Gemma's eyes.

Lastly, I want to thank everyone who read *The Dark Lake*. Books really do take on a life of their own once they are published, and receiving feedback from readers makes the solo part of the slog incredibly worthwhile.

The Dark Lake

Sarah Bailey

'*The Dark Lake* is a stunning debut that gripped me from page one and never eased up. Dark, dark, dark—but infused with insight, pathos, a great sense of place, and razor-sharp writing. It's going to be big and Sarah Bailey needs to clear a shelf for awards.' C.J. Box, #1 *New York Times* bestselling author of *Vicious Circle* and *Open Season*

A beautiful young teacher has been murdered, her body found in the lake, strewn with red roses. Local policewoman Detective Sergeant Gemma Woodstock pushes to be assigned to the case, concealing the fact that she knew the murdered woman in high school years before.

But that's not all Gemma's trying to hide. As the investigation digs deeper into the victim's past, other secrets threaten to come to light, secrets that were supposed to remain buried. The lake holds the key to solving the murder, but it also has the power to drag Gemma down into its dark depths.

The Dark Lake is an addictive crime thriller, a mesmerising account of one woman's descent into deceit and madness, and a stunning debut that has caused a stir around the world.

ISBN 978 1 76063 297 7